The Silent Parade

Text copyright © A.P.Thomas 2024

Cover image: Augusta Savage: "Gamin"

Courtesy of The New York Public Library

'We march because by the Grace of God and the force of truth, the dangerous, hampering walls of prejudice and inhuman injustices must fall.'

'We march because we deem it a crime to be silent in the face of such barbaric acts.'

'We march because we want our children to live a better life and enjoy fairer conditions than have fallen to our lot.'

Banners displayed during

'The Silent Protest,'

28th July 1917, New York City.

'You like Baseball do you, Anderson?'

'Yeah, I do. It's the only time when a black man can wave a stick at a white man and not start a riot.'

Response of Gene Hackman,

from the film *Mississippi Burning*.

Prologue
New York Nocturne

It is a hot July night in 1917, and the angry eye of the white sun has closed to be replaced by a sick scythe of a moon that sits ominously over New York. Down at the Brooklyn docks the late shift are unloading containers from a dark slab of a ship. There is not a breath of wind; even the water seems not to move. In the oppressive stillness, every sound becomes amplified: from the creak of the cranes and the groan of the load bearing cables to the holler of instructions that echo around the quay, 'Keep it comin', keep it comin'. Load 'em on the left there. Steady now, don't break 'em,' then the reverberating thud as crates hit the dockside. Dark shiny faces with eyes wide and bright from exertion get caught in the illumination from electric lamps. Everywhere there is the smell of sweat, oil, and the ocean, forming a dark salinity of industrial toil that hangs heavy on the air. All of this is happening while the good people of New York City shift restlessly under stifling bedclothes, straining for a sleep that just won't come.

The piercing drone of a klaxon wails through the night to signal the end of another shift, prompting the mass movement of men into changing rooms at the warehouse. There is tired talk of sweethearts or an after-hours beer while the men wearily gather their meagre belongings or rub at aching muscles with overworked hands: 'Sure is hot tonight,' a heavy-set man by the name of Abraham declares. 'They worked us like dogs. No wonder the regular guys have had enough. Anybody coming for a cool one? I sure could use a drink.'

'Not me,' responds an austere young worker called Jonathan, 'I have to save my money – none of us knows how long this extra work will last, and anyway, I got my Yolande waiting back home.'

'Oooh, your Yolande,' Abraham teases. 'You go on home to your woman, then. I want my cold beer. I earnt it tonight and I got a thirst on. It's too damned hot to sleep anyway.'

There is sharing of cigarettes and a quick wash of faces and hands under the cold splash from the faucet before the men set off across the yard. They hear the clank of the dockyard gates behind and the drag of the heavy chain to secure them; harsh metallic noises that drift off into the night to leave only the sounds of shuffling boots and weary conversation as Abraham walks out with Jonathan.

'You saving for anything special, Jon?'

'Just the usual, pay the landlord and put food on my table.'

'The daily grind!'

'Man has to find work where he can get it,' Jonathan reasons. 'No job means no money, and that ain't an option, least not in my house.'

'Mine neither, brother. Mine neither,' Abraham assures him.

'Still, it don't feel good to be betraying the regular guys,' Jonathan says, scratching at his stubble, 'We're all working men, after all.'

'You think they wouldn't do the same to you?' Abraham spits. 'Wise up, brother. We're black. That means we take whatever work is going because we're the bottom of the pile and we never get a break in this city. My heart ain't ever going to bleed for white folks.'

'I know that. Doesn't mean I haven't got a conscience about it though. Once a man loses his morals, what's he got left?'

'Your children can't eat morals,' Abraham lectures him. 'Just remember that when you have kids in a few years' time and then they're starving because no one will give you a job on account of the colour of your skin.'

It is just another night at work for the latest batch of employees drafted in by the New York Dock Company to counteract the damage of industrial strike action taken by the regular Irish dockers. Those families now go into stores asking for credit, some women give bread to others that cannot properly feed their children, some men hope for a lucky bet or hide behind a haze of cheap hooch. All of them curse the company and most secretly long for the strike to be over, but a stand has been made and must be seen through, even if they know they cannot truly win.

In a Harlem tenement the red bricks have cooled a little on the building's façade after soaking up the heat of the day to sit blushing like a coy mistress. On the inside a young woman waits for her Jonathan to come home. Her dark skin shines under the light as she bathes herself, the fragrance of the soap filling the bathroom, a clean smell that her man adores. She is called Yolande, the name a song on the lips of her lover who has little else to rejoice about in these poverty-stricken times. As she washes, she hums a tune softly to herself, a sweet melody about love in anticipation of her man's return. She imagines him hard at work, heaving crates on the dockside, his lithe back straining in the moonlight. Work that was born out of necessity now gives her a feeling of deliciousness. Through the open window, the sound of a clock striking eleven drifts in. Not long now, Yolande thinks, drying herself before fixing two drinks and waiting for Jonathan's return.

In the darkening confines of a dockside bar, so close to the sea that its timbers bristle with salt, the striking Irish workers drunkenly scuff at the battered skirting boards in boots that no longer see any labour. Nonetheless, more beer is bought on credit, toasts are raised, and the hot throb of hatred fuels the men, along with alcohol, towards a violent vengeance that is the only kind of language they know the bosses can't ignore. The ringleader stands at one end of the long room on a packing crate stage more used to housing folk musicians than a political agitator.

He is still, with grey-green eyes that coldly and calmly take in the chaos of the men around him. Those eyes hypnotise like an impurity burning in a flame, but they cut to being dead ashes in an instant, for he is a brutal man. His thrift store suit sits upon his lean frame with authority because he wears it like the armour of important business. He knows the rabble needs a commander in chief if they are to stand any chance of surviving. This is why he is here tonight, to make the speech and incite the action. It is all part of a bigger plan. He finishes his cigarette, grinding it under his heel, bangs his tankard down on the table three times, and waits purposefully for silence to fall before he begins. He is certain a hush will come because he is Johnny Cain.

'Gentlemen, thank you for your attendance. We are all here tonight because we have had enough. We've all worked these docks. We've worked them through winters where the breath froze out of our mouths and the hands that held the chains were still numb from the cold hours after the shift was over. We've worked them through summers where our sweat pooled in puddles on the dockside and the crates slid through our soaked gloved fingers. We've toiled and ached, spat and cursed, but we've carried on because we are *working men*. We are not doctors or lawyers, businessmen or politicians. We are dock workers and proud of it. That is what we do. That is who we are. We give good, honest, consistent labour. We take our pay at the end of the month, and we carry on. Until now.'

Cain pauses, looking around the many faces in the room, drawing them into his cause, letting them hunger for his next words.

'Why do we strike? Because our bosses refuse to pay us a wage that will keep our families fed and clothed. Because rather than recognise our legitimate concerns, they turn their backs and employ strike-breakers to steal the bread from other men's tables and from their infants' mouths. They leave us with nothing to lose but our liberty, but I say to you, what liberty? When our every drink is on credit, when we cannot walk for fear of wearing out our shoes, when we cannot eat because our children are starving and need it more than we do, when every breath we take aches with what we have lost. What is liberty worth then, I ask you?'

Cain waits, drilling his fiery stare into the space above his fellow workers' heads. When he speaks next, it is in a quieter voice, but somehow it carries even greater certainty in the hush of its tone.

'They think leaving us with nothing will break us. They are wrong. We are not desperate, we are determined. Our hunger is our strength. It drives us on to fight for our cause. Tonight, we will strike in a different way. We will lash out at those who betray us. We will smash the strike-breakers until there is no one left prepared to work on the docks under these conditions and pay, until the danger money is not enough. We will stand against the company bosses who try to take the blood from our veins, and we will not falter, we will not yield. We are as our forefathers made us, Irish and proud. When we are oppressed, we fight, and we do not give in until the war is won!'

The rousing end of Cain's speech brings cheers and stomps from the men, who chase whiskies and salute their cause, lost in the euphoria and bravado of the moment. Unseen by these crusaders, Cain turns and coughs blood into his handkerchief, an affliction that he does not want anyone to know about. His younger brother Patrick frowns as he notices what the speech has cost his heroic sibling. He resolves to lead the attack for Johnny, rising angrily and calling for the mob to join him as they take their fight out into the streets on this sultry night. Much more blood will be shed before they take to their beds. The pent-up energy of their hate must find its release so that some satisfaction might come in these troubled times.

On the sidewalk, the Harlem workers are exhaustedly walking home, dragging their feet after another backbreaking shift. They take no joy from going against their fellow longshoremen, from working in the place where others have downed tools in a legitimate protest, but poverty and need overrule the moral concerns they might have. Their boots scrape to an uneasy stop because out of the shadows step those regular workers.

'We got trouble,' Jonathan announces.

'Steady now; stick together. We need to face this down,' Abraham asserts.

They are a white Irish mob that reeks of alcohol, resentment, and definite violence. They carry crow bars, spanners and pieces of wood clenched in their taut hands. They are men ready for vengeance. The tired black strike-breakers take a step back in unison, but more white men appear behind them to cut off their escape. This has been well-planned, and now it must be executed. An electric current of fear howls palpably through the thick night and for a moment the scene hangs in suspension. Then weapons cut through the air finding flesh; there are shrieks of pain, angry shouts, and the ceaseless muffled crunch of the blows. Everything becomes animalistic in the hot night.

The whistle of a patrolling policeman issues a shrill call to arms and other distant echoes blare a response. The attackers deliver final retributive stamps and flee into the darkness from which they came, leaving their quarry a dazed and bleeding mass of broken bones, cuts, and bruises. The cops arrive and breathlessly take in the scene of human destruction, muttering to themselves.

'This again!'

'Third time in a month. Somebody needs to sort this strike out; guys are getting the hell beaten outta them.'

'Maybe they should get the message not to break a strike.'

'We're here to uphold the law. This is bringing disorder to the streets; it ain't right.'

'Tell that to the men who can't feed their kids on what they're getting paid. They got a right to be angry.'

'This goes beyond being angry. This is breaking heads!'

Some move forwards to help the beaten black men, but not all.

The white men are back in the stuffy bar. They compare war wounds and chase more whiskies. They toast their victory.

'Here's to the real dockers!' Johnny Cain asserts.

'When Irish eyes are smiling!' someone else responds. 'Down with the Harlem traitors, we saw to them good and proper again tonight!'

Nobody admits that it was not a fair fight.

Johnny's talk of retribution masks a greater purpose that has come a step closer to being achieved, but instinct causes him to survey the room. His little brother Patrick is missing, and it troubles him. He senses that despite the attack going like clockwork, something bad has come the way of the Cain clan tonight.

In a downtown hospital, nurses tend to the victims. They stitch gashes and set plaster casts over arms. Black men smoke cigarettes with difficulty through busted lips. Jonathan can barely move, and one of his eyes has swollen shut. His Yolande has fallen asleep waiting for her man in a bed lit by a guttering candle. She is unaware that other men have broken him so he cannot make love to her. The heat has completely disappeared from the bricks of the tenement building. It stands cold in the darkness now. Abraham's bruised body hurts with every breath; his mind is full of fury. He thinks about the upcoming Silent Parade and wonders whether a peaceful protest against the oppression of coloured folks will have any effect at all on the city of New York. He ponders if the only language subjugation understands is violent uprising and then realises, he is thinking like his brother the hard-line Harlem activist.

Tomorrow at dawn the dockyard gates will be opened for business, but many of these men will rise painfully from their beds, coughing through cracked ribs, unable to work for several weeks. Their families will have to rely on the charity of others to put food on their tables, but the community is used to this. West of Lenox Avenue, the coloured folks of Harlem will join together and help each other because it is the only thing to do. They know that things don't change; they just stay the same.

In the hush of Prospect Park, hidden by the cover of nightfall and a screen of trees, the two young lovers hold hands. Her blue eyes are lost in the dark brown caves of his. They whisper to each other, aware of how sounds carry through the summer dusk, but even this creates its own kind of spell.

'Can you get away tomorrow night?' he asks her.

'I told my father I'm tidying up at the restaurant, that should give me a couple of hours. He'll get suspicious if it's all the time though,' she says with a pained regret.

'I know, but I can't spend these summer nights without you. Every time you have to leave it hurts my heart. I just want us to be together.'

'Me too, it's all I can think about when I'm not with you.'

She is wearing a light blue cotton dress with tiny daisies dotted in print on the fabric. It is his favourite. When she smiles it is sunshine for his soul. She takes in the line of his jaw, firm, noble and outlined by the moonlight every time the cloud cover parts. His hand is warm, big, and soft, bringing the touch of a gentleman. They are totally intoxicated with each other. They are much too young for the past to mean anything, and the future is an abstract that cannot burn as brightly as this moment.

They savour their seclusion; two young people whose parents would not want them to be together; who would forbid it. Their love is thwarted by obstacles, but in this park, at this hour, everything seems possible. They talk of leaving New York one day, of leaving America. They both love the idea of Paris: 'When the war is over and Europe is safe, we can follow our dream,' he reasons. 'The rich French folk will fall over themselves to employ an American nanny, and I can apprentice a trade or use my experience of working in a hotel. It'll mean starting at the bottom, but Paris will allow us to be ourselves and to not have to live in fear about who might see us,' he tells her enthusiastically.

'We can rent a little apartment,' she envisions, with glittering blue eyes full of youth, energy, and promise, 'I've read all about the Left Bank, but there will be even cheaper areas. It might only have a single bed if it is a space meant for just one. It will be cramped and humble, but it will be ours, and we would never have to part.'

'A life together, away from our disapproving elders,' he says, lost somewhere in the daydream of their love's potential.

'Just you and me, living in Paris. I want it to be more than just a fantasy spoken of in whispers witnessed only by the trees,' she implores him.

'If you believe in it, then we can make it happen. You're my fantasy. It's a dream to be here with you, and because of that miracle, our future can be whatever we will it to be,' he tells her.

'So, we keep saving and wait for the war to be over,' she beams.

'We do. It can't last much longer, and then Paris can be our playground. Until that happens, we just have to go on meeting in this beautiful park.'

'We do,' she assents, squeezing his hand in delight.

He is eighteen and old enough to think of himself as a man now. He will protect her and provide for her. One day they will be married, and he knows she will look a vision of beauty in her wedding dress; even more lovely than the first time he saw her stepping off the tram in Manhattan; even more lovely than right now with the dappled light playing across her face and making her eyes sparkle.

Her fingers move under his hand, tracing its contours. She is seventeen and still apprehensive about giving him her lips because she has never let a boy kiss her before. Whenever they part, she has offered him her cheek and he has graced it with a warm brush of tenderness. In a world full of ugly human conflict, she wants them to stay pure and for everything to happen fittingly; but tonight, in this park, with the scent of the honeysuckle and the perfect silence and heat; with her hand in his and the night holding its breath; she is ready.

Their faces bend closer, as incrementally as a shadow that creeps across the land, like the frame-by-frame flicker of a movie screen played at its slowest speed or the gradual growth of grass in a meadow. When their lips touch, it is like the opening of a flower, the pulsing of a firework display seen through the eyes of the deaf, the richness of a gospel choir heard by the blind. In that moment, they have become complete. In the distance, a church clock chimes eleven times, and the spell of fantasy is interrupted by the urgent command of time.

'I have to go,' she says sadly.

'It's late, I know,' he responds in anguish. 'I wish we could stay here forever, but we can't. Let me walk you some of the way home, as far as I dare.'

'Of course,' she smiles.

They part at a street corner; he is careful not to stray too far into her neighbourhood. On this night, even more than any other, because of the kiss, they do not want to leave each other; but achingly they know that they must. He watches her walking away, drinking in the way that she moves, her wavy hair, her shapely legs. The essence of her fizzes in his brain. He watches her until she is out of sight and then turns to make the long journey back across town, lost in the energy of that kiss. In the shadows, a figure studies him intently before following.

As the young man walks, it gives him time to reflect. The night is still and warm and endless, opening up for him a whole future rich with possibilities. He is in love and can taste the magic in the air. It hums a warm tune in time to his buoyant steps. He knows that he is a young black man from Harlem, and that his country has taught him to expect no prospects other than manual labour, but he wants to better himself by being skilled. He knows that being a young man in love makes him vulnerable, that he must not allow the romance that colours his world with beauty to sway him from the truth: that he must be tough, have guile, and seize whatever opportunity comes his way. For he is a young black man from Harlem, but, oh, how love makes him fly above his forecasted fate.

He comes from a God-fearing, respectful household, with a father who believes in defending the values of America enough to have gone off to fight in the war, and a mother who has the strength and courage to defend the causes closest to her heart. She has brought her boy up well, teaching him that hatred and bitterness will never make him happy, and that if he aspires to something, then hard work and determination will allow him to achieve it. So, he grows from the example of his parents and frames his own ethos: Why not dream of better things when the rest of society is trying to confine you to a life in the gutter? Why not let love rule your heart?

This aspiration has him dreaming of a life in Paris, married to his beloved, even though the colours of their skin are different. It has him floating along the dark streets of New York City late at night, oblivious to the footsteps that quietly fall behind. It has him not recognising that here on this hot trail, with anger seething up from the sidewalks just yards away, his fragile future will disappear like smoke vanishing on the wind. The footsteps of his girlfriend cease as she reaches the safety of her front door in the white neighbourhood, but his footfall continues, echoed by another set of steps moving closer, closer. As he walks near the dockside, there are shouts in the night, cries, and police whistles that cut through the splendour of his dreaming. The noises of the affray mask a different danger, for they obscure his assailant's tread. The attack comes without warning. It is the deadly destroyer of beautiful dreams.

Chapter One
Brooklyn Baby

In the kitchen of a small house in Northwest Brooklyn, Frank Visconti sat in the darkness picking the label from his bottle of beer. From their bedroom across the hallway, his wife, Maria watched as his features were periodically illuminated by the lighting of another cigarette before he snapped out the match with a shake of his wrist. Frank was often to be found at the kitchen table. He sat there into the small hours silently contemplating the state of things, a middle-aged longshoreman worn out from hard work, poor pay, and unfulfilled dreams. Normally, Maria would go to sleep and leave him to brood; they had been married for more than twenty years and she knew that she could never change his night-time moods; but tonight, she stayed awake.

Tonight was different because Frank was waiting for their daughter, Isabella to return home. Trouble lay ahead. While she loved every fibre of her husband's being, Maria knew his flaws, oh how she knew them. The depression and the anger marked him like scars; even though they often lay hidden behind his eyes, she could still see them. Usually, it was the depression that Maria feared the most, but tonight it was the anger because she knew just what Frank had found out about their only daughter. So, she stayed awake and waited.

Isabella was seventeen and had started work as a waitress at a nearby Italian restaurant. She was working nights while studying her stenographer's apprenticeship in the daytime. The courts interested her. Maria was pleased that her daughter's independent spirit made her want to get a steady occupation while Frank was just relieved that she didn't have to work anywhere near the Brooklyn Docks. He was still worried that some of the cases his innocent daughter might be documenting a record of would expose her to the evils of the world all too soon though.

Maria knew of a different danger. She didn't see a child like Frank did when he looked at Isabella, she saw the young woman her daughter had become. She had been a seventeen-year-old girl herself, even if it had been a long time ago. Isabella was driven, vivacious, and keen to experience life. She was turning the heads of all the boys in the neighbourhood, and it was only a matter of time before her own head became filled with the thoughts of love and all that entailed. Maria understood this and had prayed for her daughter's heart. Telling Frank about any of this was, of course, out of the question.

The trouble had started when Frank called in at Antolini's restaurant after his shift ended. He'd wanted a quiet word with Marco Antolini, the restaurant's owner. Isabella had been returning home very late from her waitressing work even though Marco made a promise not to keep her after ten at night as she needed to be up early every morning to continue her stenography course. Maria had known the late nights would have nothing to do with Marco, but she hadn't dared tell Frank this. She should have realised he'd take matters into his own hands, she lamented afterwards. Three nights this week Isabella had not returned home much before midnight and when her father quizzed her about it, she blamed Marco for making her clean up the kitchen or cash up the takings. Again, Maria stayed silent, trying to catch the eye of her daughter at other moments. Isabella skilfully dodged her imploring and searching gaze.

After a beer and a sit down with the restaurant owner, Frank was unsettled. Marco swore on the Holy Saints that he had let Isabella leave early every shift, just like they'd agreed. His hesitant son was lurking by the kitchen door, and although usually mute, had backed up his father's version of events. Frank trusted the man to have kept his word, and even though the boy was strange, he had no reason to lie about this, so what was his seventeen-year-old daughter doing in those hours when she should have been at home, he asked his wife when confronting her with what he'd found out.

Maria already knew the answer. Although no one had told her directly, a mother noticed these changes in her daughter; the lightness of step; smiling to herself at the sink; humming a tune as she walked up the stairs. She wanted to tell Frank it was a boy and that it was to be expected at Isabella's age, but her husband was on the warpath. The truth would out, but it would not come from her. Neither would it come from their nineteen-year-old son, Danny. For while Maria was certain he knew all about it after a conversation they'd had earlier in the week, Danny knew better than to break that kind of news to the patriarch of the Visconti household. So, the whole place held its breath and waited for the return of the deceitful daughter.

In the heat of the night the city seemed to throb with a subterranean pulse like far away cellos tuning up for a concert at Carnegie Hall. All the houses had thrown open their windows, desperate for a sweet breeze that never came, and the sidewalks gave back the echoes of footsteps twice as loud as their original noise. The report of Isabella's heels reached her mother before anyone else in the house could recognise them. Usually, it was the comforting sound of her daughter having made it home safely, but tonight safety lay elsewhere. Tonight, Frank

Visconti was waiting, and he wanted answers. Maria could hear her son Danny shifting restlessly among disordered sheets up in his room, while at the kitchen table, Frank sat perfectly still. He'd stopped picking the label from his beer when he heard those footsteps approaching.

Cautious as she was, the girl's head was still light from that kiss in the park, and the distance from there to her house took no time at all. That kiss had made her tread less wary and blinded her senses to the foreboding that was seeping out of the Visconti house. She should have known as she slid her key into the lock that the touch of metal on metal was like an electric shock running through the building, that the closing soft thump of the door sounded like the drum before an execution, but her head was a symphony of flowers. In their rooms, Maria and Danny heard her entrance and knew it had awakened the beast within Frank. A showdown was coming that neither of them wanted to be a part of, so, they sat listening with their hearts pounding blood in their ears.

Isabella made it as far as the end of the hallway before an ominous voice echoed from the darkness of the kitchen. 'Bella, come here a minute, will you? I got something to ask you.' Frank struck another match, lighting the single candle on the table, the flickering flame catching the furrow in his brow and the guilt on his daughter's face. 'I went to see Marco Antolini today.' He let the words hang there so she might guess their meaning. His Bella had always been such a bright girl. 'What've you got to tell me about these late nights? I want the truth and not any more of that nonsense you've been trying to feed me.'

Isabella sat down across the table. She hated to dishonour or disappoint her father, but she was the least scared of him out of all the Visconti family. 'Papa, you know I'm going to qualify in three months' time, and I'll be able to get a full-time job when I turn eighteen. That means the court sees me as an adult woman. So, I want you to think about that when I tell you where I've been.'

Frank said nothing, simply hardened his expression and waited.

'I've met a young man...'

'Bella, no! Don't tell me that,' Frank responded, the hurt audible in his voice. 'I forbid you to get into anything until you were at least twenty-one. You don't know men. You don't know the ways their minds work. You need to have grown up and experienced more of life before you get yourself into any of that business. Even then, the family needs to find you the right Italian boy to take care of you.'

'But Papa, I *have* grown up and I *am* experiencing life. Falling in love is just part of that. It happened. I didn't plan it, but it's here now and I want to be able to enjoy it with your blessing.'

Frank's face changed from wounded to suspicious. 'It's not that Benny Antolini, is it? I never liked the kid. There's something creepy about him, always skulking around muttering to himself, hanging about his father's restaurant like a bad smell. Tell me it's not him, Bella.'

Isabella looked around. Her mother had appeared in the kitchen doorway. Frank's voice had risen enough to summon her to the family crisis. Quietly, the errant daughter answered. 'No, Papa. It's not Benny. It's not anyone from the neighbourhood.'

Frank took a gulp of his beer and set it down heavily on the table. He wiped the foam from his top lip and narrowed his eyes. 'Yeah, well. I guess it don't matter who it is because it has to stop, Bella. It has to stop right now! You went against my wishes, you lied to me about where you were, and you been staying out later and later. It ends here, tonight, you understand?'

Distraught, his daughter got up from the table. 'I love him! I'm an adult! I don't want to disobey you, but if I have to choose then I will move out to be with him. Three months until I get a job. I don't want to leave. I don't want to hurt you, but I will if I have no other choice.'

Frank swept the beer bottle off the table. It hit against the Belfast sink and smashed. He got up so suddenly that his chair toppled back and clattered to the floor. Isabella ran from the room, knocking into her mother as she went. Maria recovered herself enough to form a barrier in the kitchen doorway. She had seen Frank turn violent in the younger days of their marriage and feared he would chase after their daughter in his rage. It seemed as if that was exactly what Frank was about to do, but he pulled up short, hitting the wall next to his wife in frustration before resting his head into her chest and mumbling: 'Where the hell did I go wrong, Maria? Just where the hell did I go wrong in bringing up that girl?'

Up in his bedroom, Danny hung upon every word of his father's hurt. 'You didn't go wrong,' he whispered, 'none of us did. It's just Bella.' His sister had never done things the easy way, but this was something very different to her childhood waywardness. Pulling on a cigarette and blowing smoke out of his window, Danny balled up his fists and rubbed at his eyes in frustration.

The young people in the neighbourhood were talking, and all their gossip was about his little sister. What Benny Antolini had told him came without malice. Benny was quirky and quiet, but he was observant too, and rational when he needed to be. When he spoke, it was often curiously without emotion, as if he couldn't process the feelings that surrounded certain things. Yet even Benny had been awkward when talking to Danny about seeing Isabella with a young black man. As Italians, the boys knew the unwritten rules of their community. There were some things you just couldn't do.

Danny moved to sit on his window ledge. The house had fallen silent, but the tension was everywhere. There wasn't even any wind out there on the street. The night hung heavy and black, pressing in all around him. He'd wanted to doubt what Benny had told him. The kid could read people wrong and get mixed up in his head; it had happened that way when they were all at school together. But then came the behaviour from people, friends who couldn't look him in the eye, young men who shuffled their feet and talked out of the sides of their mouths to one another when he passed. He'd confronted them, gotten right in their faces, but they'd clammed up. Something was going down for sure, so, he'd asked his best pal about it, one week ago, as they sat on the swings after dusk in the recreation ground.

'Benny Antolini says he saw Isabella with a young black guy. No one else has said a word, but they all act funny around me now. People are smirking and talking behind my back, and I know I ain't imagining it. What's the word on the street, Paulie? What is it you're keeping from me?'

Paulie looked down at his shoes and scuffed at the dirt in agitation, making little clouds of dust float around their feet. 'She's been seen,' he said quietly, 'in Prospect Park, and more than once. I didn't see her myself, but the guys got no reason to be making that stuff up, especially when it's so serious. They wouldn't do that. They know what it means. I'm sorry, Danny.'

The swing creaked on its chains as Danny turned to face his friend. 'So, what do I do, Paulie? What do I do?'

'I guess you gotta talk to her somehow. I don't know.'

Danny kicked at some loose blades of grass that had sprung up out of the cinders. 'You know Bella, though,' he said sadly, 'She's never been one to listen to reason. God knows, I tried enough times.'

'So, try again,' Paulie urged him. 'What else is there?'

'There's man to man,' Danny said darkly.

'I seen too much trouble come from that way of doing things,' Paulie warned him.

Danny sat for a while without speaking, then he got up from the swing and said, 'I'm going home. See you around, Paulie.'

'You be careful!' his friend called out as he watched Danny's troubled figure recede into the distance.

Maybe there was another way, Danny thought as he walked back to the house. A showdown was fine with him, but it might get back to his father, and the old man wouldn't leave things alone if he had suspicions. Perhaps a woman-to-woman talk could make Bella see sense. It would upset his mum to know what was going on, but she was a wonderful mother who could cope with just about anything. She was the rock of their family in many ways and Danny trusted her to know what to say. Besides, he was struggling to carry the burden of Bella's secret tryst all by himself. He needed someone to share the load.

They were putting out the washing in the back yard when he told her. Maria held onto one of Isabella's blouses like the girl herself was inside of it. She closed her eyes and whispered some kind of oath under her breath that Danny was glad he couldn't quite catch, then she opened them and looked firmly at her son.

'Have you spoken to your sister about this?' she asked.

'No, mum. I couldn't,' he said, 'I didn't know how to.'

'And you think I do?' she snapped, crumpling the blouse beneath her fingers.

'You're a woman,' Danny explained. 'I just thought you could understand how she's feeling and then talk her out of it without getting angry like I know I would.'

Maria paused, stretched out the blouse, shook it into shape, and hung it securely on the line. 'I knew there was someone,' she confessed. 'I just didn't think she'd be so stupid!'

Danny ground his teeth and looked away. 'What are we going to do, mum?'

'I'll talk to her Friday,' Maria said definitely, 'when your dad's gone straight to the bar from work, and before Isabella starts her shift at the restaurant. I'll bring it home to that girl just what will happen if she carries on with this. She has no hope of keeping it quiet or of things turning out any way other than disastrously. Leave it to me, Danny. I'll snap her out of whatever daydream she's living in at the moment.'

Friday had been one day away when Frank called in at the restaurant and found out his daughter had been lying to him. One day away, Danny cursed as he flicked his cigarette butt towards the gutter in a well-practised move. This time, due to his frustration, it showered sparks down the middle of the road before laying there, glowering up at him. He wasn't sure his mother would've gotten through to Bella anyway. There had always been a wilfulness about his little sister that stemmed from her early years. Danny remembered the tree climbing competition where all the kids around their way gathered under a magnificent oak that stood at the end of the street. There had been much bravado and talk of how high each boy was going to climb, but when it came to it, most chickened out before they'd gotten even halfway up its branches. Bella had been different.

She'd seen the toughest boy in the neighbourhood pick his way more than thirty feet above the ground, higher than the houses that surrounded that great tree, then she'd followed his path upwards until she reached the ribbon he'd tied around what he thought was his victory branch. Then she climbed higher. The applause of the kids soon turned to concern, and Danny, who was no mean climber himself, knew his sister was too high for him to rescue her if she got stuck. Bella had reached the spindly branches near the top of the tree, the shouts for her to come down only spurring her on to ascend further. Then a branch snapped, and she lost her footing, falling almost fifteen feet before hitting a bough that saved her. She froze in fear and clung to it, so that her brother and protector had to use all his nerve to reach her and bring her back down to earth. Afterwards, he was furious with her and told her to never do anything like that again. Bella had just smiled, a glint in her eyes telling him there would be more mischief to come in future years.

Later, there had been a humdinger of a fight in school where Bella and another girl were locked in a fit of hair pulling and scratching. The other girl's boyfriend had waded in and shoved Bella away so hard that she fell heavily on the cement yard. Bella had flown at him, and he'd thrown her down again. One of the other kids had gone and got Danny, who arrived just in time to see his sister lash the boyfriend in the face with the belt she'd taken off her dress to use as a weapon. The buckle cut him, and blood poured from the wound. A furious melee ensued, with both boys and girls thrashing at each other until the teachers came to separate and chastise them. Bella was fearless and a fearsome opponent when provoked. She had a powerful anger in her that came from their father. Danny knew this because he had it too, and now, pacing around his bedroom consumed by the shame of his sister's actions and the hurt it had brought their family, he could feel the fury rising up inside of him like a hot, red demon that had to find an outlet.

Isabella lay sobbing on her bed when Danny entered the room. She looked up and asked him: 'Why, Danny? Why does Papa have to hurt me this way? What's so wrong with falling in love?'

Expecting him to offer her comfort, the younger sibling was shocked at his response. 'What I want to know is why you got to disrespect him like this?' he hissed through clenched teeth. 'The man has given you everything. All he's ever shown you is love and now you go and throw it in his face.'

Startled, Isabella searched for a reply. It seemed that her brother had grown wider and more menacing with his last remarks. It was like witnessing a mirror image of her father's anger. 'Danny, I thought you'd understand.'

The youth banged his fist down on her dressing table, making the little glass bottles of scent jump and tinkle. 'No, sis. I don't understand. If the old man knew what Benny Antolini claims he saw the other night, then he'd throw you out of this house. Hell, I ought to kick you out myself. It disgusts me what the boys round here been saying about you.'

To this, she had no response and so he knew it at once to be true. Storming out of her room, Danny went back to his own and threw open the window. He smoked violently, furious at the dishonour that his little sister had brought upon the family. If something wasn't done about it soon then the Visconti clan would be the shame of the neighbourhood and if his father found out the whole truth, then it would break his heart completely. He had to find out the guy's name and warn him off. Bella would have to tell him, or he would threaten to let their father know exactly what she'd been up to. With his plan clearly formed, Danny went back to her bedroom.

Chapter Two
A Fistful of Horrors

In his stale office down on Montague Street, David Young picked up the telephone. As the man in charge of the day to day running of the New York Dock Company he was under pressure, but his power and influence allowed him to have the home number of the police commissioner. It was almost midnight, and in a groggy bedroom somewhere across town a senior policeman's fitful sleep was broken by a ringing that he knew from experience was the clarion call of trouble. He sat up in bed and smoked a cigarette, using his free hand to hold the receiver to his ear. Tonight, for this, he would not leave his bed. The situation could be temporarily smoothed over with platitudes and false promises, but *Tomorrow and tomorrow and tomorrow creeps in this petty pace.* He sighed and exhaled smoke into the room, an educated man who knew there were law and order problems in his city that he just couldn't solve.

'Commissioner, I need assurances that no more of my workers are going to end up in the hospital. Until now, I've always managed to draft in replacements, but it won't be long before fear takes over and the blacks from Harlem find another way to feed their children that doesn't risk them getting the hell beaten out of them for doing it. The economy of New York relies on its docks. If we let the strikers bleed us dry, we fail. If my workforce is intimidated into submission, we fail also. The mayor can look at this any way he wants to, but that's the reality of the situation. No one's going to re-elect a mayor who busted the economy, and no mayor is going to keep a chief of police that can't keep the members of its community safe.'

Cursing inwardly to himself, the commissioner responded. 'David, I know it's hard, but you've got to see the politics of the situation. Your disenfranchised white workers have lost their livelihoods. They can't put food on the table themselves. They are tough working men, men with pride. All they ever wanted was an honest day's pay for an honest day's work. The mob won't dare to come back tomorrow; they've vented their frustration. We'll both speak to the ringleaders, but you've got to try and sort this strike out: it's no good for anybody. Tell your directors to at least start talks. They can't go on being this hard-line. The tensions in this city may not be anything like as bad as in Chicago, but I don't want to see them escalate. The mayor sees all of this. He knows the score. We've talked it through. New York City is meant to be united: we hate everybody else, and they all despise us because of our attitude.' It was the best he could do right then to diffuse the situation with a modicum of humour, but he knew it wouldn't suffice in the face of the night's violence.

Young flinched on the end of the line and then zeroed in on the culprits. 'It's the Irish boys that are responsible for tonight's beatings; they're out of control. You've got to promise to come down on them like a tonne of bricks if they so much as try anything like this again. These guys are itinerants; there's no reasoning with them. Only the threat of being thrown in jail will make them start to listen.'

Young was adamant and the commissioner knew it, but *he* also had the sensitivity of the tinder box resentments of the white dockers to contend with. 'I will do everything that I can, I promise; but you know the Irish community needs careful handling. Half of my police force drink in the same bars, go to the same churches and support the same baseball teams. Christ, some of your laid-off workers come from the same *families* as my men. We all have to watch how we tread. Diplomacy has to come before hard policing, David; you know that. Get your bosses to end that goddamn strike; find a compromise; do whatever you have to do. In the meantime, I will step up patrols around the docks, but I can't guarantee that some of my men won't turn a blind eye if they feel conflicted. Your workers will be safer, but even a truce will be short-lived and uneasy. That's the best I can offer at the moment.'

The commissioner ended the conversation on that unsatisfactory note. His wife lay in bed, a veteran of sleeping through the disturbances that came with her husband's work. He knew there was no chance of him getting back to sleep now, so, lighting another cigarette, he sought out the bottle of scotch in the living room, switched on a table lamp, and thought about the politics of the situation. Young might have a ringside seat to all of the trouble at the docks, but he didn't have access to the inner sanctum that was City Hall. He could throw his weight around and protest all he liked, but he didn't sit at the top table; he didn't have the power. Neither did his directors, for all their business acumen. The mayor had the power, and the mayor favoured the Irish.

He saw the strike as a typical dispute. *It's a labour situation. The boys need work, and the company needs the boys. Try as they might to draft in replacements, sooner or later, they'll have to give on something, and they know it. There are just too many bodies involved. It's not like the goddamn war in Europe where hundreds of thousands can be sacrificed for a principle. These workers won't stand for starvation, they've proved they are ready to fight back. The company will have to understand that. It'll play itself out soon enough, trust me. They'll not break the Irish boys' spirit, not when they've got the cops from their community backing them. The company will have calculated all this. They're just making them suffer so they can negotiate a tighter deal and ringfence their profits. These bastards know how to sustain a corporation. Everything in this city is built on the blood of the poorest, that's the way it always has been, and the way it always will be. It's a fact of life. More of that blood might get spilled, but order will be restored soon enough.*

The commissioner knew when to keep silent. He was there to take the mayor's temperature, to see how the land lay, nothing more. He was a passive observer and anyway, he reasoned, his position was hardly any less difficult or political. There were other truths he'd discussed with the mayor. He was forced to admit that the N.Y.P.D. was biased: there were too many Irish cops who sided with the strikers and allowed their violence to continue, turning the other way or disappearing at times when they were meant to be patrolling the docks and offering some protection to the black strike-breakers. His other officers couldn't be expected to break ranks with their colleagues, it went against the code of being police. There was the shadow of failing to uphold the law, but there was an even bigger spectre that kept them together, the need to be united against the organized crime mobsters rampaging through the city. He'd confessed this to the mayor, who in return, had been candid with him.

Why should I lose huge swathes of my vote over a business dispute? It was a question that he'd already answered. The black vote, what there was of it, would never get him re-elected, nor would it unseat him from power. The situation was crystal clear. The mayor would support his chief of police in the face of complaints from the dock company and the Harlem workers. They would say the N.Y.P.D. was doing everything that could be expected of them in the face of very difficult circumstances, that the strike needed to be resolved in order for the troubles and violence to stop. The politics of money and profit would resolve itself, as was always the way with these things. As the commissioner sat in his chair in the middle of the night, he thought of all of this, mulling it over once again. He just hoped it didn't escalate into deaths. That would be much harder to defend, he considered, sipping on his drink and taking a worried drag from his cigarette. He sensed there was still a lot more trouble to come, but he couldn't have known how rapidly and vividly the horrors would bear their poisoned fruit.

Somewhere across the city, Sergeant Dominic White sat on the stoop of his apartment block smoking a cigarette. He was avoiding his wife. He had somehow found himself drawn into an atmosphere of tension and deliberate silences where the two spouses actively repelled each other from rooms: when one entered, the other one left. This had been the course of their relationship for the last three days and it was born from a familiar argument. While he felt he was just about managing to fulfil his duties as a policeman, husband and father, Mona saw it differently. What she didn't understand was that the job had to get done; you couldn't just leave criminals to roam loose or go to ground. What *he* didn't understand, apparently, was that he wasn't singlehandedly responsible for cleaning up the crime in New York City. He was twenty-seven years old, driven and falsely knowing. It was only later in his life, long after the fall, that he would begin to see how little his young self really knew and how right Mona was, however acerbically she voiced it. With some things, only time will teach a man.

Forlornly, White got up from the stoop, flicking his cigarette butt to the kerb. It wasn't the heat that was making him tired, it was the relentless exercise of banging his head against Mona's unshiftable position about his work. He loved her and he had always protested that he would choose her over the job in an instant, but the way she saw it, he never once had. Their dispute was worn thin with repetition. When he argued that he took time to be with Amy, their three-year-old daughter, Mona would huff and sarcastically respond: *how very good of you to make the effort!* They had said all that could be said about it one too many times, but the avoidance and the silence was a thundercloud waiting to burst. This much he knew, he just couldn't work out how to stop the rain. He was a cop who couldn't let go of being police, and a man who couldn't hold onto being a husband.

Something had formed in him during the troubled passage of his youth, a notion that the law, and those who enforced it, brought steadiness to an otherwise chaotic world. It was a simple view formulated by a young man experiencing his own deep traumas as he grew up first in New York City and then in small town America, and one man, Bill Masters, had inspired White to become a cop. The local sheriff had proven himself to be the rock upon which the community was anchored. God put fear and righteousness into many, but for those who strayed into evil ways, the sheriff was there to stop them. For a young and impressionable White, that had been the lure of the job, a calling to pursue a straightforward and unromanticised desire to make order out of chaos, to play his part in righting the wrongs of the world when he could not repair the tragic loss of both his parents. So, he'd returned to his birth city and joined the N.Y.P.D. at just twenty-one.

As he wandered up and down the sidewalk out front of their apartment, White thought back to the moment where everything had become more complicated, and his career had gotten even more addictive. He'd been a patrolman for just two years and was out walking his beat one seemingly uneventful day in 1913 when a body dropped from the sky and smashed to pieces on the sidewalk. It had fallen from the Woolworth Building, one of the city's fantastic new skyscrapers, causing him to conduct his own unofficial investigation into what had been troublingly labelled a suicide. He had listened to the dead man's secretary, a woman by the name of Martha Marsh, and her words had set him on a path of discovery that eventually led him through the door of Detective Squad and to the tutelage of Lieutenant O'Malley.

It was a brutal learning curve with a seemingly unforgiving mentor. O'Malley had been hard on White, but then so had life. At first, the young detective thought it was down to how he'd exposed the failings of the squad with his own tenacious work as a humble patrolman, but as time went on, White figured it was just his boss' way. O'Malley was the iron fist in the steel glove, and it was a pretty brutal glove at that, the junior detective surmised, shaking his head as he wore out the sidewalk next to his stoop. It didn't matter. O'Malley was an excellent and experienced detective, his greatest guide through a world of solving crime. The Lieutenant, the Squad, and the cases he worked on were a huge part of White's life, but Mona and his daughter Amy ran far deeper through his veins. He needed both a career and a family, White concluded, coming to a halt outside his apartment, but combining the two was like trying to mix oil with water.

In the gloomy apartment, Mona stared at the pattern in the rug. It was a place she'd watched Amy play so many times and with such a carefree innocence that she'd almost resented her. The marriage had been going wrong for a long time. In the beginning, of course, there had been excitement, romance, and love. Dominic was a noble man, she knew that, but his cause had changed from back in the day when she had been at the centre of his world. Amy's birth had complicated things further. At a time when her head had been buried in the fog of new motherhood, Dominic began chasing a career as a detective. Whereas some women worried about losing their man to another girl, she had watched on helplessly as she lost him to that damned O'Malley.

He was with them and yet not with them. She thought of all those times he'd sat in the apartment, in his chair or at the dinner table, with the gramophone on or fussing over Amy, and knew there had always been a case going on in his head. She could see the vacancy in his eyes. There was always something he was trying to get to the bottom of and someone he was looking to catch. She saw the energy drain out of him, the focus desert his movement and words. The ghost of her husband lived in that place, breathing the same air, and going through the motions of being a partner and father. She had long lost the essence of the man she'd married, and it scared her what it might do to them all if she addressed the issue, but it frightened her even more what her life, and Amy's, would be like if she did nothing.

They had argued about it too many times, so much that they had reached a bitter impasse. It was impossible to talk calmly now to sort anything out; there was too much hurt on both sides. In another of his many absences, she had decided what she must do: it was time to go back home to Omaha. Both she and Amy needed the security of a man they could rely on, and what had once seemed like stifling control from her father, she now saw as care and infinite attention. Pops Ross would look after them. His ways, and the town they came from, could be trusted never to change.

 It was the kind of environment she wanted for her daughter, to grow up in a place of certainty where simple values ironed out life's creases. In her own youth she had rebelled against it, running away to look for adventure in the East, but now the shine was wearing off New York and she longed for the comfort of home, for everything that Dominic could not or would not give her. It would break his heart, she knew, but he would still have the career he loved. She had made up her mind. She had to do what was best for her and the child. She had to leave now.

Back in the apartment, through the open window White heard a clock somewhere chime eleven. Little did he know it was to mark the final and decisive blow to their marriage as his wife informed him of her decision to leave him. It was a moment from which he would never completely recover. She came into the sitting room dark eyed and serious, a look that rendered him immobile as he turned from the window to face her.

'I'm going, Dom,' she stated. 'I can't do this anymore.' Before he could shake his dumbfounded tongue loose to reply, she added: 'Nothing ever changes. We have the same argument every time and you make the same promises that you never keep. I can't be with someone who is married to Detective Squad.'

'Going?' he managed, his mind racing. 'Where are you going? How will you live?' They were stupid questions, he knew. Mona had clearly had time to make plans.

'I'm taking Amy back to live with my folks in Omaha. That way she can be around a proper family, and you can get on with making Inspector at the Squad.'

For a moment he thought about throwing an accusation at her that this was all about his application for promotion, but he knew the truth. The job had claimed him, and Mona felt she'd lost him a long time ago. She was alone in a hollow marriage, and she needed to be surrounded with love; damn it, she *deserved* to be properly loved. Growing mute with failure, he weakly offered: 'You've made up your mind, but can I do anything to change it? You know I love you very, very much, don't you?'

Mona looked away from him. Staring down at the rug, she uttered: 'I know you do, but you just never show it. Your first love was your work. I can't compete with it anymore.'

'So, when are you going?'

'My father's driving from Omaha the day after tomorrow. He'll stay over…'

'The day after tomorrow?!' White exploded. 'You're leaving New York in two days' time? When am I supposed to see Amy? How do I explain to a three-year-old little girl that she's going away, and she isn't going to live with her daddy anymore?'

Mona tried to remain grave faced, but her incredulity was given away by her tone. '*You* don't have to explain. It will be me that keeps having to explain for a very long time and I don't even know what I'll say because I can't understand it myself. I'm not removing Amy from your life; she's your daughter too and you can always visit her.'

'In Omaha? It's days away and there isn't even a rail link!' He was spitting now, a man drowning in a sea of bile because he'd just woken up to the seismic changes that were coming in the next day or two.

'It's three or four days by car. Cops get leave, or at least most of them manage to take it once in a while!' she argued, her barbed words visibly biting into him.

A fight? Now, of all times? He was confused and hurt. Wasn't it enough, he thought, that she was leaving him? Wasn't it enough that she was taking away his baby girl? Did she really have to twist the knife as well? Hating her momentarily, White took his bitterness past her, storming furiously out of the room. Mona's *I'm sorry, Dom* was obliterated by the rage he felt.

Omaha. This was Pops Ross' influence. Fucking Pops Ross and his need to dominate everyone in his life. He'd never taken to White, of course. Despite him being loving and honourable with a good secure job to boot. Even when he'd given the man a grandchild, still the coldness remained. Ross had believed Mona would find New York too difficult, that the place would be too big for a smalltown girl to cope with, and that she'd give it all up, come to her senses, and return home to her daddy. Her relationship with White had scuppered Ross' hopes and built a wall of resentment between the two men. Now, the old bastard was getting what he'd always wanted, except he'd also have a granddaughter to exert his control over. Pops would be in his element and there was nothing that could be done to prevent it. It made White's blood boil just thinking about it as he walked through the neighbourhood, furious at himself and everything.

He paced around the quiet suburban streets with nowhere to go. When he realised, an hour or so later, that he couldn't exhaust either his body or his mind by doing so, White returned to the front stoop and sat numbly chain-smoking. Mona's leaving him was so soul destroying that he couldn't even turn to drink to try and comfort himself or dispel the shock he felt. He knew if he started drinking now, then it would have no logical end. He would puke up, pass out, awaken and do it all over again until absolutely nothing remained.

His sense of hopelessness was pierced by the ringing of his telephone in the apartment above. Realising he was on call and no one but the precinct would be trying to contact them after midnight, he raced up the steps two at a time and snatched up the receiver while his wife stood watching him blankly from the bedroom door. There had been a murder. A body had been found at the Brooklyn Docks. He went because a human life had been taken and the responsibility of duty called. While he couldn't detach the horrors of his personal life and the emotional carnage whirling around his head, there was a job to do, and this, he knew, was what he did best.

Chapter Three
For a Few Horrors More

Dead bodies, especially those that have been murdered with extreme violence, always bring an ugliness to any setting. The location of New York's latest victim could hardly have been more depressing. Following a small dirt track that was sandwiched between a large wooden warehouse embossed with NEW YORK DOCK COMPANY in ten-foot-high lettering and a drab two storey site office, White shone his flashlight onto a pile of lumber and discarded pallets. There, dumped among the dockyard's detritus, was a badly beaten corpse. The face had been bludgeoned with a blunt instrument and there were footprints visible on the clothes where the torso had been stamped upon. A wound to the back of the head, coupled with no clear defence wounds to the hands or forearms, suggested the victim had initially been attacked from behind.

White considered the alleyway. It was a secluded spot either for an arranged meeting or an ambush, and the windowless warehouses hid the crime from view. He shone his flashlight over the victim again and frowned. 'Hello, what do we have here?' he said quietly. Interestingly, there was an accumulation of earth around the heels of the dead man's shoes. Moving the beam of his flashlight along the ground, White was able to follow two grooves to a place where a porter's trolley stood against the warehouse side. There was fresh blood staining the wooden boards of the trolley. This was where the body had been dragged from.

The detective continued to follow the tracks made by the iron wheels of the trolley around the back of the warehouse to where two planks had been removed from the perimeter fence of the dockyard. Beyond was a quiet backstreet surrounded by factories. So, the body was brought here after the murder took place elsewhere, White thought. After the factories and docks had closed for the night, it would be an easy place to dispose of a body without being seen, but then why leave it where a night watchman was sure to discover it?

The lack of deep colour to the bruising on the victim's skin, coupled with no onset of rigor mortis, testified the victim had not been dead for more than a few hours, meaning the murder had most likely happened under the cover of darkness. They were not too far from open water where a weighed down corpse could be sunk. Even if it were to ever resurface again, the ravages of the sea would have made it unidentifiable. 'So, why leave him here?' White asked the fetid air.

The level of violence was significant. As well as the wounds to the back of the head and face, the footprints on the torso indicated a frenzied but deliberate and hateful attack. As it was, White could tell the victim was male, aged between sixteen and twenty-five and an African American. So, after the violent attack, either something had made the killer panic, or they had simply dumped the body like trash in the closest deserted place to where the assault happened. White couldn't rule out they wanted the body to be found, possibly for reasons relating to the victim's race. He was aware there had been trouble at the docks just a couple of hours earlier, the beating of black strike-breakers by a displaced Irish mob. Looking at the victim's smooth hands though, White concluded he was no longshoreman, so, why had he ended up here? Whatever the reason, someone had hated him enough to bludgeon the life out of him.

After the arrival of the police photographer, the crime scene was illuminated by several kerosene lamps borrowed from the warehouse. The professional snapped away, flashbulbs exploding, while the mortuary attendants waited by their wagon, smoking cigarettes and talking baseball. Then the body was moved and White, aided by two junior detectives and a scrum of patrolmen, made a cursory search of the surrounding area. Given the chaos and confusion of the site, allied to the fact they were working in darkness, it was unsurprising when they found nothing. White hoped it wouldn't rain before dawn, when he would resume his search in daylight before a crowd of early shift dockworkers might disturb the scene.

Looking at his watch, he saw it was two o'clock in the morning. The lights in the main office were still on and he would need to speak properly to the dock manager. Perhaps the guy would let him hole up there until it got light. His reasons were twofold. He wanted to be there to search again at first light, and he couldn't bear to return to the apartment and be stuck in the same space as Mona. If he was lucky, he might even get some coffee thrown in for free, but then, White reflected, the night hadn't given him much fortune so far. As he walked towards the office building, the detective looked up at the dark cranes on the horizon, sullied by the drifting smoke from the factory chimneys. They formed a guard of dishonour high above the murder scene. Tonight, he surmised, he had lost a wife, but some poor young man had lost his life.

The office of David Young was far more salubrious than the dockyard it sat in. It housed a broad Victorian oak desk, glass fronted bookcases and a buttoned leather Chesterfield settee which White eyed as a more than adequate place of rest for a detective waiting to examine the site. The dock manager was understandably tired and clearly troubled by the events of the evening. White figured he didn't look like he had colluded in the beating of a black boy. Young made them both a much-needed coffee and offered White something a little stronger to put in it. The sergeant would normally have refused as part of his professionalism, but it had been one hell of a night and it didn't look like it would get better any time soon. When they were settled in, having both lit cigarettes, White began his questioning.

'So, I take it you went down and took a look at the body, Mr Young?'

The dock manager shifted uneasily in his chair and grimaced. 'Yes, and I won't forget what I saw in a hurry.'

'Did you recognise him at all as one of your workers?'

'I'm sorry, officer, I can't say I did, but then the way he got killed, even his own mother would have trouble identifying him. I can't be sure if he worked here or not. The strike-breakers are all fairly new to us and I don't have much contact with the men on the ground. If you have photographs, I could ask the foreman when he comes on shift, *if* he comes on shift. You heard we had some guys assaulted tonight? Jumped after they left the dockyard and given a pretty good beating by all accounts.'

White frowned and sucked on his cigarette. He wasn't about to tell Young the victim was no dock worker, and he was interested in the link the company manager was making between the two events. 'Any idea who did it? The beating, I mean.'

Taking a swig of his fortified coffee, Young swallowed hard and looked the detective right in the eye. 'We all know who did it. I was talking to your commissioner on the telephone a couple of hours ago and he knew the score. Are you Irish, Mr White?'

White was a little taken aback by the man's sudden change of attitude, but he hid it and probed further. 'What should that matter?'

'You'd be surprised. It seems there are certain perpetrators in this city the cops hesitate to bring to book, if you catch my drift.'

White stared back. So, that was the deal, he thought. 'Not this cop,' he stated firmly. 'I don't care if the criminal is the King of Sweden. If he breaks the law, then I go after him.'

'Glad to hear it, Mr White. It's a shame that you aren't Commissioner of the N.Y.P.D.'

White smiled for the first time that night. 'I've had occasion to think that way myself at times, but it'll never happen until hell freezes over in the mayor's office. Now how about you give me the names of these Irish ringleaders so I can get on with my investigation.'

'Your chief won't like that.'

'Let me tell you a little secret, Mr Young. When I'm hunting a violent murderer, I don't always ask my chief's permission for everything I do.'

Young considered this positive development. 'Okay, officer. There sure ain't no bend in your road. I like that.'

'No bend. That's a good one. Gets me where I'm headed quicker, I guess,' White concluded.

'I hope so,' Young declared. 'As for where the strike's headed, I just don't know.'

'I'm not too up on the politics of it all,' White admitted. 'All I know is when young men start getting killed, it becomes my business.'

'I'm not unsympathetic,' Young explained, tipping up his mug and draining the last of the coffee from it. 'I understand it's tough for those boys, but they don't seem to see there's a fine line between giving them what they want and going to the wall. We have to be competitive, or we die. We're already up against other companies, and there are cheaper ports trying to undercut us all the time. This is not the Capitalist versus Socialist moral war that some people want you to think it is. The Irish boys have gone on strike, we didn't lay them off. We can't afford to pay them what they're demanding, and containers still need unloading. The blacks in Harlem are poorer, more downtrodden, and will work for less. That's just a fact of life. I want the regular workers back; they've always done a good job here and I have nothing against them. The company will give them what they can, but it won't be the figures they're insisting upon. It can't be. That's just economics.'

'And this is murder,' White stated. 'For all the supposed political difficulties around this strike, violence is still violence, and killing is killing. My job is to bring the perpetrator, or perpetrators, to book, and I don't care who I offend in the process. Like you said,' White assured him, downing the dregs of his own coffee, 'there's no bend in my road and I don't give a damn about politics when there's a young man lying dead out there in that yard.'

'That's good to know,' Young nodded. 'You just tell me what you need, and I'll make sure you get it.'

'Let's start with a place for me to lay my head,' White responded. 'I want to resume the search at first light, so there's no point in me going home and coming back. Have you got anywhere here I can catch forty winks?'

'Sure,' Young responded. 'You can have the back room. I'll take the couch.'

So, the two men came to an understanding in the late-night hush of the hot dormant docks.

A little later, White lay on a flimsy camp bed with its springs creaking like they were about to give way every time he moved and tried once more in the solitude of the anteroom to work out where he'd gone wrong as a husband and father. The fact that he was stuck out at the docks waiting to preserve a crime scene pointed undeniably to the impossible position he was in. Rather than going home to his wife to make one last ditch attempt at saving their marriage, here he was chaperoning the dead. Even a cop imbued with the gallows humour that came with the job couldn't have found that one funny, he acknowledged bitterly. The problem was as plain as the nose on his face, but the solution continued to escape him. Who was he kidding anyway? Mona had already made up her mind, and there was nothing he could do now to change it.

Policing in New York City had never been the same as he'd seen it growing up in the Midwest. The draw of being a city cop was the energy and endless variety that surrounded criminal events: every day was a new experience to learn from in the Great American Melting Pot and he loved that. It was addictive. Yet the same principles of policing, to uphold the laws that governed society for its own good, and to help bring to justice those who wilfully and maliciously broke those laws, still existed in the backwater of a small town he'd lived in as a youth. The difference there was familiarity. The local sheriff knew everyone, and the close community saw the good he did and understood it. To Mona, the victims White sought justice for were remote. She never knew them or saw how the tragedy of crime destroyed their lives, so, she couldn't fully understand *why* he had to dedicate himself to apprehending the guilty perpetrators. She just didn't get it, and she never would. Perhaps if she'd stayed in the courtroom and stuck at being a stenographer, she'd have seen things through similar eyes, but she hadn't and there was no point in regretting their different paths now.

Recognising he had to choose between Mona and the job didn't make things any easier. White had known this all along but had chosen to ignore it because if he wasn't police, he didn't have the first clue what the hell he would be. She hated the job he loved, that was the unsolvable riddle, and White had to admit, turning uneasily on the thin mattress, that he could not give it up for her. He couldn't stop being a detective, even if it cost him his wife, that was the brutal truth of the matter. Turning over in the uncomfortable bed again, he willed sleep to come, but it seemed very far away right then. 'You made your bed, now lie in it,' his inner voice intoned to him, its sarcasm as always, an unwanted addition to his thoughts. It left White feeling nothing but sadness for the situation he was in. He didn't want to lose Mona, and the idea of not seeing Amy grow up was tearing at his mind. He felt utterly defeated and clung to the idea that solving this murder might somehow make life just a little more bearable. It was a misplaced logic, he knew, but he couldn't help how his head worked. He had to be true to it because pretty soon it might be all he had left for company.

The same thoughts kept spinning round White's mind, and he tormented himself further by constantly checking his wristwatch, marking off the half-hours where he could not get to sleep. Three turned to half-three, then four and half-four. When the detective finally dozed off, he was greeted by vivid dreams that put him in familiar places and pulled him back into his past. He was in Prospect Park and could feel the warm sun soaking into his skin. He was pushing a perambulator, and from it, Amy stared up at him with all the big-eyed curiosity of a new-born. She was drinking in everything, her father in his shirtsleeves, the dappled light filtering through the trees, passers by in their different shapes and colours. It was a beautiful afternoon, but then White found himself still walking the park in the dusk, with no pram to push, no infant to care for, and most of the people gone.

He took comfort in a young couple who were holding hands as they sat upon a bench, even though he couldn't make out their faces in the quickening dark. He envied them their youth, and how powerful it felt to be that young and have the whole world at your feet, blissfully unaware of the naivety of your hopes and dreams. Then, the darkness enclosed everything, as if the trees had come together to suffocate them all. There was a cry that seemed to echo around the park, and it was that which snapped White awake once again.

The cot creaked under him and as he came slowly to his senses, the detective recognised the small, drab room he was in. The dream had aroused in him a feeling of being young and in love, dynamic times when the world had seemed a more carefree place, even for a cynic like him. He thought back to when he'd first met Mona; he'd been giving evidence in a trial while she took everything down in her role as the court stenographer. Their paths had seemed fated to cross. He kept noticing her typing as he answered the questions, and it had prompted him to ask her out on a date straight after. He should have seen the signs when she quit her post three months later because it was too gruesome hearing the bad things people had done to one another, but those early days of love had left him blind like any other man going through the same experience. They were unwelcome thoughts now, and the contrast of being alone on the crappy bed in the even crappier room while a body slowly festered in the morgue downtown wasn't lost on White. He was in his own version of hell, he concluded.

Nothing for it now but to wait for the dawn and keep moving forwards, he thought, checking in with his wristwatch one more time. Half-past five. That meant it would soon be getting light. The early shift at the precinct was about to clock on, and he'd requested lots of patrolmen to help him search the dockyard. He might as well lay here on this terrible bed until they arrived, even if it was a form of torture. What was it someone had once told him? *Rest is the second-best thing to sleep.* No chance of either of those things happening here, he bemoaned. That was the last thought White had before improbably drifting off. The challenges of crime in the new day would all too soon slap him back into action, which was okay with White because for him, the next best thing to rest was sleuthing. That was just who he was, and it wasn't about to change.

Chapter Four
Sanguine in the Small Hours

Grace Walker sat sewing in the small hours, not through poverty or necessity, but because she simply couldn't sleep. The Harlem apartment was empty save for her quiet presence, and after a while the silence became toxic, like a deadly gas drifting over the trenches all those miles away in France. This was just one of the many worries that had Grace awake and anxious on the hot summer's night. The last three months had brought seismic changes, both to America and to the Walker household, with the threat of bloodshed hanging over the nation and her man who had taken up the draft. Grace feared for her husband and her son, two African American men who might be facing very different but nonetheless deadly dangers in the immediate future. Concentrating on the needlework helped distract her fraught mind.

For the first two hours after midnight, she had busied herself with chores. Some, like the ironing, were essential. There was a logic to heating the flat iron during the coolest hours of what had been another broiling day, and as she smoothed out the creases from the clothes, Grace thought how good it would be if she could irradicate her worries with such ease. Joseph, her only son, had taken to spreading his wings on these long summer nights, a fledgling bird flying freely on his own for the first time, tasting adulthood in the thrill of staying out late. Even so, he usually returned by midnight, mindful of his mother's restlessness over what he might encounter on the streets of New York City after dark. She had started to iron more fervidly when it was half-past twelve and he had not come home.

Everything had arrived at the wrong time, she reflected, hanging her boy's work shirts neatly in his wardrobe. She paused as she caught a glimpse of herself in front of the mirror set into the inside of the wardrobe door. When had she gotten so old, she asked? She was not yet forty, and her hair maintained its lustrous and thick blackness, but the lines around her eyes and mouth told their story of hardships faced and troubles now weighing her down. The sparkle had gone from those eyes, all the energy displaced by a fear that sniped at her stomach and had her up cleaning in the middle of the night. Her figure, always fulsome and strong, was now reduced to a frame like an unfilled sail. Her flesh hung through worry rather than hunger. The Walkers were intelligent and resourceful people, there was always food on their table, but it wasn't what she didn't eat that mattered right now, it was what ate away at her.

Grace feared for her son out there in the world. Joseph had left school and worked as a kitchen porter, but in the spring, he had taken advantage of the expansion at the Waldorf-Astoria hotel and gotten himself a job with greater prospects. He still worked in the kitchens at times, but his warm and professional manner saw him promoted to front of house. At just eighteen, Joseph was filling the shoes of the head waiter when the restaurant was at its busiest and the diners at their most demanding. Grace was brimming with pride at her son's tales from work, and the management were impressed with him also. They wanted to keep Joseph at the hotel and had told him a bright career lay ahead, but he wanted more. Exactly what that was, he hadn't worked out yet, but Grace saw something in her son, a powerful ambition, that might mark him out for greatness. The only problem was racial prejudice made that a journey full of pitfalls. Too many white folks wanted to keep black people at the bottom of the pile. Young men like Joseph made them fearful.

When there was nothing left to iron, Grace moved on to scrubbing the kitchen floor, even though she had already cleaned it that morning and there was only her and Joseph to make it dirty. One o'clock came and went, so the unsettled mother resorted to shuffling and restacking bills and other correspondence she had previously organized in that meticulous way of hers. Perhaps her subconscious had been seeking comfort from her husband's latest letter, more detailed than the first, as he waited to see action over in France. Charles was a fierce patriot who had joined up as soon as drafting called for men to defend the glorious freedoms of America. A month ago, he had been posted as part of the American Expeditionary Forces. It sounded impressive, but Grace knew it meant only one thing: war. She paused to read through the letter again, its contents drawing her closer to her husband as she heard his voice in the written words.

June 30th, Nancy, France.

My Dearest Grace,

I hope this letter finds you in fine health and good spirits. As I explained when I first wrote, there is no danger here yet, just endless organizing and drills in preparation for engaging with the enemy. Other than that, we are left to our own devices. There is a camaraderie developing amongst our division, both black and white, a feeling that we are men together that will soon be fighting for a common cause we all firmly believe in. There are moments when issues of race remind us coloured soldiers of our 'place' socially, but this is the army, and the sense that we are all facing the same danger renders the racial hierarchy somehow less important.

In the town we have been able to meet fellow fighters both from England and France. There is something deeply trustworthy about these men, a gravity and honesty that, while unsettling at first, we quickly came to appreciate. They have heard about, or in some cases faced, the unimaginable. Horrific stories of the battlefields are sometimes mentioned in passing, seeping through the cracks of their bonhomie like accidental spillages. The men who directly witnessed the worst remain mute about it. They are haunted by guilt at having survived. One spoke of being caught in a gas attack, fumbling for his mask while his eyes burned, nose streamed, and lungs heaved. He got his mask on just in time and so lived to tell the story, but the scars on his lungs will never heal. Others weren't so lucky, he said, leaving the conversation at that.

Reading through what I have written so far, I have the urge to erase the previous lines, but I promised you I would relay my experiences without censure. I want to reassure you the worst of this war has passed. There is talk in the camp we may not fight at all, that the enemy's forces are so depleted and disheartened that America's entry into the war has all but broken their spirit. They know they cannot win now. Some think the conflict will not see another winter, that the Germans have no stomach for it, let alone the supplies to keep them going. I am hopeful this is the case. While I do not shirk my responsibility, it would be better, I know, to win by the threat of our presence. Anything else carries inevitable dangers, and while I am not scared, only a fool would want to run into the fire of conflict.

I must sign off now, more drill beckons. I miss you both and will write again soon. Let us all hope this war is coming to an end and America's intervention has hastened this. Make sure Joseph is attentive to you. He knows he must take care of you in my absence. He is a good boy, but I have seen the vigour of youth within him, and that inevitably brings with it some degree of selfishness. I am excited about your news of the parade and am disappointed to be missing it. It sounds like a powerful form of protest, much *needed in the turbulent times of our nation and the suffering of our race.*

May good fortune bless your days and the Lord protect you both. I miss you, my dear wife.

Yours with great affection,

Charles.

Grace folded the letter neatly and placed it back into its envelope. She clung to the hope of cessation, an end to the war so that Charles could return safely home, but she sensed more blood would need to be shed before that could happen. Her faith had taught her to always be optimistic, but this was a World War, and death had cast its shadow over the continent of Europe so darkly that it had even reached out across the Atlantic. The reference about Joseph also made her feel uneasy. It was as if Charles had prophesied their son's waywardness, although he could not see the dangers it held because of his own far more perilous situation. There was nothing for it but to find some more chores to do, Grace thought, as the church clock announced it was half-past one.

She busied herself with dusting, inventing cobwebs where there were none, waving the broom absentmindedly at the phantom threads, distracted by thoughts of where her son might be at so late an hour. The motion kept her physically active in an attempt to stave off the nervous foreboding that was growing inside her. The foundations of her faith had been tested, first by Charles being posted to France, and now, by Joseph's absence so deep into the night. She knew he was in love, that somewhere a sweetheart consumed all his attention; she was his mother, and these things were plain for her to see, but who the girl was and where they might be remained a mystery.

So it was that at around two a.m., Grace took to her sewing, working the needle through the cloth automatically like the practiced seamstress she was. Most of her work now was mending the clothes of her people, for they were too poor to cast out the threadbare or torn. Yet, her skills extended far beyond simple darning. She had produced fabulous wedding dresses in taffeta and silk, lace, and embroidered pearls. The dresses she had created for ceremony sang out at the altar, the brides that wore them were a vision of black beauty never to be forgotten by those who witnessed them. While Grace sewed, there was some element of relief, and so, she felt able to turn her mind to the upcoming Silent Parade.

Her politics were simple. She was deeply disturbed by the treatment of African Americans across the country, and was well aware that New York remained a permissive and privileged place to live in. Recently, racial tensions had risen. In Chicago, Illinois, there had been rioting, and black citizens had been shot like criminals, condemned without trial or jury, their lives snuffed out on chaotic streets and the action justified as necessary to facilitate the restoration of order. The taking of black lives came all too easily, and Grace mourned the slaughtered while fearing such behaviour might find its way to her own town. It wasn't the burning crosses of the south, but the blood spilt onto the streets was no less red, and the victims in the graves were just as dead.

The parade gave her hope. Four years ago, she had watched the suffragettes as they took over the streets, a powerful procession that silently established a weighty cause, the eerie quiet of the normally vibrant Manhattan district casting a spell upon those who were there to experience the moment, sending a sign across the city and beyond that oppression and disenfranchisement fostered a festering discontent that would rise up, like a hot sun that could not be suppressed. It affected her, and she knew this was the statement her people should be making, a soundless stand, save for the insistent rhythm of the drums to lend the march a solemn, funereal air. The masterstroke would be the presence of so many black children.

The idea had come from William Du Bois, the N.A.A.C.P. leader who had energised the people of Harlem into unprecedented action. Du Bois was a man of strong character, a good man getting things done in the right way. While other political activists longed for revenge, wanting to fight fire with fire, bloodshed with more bloodshed, Du Bois was different. He recognised the power of a dignified stand, and the impact that the astonishing sight of thousands of innocent black children dressed all in white as a symbol of their purity would bring, both to the crowds that thronged the streets, and in the pictures the newspapers printed of the parade.

Those images would speak in a profound way of a need for peace, for the cessation of violence, exposing and shaming those who carried out such despicable acts, and leaving the nation in no doubt as to the wrongs of the crimes committed against their fellow Americans, their fellow human beings, all because of a difference in skin colour that was really no difference at all, especially in the eyes of God.

Grace accidentally pricked her finger, a bubble of blood welling on the tip. She watched as it spilled over and left a red line that ran down into her palm. The spell of her musing was broken. It was half-past two in the morning, and all the sewing in the world, all the dreams of a better America, could not banish the bad omens that hung over her. She thought again of Illinois, the fire and the fury all meted out upon black people because they had dared to try and be equal, not even truly equal, but just to taste what that world was like. She thought of the parade and worried about the white response, feeling fearful of the country she was living in. That fear found its greatest shape in her anxiety about her errant son, lost somewhere out there in the night. She licked the blood from her palm and paired it together with the other one in a prayer, that her golden boy would come back unharmed before the sun rose again over Harlem.

Grace woke up two hours later with her head resting on the table where her needlework lay. She got up and checked her son's room. The bed was empty and unslept in. Joseph had not come home. It was all she could do to remain hopeful that he was resting peacefully next to his girl somewhere. She forced herself to have faith in Him and stay sanguine in these testing times.

Chapter Five
Peccare Nel Cuore Della Notte

Isabella lay curled up in a self-protecting ball on her bed. It was the early hours of the morning, and the Visconti house was quiet, save for the muffled sound of Frank's snoring from the bedroom below. Danny had worked himself up into a rage the like of which she'd never seen from him before. The threat to tell their father everything he knew about her boyfriend if she didn't hand over his name and address hadn't been necessary. She was too scared of what Danny might do to her there and then as he hissed under his breath and gripped her wrist so tightly it shot a sharp pain through the bones and made her feel faint. He'd never laid a finger on her before tonight, but now her protector had had such a look in his eyes she thought he might strangle her if she didn't give him what he wanted.

She wished she could have warned her beloved, but Frank had been awake and prowling the hallway, aroused by Danny's going out and still mad at his daughter, meaning the only exit would have been through her bedroom window to drop into the garden below. Even if she'd escaped injury dropping all those feet, Isabella knew her brother would reach Harlem before she could. Her only hope was the black community would protect her young man, but then that got her worrying about what they might do to Danny. She hoped maybe he'd wear his anger out as he walked across the city, but she knew from the way he'd been when he was in her room that was just wishful thinking. No, Danny was hellbent on upholding the honour of his family. He was no better and just as dangerous as their father in that respect.

She uncurled herself and got up to look out of the window. She couldn't sleep, not with the frightening things that had happened tonight. The darkness only made those terrible events feel even more ominous. How quickly the beauty of her evening had turned ugly, she thought. The whispered dreams of the park had been crushed beneath the fury of the male Viscontis and she was forbidden to ever see her beloved again. Even if Danny didn't find him and do him harm, all their plans to wait and save for a passage to Europe were in tatters now. The truth would come out, it was already all round the neighbourhood according to her brother, and if her father didn't actually murder her, he would at least have her sent back to Italy to some goddamn convent or something. Pride and a good name always came ahead of love with her people. Those two things were as important as God to them.

Looking out onto the deserted street, she tried to formulate a new plan. While it was true her father might want to ship her off back to the motherland, the arrangements would take time, as would getting her mother to agree to and fully accept it. Isabella knew she must be contrite, tow the line, and pretend to show compliance and remorse. It would buy her several days to get over the shock and work out how to escape the fate that awaited her. She wouldn't put it past her father to try and imprison her in the house, but she would find a way to leave when she needed to. She had some money saved up from her job at the restaurant, enough to buy a ticket to someplace else. Where, she didn't know right then. She just hoped her love would be able to come with her because she couldn't imagine living life without him.

She was too old for fairy tales, but when he'd kissed her under the warm moon, it was as if something she'd dreamt about all her life materialised in that golden moment. His taste, his touch, and his smell were all still so vivid it was as if he were right there in the room with her. The park seemed half a world away now, and her romantic thoughts were interrupted by the sound of the front door opening then closing again. From the voices outside her bedroom door, it was clear Danny had finally returned, and her father was grilling him about where he'd been at this hour. She only heard him say that he'd been out for a walk because he couldn't sleep.

Danny had been out for hours and by the time Isabella had waited for her father to go back to sleep, the dawn light was already tinging the sky with pinks and purples. Despite her fear, she had to find out what had happened, she had to know if her beloved was okay. So, she tiptoed tentatively over to her brother's room. She found him still awake when she entered, his eyes glaring up at her from the pillow. For a while, she couldn't find the courage to speak, but she felt compelled to question Danny about where he'd been all that time and what exactly it was he'd done.

'What happened, Danny?'

'Nothing,' he scowled.

'Nothing? What were you doing out all that time?'

'I don't want to talk about it! I'm disgusted with you. Get out of my room!'

Knowing his shouting would have woken their father again, Isabella retreated to her bed. She curled up into a ball once more and rocked herself like a baby in a crib, but still no comfort would come. As soon as she was able to, she vowed to go find out for herself if her beloved remained unharmed.

It was the first hours of a new morning and Marco Antolini couldn't sleep. He kept thinking back to the visit from Frank Visconti earlier that evening and knew it boded trouble. Isabella was lying to her father, and in the Italian community that was committing a sin. Marco yawned, and giving up on his bed, headed into the kitchen for a glass of milk. Bella was a good kid, he thought, sipping at the rich drink. She'd always turned up on time for her shifts at the restaurant, she was good with the customers, and it was clear she was going to make something of herself. She was spirited, just like her father, Marco reflected. The problem was, when you got two strong people living in the same house and only one of them made the rules, things always had the potential to explode.

He thought about his own relationship with Benny, the only son they'd had before his wife Angelina died giving birth to their second child who also did not survive. He wondered if the tragedy had exacerbated the boy's condition, whatever that was exactly. After Angelina's death, they became kindred spirits, the boy who had always struggled to make sense of all things emotional, and the widower who could no longer bear to see other couples together after having his own life partner incomprehensibly snatched away from him. They co-existed quietly in the same house, father and son, and worked silently to keep the restaurant running. Sometimes, Benny's affliction worried Marco and he longed for enthusiasm and conversation, which was why he valued Bella's presence so much. At other times, he felt a deep understanding with his son, an unspoken pact to keep everyone at arms' length, because life could hurt you too much.

Now, he feared he might be losing Bella's services, and it made him sad. Marco knew he hadn't betrayed the kid. Even if he'd have lied about what time she'd been finishing at the restaurant, the rumours circulating the neighbourhood, or a version of them at least, would have reached Frank sooner or later. He wondered if Frank had confronted his daughter yet. Knowing the man, he suspected so. If Bella was smart, and Marco was sure she was, then she'd only reveal part of what she'd been up to and agree to it ending right there and then. With any luck the whole thing might die down and the gossips move on to the next scandal. If Frank found out what Benny had finally revealed, all hell would break loose in the Visconti house.

It had taken until after hours at the restaurant and Bella's departure for Marco to quiz Benny. He'd seen something in his son's expression when Frank had been making his complaint, not much, but enough for him to recognise Benny knew more than he was saying. Then again, Benny always kept his cards close to his chest. Marco knew the best way to approach his boy, so, while he mopped the floor and Benny stacked clean plates, he introduced the topic casually and began his gentle probing for information.

'Bella seemed cheerful as ever tonight. I guess Frank hasn't had the chance to speak to her yet.'

Benny put away two more dishes before he spoke. 'I guess not,' was all he replied.

'I wonder where she's been going after she finishes up here. It's a little late for a young girl to be alone out on the streets. I'm not sure it's safe, if she is alone, that is.'

Benny was not about to be drawn. The clinking of crockery was his only response. So, Marco pushed further.

'You hang out with the Visconti kids. Any idea what Bella's been doing? Has Danny talked to you about it?' he asked.

'Danny hasn't told me a thing,' Benny stated, continuing to methodically stack the plates.

'But you got some idea, right?' Marco asserted, inviting a confidence as he pretended to be more absorbed with his mopping.

'Some of the boys in the neighbourhood have been saying things,' Benny said flatly, not trying to be quizzed further, but knowing deep down he wanted the burning secret to come out.

'What things?' Marco asked, stopping to look at his son while leaning on his mop.

'They said they'd seen Bella with a boy, but not someone from the Italian Quarter,' Benny revealed through gritted teeth. Marco waited, and in the silence of the empty restaurant, he stared a little harder at his son, willing him to go on. 'They said he was a black boy!' Benny blurted out.

'Oh, Jesus!' Marco exclaimed.

Benny put away the last plate with a clatter. 'See why I didn't want to tell you?' he said angrily. 'Can I go now? I need a walk to clear my head.'

'Of course,' Marco said, gesturing to the door. He knew the kids were all close and had been since junior school. It was understandable Benny would be upset and unsettled by the taboo of what Bella was doing if it was to be believed. Much as he didn't like it, Marco resolved to get to the bottom of the matter and find out the truth. He felt like an uncle to the girl, and he'd do anything he could to avert a disaster, even if it meant keeping things from Frank.

That was what had made it impossible to sleep, Marco reflected, finishing his milk, rinsing out the glass, and putting it on the side of the sink. He ought to go check on Benny. Often, the boy had trouble sleeping and would take a walk to avoid disturbing his father. It was one of the things that helped calm the thoughts in Benny's head. He'd given the kid some space after the scene at the restaurant and Benny had returned home before Marco could become more restless, so all was well. A flicker of light from the yard caught his eye, the shadow of Benny sitting out by a small fire, smoking a cigarette, and contemplating the night, the flames another thing that soothed them both. Marco lit his own smoke and went out to sit with his boy.

'I couldn't sleep,' he told his son. 'I guess you couldn't either.'

'It's a nice night,' Benny said, staring into the flames. 'Feels calm sitting here and smoking by the fire.'

'It does,' Marco replied. 'I figure this business with Bella is worrying us both. If what you told me earlier is true and not just malicious gossip, that girl's going to be in a whole lot of trouble.'

'It's true,' Benny said resignedly, still not taking his gaze from the fire. 'I saw her with the guy myself.'

'You saw her? When was this? Why didn't you say anything?'

'It was a couple of weeks ago,' Benny confessed. 'I didn't know what to do. You don't tell a bad thing like that.'

'That's true,' Marco reflected, puffing with agitation on his cigarette. 'I hope to God she gets this sorted out. Maybe Frank knowing something is wrong will scare her into coming to her senses. She's clever enough to sell him half a story. Let's just pray the worst of it stays hid.'

'Yeah,' said Benny, flipping his cigarette butt into the fire. 'I'm going to bed now. You want to keep this fire lit, or shall I put it out?'

'Leave it. I think I might sit here for a little while longer. It's been one hell of a day. Night, Benny.'

'Night,' Benny said, lumbering his way off towards the house.

So, Marco sat smoking in the darkness with the fire playing light onto his troubled features. He offered up a prayer that the young girl and her family might be spared the shame of the scandal breaking. Benny was a difficult young man to get along with at times, he thought, but at least he hadn't brought that kind of chaos into his house. He finished his smoke as the fire died down and raked over the embers until he was sure they could be left. Then the weary Italian made his way back to bed. There was nothing more could be done today. He'd just have to wait and see what tomorrow would bring.

Danny Visconti clenched his fists and felt the knuckles on one hand tighten where they were swollen and bruised. The events of the night raced through his mind, and everywhere he turned there were bloody visions. Frank didn't know the whole truth, but he was gonna know. There was no way of keeping this a secret, not now. The storm that had been threatening their family was beginning to break, and there could be no shelter from it for any of them. He wished he could have told his mother everything that day she was hanging out the washing, but there was no way of turning back the clock. Things had been done that could never be undone. He thought about what all this would do to his parents, and it made his stomach churn. Part of him regretted making it back home after the confrontations of the night. It might have been better if he'd died out there. At least then the focus would've been taken away from what his sister had done.

He'd been hellbent on heading for Harlem, to the address Bella had given him. He knew who he was looking for because he'd seen the guy a couple of times hanging around her stenography college. That was before the rumours began and he disappeared. His blood had been up, but even as he'd walked, Danny had started to think about being a lone white boy entering a black neighbourhood late at night. He knew he should've waited until the morning, but his anger drove him on, ignoring the danger until down near the docks where he'd turned a corner and stumbled into a small group of men being set upon. They were black and bleeding, the white mob attacking them showed no mercy. Danny saw it as a sign.

Later, in the aftermath, he'd found himself keeping to the quietest streets, just trying to stay out of sight. Violent images crowded his mind, and he realised he'd subconsciously walked to the hospital. He stood outside, studying his knuckles, and wondered why he'd come to this place. Before he could move on, a pair of beaten black men emerged and began walking with difficulty down the path. He thought he recognised them from earlier, but the grotesque visions swam up before him, and he looked away.

'Hey!' one of the men called out. 'You were down by the docks. You saw those bastards beating on us. You're a witness!'

Danny shook his head and remained mute. The other man seemed to be trying to calm his friend down and reason with him, but the figure remained determined.

'He could go to the police for us, Abraham. They got to listen to the word of a white kid. We can't just let those guys get away with what they done to us.'

'You crazy if you think the police is going to listen to anyone about this,' the man called Abraham scowled. 'They don't want to know. Look at that kid's knuckles. He looks like he been in a fight himself. He ain't going to help us. All he is is more trouble.'

Danny came to his senses and fled the scene. He kept running until he found an alleyway, breathing hard and feeling sick. Still the demons of the night appeared in front of his eyes, and he wanted to be back home in his own bed. He craved for the horror of what had happened to disappear, for the rage and the blood and the violence to be washed away with sleep, so he could awaken and pretend none of it had taken place. He didn't want to face strangers. He'd never been good with new people and now, more than ever, he needed solitude to get through what had happened.

Home had brought him some sense of comfort and safety. He'd been able to present himself well enough to his father so the old man didn't get suspicious, but he'd been seen by the docks and at least two men had recognised him again. What if more people remembered his face? What if the police that had rushed to the scene recalled him being there? What then? No one had seen him between the other trouble and the hospital though. That might have been his saving grace, the presence of mind to stay in the shadows after the attack.

His thoughts were interrupted by the sound of birdsong and he realised the dawn had come without him noticing. Frank would be up soon, then he would have to face more showdowns. So far, only he and Bella knew the boy she'd been seeing was black, and they both desperately wanted to keep it that way. Danny understood he needed to help his sister now, despite still feeling appalled by what she'd done, because they both had vital reasons for the truth to never come out. Their futures depended on it. They were partners in crime, even though they now hated each other. Sinning in the dark hours had made it that way.

Chapter Six
Heartbreak in Harlem

White woke up with a mouth like a stable stall and a crick in his neck where the strange bed had done its damage, which was something of an insult given he'd barely slept an hour on it. He splashed his face with water and set his tie straight before hiding his crumpled shirt beneath his jacket. Young made him some fresh coffee and he drank it while rubbing his stubble and blinking the bleariness out of his eyes. Just before six o'clock in the morning he was joined by a group of beat cops who he instructed as to how to search the scene while chewing on his second cigarette of the day. It turned out to be a fruitless exercise.

In daylight, the vast and disordered nature of the docks became clearer. The operation was huge, with multiple quays, cranes, and loading bays. They were surrounded by heavy industry, and the unforgiving environment made White think back to last night's conversation with Young about the politics of the strike. The detective could see the hard work that went on in this place, but he could also imagine how easily it might brutalize a man, making it much easier for him to turn to murder.

There was something else about the docks though, White thought, as he stood there surveying them in the first cool light of the morning. It was as if the body they'd found was just one in a series of violent and hideous crimes that had washed up here, a dark setting where the horrors of what one man could do to another was distilled in the damp atmosphere he was now breathing in. Sometimes, being a cop made you recognize things you didn't necessarily want to.

He thanked Young and headed on back to the station to have a shave and write up his notes on the case so far. In his broom cupboard of an office, he massaged his neck while breakfasting on another cigarette. The names of the Irish ringleaders had been sent down to records to see if either of the men had any previous convictions. When the knock on his door came, he thought it was in response to his request for information, but it was the sharp and reliable desk sergeant who had made a possible connection to the identity of White's murder victim. An eighteen –year-old African American from Harlem had been reported missing by his fractious mother. Young men full of energy on a hot night in New York City didn't always return home to their mamas. It was a long shot, but it was still worth checking out. The desk sergeant gave White the address of the mother and showed him a photograph she had left. It was then the detective's heart sank. It looked like the young man wasn't missing anymore.

Another blow in a time of disaster, White thought. Mona would be leaving New York with their daughter tomorrow, aided and abetted by the dominant Pops Ross, but now he had an identity for his victim, and an age that showed the promises of life the young man had been robbed of. The pull to solve the case became even stronger as White studied the photograph. His marriage was gone, this boy was dead, and somewhere out there the killer was still at large. While one part of him chastised himself for not heading home to spend some last precious hours with Amy, another recognized time was everything in a murder investigation. The clues would dry up and the trail would go cold. He had to get on it right away. Putting on his fedora, the detective made his way out of the precinct towards the address he'd been handed. He was about to bring the worst kind of news to a mother in Harlem.

At St. Philip's Episcopal Church in Harlem, the local members of the N.A.A.C.P. were meeting to discuss their final preparations for a gigantic silent protest parade against the treatment of black citizens across America. They were all set to march through the most famous streets in New York in just two weeks' time. Taking their cue from the suffragettes who had protested with a powerful message several years earlier, their hope was to present African Americans as human beings with a dignity and civility that deserved recognition. Attitudes needed to change, not so much in New York as elsewhere, but the Great American Melting Pot was the only place where they would be permitted to make such a protest.

As a senior member of the N.A.A.C.P. and a powerful orator, William Du Bois cut an impressive figure at the podium. A handsome and smartly attired man in his late forties with a carefully waxed moustache and twinkling, intelligent eyes, he held the attention of the congregation completely.

'There are racial tensions happening in this very city, my good people. Why, only last night our brothers working at the Brooklyn Docks were the victims of an unprovoked and violent attack by white perpetrators. Their only crime was to work a shift so they could provide for their families. You have all heard about the terrible scenes in Chicago, East St. Louis, where rioting resulted in the brutal killing of unarmed African Americans. The fact is we are seen as no better than animals by the white population. They beat us and suppress us with the support of the authorities. Now they are murdering our sons in the streets. We, a brave people who will go to war against Germany to protect American values, are still not valued ourselves. The only way things can change is for coloured people to be seen as civilised and intelligent human beings, deserving of the same treatment as white folks. This is why we march. All I ask, as I stand here now before you, is that you join us to convey a dignified and sombre message. Together we can make a difference for ourselves, and more importantly, for the generations that will follow us.'

The meeting house responded with enthusiastic applause and cries of assent. Sitting among the audience, Grace Walker was both inspired and anxious. Her only son, Joseph, had not come home last night, and even though he had gotten into the habit of returning late, he'd never failed to appear before now. Grace knew her son was aware of how much she worried about him, especially now his father was away fighting in the war. She was convinced something must have happened to him, so she had reported him as missing to the police. The sergeant at the precinct had not wanted to take the picture of Joseph, preferring to wait and see if he turned up of his own accord, but Grace insisted. Now, in the house of God, she made a silent prayer for the safe return of her boy.

White entered the coloured district of Harlem and felt a palpable change. In any other area of New York, he could practise anonymity when he needed to, be the watcher and the listener unnoticed. Yet here mistrustful eyes peered out from the shadows of doorways and the tensions of race meant his every move was scrutinised. In total contrast to his years as a beat cop, he walked along the sidewalk of Lenox Avenue as humbly as a pastor, making himself small and peaceful. This was not the area for a lone detective to be waving his badge around in. Besides, he was here on tragic business and with genuine condolences. These people had suffered enough.

He recognised Grace Walker immediately; her dead son bore the stamp of her fine features like statues cast from the same mould. The noble looking gentleman accompanying her was just saying his farewells judging from his body language; he was too expensively dressed to be a resident of Harlem. White considered waiting for him to depart before bringing horror to her home but calculated such a companion might be invaluable to help her with the initial shock of her son's untimely death. So, he introduced himself and could see from Grace's expression that she had read the terrible news he carried.

Inside, the apartment was thrifty but spotlessly clean and dignified. It reflected the woman that lived there. Grace Walker had substance about her. White could read the humanity in her face, but it was also marked by the quiet determination of a woman who had had to endure much hardship, worry, and prejudice. The picture of the Virgin Mary that hung upon the kitchen wall told him not only of Grace's religious beliefs, but also fitted the powerful maternal presence that dominated her humble home. However, White thought, even a woman like this would crumble inside at the news he was about to deliver. Sitting around a battered table, White came to the point. It was no use pretending to intelligent folk like these. He spoke quietly and with genuine regret.

'Mrs Walker; Mr Du Bois. This morning, I was informed of a missing person and shown the photograph you left. I am afraid I found your son, Joseph, dead last night. He had been the victim of a homicide. I am very sorry to have to bring you such news.'

Du Bois spoke first, Grace was still falling down a deep chasm. 'Are you certain the victim was Joseph, detective?'

'I am, sir. Officially, I will need someone to identify Joseph's body. Is there a male member of the family who could do that?'

Du Bois shook his head. 'Charles, Joseph's father, is away fighting in the war. He was their only child. I met the young man briefly. I don't suppose that is good enough to suffice, but I can accompany Grace. I would like to do so. Can it wait a while, detective? If you are sure and it is a formality, it might be best to let Grace prepare herself first.'

At this, Mrs Walker anchored herself. Looking between both of the gentlemen, she quietly asserted her own wishes. 'If my boy child has been taken, then I want to see him and say my goodbyes. I have one man risking his life thousands of miles away for goodness knows what. Let me be close to my boy. I had dreaded facing death. I thought it would arrive in a telegram from overseas. Instead, you came.'

White leaned in; his hands cupped together on the table. He looked directly at Grace Walker. 'I'm sorry. I wish I had different news for you. I have a daughter myself. I can't imagine how I'd feel if I was dealt this kind of blow.' As he said the words, the detective felt a pain in his chest as he realised he was, in a less permanent way, facing the removal of his only child. Joseph's murder was something much worse though, and as she sat there distraught at her kitchen table, Grace had White see a whole other level of loss.

Nevertheless, there was something in his face, something in his tone, that struck a chord with both

Grace and Du Bois. With gentle and tentative assent, the trio set out from the apartment to take the dreaded journey to the City Morgue. Except when they walked down the front steps, a hostile crowd had gathered around White's automobile.

The leader of the mob was tall and skinny. He had a young man's body but an old man's face that bore a livid pink scar across one cheek. Instinctively, White tensed up for battle. He believed the hand the young man kept in his pocket concealed a weapon that he was fully prepared to use.

'What the hell business this white man got with you, missus Walker? He a lawman? You in Harlem now, lawman. You better watch how you be treatin' black folks down here in this neighbourhood.'

Du Bois placed himself strategically between the young maverick and the uncompromising cop. He seemed perfectly calm, but also at least a foot taller than just a moment ago. In a voice that was both mellifluous and authoritative, he said: 'No need for confrontation here. Mr White is helping us in a difficult time. Mrs Walker has just lost her son, so if you would show her the respect of letting us all pass, that would be greatly appreciated.'

The youth was unsettled by the educated talk and civility of Du Bois, but he still miscalculated the situation. Perhaps it was the issue of colour that blinded him to the gravitas of the gentleman's words, that, or a violent lust to hit out at the world and the injustices he felt.

'Mr *White*! You mean the man come down here wearing his name like a flag to stick into the black soil like another colonizer. What are you, his pathfinder?' It was not a joke and the youth's eyes blazed with anger.

Grace Walker stepped forward. 'Young man, I have a husband at war and a boy wouldn't harm a fly lying dead. If you want to cause trouble, do it somewhere else, or so help me God, I will slap you so hard to make your head spin. You ain't fit to lick their boots an' I got an anger rising in me like a tornado, so step aside.'

For the first time the youth actually took in the grieving mother. Grace Walker was five foot nothing, but she was an avalanche of hurt and pain just looking for a place to demolish. He stepped out of their way, eyeing White with malice. The car clattered off for its awkward destination and the tension was only broken a little by Du Bois' statement: 'Well, truth be told, Grace, I believe I was more frightened of what you might have done to him than of what he might have done to us. I sure am glad to be your friend and not your enemy.' In his rear-view mirror, White could see Mrs Walker still staring down the evil in the world. It was a stare that would turn her eyes into tunnels as she identified her only son's body at the morgue.

Joseph Walker lay on a slab in the cool tiled mortuary, his body covered to the neck by a sheet. The technicians had cleaned him up, but there was still the evidence of a violent beating present on his face and upon seeing it, Grace broke down and wept. She was comforted by Du Bois, who remained stoic on the surface, but was deeply troubled underneath. While she was signing the necessary paperwork, the N.A.A.C.P. leader took White aside and began to ask him the difficult questions the detective had known would come from the killing.

'You say Joseph was found down by the docks? Those are the same docks black workers were attacked coming out of last night. Do you think some of those attackers might have hung around and seen a lone young man who they could take their frustrations out on further?'

White chewed on a hangnail and frowned. He was mindful his words might escalate the already high tensions between the races in New York. 'It's a line of enquiry I will investigate fully, but the police had already scared off the assailants. It would be highly unusual for any of them to make a return to the scene. Why take the risk?'

Du Bois gave a sharp intake of breath and exhaled frustratedly through his nostrils. 'Forgive me, detective, but are you already ruling out the most obvious suspects because you don't want to cause trouble within the Irish community? The men who handed out those beatings are still roaming free while several of my people are in the hospital. I would expect that in Chicago, but I'd hoped New York was a better city.'

Grace had now joined the men and White felt himself picking his words with even more care. 'When a crime takes place, especially a violent crime, I do everything I can to track down the perpetrator. I have names and will be pursuing those men today. Anything I can find out about Joseph's murder will be followed up. I have no loyalties except to the victims, truth, and justice.'

'I hope so, detective,' Du Bois replied.

White offered the pair a lift back to Harlem, but Du Bois preferred to make other arrangements. It was useless for the detective to ask the N.A.A.C.P. leader to try and dampen the mood in the black neighbourhood. In Chicago there had been riots, and the dock strike coupled to the assaults and murder made White fearful New York might be about to descend into the same kind of chaos. He had to find Joseph's killer sooner rather than later. His leads were two names and a boot print, hardly much to go on. The notion the body had been murdered elsewhere and then brought to the docks still nagged at him. He would investigate the Irish workers because there was a clear motive, means and opportunity, but he felt there was something else to the case, something he just wasn't seeing yet.

It was hard for him to think straight when his mind was constantly being drawn back to the chaotic change about to happen in his home. Everything but the job was being ripped away from him and he felt powerless to alter it. All of this sat among a backdrop of industrial action and racial tensions that may or may not be tied into the murder. He had to find the answers, and he had to find them soon before the whole thing boiled over and more deaths occurred. He couldn't just go home, and even if he could, White knew he wouldn't know what to do or say anyway. So, he headed back to the precinct and carried on with his investigation of the case.

After finally managing to persuade Du Bois she would be okay on her own, Grace sat in the empty apartment. There was a profound silence in the place, as if the whole tenement block had heard of her bereavement and was quietly taking in the shocking news while respectfully giving her some space to come to terms with what it meant herself. Perhaps they had heard, Grace thought. News always did travel fast in Harlem, and bad news travelled the fastest. She had wanted to be alone to begin the impossible process of trying to collect her thoughts, but everywhere she looked were objects that reminded her of Joseph's childhood, each one more heart-breaking than the last. So, she began to pick them up and put them away in cupboards, carefully so as not to damage the artifacts that were the only things left of her son but were items she could not bear to see right then, and maybe wouldn't look at for a very long time to come.

A small wooden spinning top Charles had turned on a lathe, varnished, and capped with a brass point took pride of place on the mantlepiece, having long since ceased to be played with by her son. Joseph had been keeping it safe to pass on to his own child, when he had one, which was why Grace couldn't bear to look at it a second longer. She wrapped it in a blanket and laid it at the bottom of the airing cupboard, but in her mind's eye she could still see it skittering across the living room floor while young Joseph, wide-eyed with wonderment at what it could do, tracked its every magical movement.

She took down the certificate from Sunday School last of all. Joseph had been presented with it when he was eleven years old after memorizing more bible passages than any other child in his group and speaking about what each one meant to him in front of an audience. Parents had been invited to the church to hear the recitations and Grace had sat proudly in her best clothes while her son shone from his place in the pulpit. The reverend had praised Joseph for both his gravity and the zeal with which he spoke, saying that he might make an excellent minister one day if that was what he wanted. Grace wished that it had been, then maybe he would never have ventured out late at night and found himself down by the docks where trouble from white men lurked.

The beautiful boy at the altar had been turned into a lifeless corpse laying on a slab in the cold antiseptic morgue, and Grace wept as she took down the framed certificate, her tears falling onto the glass and blurring his name. One day ago, she had had a living, breathing son, a wonderful child with his whole life ahead of him, and now it was all gone, taken by someone she did not know for reasons she could not fathom. She wished her Charles were here. How could she tell him this life-altering news when he was so many miles away? A letter seemed so cold and impersonal, so utterly inappropriate, when it was detailing the greatest loss imaginable. It would arrive like a shrapnel wound, and she couldn't do that to the man she loved so dearly.

She didn't know what to do, or how to make sense of any of it. Her head felt like that spinning top whirring round and round out of control in the lonely apartment. She took the detective's card from the pocket of her dress and held onto it tightly. He had been a good man, a sensitive soul, she thought. Her only hope now was that he could find her son's killer and explain why Joseph had been taken from her. Sometimes, even a devout Christian like herself needed answers and comfort from someone other than God. It was a sin to think that, she knew, but it was the truth, and right now, the truth felt very real indeed. It was closer to her than His love. She didn't want it that way, but that was how it was. The card in her hands ripped a little as she clutched it between her desperate fingers. *Give me answers, Mister White. Let me understand why my boy is gone,* Grace pleaded in her tormented head. Her faith was wavering, and she had poured a little of it into the eyes of the detective as he'd faced her in the nightmarish corridors of the city morgue. He'd said that he'd do everything in his power to find Joseph's killer. Grace just hoped those powers were strong enough to succeed.

Chapter Seven
Careful With That Gun, Eugene

White spent the afternoon secreted in his tiny office reading up on what little there was in the records about Mick Nevin and Pat O'Brien, the two Irish ringleaders whose names Young had given him the night before. Nevin had been brought in for affray but let go with a warning. O'Brien was known as *the butcher*, a bare-knuckle fighter and tough guy who had charges of illegal boxing and gambling levelled against him; but it seemed someone at Tammany Hall liked prize fighting and so O'Brien escaped prosecution. Sometimes in New York it wasn't what you did but who you knew. There was a history of violence, but White would probably have every Irish dockworker in New York as a suspect if that were the only criteria to pursue.

Nevertheless, he had arranged for two junior detectives, one from the Irish neighbourhood, to accompany him to the bar where the suspects drank. He could have gone to their home addresses, but he wanted to be seen to act publicly with no fear and no favours. It had the potential of being a dangerous move and his colleagues were less than delighted at the prospect, but White didn't care. Sometimes you had to go and enforce the law, especially in the places where they thought you'd let it slide.

They hit the bar at five o'clock, hoping for a smaller audience and the two men in question to be less likely to resist through intoxication. There was no way of them not looking like Detective Squad as they entered the building. White recognised O'Brien from his mugshot in the file but could have guessed his identity from the way he perched pugnaciously on his barstool, a fighter's crouch with bent elbows and the instinctively ready fist clenched at belly height. The other hand was poised to slam a heavy mug of porter in his direction. Standing sideways on to the bar was a thicker slab of a man, short, but with powerful looking forearms. He turned to reveal a pair of hooded green eyes and a cigarette that dangled hopelessly from his bottom lip. Mick Nevin, White presumed.

The joint was quiet, but it switched to full blown silence as the detectives crossed the room. White was the first to speak. 'Relax a little, O'Brien. I'm not going to invite you to dance. Sergeant Dominic White, Detective Squad. I just need to ask you a few questions.'

O'Brien stayed in his crouch, gripping the handle of the mug a little more tightly. 'White? That sounds like an English name. I don't like the English and I don't like the police. You want to question me? Go and get an arrest warrant. Otherwise, I'm staying here and getting on with my drink.'

White chuckled. Twice in one day someone had taken objection to his name. 'And there I was thinking a public-spirited man like yourself would be only too happy to help me with my enquiries. I can do this the hard way if you want, O'Brien, but I'm not a fan of paperwork. Just from those grazed knuckles you've got there I could arrest you right now on suspicion of assault, but it's a bigger crime I'm investigating. I'm hunting a murderer and I don't have time for your attitude.'

Something in the words triggered O'Brien, for he slipped from his stool ready to swing his mug of beer. Before he could plant his front foot to throw it, White had drawn a revolver and pointed it at his stomach. 'Sit down,

O'Brien, before I shoot you in self-defence.' The prize fighter paused. 'You think I won't? Try me,' White added. O'Brien remained standing but lowered his mug.

'Well, isn't it just like a cop to not fight fair,' O'Brien spat. 'Check your back, detective. Looks like you've upset my friend.'

Moving around slowly, White could see a figure sitting in a booth. The man was pointing a pistol at the three policemen. He was thin, with a face as white as marble and cold-looking like a corpse. His narrow black eyebrows and slit of a mouth accentuated the icy meanness of the man. His blue eyes were devoid of any warmth, like two frozen lakes set into the hard landscape of his face, and they studied the cops like an alligator sorting out which chunk of meat to take first. He looked more like a killer than any man White had ever seen. His voice, when he spoke after enjoying the deathly silence for a moment, had an Irish brogue, but was cold like the wind that whipped in off the sea, each word stinging saltily as it left his lips.

'Looks like we have ourselves a stalemate, gentlemen. There will be no arrests and no questioning. No one here had a hand in any murder.'

White had turned to face the man. Both guns were still raised. 'Who might you be?' he asked, hiding the chill he felt. The detective had had guns pointed at him before, it was an occupational hazard, but this man exuded a dark and powerful sense of death. Looking at him gave White the same feeling as staring at a graveyard on a winter's day.

The man smiled through those thin, closed lips. 'Who I am is of no concern to you, sergeant. I have my own arrangement with the N.Y.P.D. that goes a lot higher than you. Best you be on your way now.'

White bristled. Despite the ice in his blood the presence of the man had introduced, he'd never been one for backing down. 'No one bought *me,* and you won't have protection from shooting an officer of the law. So, I'm going to take those men in, and you can use your influence later, if you like.'

'I don't have to kill you, just teach you a lesson,' the figure said coolly and steadily. 'I can shoot you and testify it was a total accident. I thought you were a gangster holding the place up. Juries can be bought so easily these days. Do you leave now, or do I show you how quick I am on the trigger?'

Before White could decide what to do, a voice from behind the figure answered: 'He's going, Eugene.' From the booth behind the man with the pistol, Lieutenant O'Malley stood up. He was unarmed, but apparently unfazed by that. O'Malley was White's boss and mentor. He was neither tall nor especially broad, but there was a presence about him that could not be ignored, an energy in his eyes, a power in his large hands, and a robustness to his stomach that would have been called a paunch on any other man. He stood stock still, legs planted slightly apart, staring unblinkingly into the eyes of each gunman in turn. 'Gentlemen, put your guns away, it's bad for the takings at the bar. Mr O'Brien and Mr Nevin will present themselves at the police station at nine o'clock tomorrow morning to help us with our enquiries. That agreed, we shall take our leave.' He said all this in a low and reasonable voice, but with an edge to it that couldn't be mistaken for anything other than a command.

Eugene kept the pistol where it was but had turned to face the Lieutenant. 'What if they, or I choose not to comply?'

O'Malley crossed his arms and smiled the coldest smile White had ever seen from him. 'Now, Eugene. I'm being friendly. I don't have to be. In fact, I can be the meanest son of a bitch in the whole of the N.Y.P.D. if I want to be and you know that. They'll comply. Put that gun away. I don't like you pointing it at my boy.'

'Your boy?' Eugene checked, something less confident flickering across his cold face momentarily.

'You heard right,' the lieutenant curtly affirmed.

Eugene slowly holstered his weapon and O'Malley gestured for White to do likewise. When the tension had been brought down a level, the lieutenant strolled over to the bar and stood between Nevin and O'Brien. 'Bartender, a Bushmills before I go. Eugene will pick up the tab.' The drink was poured, and O'Malley took it in one draught. Turning to the two Irishmen, he reminded them: 'Nine o'clock, and don't be late. I have a very busy day tomorrow. If I'm kept waiting it can make me extremely cranky. You go ask Eugene over there what I'm like when my mood turns sour. Nine o'clock.' With that, he ushered the three detectives out of the bar to safety.

Outside on the street, White turned on his superior officer. 'Do you mind telling me what the hell just happened in there, sir?'

O'Malley lit a cigarette, savouring the hit of nicotine. 'Politics and experienced policing, sergeant. You see, you investigated those two men, but you didn't find out who owns them. Insider knowledge is a valuable thing.

When your sidekick here called me because he knew the community and was worried about where you were taking him, I decided to lend a hand. There are ways of doing these things, Dom. You can't just turn up and wave a badge. Anyways, now they know you.'

White was fuming. 'That guy in there pointed a gun at me. Is that how we do law and order in this city now?'

O'Malley shook his head. 'No, it isn't. Did you see me draw a weapon? Ask yourself, how comes I got what I wanted when I didn't even have a gun? You still have plenty to learn, detective. Those men will get questioned; I will see to it personally. One day before too long, I'll also stand by the side of Eugene's grave and be sure to throw a big handful of dirt on top of his coffin. So, rather than chewing me out right here in the middle of the street, why don't we go back to the precinct and you can fill me in on the case.'

Sore as he was, White had to trust his mentor, so they returned to the precinct and over a drink went through everything from the assaults to the murder, the victims, the suspects, and White's theories from the evidence so far. In the back of his mind, the clock ticked down to Mona's departure.

O'Malley took a slug of Irish whiskey and set the glass down firmly on his desk. The office was stuffy and had a musty smell that echoed the one coming from the lieutenant whenever he moved. Scratching at his stubble, the senior detective shifted in his chair and peered through the blinds at the outer room that usually thrummed with a melee of cops chasing leads or discussing cases. Now, it was quiet. Being after six, most of the men had gone home to their long-suffering wives, headed to the bar, or crawled back under whatever rock they had earlier emerged from to work their shift. Of the one or two who remained to work late, no one was interested in the murder of a young black boy. O'Malley, to his credit, seemed to be.

'Run me through the details, Dom,' he said, refilling his glass sloppily. White held his hand over the top of his own glass, then relented and let his boss pour him another one as he remembered the awfulness of the situation at home.

'The dockers clocked off at eleven,' White stated, 'that is, the black strike-breakers from Harlem. They took a few minutes to get a wash, it was a hot night, remember, and then they headed out of the dockyard. The gates were shut and locked about eleven twenty-five. They were barely down the road a way when the Irish mob ambushed them. The first patrolmen were on the scene by eleven forty. The mob fled and the cops called ambulances to carry several of the battered black men to hospital, which they did around midnight.'

White paused in his account, taking a draught of the smooth spirit and allowing O'Malley to catch up with the notes he was scribbling down with the stump of a pencil. The lieutenant looked up. 'Go on,' he said.

'The body was discovered at twelve fifteen and called in immediately by the New York Dock Company foreman, David Young. It was found because he'd instructed the security guard to make a careful patrol of the site following the evening's trouble. He was on the phone to none other than our glorious commissioner while that happened and had just ended the call when the bad news came.'

'What had they been talking about?' O'Malley asked, his interest piqued.

'The strike and the assaults,' White replied. 'Apparently, it wasn't the first time black workers had been set upon in the course of the dispute. Young thinks the commissioner won't do anything about it because of the Irish connection,' he stated flatly, not caring what his fiercely Celtic boss made of the accusation. O'Malley simply looked at White and took another slug of his whiskey.

'I arrived at the docks just after one in the morning,' White continued. 'They showed me where the body had been dumped and, following a trail of tracks left both by the dragged body and then by a porter's trolley, I located a spot where the perimeter fence had been breached. It looked odds on the body had been carried into the dockyard from outside. That would fit with the fact Joseph Walker never worked on the docks.'

'So,' O'Malley theorized, twisting his glass around in his large hand, 'your boy was killed outside the docks and dumped after the workers had ended their shift at eleven, probably after the gates were locked at eleven twenty-five. Someone would only risk leaving a body in the yard when it was deserted, otherwise there would've been too many men around that could've spotted them. You say they used a porter's trolley to move the body some of the way?'

'Yeah, so I'm thinking the killer wasn't the biggest or strongest of guys,' White offered.

'So, not a docker then,' O'Malley reasoned. 'Those guys are used to lifting heavy loads day in, day out.'

'I originally wondered if dumping the body in the dockyard was a statement,' White admitted. 'All those black strike-breakers and the violence against them recently. Maybe a beating got taken too far but the Irish boys saw how they might use it.'

'Except the Irish boys were a mob,' the lieutenant asserted. 'Strong men that hunted as a pack. They wouldn't have needed to use a trolley to transport the body. You also said it had been dragged part of the way. That suggests a lone killer who didn't have the strength to lift a young boy. How much did your victim weigh?' O'Malley asked.

'I'm not sure, but he was skinny, so, not that much. No more than a hundred and fifty pounds, I'd say.'

'The body was found at twelve fifteen,' O'Malley mused. 'That's less than an hour between the workers leaving and the security guard making his gruesome discovery. Was there any rigor mortis? What was the estimated time of death?'

'He was still warm when I got there at one,' White said. 'It was a hot night. The Medical Examiner puts time of death somewhere between ten and twelve.'

O'Malley lit a cigarette. 'How do you see it?' he asked his protégé.

'The killer didn't have an automobile, otherwise they could have taken the body down to the shore somewhere deserted and thrown it in the sea. Or, if they did, then they committed the murder, deliberately took the body down to the docks, and placed it in the yard sometime after it closed for the night.' White stopped and lit his own cigarette. He frowned as he did so.

'What's bothering you?' O'Malley asked.

'This doesn't feel that well-planned,' White replied. 'Joseph was viciously stamped upon several times after being initially attacked from behind. This was an assault carried out with a lot of rage and fury. There was a footprint left on the body that points to the killer being male, and as we said, not very strong. Even so, they still managed to beat a man to death. On the one hand, it could've been one of the Irish mob mistaking Joseph for a strike-breaker, a case of him being in the wrong place at the wrong time. I've been thinking about the anomaly of a tough dock worker having to drag a light body. If the assailant had been injured in the fighting, he might have struggled to carry the body, but then why would he attack someone when he was already hurt himself?'

'Anger, opportunity, or he miscalculated. He started by hitting the guy from behind. Perhaps he didn't do it hard enough and was injured in a struggle with the victim. Who knows?' O'Malley offered, 'but I see what you're saying. So, why do you think they left the body where they did?'

'If this has nothing to do with the industrial dispute, and it isn't a case of mistaken identity, then the killing, the fighting between the workers, and the arrival of the police could all have been coincidental,' White posited. 'A murder goes down next to the docks, it's unplanned, but full of rage, suggesting perhaps the killer knew his victim and was angry with him over something, angry enough to take his life. The second it's committed, a police whistle blows, then another, and another. Our killer panics. He might have been about to leave the body right there on the street, but that feels too risky now. Then he notices the gap in the fence. He thinks, *why risk walking away and being seen by the police in the close vicinity of a corpse when I can just hide it in here?* So, he takes his opportunity and avoids the patrolmen who would've been converging on the scene from all directions. Then, he uses the fleeing of the mob and the injured strike-breakers as a diversion while he coolly walks off into the night.'

'It could've happened that way,' O'Malley considered, 'but that would've been one hell of a coincidence.'

'So, you want to still figure one of the Irish mob for the killing?' White asked, trying not to sound too cynical.

'They're coming in at nine o'clock tomorrow morning, aren't they?' O'Malley reminded him curtly. 'We'll see what they have to say for themselves then. Anyways, if one of those boys *did* do it, Eugene will find out about it and tell me.'

'What is it between you and this Eugene?' White questioned mistrustfully.

'It's a long story,' O'Malley responded, stubbing his cigarette out in the overflowing ashtray, 'and one it's better you don't know. What's your plan in the meantime?' he asked, shutting that part of the conversation down.

'Well, I want to know why young Joseph found himself down by the docks at that time of night, and most of all I want to find out who might have wanted him dead, if anybody,' White answered.

'That always helps,' O'Malley observed, folding his meaty arms. 'Better go figure, then,' he added.

'Before I drink too much of your whiskey,' White quipped.

'I wasn't offering you any more,' O'Malley grunted.

'I was going anyway,' White said. 'The décor in here is kinda faded. There are much plusher bars in town.'

'Just not cheaper,' O'Malley retorted.

It heralded the end of the conversation and left the two detectives to think separately about the puzzling elements of the case. White remained uneasy about his boss' association with the deathly Eugene and was sceptical about the Irish boys turning up to be questioned in the morning. Still, he thought, as he walked down the steps of the precinct, he would have to wait and see. There was nothing he could do about it right now, nothing he could do about anything come to that, he surmised, troubled by his own failings and unable to shake himself free of the dark clouds that massed within his head.

Chapter Eight
Burning Crosses

Brother Paul sat in the rented Harlem basement and watched as Abraham took more whiskey through his bruised mouth. Paul did not drink. He liked to keep a clear head and be free of vices. He did not use women either for much the same reason. They had been discussing the assault down by the docks, arguing over the significance of the mob's actions and what should be done next. Paul saw his younger sibling as angry, but flawed, and although perhaps not furious enough, it was a rage that might be useful to his cause. While Abraham could react with a passion to the racial injustices they faced, his temper would flare up only to dissipate into something smaller, a sense of subjugation he muttered about in dark corners like this one. Paul was different. Everything was measured, from the austere but carefully fitting suit he wore, to the thin and neatly trimmed moustache he sported, and he was willing to sacrifice much more than other men to achieve his cause, even at the expense of his own brethren if it must be so.

He sat and watched Abraham, who was snarling and whinging like a chastened dog that had been put in its place by the pack leader, and Paul understood this was still a hurt he could use. After all, somebody had to communicate with Eugene. Brother Paul did not deal with these matters in person, nor did his organization have a name. It was all part of the plan of subterfuge, of not getting caught. Some had referred to the group as *The Brotherhood* or used such undermining attachments as *negro* or *black*. Paul did not sanction these names. He wanted the movement to remain untraceable and knew the absence of a name not only made them harder to pin down but was also more frightening to white folks. Every action where the perpetrators remained at large, every time a blow was struck anonymously, would be attributed to them. What was scarier still in the minds of the white oppressors, was that *them* could not be defined. They just existed. A malevolent force that could be any black man or woman in the district, in the city no less. To take *them* on would be to take on the whole of the black community, something the white people in the north still hesitated to do.

'You listenin' to me?' Abraham demanded.

'Yes, I am,' Brother Paul coolly responded. 'You were talking about the effect of the beatings.'

'It's an injustice that makes the newspapers,' Abraham continued, awkwardly taking another slug of drink through his injured mouth. 'It's fuel for the Silent Parade. Black citizens trying to earn an honest living, set upon repeatedly and with no protection from the police,' he added.

Paul folded his arms and looked hard at his brother. 'That really how you see it?' he asked, his tone as the older sibling undermining as ever.

'What's your opinion?' Abraham shot back.

'My opinion,' Brother Paul began, unfolding his arms and leaning forwards to place both hands upon the table, 'is nobody white will care about a few busted up black dockers, especially not when they read about how they were breaking a strike. People will think they got what they deserved.'

'So, what are you doing to get us noticed?' Abraham retorted sorely.

'In one part, I would have thought that was obvious,' Paul said. 'We destabilize the white dockers' position by breaking the strike and showing there are men in this city willing to work for less. Both Eugene and I want black longshoremen to become the go-to labour force, so the bosses begin to rely on us, and then we can squeeze them for a little more pay. Infiltration into the white world has to come gradually. It is the only way we can begin to undermine their institutions. We become familiar, we become necessary, then we start to hold some power. It has to begin somewhere.'

'You think we can trust Eugene?' Abraham asked.

'Absolutely not, brother. He may have his own war to wage, but to him, we are nothing more than pawns in his game, and as such, we can be sacrificed if necessary. This is why our work with the Irishman is only one strand of our operation. To be successful, we must think in many directions.'

'Brother, you talk in riddles,' Abraham said, chasing the last of his whiskey and slamming the glass down upon the table. 'You always speak of tactics and strategy, but I don't see a whole lot going on besides this thing we got with Eugene.'

Paul frowned a little in annoyance. 'The business at the docks serves its purpose, but bigger waves need making. Forget your Silent Parade, it is a spectacle that will come and go like all peaceful protests, to be forgotten with the changing of the weather. What's required is something far more radical and confrontational.'

'Like *The Messenger* magazine?'

'Words,' Brother Paul spat dismissively. 'Philip Randolph is an intelligent man, but revolutions are built on actions, not words.'

'Well, you sure didn't like what Marcus Garvey proposed when he set up the U.N.I.A. here in Harlem last year,' Abraham observed, 'and that was certainly a call for action.'

'To repatriate black people back to Africa. Hell, that's doing the white man's work for him! I admire Garvey's energy, but he, Du Bois, and Randolph are all wrong. What we need is a call to arms, like the one in Chicago.'

'Those were riots,' Abraham corrected, 'and only one side was properly armed. Too many black people died because of violent protest. All it does is get us killed.'

'Dear Chicago,' Paul mused, 'violence without proper direction or a telling cause. It's a lesson for us to learn from, but even as a loss it was useful in generating greater anger among our people. Here in New York, it might only take the death of one innocent to justify a more vitriolic parade.'

'What innocent?' Abraham questioned. 'And anyway, didn't you hear about the support for Du Bois? The N.A.A.C.P. is strong here in Harlem. The protest is going to be thousands of people, all campaigning peacefully, but in such vast numbers that they will create a powerful spectacle. It worked for the suffragettes. The authorities can't ignore such a large turnout.'

'While our people are silent, it allows those in power to placate us with words. Murder cannot be ignored,' Paul stated.

'Murder? There hasn't been any murder in New York.'

'A necessary casualty to properly ignite the real race war in this city,' Paul continued, as if deaf to his brother's words. 'Let's see how many people follow Du Bois' Silent Parade when the tragedy becomes known. Let's see how many mothers send their children to march once they know a boy has been killed.'

'What boy? Killed by who?' Abraham asked.

'By the mob, of course. By the rampaging Irish,' Brother Paul smiled.

'There was beatings, nothing more,' Abraham declared. 'Bad beatings, but nobody got killed.'

'You need to keep up with the word on the street,' Paul said.

'All the talk's about the assault and the parade. I keep up just fine. I know what's going on. I was *there*. No one got killed, and nobody's talking about no murder.'

'They will,' Paul said defiantly, 'They will. There don't have to be burning crosses for people to see the hatred and know what can happen to them. They witnessed it in Chicago, and now they'll feel it here. When the protest comes, it must be bloody, or it will be of no true significance.'

'You talking in riddles again and it scares me,' Abraham said. 'Whatever you got in your head needs to stay there. Don't be talking to anybody else this way. Promise me, brother.'

With a look that seemed to take in his younger sibling, all the room, and far beyond it, Paul announced: 'Then they cried out with a loud voice...and ran upon him with one accord...and stoned him. And Saul was consenting unto his death. New Testament, Acts Seven and Eight. It's all there, brother. It has all been written to guide us.'

'Riddles!' Abraham hit back. 'When you get to talkin' like this, it makes you sound crazy. I'm going out for more whiskey. This bottle's finished.'

He got up and moved heavily out of the room on drunken legs, shaking his head as he went. There was the noise of his feet as he climbed the basement steps, and the slam of the outside door. Then all was quiet.

Brother Paul cast his eyes up to the cement ceiling. 'And I persecuted this way unto the death, binding and delivering into prisons both men and women…breathing out threatenings and slaughter against the disciples of the Lord.' He made the sign of the cross in the air in front of him and chuckled. 'Lord, you made me bad so you could redeem me, but my road to Damascus is yet to come, and you know no murderer has eternal life abiding in him. I doeth evil, I am a sinner, but you made me so. Amen.'

Joseph Walker was dead, brutally murdered on the streets of his hometown at just eighteen years of age. A young black boy whose future had been taken away from him. Brother Paul hoped the boy would come to represent the potential fate of all black people living in this violent and hateful nation, that his murder would engender feelings of indignation and wrath, because vengeance must be had. True peace could only be felt after a war, and he was intent on bringing that war to New York. Emancipation would be written in blood because the law kept his people down. He would work on Abraham some more. He needed his brother to spur Eugene into action. The people must link the Irish mob to the killing, even if the police found no evidence to convict them. Strings must be pulled, he thought, and he was the puppet-master. The upcoming parade must not pass off peacefully. There must be blood, and war, and progress.

William Du Bois walked around the empty pews of St. Philip's Episcopal Church trying to collect his thoughts. The image of the murdered boy at the mortuary, and the sensation of Grace's grieving were powerful disturbances he could not forget. He had seen such things before and witnessed the shockwaves as they spread through a community. Now, circumstances would inextricably link the vigil over Joseph to the Silent Parade if it could be held as planned. Du Bois knew how such a killing could ignite the fires of bitterness and anger. It had happened in Chicago, and he did not want to see it happen here. Lord knows, he thought, pausing to rest his hand on one of the cool benches, there has been enough bloodshed already.

He was supposed to be a man of substance, and yet he'd left Grace all alone in that apartment. She had insisted she needed time by herself in the wake of her son's murder, and he'd understood that and respected her wishes, but it didn't sit right with him. He'd suggested they call for the reverend to speak with her and offer the comfort of God's words, but she had dismissed that also. Grace was a proud and stoic woman, of that there was no doubt, but no one should face what she was going through on their own. He decided to go back to her apartment to at least offer some company before she spent the whole of the night by herself in mourning. He exited the church with a feeling he should take something, that going to her door empty handed seemed wrong, but no gift felt appropriate, and she would only stare at it after he was gone, its presence marking the day she'd identified her son's body on a slab.

When Du Bois reached the tenement block, he stopped. He wished he had his wife, Nina with him for moral support, but she was away visiting old friends in Atlanta. Never mind that now, he told himself. Grace Walker looked up to him as a civil rights activist, and he would allow her faith in him to comfort her in her time of need. She had done so much preparation for the parade, he felt it was the least he could do. With that, he entered the building and made his way up the stairs to her door, knocking lightly so as not to startle her.

'Tell me again, about the certificate,' he said, taking a little more of the tea Grace had given him. They were at the kitchen table in the fading light of the evening, the rays coming through the window picking out rawness around her eyes and nose, betraying her demeanour of weariness as something more serious, more crushing.

'He got it for reciting bible passages he'd memorised. We were so proud. We framed it and hung it up on that wall for everyone to see. Seven years it was there. Now, there's just a dirty-edged space where it used to be. I scrubbed the wall, but it won't come off and I don't have any paint. Anyway, it would still stand out unless I did the whole kitchen, and I'm tired, Mr Du Bois, so very tired,' she said defeatedly.

'I'm sure it could be arranged,' Du Bois offered. 'I can get one of the young men at the church to lend a hand. It wouldn't take long.'

'No,' Grace said definitely. 'Thank you, but I cannot set myself to tasks pretending everything is normal and it's just another day. The mark will have to stay for now.'

'Of course. I apologize. It's really none of my business,' Du Bois said awkwardly, fiddling with the waxed tip of his moustache as he always did when agitated.

'It was good of you to call,' Grace said, aware she had rebuffed his kindness more than once today. 'I'll try my best at conversation, but my mind is taken up with Joseph and Charles. I want to make sense of everything, but that won't happen for a long while, if at all,' she added, smoothing the tablecloth back into place. 'So, in the meantime, let's talk about the parade.'

'Are you sure?' Du Bois questioned. 'Like I said, I can leave you to mourn as soon as you feel you don't want company.'

'It is the greatest of causes, and it matters even more to me now,' she said, shifting the salt cellar, then continuing on a different tack. 'I think that detective will investigate properly. I believe Joseph's death meant something to him. I saw a great sadness in his eyes, and even though I know it wasn't just for my son, the killing touched him. I saw something else too, a steadfastness, the sign of a man who keeps his word.'

'You saw all that?' Du Bois considered. 'Well, I guess it's true women read these things more readily than men can.'

'You have it too,' Grace stated.

'The gift of weighing up a man through the windows of his eyes?' Du Bois frowned. 'I'm not sure I do entirely.'

'No, the steadfastness. It's why I believe the parade will be an even greater success than the one staged by the suffragettes.'

'Well, I hope so,' Du Bois said a little hesitantly.

'I'm sorry, I didn't mean to embarrass you with that compliment,' Grace said, sensing Du Bois' discomfort.

'It's not that,' the activist said. 'It's…well, the *tensions* surrounding everything.'

'You mean Joseph's murder,' she said bluntly, dismissing his attempt to protest to the contrary. 'It's okay, Mr Du Bois. I've worried about it myself this evening, strange as that may seem. Lord knows, the mind flies off in every possible direction when it is disquieted. Your fear is the community might want to react angrily, that they will make the protest aggressive rather than peaceful and dignified.'

'It is,' Du Bois nodded thoughtfully. 'The whole thing about New York, the reason why we are able to have a parade here when we couldn't anywhere else, is there are white sympathies in this city. There is racial prejudice, of course, and even a minority who think it justified to act with violence towards our people, but there is far less of the backwards, ingrained hatred of the southern states, where white folks still remember the days of slavery with fondness and behave like nothing has changed since then.'

'We have an opportunity to show our worth as a civilised people,' Grace affirmed, 'but you are right to fear a backlash. Our men have been beaten in the dockyard; my son killed for no reason. Retaining a peaceful stance becomes even harder with those crimes hanging in the air unpunished.'

'It does,' Du Bois agreed, 'but an angry response will only serve to support the misguided view our people are savages, and I do not wish to fuel that lie.'

'Joseph would have wanted peace. He adored children and he loved sunshine. Hopefully there will be both for our parade.'

'I hope there will. Meanwhile, I must work to dampen the inevitable fires of racial hatred in the community generated by your son's murder. We must promote righteousness as the true way forwards.'

'We must,' Grace agreed.

Du Bois remained agitated beneath his assured exterior. He felt a desperate need to smoke wash over him and could almost smell the tobacco sitting in the pouch in his pocket but didn't want to be presumptuous in Grace's house. Instead, he steeled his mind to focus on what the parade meant to the grieving mother.

'Grace, I sense you need this parade more than ever now. If you feel able, I would like to involve you further in the organization. I want you to be at the heart of what we are doing. I know you're exactly the person to help us make a real difference.'

'What I want,' Grace said in a measured and thoughtful tone, 'is for the protest to be dignified and meaningful. It must be a stand against *all* violence if it is to bring any healing.'

'Then I will work, with your support, to make it so,' Du Bois declared.

'Good,' Grace said. She looked sharply at the kind activist. 'You keep touching your breast pocket. It's too high up for you to be feeling for your watch, subconsciously wondering about when you should leave, but there's something itching you.'

Du Bois smiled. 'Truth be told, I'm gasping for a cigarette. I didn't want to act too familiarly in your home.'

'Go ahead. The smell of tobacco calms me. My father used to smoke a pipe. Cigarettes don't smell as good, but they're not a bad substitute.'

Du Bois swiftly assembled his cigarette, noticing how his host watched him as he did so. 'You don't…want one?'

'I thought you would never ask! I know it isn't ladylike or the done thing, but I'm not sure I care anymore.'

'Fair enough,' Du Bois said, handing her his cigarette and rolling himself another one. When they had lit up and enjoyed several drags, he asked, 'So, you trust this Detective White?'

'I do. He's suffering. He's damaged by something, but that brings the best out of some men, even if they don't know it will.'

'You're a very wise woman, Grace. I will trust your judgement.'

'You suspect he's just another white cop who only cares about his own kind, or at least you worry that might be the case, but you're wrong. I've seen his pain and felt his goodness. If the killer is to be found, he will be the one to find him.'

'I hope you're right,' Du Bois intoned, drawing thoughtfully on his cigarette.

Grace found an ashtray, her movement breaking the intensity of their conversation. The hour was getting late, and Du Bois, feeling he had brought some comfort and renewed purpose to Grace, knew it was time to be on his way. He lay his cigarette down in the ashtray, his intent to leave clearly signalled, and Grace, understanding the gesture, placed her own smoke on top of his. The cigarette lay across the dead one, smouldering like a hurt that could not be extinguished.

He said his goodbyes, promising to keep her updated on the progress and planning for the parade. Once outside, he took in the air on the street, feeling it had somehow changed. Grace's son had been pointlessly slaughtered, and here he was, trying to steer the ship of protest in a peaceful direction. The body on the slab, the grief-stricken mother, and now, another image added to the pile: two white cigarettes forming a cross and burning away in a Harlem house. Whose anger it symbolised, he could not know, but it haunted him as he made his way home. It had been an horrific day, but he feared there was worse to come.

Chapter Nine
The Coward's Way Out

While the case had been firing his senses, he was just about okay, but White left O'Malley's office dreading the night that lay ahead. Everything was falling apart and there was absolutely nothing he could think to do to stop it, so he went to Rick's Bar to top up O'Malley's whiskey with some more straight shots. His only solution was to get as physically and emotionally numb as he possibly could, even though he recognised it was the coward's way out. The Irishmen had been confrontational. White certainly figured O'Brien as a man who could bludgeon a young black boy to death for no great reason, but his reaction to being accused of murder had seemed genuinely incandescent, and he certainly wouldn't have needed the help of a porter's trolley to bear the body back into the yard he knew so well. Something wasn't right. In fact, scratch that, White thought. Nothing about anything was right. The scene in the bar with O'Malley and Eugene had gotten completely under his skin, so much so he couldn't look at his mentor in the same way anymore. Then there was Mona. Nobody was who he thought they were. All his points of reference were disappearing.

The whiskey went down easy in the clean and friendly bar with its polished brass rail and soft white lighting, but staring up at the globes above his head, the detective didn't feel drunk, just full of misgivings. Rick, as ever, presumed his cop customer's woes were work related, and, following the bartender's code, he cleaned glasses and served other folk while waiting for the revelation as to what was troubling White. You never asked in his profession, because more often than not you really didn't want to know, and anyways, it was better to stay neutral than try to offer any genuine insight. Insight involved folks facing up to reality, and Rick knew nobody came into his establishment to do that, quite the opposite, in fact. So, he tidied and waited.

White knew they had a long enough history together that he'd say something to Rick, however small or swathed in hypothesis it might be. The detective had a reputation for playing his cards close to his chest. He had to in his line of business, and Rick understood that. Nevertheless, he wanted to engage the savvy owner, so, as he finished another whiskey and motioned the bartender over to pour him some more, White revealed some of what troubled him in the form of a question.

'What's your take on police corruption in this city?' he asked.

Rick had the time it took fixing the drink to consider. He didn't for one second believe White could be involved in anything sinister, the guy had always played things straight, but it was clear something was leaving a bad smell down at the precinct. You had to think fast as a barman, so, choosing his words tentatively, Rick replied.

'Corruption happens everywhere. It's part of human nature. Cops are human beings just like everyone else. There will always be rotten apples in the barrel, and people can't always be trusted if they have an agenda. That's life.'

White took a sip of his whiskey and looked over the rim of his glass at Rick. 'But we're the police,' he said, 'we're here to uphold and enforce the law. If we don't abide by it ourselves, what kind of message does that send out?'

Rick thought for a moment. He'd known the detective a good while and felt, in this instance, he could be honest with him. 'Is the law always right?' he asked.

'No,' White replied, 'it can be wrong on occasion, but corruption is always indefensible, period.'

'Agreed,' Rick stated, 'but there's a difference between being on the take and doing somebody a favour, as long as it doesn't hurt anybody else. It's part of what this city is built on.' He waited, watching as White wrestled with that last statement. 'It might help me if you could be a little more detailed, give me a scenario so I know what you're driving at, if you can,' he added.

Swallowing more drink, White signalled for a refill and grimaced as the whiskey, a difficult thought, or both hit home. 'Consorting with criminals is part of how the job gets done,' he stated. 'You make deals, trade information, and let certain people stay out there on the street because that's where they're most useful to you. You can catch bigger fish and solve more serious crimes operating that way. They get you things you could never obtain otherwise, being outside the criminal network.' He drank determinedly from his new measure, lit a cigarette, and homed in on one of the episodes that had unsettled his mind.

'I ran into a guy today, an Irishman named Eugene. He was gangland for sure, and one of the bigger fish I just mentioned. I drew my gun, and he drew his, then my boss stepped in and settled our altercation. They know each other, but he won't say from where. I don't like it. I'm handling a case, a murder down by the docks, and the foreman there was telling me about how the cops are turning a blind eye to black strike-breakers getting beaten up by the regular Irish workers because a lot of cops come from that community and have sympathies, even loyalties to these guys. So, they don't get involved, which means they don't uphold the law. How are those black folks meant to feel about that?'

'Like I said,' Rick reasoned, 'people can't be trusted fully when they got an agenda. You think your boss has been doing deals with this Eugene?'

'I don't know,' White admitted vaguely. He was distracted by Rick's comment, about how you couldn't trust a person when something was bending the way they thought and the actions they took. His mind leapt to O'Malley taking over the interviewing of Nevin and O'Brien, how his boss had smoothed things over so quickly with the gangster, and how he wouldn't be drawn into divulging what his connection to the shady Eugene was. O'Malley had an agenda alright, it was just White couldn't see exactly what it was yet, and that was troubling him deeply. Then his mind lurched, probably courtesy of the large quantity of whiskey he'd taken on board, to the imminent arrival of Pops Ross, driving halfway across the country so he could control Mona's life once again. Now, *there* was an agenda, the detective thought sourly, finishing what was left in his glass in reaction to the bitter reminder of what was about to come.

'I lost you there for a moment,' Rick observed. 'Another, or are you quitting while you still have a chance of rescuing tomorrow and whatever it brings?'

'Boy, you're really hitting the nail on the head tonight,' White said grimly. 'More drink. You just reminded me I don't want to be myself tomorrow.'

'I didn't mean to upset you,' Rick said, pouring more whiskey into White's glass. 'I didn't mean nothing by it. Look, people always have an agenda, especially when it comes to anything big, anything that matters. You just got to realise that, then you got to try to make the right call, that's all. I seen plenty of folks mess that up, it's where the best of my business comes from. Do me a favour, will you? Don't be a part of that. Take a walk and think things through, do whatever you need to do. I know I shouldn't be saying this, given I'm a bartender, but drinking yourself into a stupor isn't going to solve anything, it won't even let you forget. Go home.'

'Home,' White repeated heavily.

Those words, especially that last one, resonated with the detective, but for all Rick's good intentions, they just made him feel even more despairing of the day. Silently, he finished his drink in one go, paid, picked his hat up off the bar, and waved goodbye to Rick in a way that was as much a motion to push everything they'd discussed out of the window as it was a farewell. He didn't want to cause a scene. Weaving slightly as he exited the bar, White started to make his way reluctantly back to the apartment.

He couldn't call it home anymore, but he had nowhere else to go and there was a bottle of rye unopened in the cupboard. As he made his way through the hot and sticky streets, White thought about Joseph Walker. If the Irish didn't kill him, then who did, and why? Grace had spoken of a sensitive and respectful boy without an ounce of violence or malice in him. Had he just been in the wrong place at the wrong time, or was there another explanation? White's steps slowed up. He had reached the corner of his street.

When he got inside, drunk though he was, he was sensitive enough to notice the air in the apartment already seemed changed, like it was charged with a negative energy or waiting solemnly for two of its three occupants, and probably its favourite two, White surmised, to leave. He looked around the darkening rooms wondering what objects Mona would take and whether he would notice their absence immediately or be cruelly stung by their removal in the weeks and months to come. He wondered, and this was an even worse thought, what she would leave that would remind him of her, and what he would have to give away because it brought back memories too painful for him to cope with. How hard would he have to scrub the place to erase her scent, and would he even want to?

He stumbled towards the kitchen, believing he would be safest in there because it was utilitarian and contained nothing he could become emotional about, but the sight of Mona's suitcase and another, smaller one accompanying it in the hallway hit him like a bullet in the chest. He found himself struggling to breathe, the loss was so great within him. Automatically, he fetched the bottle from the cupboard and not even bothering with a glass, uncorked it and took a swig. The lights in both bedrooms and the living room were out, and he found himself creeping through his own house so as not to wake his wife and daughter. He couldn't bear to see either of them right now, even though he would be losing them in the morning.

He eased open the window, and with the bottle in his pocket, climbed down the fire escape to the shared yard below. The night was muggy, and looking down at his dishevelled clothes, White realised he'd neither washed properly nor changed for nearly forty-eight hours. He took off his tie and opened his shirt right up, but there seemed no air to bathe his chest. Rubbing his neck and smoking a cigarette, he took another swig of the burning spirit, but it did little to fill the hollows of his insides.

From the darkness of the bedroom she was now sharing with their daughter, Mona listened as her husband blundered around the small apartment. From the heaviness of his movements, she could tell he'd been drinking. She held her breath, not wanting him to come in and disturb them both. Dominic had never been a violent man, or even one to look for an argument, but he knew they were leaving, and it had hurt him deeply, so she couldn't be sure of anything anymore.

When no lights came on and the noises ceased, she waited for what seemed like an eternity, then slowly opened the bedroom door. She tiptoed tentatively along the hallway, but there was neither sight nor sound of him in the living room or kitchen. Then, a faint noise drifted up from the yard, reaching her highly attuned ears through the open window. She peered cautiously out to see Dominic laying on his back, moaning and looking up at the sky through heavily lidded eyes, with a cigarette dangling from his mouth and a bottle by his side. In that moment, she could see his pain, but she couldn't go to him. She had convinced herself their futures lay in different directions.

She quietly drew out a chair and sat motionless in the silent dark kitchen, illuminated only by the moonlight that was falling through the window. She sat doing nothing but thinking. She reasoned the fact she could see him like that, sprawled out drunk and despairing on the patchy grass, and not feel the urge to go to him and soothe both their pain, meant their love was damaged beyond repair and she was doing the right thing by leaving and going back to Omaha. She'd felt so hurt all the times he'd not been there for her, either physically or in his mind, that it had had a withering effect on her love for him. Mona realised, sitting stock still on the kitchen chair, that she couldn't feel the way she used to do about him. The love wasn't dead, it was just bled completely dry by all the things that had been eating away at it for such a long time now, things that could never, or would never be put right.

Everything about New York was hot, dirty, and oppressive. The city was consuming her, and she longed for the open plains of the landscape she'd grown up in. Soon she would be back there again, giving Amy a future that would contain more love and security, taking her away from the chaos and unpredictability she would otherwise have faced. She took no pleasure out of separating Amy from her father, but it had to be done, for her sake and for the child's. Whether Dominic would ever forgive her for doing it was another matter. Only time would tell. She got up from the chair and placed it quietly back in at the table, looking at the suitcases in the hallway as she did so. Then, leaving Dominic to his drinking down in the yard, she made her way back into the bedroom to wait for the morning and Pops Ross to come.

Around three o'clock White was just about able to consider that he might never love anyone again if this was how it all ended. For all her concern surrounding the burgeoning crime and violence within the city, the safety and social development of their daughter, and her own sense of feeling neglected, the one thing Mona had never seemed to worry about was how her actions or outbursts affected him. For nearly everyone else, she was able to show compassion, but towards him, Mona was like a blunt instrument, unable or unwilling to have any emotional sensitivity when it came to his feelings. She simply didn't understand the hurt she caused him, and thinking back across their whole relationship, White realised it had always been thus. It wasn't that she hadn't shown him love, although she was never a naturally affectionate woman, just that it had been too thinly spread over their time together. If she had felt unloved by him, then perhaps it was because he'd given up sounding his heart into a deep well that never gave back a loving echo.

He'd thought having a baby might change things for the better, that somehow the idea of them becoming a family unit would strengthen her feelings about him, but it had not. If anything, the arguing increased. That was why he'd thrown himself into his work more than he'd needed to, going above and beyond what the job demanded. He'd always been a highly committed detective, but at some point, and he couldn't remember when, his love of the job had turned into an obsession. Now, here he was as it all fell apart, drinking to obliterate the pain he felt, but with his mind still split between the loss of his wife and child and tracking down the killer of an innocent black boy.

The whiskey had made him suitably numb enough to explore the pit of his despair without being consumed by it. As a matter of interest, he checked the level of the bottle. It was implausible and confusing. He realised he'd also dropped his cigarette somewhere in the process. The heat of the night didn't seem to be letting up and he was sweating with concentration as he forced his fingers to focus on the rolling of another smoke; something he could normally do without thinking. Eventually, he managed to find his matches and get one to strike without bouncing off into the yard unlit. He drank more whiskey, even though his subconscious was warning him he was way past having too much. He didn't like his subconscious right now; every time he closed his eyes it was dredging up images of Mona and the battered body of Joseph Walker.

Besides, he reasoned, taking another swig from the neck of the near empty bottle, he was already too drunk to think clearly anymore about who might have wanted the youth dead or why they'd carried out the murder with such fury before leaving poor Joseph discarded at the docks. It was a case he was in no fit state to fathom right then, and it made him feel even more terrible to be drinking himself into a comatose state when he should've been sleeping so he could get up early and start asking the questions that would lead him to finding the killer and solving the case. Also, so he could say goodbye to his family without reeking of booze.

Around four o'clock, White finally became horizontal with hurt: a destroyed detective wrecked on rye whiskey and asleep in his dirty clothes on the damp grass of the shared back yard, an unlit bent cigarette dangling from his mouth. He had reached an all-time low.

Chapter Ten

The Way of the World / The Weight of the World

White immersed himself in the water of his lukewarm bath. He had filled a two-pint pitcher from the faucet in the kitchen and forced himself to drink the lot with a double dose of aspirins. After his soak, he shaved and put on a clean set of clothes. Everything was happening in slow motion and taking twice as long to do as normal. It was the monster of a hangover dragging him down, but he wouldn't let it. There were important things to be done, and he had to redeem himself for both his own sake and Joseph's. So, he set out for Johnny's Bar and Grill, eating the biggest breakfast he could order. He drank four cups of coffee and swallowed another dose of aspirin. Then he dragged himself up and headed off for the precinct. Despite the gargantuan intake of restoratives, he felt like he had been thrown out of an aeroplane without a parachute and landed in a cess pool. He had run out of cigarettes and run out of luck. It was just before ten in the morning.

With a headache that gave a new and deeper meaning to the word pain, the hampered detective made his way down to the interview rooms. He may have been falling apart, but he still had a purpose driving him forwards. The rooms were all empty. Then he took in all the holding cells, but there was no sign of either Nevin or O'Brien. He didn't understand. Eventually, after bumming a cigarette from another detective, White cleared his head a little and tracked O'Malley down to the precinct canteen. The lieutenant was wiping up egg yolk with a slice of toast and greeted White with a curious gaze. 'What happened to your face? Looks like you let an excited monkey shave you on the promise of some peanuts.' White was unmoved by the comment. He craved more aspirin, but most of all he wanted answers. After a night of trying to annihilate himself, he had learned the last thing that would die in him was his detective spirit.

'Where are my two Irishmen? They're not in the cells and they're not in the interview rooms.'

'*Your* two Irishmen?' O'Malley retorted. 'And there was me thinking they were owned by Eugene. You've got here a little late, kid. They arrived bang on the stroke of nine and I interviewed them both, separately of course. I'm going to write it up and send you a copy straight after I finish my breakfast; make it official. Don't hold your breath though, detective. They have an alibi for the beatings which means they also have an alibi for the murder.'

White narrowed his eyes. 'You got a cigarette?' he asked. When O'Malley obliged and the nicotine allowed him to get a better grip on reality, he continued. 'I got here before ten. You've had time to conduct two interviews and eat breakfast in just over an hour? Just how hard did you work those Irish boys, sir?'

O'Malley took a slurp of his coffee and eyed his sergeant over the rim of his cup. 'You need to take a rest, detective. You don't look so well, and your mouth is starting to offend people it really shouldn't on a daily basis. I used my interrogative techniques, the ones I've honed for more than twenty years on the Squad, and those men came up clean. Now, I'll admit I figure them for the beatings. Hell, if I press Eugene enough, I may even get them to cough for it. A bar full of Irishmen, some of them off-duty cops, will swear they never took part in any murder though. You see, I already asked my people. Sure, some workers left the bar and came back an hour later a little bloody around the knuckles but get this straight: they went out to deliver a beating, nothing more. If one of those men had stepped over the line, talk would have got back to me. Whoever killed your boy, it wasn't them.'

White was fully awake now. 'So, threaten to prosecute them for the assaults. Pitch them against each other. Tell them one of the guys in the hospital has got a fractured skull and might not live. Up the ante and see what comes out of their mouths at least. What's wrong with you, boss? It's like you don't want to investigate these guys. Did Eugene buy you? Is that it?'

From his seated position, O'Malley hit White low in the guts. As the detective doubled over, ready to spill the breakfast from Johnny's, the lieutenant grabbed his tie and drew him in so their faces were just inches apart. Through clenched teeth, he hissed: 'You accuse *me*? Who the fuck do you think you are? You're all over the place; you're flying into things without thinking and you stink of last night's booze. Whatever the hell is wrong with you, get it sorted out…and quickly. You just used up your last life with me.' O'Malley let him go and sat disgustedly at the table muttering to himself: 'canteen full of people…and he has the nerve…after all I done for him.'

White skulked off back to his office. He figured he'd lost his wife and child, what did it matter to also blow his chances of making inspector? No, he thought, finally remembering he had an emergency packet of cigarettes, and taking them from their hiding place, the only thing he could do now was to find Joseph's killer. For all the crap that had happened to him in the last few days, it was nothing compared to what Grace was going through. He knew he'd been wrong to accuse O'Malley in public, but he had his reasons. If those Irishmen were the murderers, then he would have to obtain airtight evidence no senior officer or jury could dismiss. The loss of his wife and daughter was no excuse. He needed to do his job. He needed to bring Grace Walker the small comfort of a conviction.

Flipping open the file on his desk, he studied the photographs of the shoeprint on the body with a magnifying glass. Then he thought about all the footwear and tread patterns he had ever seen. There was a depth to the imprints left on the body, and a configuration designed not to slip. The killer had worn boots, and most likely industrial boots at that. If he could find a matching pattern, then he had some kind of evidence, not enough for a jury to like, but something to get his teeth into. The hangover took a backseat. He needed to see Nevin and O'Brien in their homes. He needed to examine their boots.

O'Malley took himself up to the roof of the precinct. Detective Squad could go about its business without him for a while. He wasn't in the mood for people. The roof didn't offer any particularly good views, the precinct being a squat brownstone building surrounded by the not too distant and dizzying development of skyscrapers New York had become synonymous with. O'Malley didn't care. He was here for the solitude, not the scenery. He needed to think. The morning had not begun well, and the lieutenant knew it had probably set the tone for the rest of the day. Mostly, he was troubled by White.

His protégé was going off the rails right in the middle of investigating a racially sensitive murder. A promising young detective who had made sergeant by impressing everyone around him and who, by rights, should be heading straight to becoming an inspector in the coming weeks was now, through his naivety and wildness, doing nothing but causing trouble. White was the discarded cigarette in a tinderbox forest, ignoring the politics that surrounded him and just looking to burn his way furiously to a solution whatever the cost, leaving a trail of scorched earth in his wake. It wasn't like him, he was normally such a sensitive and thoughtful guy, and O'Malley couldn't understand why White was suddenly behaving so recklessly.

Walking into that bar yesterday just to rattle the cages of Nevin and O'Brien, two men who were neither here nor there in the bigger picture of the dispute at the docks, or with the crime wave sweeping the city, showed a total lack of guile on his junior officer's part. Everybody knew the Irish situation was a delicate one. The beatings could be seen as skirmishes where those who felt wronged had the chance to let off steam about it. The black strike-breakers understood the dispute, they knew all about the poverty faced by those taking industrial action, and they realised the dock company would show no loyalty towards them: they would be discarded as soon as an agreement was reached between management and the Irish boys. This wasn't about race; it was about workers standing together and showing solidarity in the face of corporate oppression.

Kinship was what you fell back on when outsiders were trying to damage you, O'Malley recognised, facing into the warm wind that blew across the roof of the precinct. It was why the cops were taking no action beyond breaking up the mob before it could get too carried away with its retribution. That was how the thing worked on the simplest of levels, but what White had done yesterday jeopardised an agreement that operated on a higher plain. Eugene had his own interests to protect, but there were no drugs to be found in his neighbourhood, and no violence was ever meted out to civilians. Also, and far more importantly, there was the promise to hand over anyone who acted outside of that code. Those were the unwritten rules of the agreement, and Eugene had come good in giving up violent criminals and murderers before now. If they had come from his Irish clan, he wouldn't protect the killer of the young black boy because it just wasn't in his best interests to do so, of that O'Malley was certain.

The lieutenant didn't like the arrangement one bit, but he was wise enough to know Eugene would one day be cut down by a hail of bullets from an enemy gun. Gangsters never made old bones; they were retired permanently long before they reached the seventh age of man. Besides, O'Malley thought, while it was possible to police the city in a more noble way, the pact got lunatics and killers locked up quicker, before they had the chance to destroy even more people's lives, and O'Malley realised that protecting human life was far more important than feeling honourable.

When White had experienced several more years of policing, rising through the ranks, he'd understand the responsibility that rested on a lieutenant's shoulders. Nobody above or below him had as much influence on what happened out there on the mean streets every single day. So, the Eugenes of this world were a necessary evil, and White would see that eventually, even if he couldn't see it now. In the present, O'Malley just hoped to God his protégé managed to put right whatever was wrong with his head and find the killer before New York descended into the kind of riots that were ripping the heart out of the town over in Chicago.

White looked at his watch and exhaled heavily. Before he could work the case any further and try to get justice for Joseph Walker there was the leaving of his girls. From the den of his office, the detective headed back to the house at a time when he knew they would be departing for Omaha. He didn't want to be there, but like a witness drawn to watch human wreckage, he felt compelled to at least be a helpless bystander. He had timed it on a hunch, Mona's father checking out of his hotel and driving over to their house. He figured neither father nor daughter would want to hang around, so put their exit time between 11.15 and 11.45, given that Pops Ross would never turn down the consumption of a full hotel breakfast and checkout time in most places was eleven. He had been very calculated about it all; keeping emotion at bay was the only hope he had of getting through today without disintegrating.

Sure enough, Pops Ross' car was parked outside the apartment when he got back. He had planned an impressive range of ways to handle the tragedy of his family deserting him, but he knew the reality would see him fall woefully short in every department. As if by fate, the three generations of Ross came out of the building to find him standing there in his own private nightmare. Mona was carrying Amy in her arms while Pops took care of the cases. White knew right then he would barely be able to speak. While husband and wife both succumbed to tears, he lent in to kiss the head of his daughter, smelling both her toddler freshness and Mona's familiar scent. These were the odours that would drift through the empty apartment like ghosts after they had gone.

'I'm sorry,' were the only words he could get past the lump in his throat.

'I know,' Mona replied, the tears streaming down her cheeks. Amy just looked perplexed. A rabbit caught in the headlights of her parents' pain. There they stood, two adults who had met, fallen in love, got married, had a child, and started to build a life together, now unable even to speak to each other, let alone do anything to stop their relationship dissolving away into nothing right in front of the eyes of their tiny daughter.

Pops Ross closed the trunk of the car and opened the door for his daughter. As Mona slid into her seat, she turned around to White and said: 'I'll call you when we get there. I'll keep in touch. You can come and visit Amy whenever you want, you know that Dom.'

The engine coughed into life and the car moved slowly away from the kerb. White watched it go, with his little girl waving at him through the rear window, then stared down into the gutter, blinking away impotent and devastated tears. The image of her tiny hand, accompanied by the screeching of the fighting magpies on the rooftops, all made for a disturbing spectacle that would stay forever etched upon his mind.

He stood staring at the meaningless cracks in the sidewalk, watching ants labour between them without really seeing a thing. Everything was a complete and utter mess. He was experiencing a life-shattering moment of loss, living in a world where everyone had their own agenda, and no one could be trusted. Everything felt broken now, and White realised he had to start from this, the lowest point, and begin fixing things, or give up on life entirely. When he finally moved, it was not to go into the house. There were suspects to see and he was sick of failing people. It was time to start getting some results.

Pops Ross cursed a little under his breath as he navigated the Model T through the traffic of central New York. He wasn't used to the melee of a big city, and a line of sweat had already formed upon his furrowed brow. Mona noticed this, watching him in the rear-view mirror from her position in the back seat where she sat clutching Amy's hand, as much for her own comfort as for the child's. The toddler had not let go of her favourite teddy bear since their final exit from the apartment. She had seemed bewildered at the idea she would be living somewhere else from now on. It had stunned her into absolute silence, and she had maintained that from the previous evening when Mona had given her the simplest of explanations.

'I never seen so many automobiles,' Pops Ross said, more in exasperation than in wonder. 'You all okay in the back there?' he added, showing a note of concern.

'Yes,' Mona replied monosyllabically. Amy still said nothing.

After a minute's silence, Ross declared, 'You done the right thing. You know that, Mona. Sure, it hurts now, but give it time and you'll see this was all for the best.'

His tone didn't sound convincing to her ears, especially when she was feeling like some heartless abductor who had trampled all over her husband's emotions before taking his daughter away from him. She'd brought an end to their life as a family, she thought, watching out of the window as the theatres on Broadway rolled by, denuded of their bright lights and glamour, looking ordinary in the reality of the daytime like a showgirl who had exposed her face to the world without the mask of her makeup. The lights may have faded on her marriage a long time ago, when she'd lost the warmth and attention of her man, but today was definitive. It marked a line in the sand that, once crossed, meant there was no going back. The show was over, and the theatre closed down. There would be no more music, romance, or drama between them.

Every building they passed seemed composed of harder, sharper edges, picked out by the hot eye of a high glaring sun, and it felt like the car was dragging its way through treacle rather than a traffic jam. It was as if the Gods of New York City wanted to torment her because she was leaving Detective Squad's golden boy behind having forever damaged the man they prized as their sleuthing son.

While she wasn't sorry to be leaving New York, Mona was hit by the overwhelming feeling she had caused all this devastation to not even be back at square one. Sure, she was returning to Omaha with a beautiful little girl, not to mention the fact that the time she'd spent living independently had made her wiser as well as older. She had left as a girl and was coming back as a woman, but that just made the prospect of living in her parents' house feel like even more of a backwards step. Most of all, she had been wounded in love. She had lost Dominic, and she couldn't imagine being with anyone else in the future. He had been special, but their separation had rocked her faith any relationship with a man could ever truly work. They shone like gold then they let you down. That was what they did.

Omaha, Amy, and Pops. That was all she could focus on now. Whatever ghosts followed her around her childhood home, however many phantoms from her past appeared on the streets of her town, it was still a place where she would always feel secure, a little piece of America that offered a mother and her child the chance to live in a stable community where nothing incredible happened, but the warmth of the citizens towards their own was constant.

As the traffic eased, the Model T gathered speed and they moved through the outskirts of the city and beyond it to long, empty roads flanked only by rolling fields of corn. Like her love, it had been cut down, but new shoots had emerged growing tall and golden once again. The metaphor was not lost on her, and although she sat in the back of the car still holding on tightly to Amy's little hand and reeling from the disastrous slide through love into hurt, failure and recriminations, Mona had to believe a better future lay ahead. She hoped Dominic found the killer he was hunting and then completed another difficult journey across America so he might still be a part of his daughter's life.

Chapter Eleven
Slaughter and Solution

Patrick Cain came home unharmed, but Johnny knew something wasn't right. His brother had explained not returning to the bar after the assault on the strike-breakers by saying he hadn't wanted any more drink. Johnny let that one go, even though he'd never known Patrick turn down the chance to celebrate anything. Now, Johnny sat in their small house deep in the Five Points, brooding over industrial action and Patrick's recent behaviour. Before, there had been a sizeable problem, but Johnny feared he had something altogether trickier on his hands now, something he wouldn't be able to deal with on his own. He nipped the top of his cigarette and saved it just as another fit of coughing took over and he once more clamped the handkerchief to his mouth. No time for this, he thought of the affliction, not that anything could be done about it anyway. It was amazing how living on borrowed time focused the mind.

Patrick had been on edge ever since that night, shouting out against his tormentors as he slept, and unable to roll his cigarettes without spilling tobacco everywhere. It wasn't the fighting had put him in that state, for Pat delighted in a good scrap whenever one came his way, and when they didn't, he ignited them himself simply to kill boredom and feed the hatred in his heart. Something had happened that had nothing to do with the strike, Johnny was sure of it. His brother always confided in him eventually, but this time it felt more serious. This time something inside of Patrick had come away from its moorings. The cough came again, and Johnny seized up with it. When he was done there was more blood than before spattering the handkerchief. He wondered if he would live long enough to see his brother escape a hanging. That was when Patrick appeared. He already wore the look of a condemned man.

'I heard you coughing, Johnny. You need to go back to the doctor, see if he can give you anything.'

Johnny took in the dishevelled hair, the overgrowing moustache, and the bloodshot eyes of his brother. There was grime under his fingernails even though there was no work to be had, and Patrick was looking scrawnier by the day. What was once sinew was now wasted flesh. Since the night of the assault, Pat couldn't eat a meal and would chew a piece of bread endlessly before he could manage to swallow it.

'There's no use in me seeing a doctor. You know it and I know it,' Johnny said matter-of-factly. 'What a mess we both are, Patrick. The Cain brothers, once feared across the Five Points and beyond, now reduced to this: a consumptive and a nervous wreck. What did you do, Pat? You might as well tell me. You've no hope of keeping it to yourself. Everything you do betrays you. What did you get up to that night of the beatings?'

Patrick shuddered and sat down quickly on a stool. For a time, he wouldn't meet Johnny's eyes, then, still not looking up from the floor, he spoke. 'I've done a terrible thing.'

'I know,' Johnny said quietly and with reassurance. 'I always knew you would one day.'

'It was the fighting,' Patrick continued, still unable to face his brother. 'It got my blood up. All our suffering and frustration with the strike, and when we do finally meet the men who've taken our jobs, the police turn up and we have to scatter. It wasn't enough, Johnny. It wasn't enough.'

'So, you went looking for something else,' Johnny said, going down a road he'd already travelled in his mind, 'and you must've found it because you didn't come back to the bar. But whatever you did in anger, you can't live with now. What is it, Pat? Did you cool down and hate the beast inside your bones, or is it just the hangman's noose you fear?'

Now, Patrick looked at his brother. Somehow, having his own confession taken away from him lifted the burden a little, and he wanted to set the record straight. 'I killed a man that night. He was hardly a man, and he was nothing to do with the strike neither. I did to him what I wouldn't have done to a dog, and worse still, there wasn't no reason for it, just the red mist, Johnny, the red fucking mist. When I close my eyes, I see what I done to him, and I know it was hate, a blind hate that didn't care who it hurt and didn't want to stop. I'm a killer, Johnny. How can I trust myself not to do it again? Don't ask me to turn myself in though. I've no stomach for jail, and I certainly can't face death. I'm a coward, see Johnny? A fucking coward.'

Relighting his cigarette, even though he knew it'd kill him all the quicker, Johnny shifted in his seat so he was closer to Patrick. He felt tired, as if everything he'd once hoped to do just kept receding into the distance until he couldn't see it anymore, couldn't even remember what it was. No matter now. 'Here's the thing, Pat,' he said wearily, but still summoning up enough authority in his voice to make it stick. 'You're going to tell me all the details, everything that happened after you left the scene of the beatings when the police arrived. Then, I'm going to talk to Eugene, see what can be done.'

'Eugene?' Patrick repeated anxiously. 'He can be worse than the law.'

'Yes, he can, but he's our friend. He'll do right by me, and he'll help you because you're my brother. Johnny Cain is not dead yet, and Eugene still needs my assistance in this district. I hold the ear of the strikers, and they are an army that Eugene wants. So, he'll clear up this problem and I'll give him soldiers for his dirty war. We already live in hell, Patrick. Doing a deal with the devil is just common sense. Now, tell me everything.'

Johnny Cain stared into the empty grate of the fire. It felt dead and bare, but as yet another hot night ensued, there was no need for it to be lit. The weather had drawn the soul out of the small house, and they'd taken to cooking in the tiny yard. Inside, the walls were still illuminated by the flickering play of a candle, but the room felt too hot. Opening the window let in the stench from the inadequate sewers, and there had been no rain to wash the shit away, so it festered, like a metaphor for the troubling thoughts in his mind.

For all the scheming, the speeches, and the fighting, he still only amounted to this: the poorest of houses in a slum neighbourhood – the bottom of the pile if it wasn't for the blacks of Harlem, and even they now threatened to overtake him. His gambling took away most of the money he'd got from deals, and what was left went on his whores. Political activism didn't pay well enough, and now, just as he was on the verge of making real money through his collaboration with Eugene, it would only serve to pay for his funeral, so that he might not be buried in a pauper's grave.

'A political arrangement,' was what Eugene had called their plan, laughing sickly as he did so, and Johnny reflected 'politics' was as dirty a word as 'murder,' perhaps dirtier still in these circumstances. Dusk had fallen as Patrick told his story of brutality, weeping and lamenting as he did so, a line of snot trickling unwiped from his nose. Johnny remained unmoved by what he heard. He should have been the killer, not Pat. His brother night be incendiary, but he was a sensitive man and carried remorse. Johnny had a much darker heart, that was why he was able to sacrifice his fellow men at the altar of Eugene's criminal needs.

The candle guttered, struggled, then recovered. Johnny stared into the near-dark and thought about the meeting he'd arranged. He was taking the necessary steps to protect Patrick. It would make no difference to Eugene if Cain junior was sent down for murder, it might even help his cause, but things would falter if Johnny wasn't there guiding the dockers. He was the engine that drove the wheels, and neither man could afford for the scheme they'd agreed upon to be derailed, so, help each other they must.

The cough strangled Johnny's chest again and he spat blood into the empty fireplace. Through the thin walls, he could hear the hideous wailing of next door's baby, and he realised he felt nothing but contempt for his people, the Irish, who drank and cursed, but never raised themselves up out of the pit they lived in. They had come to this land from famine, and now, more than sixty years on, they were still going hungry. Any man who did not seek out and grasp whatever opportunity came his way was a fool in Johnny's mind. He wasn't selling his people out, he reasoned, watching as the candle finally gave in and died. They'd betrayed themselves a long time ago.

He was the Pied Piper, leading the ignorant, filthy rats to the place they deserved, to the poisoned river to do Eugene's bidding, because they were too feckless to do their own. It was a hellish future, but what did he care? He wouldn't be alive to see it, and Patrick would have to learn to survive on his own. Johnny was fed up with the whole stinking show. He lit another cigarette in the darkness, the light from the match making his face seem deep, demonic, and hollow, like some wicked spectre summoned into being. As he smoked, he thought about tomorrow and what he would say at the meeting with Eugene.

The smell of the slaughterhouse was ripe at the best of times, but in the summer months, on the hottest of days where no breeze disturbed the fetid air, it clung to the nostrils like your very own sour nosebleed. Eugene did not mind the smell, nor the shrieking of the pigs as they were wrestled towards the long curved knives that dispatched them. This was his abattoir, and the sticky flow not only brought home the bacon in every sense, but it also reminded him war was a deadly business which would not wait for the slow or the stupid.

The place taught him a simple lesson: you must dispatch or be dispatched; kill or be killed. Daisy, the giant mastiff who was often to be found lumbering loyally and protectively by Eugene's side, would fearlessly face down a man carrying any weapon. She had once kept a whole mob at bay with her utter conviction to defend her master to the death, but here she was frightened. She understood the fate of the pigs, and her animal instinct had its hackles up at the danger. Still, she kept at Eugene's heel. She'd follow him into hell if he went there.

The workers kept their heads down and never asked questions. Many men came and went, talking to the boss in private, but then everyone ate pork except for the Jews, so there was nothing unusual in these people coming to the slaughterhouse, even if the visitors didn't look like businessmen and often had the appearance of butchers of a different kind. For Eugene, it was the perfect meeting place. No outsiders ventured here unless by invitation, and the folks he spoke with were usually made uneasy by the brutality of the scene. It advertised Eugene as a callous man surrounded by bloodshed, and he found that an effective business tool when it came to negotiation.

Today, there would be two visitors, separately, of course. The first one drew unwanted attention, stolen glances from the slaughterers, on account of the colour of his skin and the bruises he was sporting. Eugene ushered the man into the small and functional office where he poured them both a Bushmills, even though it was before midday. The man was a dock worker, and Eugene's experience of these people was they drank by their own clock, having worked so many night shifts. Daisy the mastiff raised her head and studied the new guest. Once she had appraised he was no threat, she rested her muzzle back down on her paws again. The man's injuries were superficial, Eugene noted. Good, he thought. Johnny Cain had managed to identify him and control his boys. Abraham had had to take a beating, otherwise his co-workers might have become suspicious, but Eugene needed him active, the plan depended on it.

'So, what troubles you?' Eugene asked.

'My friends took it bad the other night,' Abraham stated, eyeing the dog in the corner nervously, but intent on saying his piece. 'Lots of them still can't work. These beatings of yours need to be less violent. Can't you get the police to come quicker?'

'It was a small number of men,' Eugene said coldly, sipping his whiskey. 'The damage to your people is being controlled. The whole point is that they weather serious opposition, earn their place with the company, and then get to take over the Irish dockers. That's all still on track to happen.'

'You think the damage is controlled?' Abraham spat, angry at the mobster's dismissive tone. 'If that's the case, tell me why a young boy got killed by one of your crew.'

'Killed?' Eugene responded, putting out an arm to placate the snarling Daisy. 'No one's said anything about a murder,' he added, lying smoothly and feigning concern.

'A young black boy got beaten to death and his body was dumped in the dockyard all around the time your boys were smashing the hell out of us. You call that controlled?' Abraham asserted.

'This is news to me,' Eugene declared deviously, taking a longer drink. He didn't care about the black life, but this was trouble he didn't need. O'Malley had filled him in on all the details, so he knew the police couldn't be certain the killer was one of the Irish mob, but he didn't want to reveal the information and the connection to Detective Squad to Abraham. 'I'll look into it. You know we don't want any deaths; it goes against our shared purpose. If this was anything to do with one of those men, they will be severely punished, you have my word on that.'

'You'll turn them over to the police?' Abraham demanded.

'If I have to, yes,' was Eugene's honest reply.

Abraham drained his whiskey in one go. 'You sure about that?'

'If there's proof. I won't protect a murderer, not unless…'

'Unless!' Abraham exclaimed.

'Unless it aids our cause, yours, and mine. You think I don't value your people, but you're wrong. I'm a pragmatist. I couldn't give a damn what colour someone is if they can do me a service. I need your men in the docks for my own reasons, and you need them to be there so they don't starve. If one life gets sacrificed for that outcome, that's too bad, but if I find out the killer was one of mine and he proves expendable, I'll go to the cops, *if* it doesn't jeopardise the whole project. Understood?'

'You're the coldest human being I ever met,' Abraham said disgustedly, uneasy to be doing his brother's bidding when he still had his doubts about how and why Joseph Walker had died. It occurred to him perhaps Eugene wasn't the only man close to him who saw murder as a necessary casualty to the greater cause. Could Paul have arranged the boy's death and had him dumped at the dockyard to make it look like the Irish mob had committed the killing? He knew his brother would stop at nothing to create racial unrest within the city.

'That's as maybe, but you know I'm right,' Eugene countered.

'You just better make sure no one else gets killed, that's all,' Abraham declared, putting thoughts of Paul's potential involvement from his mind.

Eugene finished his drink and stared hard at Abraham. 'Watch yourself,' he said. 'I can have this strike succeed or fail, it's in my hands. The future of your people rests with me. Now, if there's nothing else and we understand each other fully, I have business to attend to.'

Abraham drew in his resentment. This man was a snake, he thought, and you didn't poke a snake twice for fear it might strike you. He'd had plenty of practice biting his tongue around white folks, so, he nodded, got up, and left the office.

First O'Malley, and now Abraham, Eugene thought, smoothing out the creases in his trousers. There was too much fuss being made over this body at the docks, it threatened to disrupt his good work. He resolved to question Johnny Cain about it when the agitator visited him. As luck would have it, this was Eugene's second meeting of the day, and although it was Cain who had asked to see him, the timing of the request couldn't have been better. He'd meant what he'd said to Abraham. If one of the Irish boys had overstepped the mark, he would take whatever action necessary to set the matter straight. The problem would be removed. In her agitated slumber, Daisy gave a short bark of assent.

Early afternoon and the flies had increased in number around the slaughterhouse, the smell of blood congealing in the heat enticing them to congregate for a feast. Eugene felt impatient and headed out to the perimeter of the abattoir, making Daisy stay back at the office. Just then, the figure of Cain appeared at the end of the road. The mobster waited until eye contact had been established and then set off at a stroll. He reached an alleyway between two tall buildings where a couple of lowlifes had overturned some packing crates and set up a craps game away from the glare of the sun and any prying beat cop who might disturb them.

'Game's over, take a walk,' Eugene said, before sweeping away the dice and using the crate to set his whiskey and two glasses on. The lowlifes stared. 'I got business here, now beat it!' Eugene commanded, and the look in his deadly eyes meant he didn't have to say any more. The deadbeats picked up their dice and scuttled out of the alleyway. Johnny Cain checked he wasn't being followed, entered the space, and sat down opposite his contact.

'You wanted to see me,' Eugene said, 'so here we are. Shoot.'

Cain looked around the dead-end street and replied. 'Since when did you conduct your business in back alleys? What was wrong with the slaughterhouse?'

'You don't trouble me over trifles, Johnny. That's what I like about you,' Eugene said smoothly. 'When you rang me, you sounded burdened. I don't want your serious personal matters reaching the ears of my workers, however much I trust them. What's all this about?'

Cain took hold of his whiskey, his steady hands belying his rapidly beating heart. 'Patrick's in trouble and I need your help,' he said directly, wincing at the large drink he'd just taken for Dutch courage.

'What sort of trouble?' Eugene asked, studying the man across from him intently. 'Will I need a whiskey for this?' he added.

'You might,' Cain admitted.

Eugene took his glass up and raised a toast to Cain. It was calculated. He needed the man's confidence. He wanted the whole story, not just some selected highlights that would leave him to operate in the half-dark.

'Patrick has killed a man. He didn't intend to, but there was too much drink and fire fuelling his blood. Now, he's filled with regret and going to pieces. It's dangerous for him, which means it's also dangerous for us,' Cain stated.

Eugene considered the information, the cogs turning in his mind. 'When was this?' he asked.

The news was what he had been fearing. 'The night of the beatings down at the docks,' Cain replied.

Eugene kept his face poker-straight, but the heat of the situation prickled under his collar. 'What do you want me to do?' he asked heavily.

'I'm reckoning the police will come asking questions. If you can reassure them the killing had nothing to do with us, it would be in everyone's interest.'

'You said Patrick was cracking up,' Eugene coolly observed, taking a shot of his whiskey. 'How can you be sure he won't break and talk to somebody else?'

'I'll arrange for Pat to take a trip out of town on family business. If you cover for us, it will ease his torments and in a little while, when it's safe to, he can return. I don't ask for anything other than you put the word out no Irishman was involved in a murder that night. My brother needs your protection. You have the confidence of the police, and I control the will of the strikers. Help me, and I will deliver on my promise to give you those men. I cannot let my brother hang for this.'

'There have been enquiries already,' Eugene announced. 'The cops are hot on this one, it won't be easy.'

'But you'll help me?' Cain asked insistently.

'I'll do what I can,' Eugene said uneasily.

'You'll give them your word?' Cain pushed.

'I'll handle the situation,' Eugene stated more definitely. 'Send your brother away and make your alibi a solid one. I can't stop the police asking questions.'

'I will. Thank you,' Cain offered.

The two men finished their drinks and Eugene gestured for Cain to exit the alleyway before him. When the agitant was gone, he kicked out at the crates and swore. He stormed off back to the slaughterhouse, cursing the day and trying to figure out how to resolve the issues at hand. When he reached the office, one of his men had arrived with the Rolls Royce. That meant another problem was looming.

'We got the call from O'Shea,' the driver stated. 'Your man's being paid a visit. You were right. That damned cop just won't stop digging.'

The day had come to test him, Eugene thought. Enough was enough. It was time to take some action. He summoned Daisy, got into the Rolls, checked his revolver, and tightened his thin mouth. The dog looked at him with concern. She knew when her master was in a dangerous mood. Yes, he snarled inwardly, it was time to start putting people in their place.

Chapter Twelve
Fighters from the Five Points Slums

The Irish Bar was dead apart from its most helpless inebriates. The bartender recognised White immediately and gave a look of apprehension at his return. 'It's okay,' White assured the man, 'I'm not here to cause trouble. I just wanted to catch O'Brien so I can eliminate him from this murder I'm investigating. Between you and me, I don't figure him for it, but he knows the area and he might have seen something that could help. Where can I find him when he's not here?' The bartender looked both ways to check no one was listening in and then whispered: 'He's at home. His wife's sick, so he's doing her work for her, but don't tell him it was me that let you know.' The man scribbled something on a piece of paper and handed it swiftly to the detective. White tipped his hat and left the bar quickly. The smell of stale alcohol was beginning to make him feel nauseous.

The bartender waited until he was sure the snooping detective was gone, then he crossed over to the telephone hung on the far wall of the joint, dialled the operator and waited to be connected to the number he'd requested. A voice came on the line, and he informed them 'It's O'Shea here, from the Lucky Dime Bar. That cop from the other day came back looking for O'Brien. I gave him the address just like Eugene told me to. He left here a couple of minutes ago.'

'Okay,' the voice said, 'we're on it.'

Then the line went dead, and the bartender returned to his work.

The Irish Quarter felt every bit as poor as Harlem. White had been here before on less serious business but was always struck by the hardship of the area. Unwashed kids prowled around in packs, shoeless and a long way from innocence. There was grime on the windows and broken bottles in the gutter. The washing that was strung out across the street looked dirty and threadbare. Rats scurried for cover, picking their way through the garbage as the detective walked towards the address the barman had given him. When he knocked on O'Brien's door, it was opened by a filthy boy with a nose that needed wiping, who stood there staring at him. A voice from inside bellowed: 'Who is it?'

Handing the kid his handkerchief, White headed down the narrow hallway to where the sound had issued from. What he saw took a moment for him to process. Pat O'Brien, bareknuckle fighter, was sitting at a washboard scrubbing clothes. A pile of clean laundry hung from makeshift lines strung across the room and an even bigger stack of dirty linen sat beside O'Brien waiting to be soaked. Pat O'Brien: the great hulking washer man.

O'Brien looked up from his chores as if he'd been caught with his hands around another man's throat. White sat down and lit two cigarettes, offering one to the ashamed dockworker. 'Maybe I got you wrong,' he said. 'Any man who does whatever it takes to keep his family fed deserves at least some respect.' O'Brien smoked, staring at the cop just like his little boy had done, except the look carried even more distrust. The detective pressed on. 'I know you already made your denials to my lieutenant, but I've got something I need to follow up on to put my mind at ease.' Gesturing to the pair of heavy boots in the corner of the room, he asked: 'are those the only pair of work boots you own?'

O'Brien spat into the empty fireplace and retorted: 'If I had the money to own two pairs of boots, do you think I'd be sitting here scrubbing other people's sheets? There's a strike on, detective, which means no pay and no food unless I find some other income. My wife is ill upstairs with a fever. I can't afford medicine. So yes, those are the only boots I own.'

Crossing the room, White examined the soles of O'Brien's boots. They didn't even come close to matching the imprint on Joseph Walker's clothing. He reached inside his jacket and brought out a bottle of aspirin he'd hoped to keep his hangover at bay with. He tossed them over to the Irishman, saying: 'I'm sorry to hear about your wife. Maybe these will help a little with her fever.' O'Brien continued to stare hard at the detective but followed it with a curt nod of his head in acknowledgement. 'I'm just trying to do my job,' White added.

O'Brien finished his cigarette and pinched the end, saving the stub for later. 'If you're looking for something on the soles of my boots, detective, I can tell you this much. All of us Irish boys get our boots from O'Shaunessey's store. He gives us a discount. We all buy the same type of boot: he only stocks one type. So Nevin's are identical to mine. I'll tell you what I told your lieutenant. Sure, we may have been in the area of the docks the other night, but nobody killed no one. We acted to defend our jobs. We are longshoremen. It's all we can do to make a living. We just want enough pay to survive on. If the blacks keep breaking the strike, our people will start starving to death. If you were in that situation, wouldn't you want to fight for your survival?'

White gave a nod. 'I don't know what to say. I don't hold with violent protest but coming here and seeing the neighbourhood…I been here before. It was a year or so back. It was poor then, but it seems even more desperate now. I sympathise, but I got to uphold the law. Try and keep your head down for a while. Your wife needs you here, not in a jail cell.' He got up and headed for the door.

'Thanks for the aspirin, cop,' O'Brien called out as he exited.

The moment White stepped out onto the slum street he knew something wasn't right. The shoeless, feral kids had slunk away like a pack of animals sensing danger and the broken sidewalk was deserted. The prow of an expensive automobile stuck out beyond the street corner, its flying lady mascot glittering in the sunlight, sitting there almost as incongruously as O'Brien had over his washboard a few minutes previously. White smelt trouble. The driver noticed him and slid the car forwards until the occupant in the back seat was able to make eye contact with the tense cop. White had been right to trust his instincts. Eugene was the man beckoning him from the back of the car.

The detective thought about turning around and heading back into O'Brien's house, but knowing there was a kid and a sick woman in there made him quickly change his mind. Besides, his default setting had always been to make a stand regardless of who it was that confronted him, and although Eugene trailed the shadow of death after him wherever he went, White had already lost a wife and a daughter, as well as having argued with his boss and mentor, so he was in no mood to concede any more ground. He figured if the gangster did shoot him, it couldn't be any worse than the pain he was already feeling. So, do your worst, Eugene, he thought, walking towards the waiting car.

'I got a call saying you'd be here,' Eugene stated tersely, 'Get in.'

White remained where he was. 'You come from Five Points originally?' he asked.

Eugene looked impatient, but the question threw him a little, just as the detective hoped it would. 'Yeah, I grew up around here,' he confirmed.

'Good,' said White emphatically, 'Then we can take a walk while you show me the neighbourhood. I'd like to get a better feel for the place and its people. It might stop me being prejudiced. I already know O'Brien isn't my killer, he's just a tough guy. Shall we go?'

Eugene regarded the itinerant cop through narrow, burning eyes. His driver had tightened up a couple of notches as White was speaking. 'The more I see of you, the less I like your manner,' Eugene spat.

'I do tend to have that effect on certain people,' White considered. Looking at the mastiff sitting in the back of the car, he added, 'I'm just not the kind of dog that needs its belly tickled.'

'More a yappy little nuisance with attitude above his station,' Eugene said, pushing open the car door and making a show of stretching his legs. 'We'll walk, this time. The dog could do with the exercise.'

'Walking is where I often find the answers,' White told him.

'Well, let's hope you're not disappointed,' Eugene replied.

Strangely, the gangster decided to be an excellent tour guide, taking White through a history of the area in his own factual way, but the detective noted Eugene was not without emotion for the hardships and suffering his people had endured. Stopping by a patch of wasteland, the Irishman pointed to an indeterminate spot and revealed 'That was where I had my first fight. Nowhere to hide and plenty of space for everyone to watch the punishing contest. I won, but not immediately, and at a cost. I've never been able to breathe properly through my nose since. The bone overheals, you see?'

'Should I be readying myself for a message about something now?' White asked.

'You should,' Eugene said flatly. 'There's an arrangement in place. You're riding roughshod all over it and I can't have that. While I'm mildly curious why O'Malley wants to afford you so much protection, both he and I know it'll count for nothing unless you start doing as you're told. There are politics to the situation everyone needs to be aware of. There's nothing can be easily done about it. We all have to navigate around what's happened. If you don't understand or can't live with things being the way they are, then action will be taken. There will be consequences. Don't misunderstand me. I don't kill cops, it's too messy, and besides, I don't need to. I'm here to tell you, keep up your current behaviour and you'll be busted back down to being a beat cop. It'll be the end of Detective Squad for you. This goes far higher than O'Malley, that much you need to know.'

White waited a moment, looking out over the barren ground. Then, levelly, he stated, 'I will have that murderer, whatever it takes, be it my badge, my honour, even my life.'

'Those are bold words, detective. Your boss warned me you might be this way. He also told me you've gotten even worse of late.' Eugene paused, weighing up something privately in his own head. 'You know,' he continued, as much to the wasteland as to White, 'I've changed my mind about you and I'm not even sure why. I can see having an arrangement with O'Malley isn't enough in this instance, so, I'm willing to deal directly with you. I can find out whether your murderer came from Five Points a hell of a lot quicker than you can. I understand that boy was only eighteen and had nothing to do with the dispute. Is that right?'

'It is,' White confirmed.

'Then I give you my word I'll not protect the killer if I find out he's one of us.'

'You'll tell me, immediately?'

'I will.'

'How do I know I can trust your word?' White asked, looking straight at the gangster.

'You don't,' Eugene said, 'but if you do things any other way, I'll guarantee you'll lose the fight. That's how it is.'

White nodded. 'I still need to make my investigation,' he said.

'Which you can do, just in a different way. Let me make it plainer,' Eugene declared. 'You don't go into the Irish bars, and you stay out of this neighbourhood.'

'In the spirit of clarity, I have to go wherever the investigation takes me. I can't do anything less,' White stated.

Eugene's jaw tightened and he hissed his next words. 'I didn't win that first fight here on the wasteland where I got my nose broke. About a year later, the boy who did it was still swaggering around until he met a tragic end. A wall collapsed on him, and he was crushed to death, or so it seemed. You see, I was smart, I bided my time, and I made sure I won. Somebody was there to push that crumbling wall onto the body after it had been dealt a knockout blow. It took some effort to arrange and execute, but it was worth it. You stay out of Five Points, or I promise you won't be around to finish your investigation. O'Malley can't help you now, it's just you and me. Don't think about tracking that story I told you either. You won't get anywhere. My name's not even Eugene.'

Before White could reply, they were interrupted by two cars, one, the expensive automobile that Eugene had emerged from, swept down one side of the slum street, but it was the other car caught the detective's attention because of a glint of sunlight that reflected off the barrel of a gun sticking out of its window. The mastiff was immediately on her guard, emitting a low growl. White grabbed Eugene's collar and hauled him behind a line of trash cans, dropping on top of the stunned gangster as he did so. Bullets tore through the cans in a series of clangs. Keeping his head down, White could hear another set of gunfire in reply and hoped it was Eugene's driver coming to their rescue. Then the noise of an engine revving, more gunshots, and tyres squealing as the enemy car made its getaway around a corner.

'Jesus Christ!' White exclaimed.

'You okay, boss?' the driver yelled, his gun still smoking in his hand.

Eugene forced his way up from under the heavy bulk of the detective. 'Those fucking Bowery Boys! I'll murder the lot of them!' he seethed, standing in the middle of the street, and looking in the direction his adversaries had come from.

'Jesus Christ!' White said once again, 'You know some swell people.'

The driver chipped in. 'I came as soon as I saw the car cruising the neighbourhood. I knew they were looking for you. They were making a hit.'

'You don't say,' Eugene retorted, then, turning to examine the bullet-riddled trash cans and the dog that remained somehow unharmed, he addressed White. 'You did well, detective. That was fast thinking.'

'Funnily enough, I'm not a fan of getting shot. It makes me move quickly,' White answered, retrieving his hat from the gutter and patting the stunned dog on its head, as much to comfort himself as her. 'What a week,' he added. 'First, a boy gets his head caved in, then I wake up with the mother and father of hangovers. I fall out with O'Malley, and he hits me in the guts. Next, my wife and child leave me, I get threatened by a gangster and nearly cut in half by a hitman. I might just quit and spend the rest of it in bed!'

Eugene looked at the detective and gave a sinister smile. 'Well, you've had two pieces of luck, as I see it,' he announced. 'Everybody's going to be talking about the Bowery Boys and keeping their heads down while they wait for me to exact my revenge, which, of course, I will. Also, I'll make it known I was under the protection of the N.Y.P.D.'s finest. My people will be okay with you from now on. You just got a taste of what my world is like. Now you know, you can make your investigation, but I'm sure you'll stay out of it as much as possible. Understand?'

With that, the gangster dusted himself down, gestured to his dog, and got back into his swanky car. Through the open window he called, 'I have business to attend to. I can't offer you a lift, but I'm sure you'll find your way back just fine.' The car pulled away, leaving White staring at the wrecked line of trash cans that had helped save both their lives. 'Jesus Christ,' he muttered again under his breath, but he didn't quit and go home to bed. Instead, he made his way over to O'Shaunessey's store to check on the information O'Brien had given him.

The store was cluttered with buckets, tin baths, brooms, and shovels that either hung from nails above the shop front or rested against its plywood façade. Inside was even more chaotic, with every essential a home could possibly need crammed onto shelves or stocked high behind the counter. Sure enough, several rows of boots were piled upon each other, their tongues lolling and their laces hanging loose like they'd just been taken off after a long shift. White pointed to the pile and asked the burly middle-aged man wearing a scruffy brown overall, 'Do you mind if I take a look at those boots?'

The shopkeeper coughed into his fist and responded sharply, 'What size?'

The detective smiled, and showing the man his badge, said 'All of them.'

'What's this about?' the shopkeeper questioned, becoming a little less assured.

'You O'Shaunessey?' White enquired.

'Yes. I'm not in any kind of trouble, am I?'

'Not that I know of. I'm just looking for information. Eugene told me you might be able to help me out.'

At the mention of the gangster's name, the shopkeeper's demeanour changed further. He stood up straighter and became more candid.

'I just need to know two things,' White told him, 'If this is the only place the Irish workers can get their boots from and if they've always been the same type of boot with this exact tread pattern.'

O'Shaunessey nodded in understanding. 'Folks *could* buy their boots from a different store somewhere else in the city, this is a free country after all, but I keep my customers coming back loyally and recommending their friends because I always sell my boots at a knock-down price. I find it's good for business doing things that way. First, you get the men in here buying boots, then their wives come along for everything else. So, you makes your money back. At least, it used to be a sound move, but now everybody's asking for credit because of this goddamn strike. As for the soles, they don't change on account of them giving a better grip when it gets wet or icy. Dock workers have to rely on their boots, they get fussy about these things.'

White examined all the boots anyway, in the interest of being thorough and methodical, but they were identical and none were a match for the footprint left on the body. He thanked the shopkeeper, and as he was leaving, asked the question he'd been keeping in reserve. 'One more thing. I don't suppose you know where the other dock workers get their boots from, the Italians and the blacks?'

'Harlem's like a foreign country to me,' O'Shaunessey said dismissively, 'but I can give you the address of the shop where the Red Hook longshoremen get their stuff.' Writing it down and handing it to the detective, he added, 'I think Eddie Millarini still owns the place. A good guy, Eddie, always ready to help out folks in his community that are struggling. We do what we can for our own,' he explained.

'Yeah, I'm beginning to see how things are,' White said. 'So long.'

He left the store and walked back to his car, passing the bullet-scarred trash cans en-route. He wondered why he hadn't let Eugene take the flying lead and surmised it was just his instinct to protect and serve, no matter how undeserving the recipient might be. He headed over to the address in Brooklyn, driving through a neighbourhood that gave off a different kind of attitude to the Five Points slums: less desperate snarling poverty and more pent-up pride, with the older men naturally stern of face and fiery of eye while the young cocks strutted with their little chests puffed out, smoking aggressively, and letting everyone who wanted to know they were ready for trouble if it came.

Eddie Millarini exhibited neither kind of malice, White was happy to find, as he talked about the history of the place with the smiling old Italian. Eddie responded to his request to see the boots he fitted out the longshoremen with by going into the back room and bringing out two kinds for inspection. He explained that while one type was harder wearing, the others were far more comfortable. 'Italian leather,' he said, winking and stroking the top of the boots. 'Some of those guys won't ever wear anything else.'

'Even on a docker's wages?' White asked.

'Pride in the old country runs deep here in Brooklyn and Red Hook,' Eddie explained.

Neither type had tread that matched the pattern found on Joseph's body. Elimination was all part of the process, but it still didn't bring him any closer to finding out who the murderer was. He thanked Eddie and drove slowly back through the Italian neighbourhood. Something troubled him about the attitude of the place, but he couldn't put his finger on exactly what it was. He headed back to the precinct and began writing up his notes, all the time doing his best to avoid bumping into O'Malley.

After writing down everything he had found out, White made a second visit to Johnny's Bar and Grill to top up his hangover cure with a steak. As he ate hungrily, the detective thought about the progress he'd made in the case. Joseph had no connection to the New York docks or the dispute raging around it. Whoever killed him had dumped his body at the yard, but they didn't wear the usual dock worker's boots and they hadn't had the strength to carry his body to its final resting place. Whoever the killer was, they had shown great violence, but it didn't seem like they were a longshoreman with a grudge about black strike breakers. There was something he wasn't seeing, but it would come in time, if he kept looking closely enough.

It had been quite a couple of days. He'd been hit, deserted, threatened, and shot at, but he was still rolling. Eventually, though, he realised he couldn't put off going back to the apartment forever and so returned to the place where his wife and daughter no longer waited for him to come home. He figured Grace Walker wouldn't be the only person with the ghosts of missing loved ones tormenting them tonight.

Chapter Thirteen
Turning to Martha Marsh

After half an hour of wandering around the empty space, and with the silence eating into him, White put on a gramophone record and sat smoking a cigarette. He tried to distract himself further by thinking about the case, but being in the place was driving him mad. There was something terrible about the inertia of the apartment, an atmosphere where everything lay dead apart from the alarming spinning of the phonogram platter that seemed to be revolving in an almost panicky way to make up for the lack of movement anywhere else in the dwelling.

The voice on the record was a godsend, bringing the semblance of another human being into the apartment and fitting perfectly with the plaintive mood that had fallen on the place since its female occupants had departed. After a while though, even the record seemed to have taken on a haunted quality, as if the singer was, like White, walking around the vacant space regretting the loss of his loved ones while voicing his heartbreak through songs that echoed off the walls like painful memories. The detective lifted off the needle and the silence returned to the apartment, only this time it felt twice as loud.

White sat there willing the telephone to ring, for a lead in the case, or for news of another crime occurring. Mona hadn't called to say they were making their way safely towards Omaha, but he wasn't sure he could take hearing her voice long distance anyway. The conversations between mother and daughter that had formed the ambient noise of their family life, sounds he had taken for granted, was the first absence that tormented him. In desperation, he grabbed another record from the small pile he owned and put it on without even looking at the title. Henry Burr's rich tenor filled the room, singing Irving Berlin's *When I lost you*. It caused the detective's chest to heave as the line: *I lost the gladness that turned into sadness when I lost you,* hit home.

He felt like he couldn't stay in the place a moment longer. After last night's blackout, there was no way he was setting foot in a bar, so it seemed he had nowhere left to run to. He had a head full of traitors: O'Malley for selling out to a local gangster, Eugene for disregarding the law and waging a war between the Five Points and the Bowery, and Mona for deserting him and taking their daughter away to live with Pops Ross. The record jarred something else in White's memory, a case and a person that had led to him becoming a detective in the first place. It all seemed to make sense, the serendipity of that record in that moment. So, it was on with the hat and out into the humid night. He was a restless spirit much in need of some sympathetic company.

After peering through the window, her door was opened. They stood there, two old acquaintances with something uncharted still between them. It had been nearly four years since he'd looked her up, but time couldn't diminish what had passed between them. Standing in her front yard like a picture of loneliness, he greeted her: 'Martha. I didn't know who else to turn to. Can you let me in?' She was taken aback, but smiled and held out her hand, leading him into a place where he could feel the comfort he needed just to get through the next hour.

She poured them both a drink and he tipped the contents of his glass into hers. 'I just need to catch up with you,' he explained. 'Make me a coffee and I'll tell you what's happened the best I can.'

They sat opposite each other, and he spoke candidly about the failure of his marriage. There was no need for small talk; they had gone way past that all those years ago when he visited her in the wake of her partner's death and provided her with a blanket to wrap her grief in. Now, she understood, it was time for her to reciprocate. Anything else they felt for each other was just as inappropriate tonight as it was back then, so taking the lead, Martha concentrated on listening and healing White the best she could platonically and spiritually.

'So that's where I'm at,' he confessed. 'Six years, a child I adore, all gone before I even had the chance to work out where it was I was going wrong. Who am I trying to kid? I always knew where I was going wrong, I just couldn't bring myself to change. That's why I lost them. Is what I do really so wrong, Martha?'

She sighed and smiled at him; her brown eyes full of solace. 'How can I answer that? You came to me doing your job, but you went beyond that. You showed me compassion when I needed it most. You were genuine and warm. You comforted me when I thought I might die of grief. You stopped me from falling down somewhere I may have never climbed out of. You were my gentle white knight. I will never forget that, so you stay as long as you need to. Call round every night if you have to, but I promise you this: I won't let you confuse me with some kind of romantic replacement for your wife. You didn't take advantage of me after Thomas died and I won't do that to you now. I'm lonely, Dom. I was glad when you came to my door and I will show you tenderness, but there's a place we just can't go to, at least not in this chapter of our lives.' She hoped this would set him straight on where they were at.

White felt a warmth and a stirring when he looked into Martha's eyes. It was wrong, he knew, but it restored some faith in himself that another woman had intimated he meant something to her. There was no ego in it, just the need to feel he wasn't the worst man in the world right then. Of course, deep down he knew that; he just needed somebody to show it because it hurt so much that Mona couldn't. They had four years of each other's separate lives to catch up on and so they talked, two people comfortable with each other and enjoying the chance to reconnect.

'Old man Easton was good to me after you solved that case at Columbia Recordings,' Martha said, drinking her whiskey freely and opening up like a flower in White's company. 'I think the idea of folks eyeing up the presidency because of his illness made him fight back and gave him a new lease of life, even if he knew he was living on borrowed time. He offered me a role beyond just being the vice-president's secretary. He wanted me to meet potential recording artists and persuade them to join us in the way Thomas used to do.' She paused at the mention of his name again, shifting her legs under her as she sat on the settee. 'I couldn't do it,' she stated forlornly. 'It wasn't just about working in that building where Thomas had died, with all the times we'd shared together in that office. To me, at least, Thomas *was* Columbia Recordings. Without him, the place was just a shell. I tried to listen to some of those records he cut to get something of him back, but they didn't sound like sunshine the way they used to, they were just scratchy and thin.'

'I put on Henry Burr tonight,' White admitted. 'I didn't do it consciously; I was just trying to obliterate the terrible silence in my apartment. It made me think of you and sorta guided me here. So, not all bad.' He sipped his coffee and added, 'You're not at Columbia anymore then?'

'No. I floated around as a temp for a while. I couldn't bear to commit myself to working for someone else on a permanent basis. That sounds crazy, I know.'

'Not crazy,' White assured her. 'I know what Thomas meant to you, what you had together. I saw your grief, remember?'

Martha drank again, fidgeting awkwardly on the settee. 'I should never have taken up with a married man, and an older one at that, but I was younger then and wanted to ignore the mess it would all have ended up being. Even so, Thomas is still in my heart. I decided he would've wanted me to make something of myself, so, when a job came up at the Winter Garden Theatre, I went for it. No one was more surprised than me when I got hired.' She got up and went to get more whiskey, shaking the bottle in White's direction. 'Sure I can't tempt you?' she asked.

White winced. 'I got wrecked on rye last night. I drank enough to beach a whale and I'm disgusted with myself for having done it,' he admitted. 'So, much as I don't like the thought of you drinking alone, I couldn't touch a drop of whiskey without wanting to curl up and die.'

Martha grinned. 'Okay, wounded soldier. I might have a beer in the cupboard. I kept buying it out of habit, even though I never drink it and don't tend to have any guests.' She grimaced at the revelation and White knew she'd have carried on getting the brand Thomas liked.

'A beer would be good,' he lied, trying to smooth over the awkwardness of the moment. He wanted to put her at ease and keep her talking. He sensed it was doing them both a lot of good. Martha hurried to the kitchen and returned with the bottle and a glass. Setting both down on the table, she uncorked the beer and poured it for him. He watched her as she did so, taking comfort from the simple act of a good woman looking after him, but all the while with a conscience about doing it. When she was settled again, he prompted her. 'Tell me about your work.'

'Well, I'm the Theatre Director's secretary, but given my experience with Columbia and the terrific reference Mr Easton wrote me, they let me do some of the booking of acts. There's a lot of crossovers, you see. There are concerts every Sunday night and we've put on some really good musicals. I've even met Al Jolson!' she said excitedly. 'So, as a job, it's interesting and very fulfilling.'

'I sense there's a *but* coming,' White said, taking a swig of beer which tasted good in spite of the fact he'd nearly poisoned himself the night before.

'Theatre people,' Martha stated. 'It's not so much their egos or the business of having to be so showy, it's that they're fickle. They aren't so steady or easy to trust. I've had a lot of difficulties with that sort of thing after what happened to Thomas. He was such a genuine man. I know this is going to sound dubious, what with you knowing he was having an affair with me for all those years, but he was very straight, and I always knew where I stood with him. These people aren't like that. They're disingenuous.'

'You mean you have to count your fingers after shaking hands on a deal with them?' White quipped, taking another slug of his beer.

'It's not funny,' Martha mildly admonished him. 'I...I've been wanting to meet someone. It's been four years now and I get lonely. I turned thirty this year and I don't want to end up an old maid. It can drive you out of your mind, the empty house and no one's company of an evening but your own. I'm never going to find the right man working in showbusiness, that's for sure.'

White took out a cigarette, offered one to the unhappy Martha, and lit up for both of them when she accepted. The move was strategic, partly because he felt she might have said a little more than she'd intended to, and also as he had no idea of how to respond without revealing feelings for her that would incriminate him. He was starting to think the impulsive journey to her house had been a mistake. They were two people who'd had love ripped away from them. They were hurt and they were lonely. He wasn't sure the level of mutual platonic comfort they were giving each other could remain just that: platonic, despite the assurances she'd given him and the guilt he was experiencing over having feelings for her once again. As if sensing all this, Martha broke the silence in order to change tack and diffuse the atmosphere that had been building in the room.

'Are you working on anything big at the moment?' she asked.

Relieved, White blew a column of smoke up at the ceiling. 'I sure am,' he responded. 'It's a particularly heart-breaking murder, even though I've seen plenty of those in my time as a detective,' he admitted.

'What makes this one so disturbing?'

'It's a young man, eighteen years of age. A boy who by all accounts wouldn't have harmed a hair on another soul's head, with all the promise that comes with the energy and naivety of youth just snuffed out. I visited his mother to tell her the news. She's a decent and sensitive woman who now has to try and understand why her only son has been taken from her, and with a husband who's off fighting in the war and might not come back. Here I am moping through the night and turning up at your door when I don't even have anything like the pain and suffering that poor woman has. So, yeah, I guess this one has gotten to me.'

'What was his name?' she asked, her big warm eyes making him know how much she cared.

'Joseph Walker. He was from Harlem but got killed down by the docks. I still don't know if it was a case of mistaken identity or if he was murdered because of the colour of his skin. Grace, his mother, needs answers and I haven't got any for her yet,' he said bitterly, taking a long drag on his cigarette.

'You will,' Martha assured him. 'You'll find a way of solving the case because you care, and because you're a brilliant detective. Look at what you did for Thomas when every other cop had failed him. You'll be okay. You just need to focus and get through the next few days.'

'Thank you,' he said, 'for everything.' Then, sensing that the room had become too intimate once more, he added, 'It might just be me topping up last night's booze, but this heat is really getting inside my veins. Do you have a back yard or somewhere outside I can sit with my beer? I'd be happy for you to join me if you don't mind having to watch a man trying to put himself back together.'

'I don't mind at all,' Martha said warmly. 'This house has a lovely garden, although it may be too far beyond dusk to smell the honeysuckle. There's a bench I like to sit on, and it'll be good to have you sitting on it with me.'

The garden was small, but carefully tended, with everything turning blue, or white, or yellow in the moonlight. The heat had dried up the earth, but the warm baked smell of the soil soothed him as he breathed it in and relaxed. They sat out on the bench, smoking and remembering the jovial Henry Burr with his beautiful voice. She sang quietly to him in the still of the night, it lifted his heart and destroyed him all at the same time. Something in her must have recognised this because she ceased it and returned to telling him about the musical stars she'd met, which ones were charming and which ones were absolutely loathsome beneath the greasepaint, sweet notes, and smiles. He laughed gently, happy to sit on that bench in the blue back garden and listen to the melody of Martha's voice.

The sadness was always there though, like the blemish on a beautiful painting or the broken bone mended that still ached in the cold of winter. Even watching the light blue clouds as they floated smoothly across the dark blue sky at midnight in Martha's garden, with the nearness of his companion settling him as only a woman could, White still thought of Omaha and his empty apartment. Some things could never be put right or forgotten. For all his heartache, guilt, and self-recriminations, he still wanted to do his job. He needed to find whoever killed Joseph Walker so he could provide Grace with at least some sense of closure.

Feeling very confused, he took Martha's hand and held it tight. He hated himself for needing her, but what difference did a little more self-loathing make? He kissed her cheek even though it was forbidden and he knew he would chastise himself for it in the morning. When they parted, he didn't know whether to feel relieved or sorry he hadn't attempted to spend the night in her arms. No. He knew leaving to return to his lonely dwelling was exactly what needed to happen right then. Nothing else would ever begin to sit right with his conscience. So, he walked back through the now breezy night with the wind alternating between being a tempest and a lullaby to his senses, always moving forwards, but haunted by the recent past. If cops were meant to be heroes, he felt a long, long way from that.

Alone once again in her house, and with the silence of the small hours sitting heavily upon her mind, Martha had time to reflect on what the unexpected visit had brought. To have White walking back into her life not only produced upsetting memories of Thomas' death, but also refreshed the awkward feelings she'd had about the detective. He was a man who had offered her great comfort and strove to deliver the truth when no one else cared. Had she met him at any other time, under different circumstances, she was sure she would have been romantically drawn to him, but the confusion of raw grief, shock, and loneliness all clouded how she had felt back then, and that left everything distorted.

Now, here he was, returning from the wilderness after several years, and at a time when his wife had just left him. What that said about how he viewed her was something she didn't want to acknowledge. And yet, as he stood there on her front stoop, she had felt a rush of pleasure to be seeing him again, handsome as ever. The fact he was wounded brought her closer to him. As he had helped to heal the terrible pain she felt back then, so it seemed right she should be there for him in his hour of need. That she wanted him, even though she knew it was his departed wife he was really looking for, made her feel both guilty and ashamed. She had spoken out and set down clear boundaries, but she hadn't been unequivocal because the need in her had meant she wasn't able to slam that particular door shut in his face.

She got up from the settee and moved across the room to where the single table lamp cast its small reflection onto the empty bottle of beer he had drunk from. She touched it lightly with her fingertips and then shook her head, snatching it up and depositing it in the trash. She was foolish, she told herself. These were dangerous times for them both, and she knew this wouldn't be the last time they met. She would have to be very careful not to be drawn into something they would both later regret. She needed to be clear in her role, to offer White her support so he could regain some equilibrium and solve the murder of that poor young boy.

She walked through to the empty bedroom as the clock in the hall chimed twice. A sleepless night lay ahead where she would shift from side to side, remembering his face as he had stared up at the sky in her garden. That calming voice, the steady and beleaguered way he moved, like he was carrying the weight of every crime he'd ever had to deal with, endeared him to her, and she realised just how much she'd missed him during their time apart. Thumping the pillow her head rested on in frustration, she vowed not to let those feelings take over. Help the man, give things time and resist, she told herself. Anything else would be sure to end in disaster. She shut her eyes tight and tried to sleep, but in the darkness, White's face still shone and there was nothing Martha could do to stop it.

The apartment sat just as White had left it, with the gramophone record still resting silently on the static platter. This was his place now, he thought, wandering through the rooms and taking it all in with new eyes. There was both the haunting and the familiar here, and he knew he would have to start again, alone, seeing the same things from a different angle. He had to reset himself. He had a job needed doing. Now, he thought, the fact it would occupy his mind so much acted as a positive. It would chase away the hours of lamentation and replace them with action. He needed to think more clearly about the case, control the emotions he felt about it so he could channel them in a more productive way to find Joseph's killer.

He needed to be able to put on a record without going to pieces, for God's sake, he thought, staring at the disk that had prompted his journey to Martha's door. He played it again, quietly in the hush of the night so as to not wake the neighbours. Martha Marsh. He felt guilty to have gone there, tonight of all nights. It had been wrong, and he would need to be tougher with himself in the future. He and Mona were over, but the pain he felt at losing her, and the love that would always be there alongside the regret that he couldn't have been a better husband and make it work between them, meant there could be no other woman on the horizon, at least not for a very long time.

He looked over at the telephone, knowing it probably wouldn't have rung in his absence, but still admonishing himself for not keeping up a vigil over it. Mona wouldn't arrive in Omaha for at least another two days yet, they'd be stopping over in some low-rent motel knowing Pops Ross, and her first thought would not have been to call home because it wasn't where she lived anymore. There needed to be some silence and space between them, he understood, whether he liked it or not. Still, no use wallowing in those feelings. Others had lost far more than he had and were surviving. He thought of Martha and her grief in the wake of Thomas' unexpected death, then of Grace Walker, with her only son brutally murdered and a husband facing danger in some foreign field. They were both women living in empty homes, and they coped with the situation. He would have to learn to do the same.

He smoked a cigarette and looked at his wristwatch. Two o'clock. He had behaved badly, and he was in a mess, but there was still time to put some things right. The key evidence was both the brutality of the killing and the boot print on the body. He needed to piece together Joseph's last movements on the day of the murder and find out why he'd ended up dumped in the dockyard. He needed to fathom who'd had the fury to commit the crime, then he had to find the boots they'd been wearing in order to prove their guilt.

He had to look beyond the white dockers, that much he knew for sure. He wouldn't ignore the politics of the strike, but he wouldn't be distracted by them either. A good detective never assumed. They examined the evidence, pursued the facts, and used their powers of deduction, with a lot of legwork and brain work in the process. Now, he must get some sleep in his own apartment for the first time in a couple of nights. Tomorrow he would widen the search and gather more clues. He was not a hero, just a detective who refused to give up until he caught his man.

Chapter Fourteen
Business, Butchery, and Betrayal

In the New York Dock Company's downtown offices, all the blinds were lowered. The managing director had a visitor he didn't want anyone seeing. Eugene sat impatiently like a racing driver pulled into the pits, waiting for Richard Zimmerman to get to the point about what he wanted. Zimmerman was in his fifties, a big man with a fading physique gone to seed through too many long lunches. The flesh on his face was beginning to sag, but his suit still gave him an air of power and those light blue eyes remained penetrating as ever. When it came business, nobody made a fool out of him, and Eugene knew this. The Irishman was here to protect his interests. Zimmerman was no gangster, but his kind would cut your throat and bleed you dry in a different way if you gave them the chance, and Eugene wasn't about to let that happen.

'I called you here because things are getting out of hand down at the docks,' Zimmerman stated. 'The cheap black labour works for us both, but not when there's a murder attached to the company name.' Zimmerman picked the newspaper up from his desk, holding it out in front of him. 'I trust you've read this.'

'I've read it,' Eugene said calmly. 'No mention of the boy having worked as a docker though. In fact, it says he was an employee at the Waldorf-Astoria hotel.'

'That's not the point,' Zimmerman said irritably. 'The article goes on to mention the beatings at the docks and it links the strike and our company directly to the violence. People are beginning to associate us with assault and murder against young black men. That's definitely not good for business.'

'The killing had nothing to do with the Irish boys,' Eugene said smoothly.

'How can you be so sure?'

'Because I own the Irish mob. Their chief agitant reports directly to me. Also, the police are in my pocket on this one. Give it a month and no one will be talking about murder. The Irish workers will have been squeezed dry and the strike will come to a head. There'll be turbulence, but I'll have already found alternative employment for the most disruptive men. I can use them. I have my own dispute with the Bowery Boys needs settling and I must have strong, angry men to help me do that. The company will end up clean, financially competitive, and with an enhanced reputation for integration. What more could you want?' Eugene said, sitting back confidently in his chair.

'I want these headlines to go away!' Zimmerman said angrily. 'Before this, we were working in the shadows, little articles on inside pages. Now, we're front-page news.'

'For a few days, yes,' Eugene agreed, 'but after that some other scandal will break or the focus will be on the war.'

'No one gives a damn about the war in this country. It's thousands of miles away!'

Eugene let Zimmerman's vitriol wash over him. The man was worried about his money. Like all businessmen, it was his motivation and his Achilles heel. 'The murder's a setback, I agree, but overall, we're still on course to achieve what we set out to do.'

'The blacks will be frightened,' Zimmerman warned. 'Some of them won't be able to work for several days, and those who return won't want to. Breaking a strike isn't worth losing your life over.'

'I've already spoken to both ringleaders,' Eugene reassured him. 'The killing will provide Johnny Cain with a good reason to call off the mob for a while. The police have been around questioning some of them, that'll spook most of the men into lying low. The black dockers are unhappy, but they don't have a whole lot of options when it comes to making money in this town. If you really want to secure their services, have the company pay a little compensation to the men who took a beating. A small sum could go a long way to making them feel recognised and valued. You wouldn't need to go as far as increasing the wages of the whole workforce.'

'I should hope not!' Zimmerman declared. 'That would cost hundreds, even thousands of dollars over time. The whole point of employing the blacks is they're cheap labour. If we start paying them what we paid the Irish, then what's the point of all the unrest and bad publicity?'

'I understand,' Eugene said, placating him. 'I have the situation in hand.'

'You need to make doubly sure of that. How much sway does this ringleader of the strike-breakers hold?'

'He's the man inside the dockyard, he's with them on the quays. They trust him. Politically, he's got someone else working alongside him pulling the strings. A brother as I understand it, although they all call each other *brother* in this organization they have,' Eugene explained.

'What organization?' Zimmerman probed. 'Is it a union?'

'No, not a union,' Eugene reassured him. 'I'm not sure it even has a name.'

'You've not met its leader?'

'No. He likes to keep a low profile as a way of increasing rumour and notoriety about him within his own people.'

'You need to speak with him,' Zimmerman firmly instructed, pointing a finger at the gangster as he did so. 'If he's the one with the real kudos, then only he can convince those men to keep working. Deal with it, Eugene. I don't want any more mistakes in this thing.'

'I will,' Eugene said tersely, doing his best to contain a growing anger at being spoken to in this way. 'You seem to be forgetting I have a lot invested in this scheme myself, the money I've put into your company, and more importantly to me, the men I stand to gain from the way things should end. It means I don't need any prompting to make this work.'

'There's a problem here. I need it sorting out and you're the only one who can do it. That's how it is. So, make sure you sort it.'

Eugene took that to signal the end of the meeting. The pair never shook hands because Zimmerman saw Eugene and his dirty money as a necessary evil, tolerated only because he could control crime around the docks and make the company even richer in these ever-testing times. For his part, Eugene just didn't shake hands. In his world it meant nothing. As he left the offices, walking out into the sunlit street, the Irishman was still piqued at Zimmerman's behaviour. He'd faced bullets this week, and here was a fat old man in a comfortable office talking down to him. It was that fucking murder causing all the trouble once again, making people scared when they had no need to be. He'd have to meet with this Brother Paul, or whatever he was called. He just hoped Johnny Cain had dealt with that idiot sibling of his. He looked over his shoulder, a habit these days after the attempt on his life by the Bowery Boys, but the way was clear. It was time to sort some business of his own. Zimmerman was right about one thing: no more mistakes could be made.

It only meant buying a train ticket, that, and some simple lies about why Patrick needed a holiday. The stressfulness of the strike accounted for that. So, Johnny thought they were all set and everything would be okay. Then the consumption got him. It shouldn't have worsened in the hot, dry weather, but it had. In the small house, and with no work to occupy them, it was impossible to hide the severity of his condition from Pat. Johnny knew nothing could be done for him, that it was worse for Pat to stay and see him this way, never mind the threat of jail or worse still hanging over him, but his little brother refused to leave New York.

'I won't do it, Johnny. Blood is blood and family is everything. I won't go away knowing you need looking after.'

They were sitting on boxes out in the cramped back yard, with the mid-afternoon sun beating down hot on the stones and casting two sharp shadows of their forms. Patrick was smoking a cigarette as he spoke, the grime around his fingernails worse than ever and a yellow stain of nicotine making a crowning spot of anxiety on his filthy hand. Johnny didn't smoke. His lungs just couldn't take it anymore.

'I don't need looking after!' Johnny hissed, feeling the bubbling in his chest rising once again. Then, more reasonably, 'When I require care, I'll hire a nurse. Right now, the only thing that matters is getting you on a train and out of this city. The cops are still asking questions in the neighbourhood. It isn't safe for you to be here.'

'You told me Eugene said he would put them off,' Patrick stated. 'That he had people in Detective Squad and an arrangement was in place. Besides, where are you going to get the money for a nurse from? Neither of us is working because of this fucking strike!'

Johnny's reply was overtaken by the boiling in his lungs, and another violent fit of coughing shook him. He didn't even bother hiding the blood from his brother anymore. When the wracking had subsided, and after Pat had finished thumping him on the back to draw more of the poison out, Johnny was able to argue his point.

'There's money…from the work I'm doing with Eugene. He needs me to keep this strike going…for our resistance to stay strong. He'll pay for any care I need.'

'I don't trust Eugene,' Patrick said, 'and I don't understand how he can benefit from the strike carrying on.'

'I've told you,' Johnny struggled. 'It's safer if you don't know. You're in enough trouble already without…getting caught up in the politics.'

'I get that he's a gangster and has something to do with the dock company. Does he need our boys' loyalty to turn the other way when they're back on the quayside? Is it smuggling, Johnny?'

'It involves making money, Pat…that's all I can tell you. It'll be good for Eugene, and good for both of us. Saying any more about it…will just put you in danger, and I can't have that to worry about now. Do you understand?'

'Okay, Johnny,' Patrick said begrudgingly, throwing his dead cigarette over the wall.

'Eugene is not a man to admit being associated with. It's dangerous to know him. The Bowery Boys…tried to shoot him yesterday.'

'I heard.' A pause. 'Johnny, if Eugene gets killed, will I still have protection from the police?'

'I'm not even sure you've got protection now,' Johnny wheezed. 'That's why I want you to go.'

'I've told you, brother. I'm not going to Boston when you're like this.'

Johnny smacked his fist against the wall in frustration. 'They visited Pat O'Brien's house and questioned him…a cop from Detective Squad! Eugene intervened, but that was before he got shot at. He has bigger things to worry about now.'

'He needs you,' Patrick reminded his brother. 'So, he'll look after me. I've calmed myself down about it all. I've laid low like you told me to, drinking at home and not in the bars. I'm not about to shoot my mouth off, Johnny. No one will see me, and if a cop comes to the house, I'll hide in the cellar. You can tell them I'm in Boston,' Patrick joked.

'Enough,' Johnny spat. 'This is no laughing matter. When I was out today…there was talk of the beatings making the newspapers. They made it because they're being linked…to a murder.'

'What?' Patrick said, his face turning ashen. 'What did the papers say about the murder?'

'I haven't seen them. I thought it better…to come back here…to get you away to safety. But you…you refuse to go,' Johnny said, fighting for his breath.

'Because someone needs to look after you! Let me go to Eugene, explain the situation. He's got to keep the police away from us.' Patrick's voice betrayed his fear, the old instability returning and causing him to go to pieces in panic. Johnny suppressed another bout of coughing, just managing to hold it at bay. He raised a hand to silence his brother, and when the affliction let him, gave his orders.

'You need to stay out of sight. I'll go to Eugene…and impress upon him that he needs to keep the police…away from this house…from this area.'

'But you're *ill*, Johnny.'

'No matter. There are things I still must do…and this is one of them. Hide, brother…and don't show your face to anyone until I come back. Promise me.'

Patrick had tears welling in his eyes he couldn't control. 'I promise, Johnny.'

'Good. I'm away to the slaughterhouse now…that's where Eugene will be.'

From his yard in the Five Points, a dying Johnny Cain made his way across town, fighting his consumption every moment of the journey, taking the tram while trapping the cough in his chest, then walking in the blazing heat of late afternoon, his illness bringing spots in front of his eyes every time he was forced to stop because of another attack. How long could he go on for, he asked himself? Long enough so Patrick had some money to get away with and he could be buried properly, that was how long. So, sweating in his shirt sleeves and pale with the death that clung to him, he headed on to the gangster's palace of blood.

Daisy the mastiff had been shut out of the abattoir office. She had not taken kindly to Brother Paul, a fact that was not lost on Eugene. The activist was a big man, larger by a head than Abraham and wider too, but the family resemblance could still be seen. Eugene couldn't work out whether his completely bald head gave Paul an air of benevolence or pugnacity. Daisy certainly hadn't liked him and there was usually a reason for that. Those hands, resting on Paul's knees while he dwarfed the office chair, looked more than capable of snapping a man's neck like it was a twig. Eugene sensed he should be wary of Brother Paul.

When the activist spoke, it was deep and low, a rumble from underground that unsettled Eugene further. He'd also noted how Paul did not react to the sounds and smells of the slaughterhouse. He'd taken in a member of staff's bloody apron without any sign of being affected by it, and this troubled Eugene. He knew he was dealing with the coldest of characters, a man like himself. The sooner he could get his business here done, the better, the Irishman thought.

'I'm glad you asked to see me,' Paul said. 'There are matters at hand needing clarification. These are important times, not just for our arrangement.'

'There's been disquiet about the unfortunate murder,' Eugene responded. 'As I told your brother, if any one of my people acted out of turn, it will be dealt with. The dock company, who I unofficially represent, want no part in such things, and neither do I. If I find the murderer, I'll do the right thing.'

Eugene studied Brother Paul's face for a reaction, but the man opposite him gave nothing away. In the interest of concluding the meeting as swiftly as possible, he added 'Now, what did you want making clear?'

Paul waited a moment before responding, as if considering carefully how to best phrase his request. 'Dock workers have been beaten, some badly, but I have no problem with that. It fuels anger, which aids my cause. However, these people need to trust me, so I am here to procure something for them. Like I said, the beatings can help all sides; I don't want them to stop. What I ask for is danger money. The company must increase pay on the day shift by five cents an hour, with an extra ten cents an hour for those working on the night shift. Money will override the fear my people are feeling.'

Eugene shook his head. 'That can't be done. I've already discussed financial incentives with the owners. I figured you would ask for something like this. They'll go as far as to compensate any man whose beating means he cannot work. Taking a pasting will be better paid than lifting crates, but that's all they're willing to give. Otherwise, they feel it would be cheaper to get the Irish workers back, and neither you nor I want that to happen.'

'How much compensation?' Paul asked, narrowing his eyes.

'There would be an extra dollar a day on top of normal wages for the number of days missed through injury, to be capped at one week. Nobody's being beaten that badly.'

'It isn't enough,' Paul rumbled.

'But it's *something*,' Eugene countered, 'and it carries with it the longer-term prospect of regular employment, so, make it work and persuade them.'

'There's something else,' Paul continued. 'So far, the mob has gone unpunished for the assaults. There needs to be some change in that, and I'm told you have influence over the N.Y.P.D.'

'You're misinformed,' Eugene said, not liking the way the conversation was going. 'If the cops aren't arresting anyone, it's because the mayor doesn't want to go upsetting Irish voters. He's the one with a direct line to the chief of police, not me.'

'So, you can't arrange a few token arrests, just to make the strike-breakers feel a little safer?'

'I can't,' Eugene confirmed.

'Not even through Detective Squad after the event?'

Eugene was unable to hide his surprise, being caught off-guard by how much this activist knew.

Brother Paul seized on the reaction. 'Good information is vital to my organization. I know you have an arrangement, just as I know you were with a cop when your enemies tried to take your life.'

'Then you'll also know the situation is delicate. I'll see what I can do,' said Eugene, recovering his composure.

'There's time yet,' Paul declared, 'which brings me onto the subject of the murderer.' He watched for another reaction, but this time Eugene gave him nothing. 'A man must be arrested and face trial for the killing. The individual will be handed over to me personally so he can be taken to the police.' This time Eugene did look incredulous. 'You want to deal with the Harlem blacks, you'll do it through me. I hold the power,' Paul announced. 'Also, there's a parade happening in just under two weeks' time. I don't want the arrests or the handover to happen until *after* it has passed. Those are my terms.'

'You seem to want to dictate a lot,' Eugene coolly observed. 'What makes you think I'll agree to any of this?'

Brother Paul folded his huge arms. 'Because I don't just own Harlem,' he said, his voice weighty like an ocean liner engine. 'I can call on black support from all over this country. I've got a whole bunch of people from Chicago headed down for this parade ready to unleash hell on my command. When we mobilize, we can come in our *thousands*. That's why it'd be good for you to keep me on friendly terms.'

Eugene considered this. 'And if I can't find the murderer?' he asked.

'Then bring me a scapegoat,' Paul replied impatiently, 'a sacrificial lamb or whatever you want to call him. I want my riots, but I also want my workforce permanently installed at the docks. Your company needs cheaper labour and men you can keep in check. Give me what I want, one man for the killing and a few measly arrests, and you can have it all, no problem.'

Eugene gave an icy smile. 'When you put it so persuasively,' he said, letting the unfinished sentence hang in the quiet office. 'I'll get you the arrests, and I'll give you your lamb to the slaughter. I have just the man in mind, a feckless relation of the Irish ringleader, no less.'

'Two weeks' time, not before,' Brother Paul reminded him, rising from his seat to fill the room.

'Like you said, no problem,' Eugene replied, getting up also and showing his powerful visitor to the door. When Paul was gone, the Irishman appraised the situation. Zimmerman wanted an end to the headlines. Two weeks would give the managing director enough time to erase Patrick Cain from the employment files. The killer must not be connected to the New York Dock Company. Eugene would just have to pretend it had all been done without his knowledge. Johnny couldn't prove anything, and by that time the strikers ought to be on their knees. Then he would make his move. Cain could still get his cut from the deal if he wanted it. With the Irish workers sacked from the docks, he'd be of little significance or threat by then. It would all work out as planned. Eugene would inherit a bunch of hungry, angry men. Brother Paul's riots would be nothing compared to the gangland war he'd wage on those Bowery Boys.

A hot day and the blight of consumption forcing him to rest. The smell of blood thick upon the air. He'd needed to collect himself anyway, he didn't want to face Eugene looking like death had already claimed him. So, a pause to try and right himself in the grounds of the abattoir, and as fate would have it, right under the open office window. He didn't even look like he was loitering, what with the mastiff knowing him and glad to be stroked after having been shut out of the building. It was there, in those moments, Johnny Cain overheard it all.

There would be no seeing Eugene now, Johnny thought. He couldn't face the gangster with what he'd just heard still ringing in his ears...*a feckless relation*. The betrayal was a fresh wound added to the damage done by illness. Just like the consumption, it was a ticking time bomb, but it had one important difference, Johnny realised as he got away from the slaughterhouse as fast as his condition would let him. It remained within his power to do something about it. This was the moment of epiphany. Everything else was gone now, all his plans laid to waste.

Sure, Patrick could be hidden in Boston, but the police wouldn't have to look too hard to find him there and a life on the run was no good for anyone, especially not his vulnerable little brother. No, Eugene must be stopped before he could give up Pat to the Harlem activist. Drastic action was needed, and it had to happen fast. I'm dying anyway, Johnny thought, limping his way through the hot streets, reeling from the sudden turn of events, from the betrayal. His race was almost run, and it put an ice in him that reasoned: what have I got to lose?

Chapter Fifteen
Finding the Answers

White thought of patterns; of the everyday behaviours of people thrown into disarray by disturbance. A shift at work followed by an unforeseen beating, a familiar argument escalated to a broken marriage and a night out in New York City ending in a brutal murder. Now a pattern on the victim's body was all he had to go on. The detective had all but ruled out the boots of the Irish mob and he'd eliminated the treads of the Italian longshoremen. A thought occurred to him that had sat in the back of his brain ever since he analysed the moving of the body to be left at the dockside like a red herring: Was the killer trying to make the crime look like it had come from an industrial dispute?

The soles of the boots that had done the stamping on Joseph Walker's body were deep, non-slip and intricate in their design, but it wasn't only longshoremen needed those kinds of boots. The city was teeming with construction workers; it could just have easily been one of them that found fury with the black youth. Out of an irregular event, something that broke the natural order of things, he had only a regular and forensic pattern to help him catch the perpetrator. This was the irony that was getting him nowhere fast as he sat in his tiny office, sipping coffee just an hour after dawn had broken. His suspects numbered in the thousands, and he felt like he was hitting a dead end.

It was time to chase things up from another angle. He still didn't have any answers about what Joseph Walker had been doing the night he died. He'd been working at the Waldorf from the morning until afternoon teas had stopped being served, but the evening had been his own. Grace had given the detective the names of Joseph's two closest friends, and although neither had been with him on that fateful night, White figured they might know who had kept him company for those missing hours. Young men didn't tend to stay out alone for that long. Time for some legwork. He was reaching for his hat when O'Malley burst into his office in that bombastic way he had.

'I got something for you. Read it. This morning's edition of the Times. Looks like the boy's death made the news despite our best efforts to keep the killing under wraps. You still look terrible by the way.'

White studied the headline and then skimmed through the article, conscious of O'Malley's proximity to him in the tiny space. He'd always wanted a bigger office, but not as much as he wished he hadn't fallen out with his boss, now, of all times. For his part, O'Malley seemed to have forgotten the whole unfortunate episode. 'I guess we couldn't keep it quiet forever,' White commented. 'At least they've got their facts right and haven't sensationalised things too much.'

'It's a hot topic, what with the beatings at the docks and the upcoming civil rights march. The Times is riding a wave that will sell papers, they're no fools,' O'Malley observed. 'Where are you with the investigation?'

'I've ruled out Nevin and O'Brien. The boot marks found on the body aren't anything like those worn by either the Irish or Italian longshoremen. I'm beginning to think this murder has nothing to do with the dispute.'

'But you've still got Eugene keeping his ear to the ground for you,' O'Malley said pointedly. Then, in reaction to the look White gave him, he added, 'Yeah, I heard about you saving his life. First, he aims a gun at you, then you stop him getting shot. What a difference a couple of days make.'

'The less we talk about Eugene, the better,' White said.

'Agreed. I visited the victim's mother to pay my condolences. I don't want anyone thinking just because the boy was black, the police aren't doing everything they can to find his killer. I didn't need to worry. Mrs Walker spoke highly of you. Maybe you're getting back to being a good detective after that crazy spell you decided to have. I hope so.'

White bristled at the comment. He wanted to say at least *one* cop was doing all he could to trace the murderer, that *he'd* made no deals with Eugene, but he bit his tongue. It had always been O'Malley's way to make incendiary comments, but right now, with Mona leaving and the pressure to find the killer for Grace weighing heavy on him, he didn't need it. Checking his watch, he got up and collected his jacket from the back of the chair. 'I have to go to Harlem,' he explained. 'I've got Joseph's friends to see. I'm trying to piece together where he spent the hours leading up to his murder.'

'You go do that,' O'Malley said, turning to make his way out of the tiny office. From the doorway he added, 'You okay?'

'I had better weeks,' White admitted, 'but I'll be just fine when I catch this killer.'

Despite reaching the address he'd been given by eight that morning, White was told he'd missed Harold Tubman. The mother, Mrs Tubman, hadn't exactly given him a warm welcome, peering out mistrustfully from behind the shield of her front door. He was white and a cop, neither of which worked well in Harlem at the best of times, but in the wake of the murder and headlines blazoned across several New York newspapers, the hostility of the place seemed even more intense than usual. At least the youth with the livid scar who'd challenged him the other day was nowhere to be seen. Perhaps it was too early for would-be gangsters to be coming out to play, White thought, exiting the tenement building.

From her open window, Mrs Tubman yelled down to him. 'Harry's at the Walker house. He's painting Grace's kitchen for her.'

'Thank you,' he called back. So, she'd reconsidered and decided to be helpful after all. He guessed he had to be thankful for small mercies. As much as he didn't want to visit Grace with no news of concrete progress in the case and with her son's death now splashed all over the papers, White felt Harold's actions proved his closeness to Joseph. If anyone might know the victim's movements on the night he was killed, it was most likely to be his best friend.

Grace Walker looked shattered. If she'd slept at all since receiving the news of Joseph's slaughter, it didn't show. The rims of her eyes were red, the whites bloodshot, and she moved with the heavy slowness of extreme grief. She still managed a weak smile for White though, and that was enough to almost break his heart. I've got to toughen up, he thought, but not here, and not right now. He found Harold among the chaos of dust sheets, paint cans, and ladder, a brush in his hand and splatters already adorning his overalls.

'You've got a bit on your nose,' White told him in a friendly way, watching as the boy went cross-eyed trying to see it. Harold wiped at it with a paint-stained hand, making matters worse in doing so. 'Here, hold still,' White said, producing a handkerchief and proceeding, like some overbearing auntie, to clean up the kid. It was a deliberate gesture from the detective. These little things were the ones that often bought the confidence of the person you were questioning. They sat down, Harold telling him to be careful of his suit on the covered chairs.

'Thanks,' White said. 'My boss already thinks I look scruffy. Don't want to give him any more cause to moan at me.' It was another move designed to put the young man at his ease. Looking around the kitchen, White added, 'Nice first coat. Good and even.'

'Everyone rushes the first coat because they think it's the final one that matters, but they're wrong,' Harold told him. 'The first coat's the most important. It sets everything up.'

'I guess you're right,' White said. 'I never thought of it like that, but it makes sense. You do a lot of painting?'

'I turn my hand to whatever makes me some money. You have to in these parts.'

'Do you always take this much pride in your work, or is this a special job because it's for Grace? You were close, you and Joseph,' White said, looking for a gentle way in.

'We were,' the boy said, concealing his pain with a steady voice, but his eyes told a different story.

'From what I've heard, he sounded a fine young man.'

'He wouldn't have harmed a fly. He didn't deserve that to happen to him,' Harold said, fighting back an emotion that threatened to overtake him.

'He didn't,' White agreed. 'A good, church-going boy who was making something of himself at the Waldorf. Grace is very proud of him.'

'He was ambitious,' the boy stated. 'Even when we was little kids, I could see he was always going places. He never let coming from this area hold him back.'

'Do you think that might've got him into trouble?' White asked, probing a hunch he'd had for a while about Joseph. Something in the perfect picture of the victim masked a flaw, or at least it might do, White felt. It was only a brief downward glance, but he caught it, the hiding of a reaction that meant he'd gotten close to something, to what, he couldn't know yet. At that vital moment, the kitchen door creaked open, and Grace entered. She blustered about not having offered him a drink, even though the kitchen was in an obvious state of upheaval, and White wondered if her appearance was strategic. Had she been listening just outside the door and heard something she didn't want him pursuing? Her presence certainly shut down anything Harold might've been about to say.

'He's been such a good boy, coming over to help me like this,' Grace announced. 'I didn't want any fuss making, but it needed doing. It was silly of me telling Mister Du Bois to leave it, so I called on the Tubmans last night and Harry said he'd see to it straight away. He's been lighting a candle every day down at the church in remembrance for Joseph. They'd known each other since before they even went to school.'

White looked between the adoring Grace and the awkward young man. He wasn't sure if Harold's uneasiness was because of his questioning or the idea that the grieving mother of his dead best friend might be lining him up as a surrogate son. Whatever it was, the boy seized on the excuse to get himself away from the kitchen. Unbuttoning his overalls as fast as he could, he explained to the pair of them.

'I forgot the candle. I usually do it each morning before I go to work, but my mind was on getting everything together and coming over early to get the painting started. I should take a break and go light one now or I'll feel bad about it.'

'You do that,' White said, giving Harold the release he needed. It was clear the boy wasn't going to tell him anything else here in the apartment. When Harold was gone, he stayed a while, calculating the time it might take the boy to visit the church. He talked with Grace, filling her in on the progress he'd made and exaggerating a little to have it seem more positive than it actually was. He could tell she was disappointed and distracted.

'He's a good boy,' she said once again of Harold, 'but he's hurting. You don't expect to lose your best friend when you're that age. The young don't know about loss or how to cope with it.'

'He's religious too, that should help him,' White noted. 'Is it St Philip's you all go to, that's the church a couple of blocks away, isn't it?'

'That's right, the Episcopal church,' Grace confirmed.

'Very good. Well, I'd better be getting on with the investigation. I have one or two promising leads to follow up. I'll call by again soon; see how you are and keep you updated.'

'Thank you. I appreciate that, Detective White. Do you think you'll get him, the man that killed my Joseph?'

'I'll do everything in my power to, that much I can promise you,' White assured her. 'Take care, now,' he said, as he left the apartment in search of the truth.

His hope was that the story about forgetting to light the candle was genuine, otherwise it might take some time to find Harold and that could harden the boy's resolve against telling him whatever he was holding back. Despite the agitation, his reaction to the reminder about the church carried a more immediate guilt, so White felt sure he was headed in the right direction. When he reached the church, he entered quietly. Harold was sitting in a pew by the altar, and the detective sensed he was taking some time out before having to return to face the attentions of Grace. I don't blame him. He's much too young to know how to handle this, White thought. He walked slowly forwards until he reached the boy's side, then stood in silence, taking in the row of flickering lights that faced him. It was as if the whole building was holding its breath, so profound was the hush.

The boy turned to look at him, and White gestured to the neat row of candles. Speaking softly, he asked, 'Would you mind if I lit one? I feel like I want to.'

Harold simply nodded, so the detective went ahead, inwardly apologising to Joseph for what he was about to do. Returning to sit next to the boy, he took a moment, then sombrely began afresh.

'You believe in *Him*, don't you? God, I mean.'

'Yes. Don't you?' Harold asked.

'I'd like to, but in my job, you get to see more of the devil's work. I guess it erodes your faith. Yet here I am. I've lit a candle and offered a prayer that I'll catch the man who killed your friend. So, I'm trying, Harold. Believe me, I'm trying.'

'If you take away the faith,' the boy said slowly, 'it don't seem like there's nothing else left.'

'I can see how that might be,' White said quietly, his voice calm and reflective. 'It's a good thing, belief in Him, a powerful thing. The almighty God, all-seeing and all-knowing. I wish I had a direct line to him; it'd make my job a lot easier.'

'I guess it would, sir,' Harold agreed, still wrestling with whatever was inside his head.

'Maybe you could help me instead. I saw something back at the house, something you were uneasy over, but didn't want to tell me there.' White paused, letting the pressure of the sentence build before adding, 'No place for lies in His house, but the very best place to do the right thing and give me the truth, give me what I need to track down Joseph's killer.'

Harold looked up at the image of Christ hanging on the cross above the altar. His eyes were wide and brimming with tears, and he seemed to be asking forgiveness from the statue. White gave one last careful push.

'I'll find out anyway, eventually. The truth always has a habit of coming out. I'd just prefer it to come from you, his friend.'

'He was seeing a white girl', Harold quietly said, the tears releasing themselves down his cheeks. 'Joseph was in love with a girl from the Italian Quarter.'

'Thank you, Harold, that's good,' White said, trying his best to mask the euphoria he felt at the breakthrough. 'This girl, did he tell you her name?'

Harold shook his head, the tears falling onto his trousers. White tried again. 'No name at all?'

'He kept it from me. The whole thing was such a no-no. It was forbidden. He swore me to secrecy,' Harold explained.

'I see,' White said, unable to hide his deflation. 'But he mentioned the Italian Quarter.'

'That's all I could get out of him. He went off to meet her every night, but he wouldn't tell me where they went and he made me promise never to follow him,' the boy explained, stopping to wipe the tears from his face with the heels of his hands.

'And you kept that promise?' White asked, already knowing the answer. Harold simply nodded again, too full of remorse over the whole thing to speak. 'Are you sure he told nobody else?' the detective added.

'He wouldn't have,' Harold said more assertively. 'He couldn't have trusted anyone else with that. You don't brag about being with a white girl when you come from Harlem,' he declared, pulling up short because he realised the dreadful implications of what he was saying.

Because it might get you killed, White thought, but he didn't give voice to it. 'I take it Grace didn't know anything about this and still doesn't?' he asked, but Harold's face answered the question for him. 'No, of course not,' White said. 'Better to keep it that way, for now, at least. That poor woman has enough to deal with.' He patted Harold on the shoulder and got up. 'You did the right thing, telling me,' he said.

'I should've tried to stop him,' the boy blurted out.

'A young man with his head and heart full of love?' White replied. 'You wouldn't have stood a chance. You know that. No lies in His house, remember? Don't blame yourself. There's absolutely nothing you could have done. Nothing. I'm telling you. I've seen it too many times. You're a true friend and a good man. Now, get yourself together, and then go back to helping Grace. It's what Joseph would've wanted.'

He exited the church, lit a cigarette, and stared up at the bright sky. In any crime there was always a motive, and he'd just found his. Harlem felt angrier than ever as he made his way through its streets to where his automobile was parked. It was a world grown dark with segregation and social taboo. They had always been there, but somehow Joseph's murder made them all the more real. He believed Harold Tubman; the thing was so forbidden that Joseph would only have confided it to his oldest friend. Someone else had found out though, and whoever it was killed Joseph over it. Feeling he didn't want to be on these streets anymore, White headed back to the precinct and the security of his office. He had a lot to think over.

In his broom cupboard sized den, the detective considered what he'd learned at the church. It was progress of sorts, he thought, sucking on a cigarette and filling the room with smoke. An angry Italian, or even another black man who didn't agree with interracial relationships, had most likely taken Joseph's life. They'd worn industrial boots to trample his bones in their hatred, but this was nothing to do with the docks. This was a different kind of anger, one that was a whole lot uglier. He knew he had to find the girl, but he didn't even have her name. It would take more detectives, and plenty more leg work to track her down, if she could be found at all. No one was about to admit to a secret that could cost them everything.

White went to make another coffee. He was wide awake now, but mentally fatigued by the horrors of the case and his loss of Mona, not to mention the expectations of Grace and Du Bois, and the complication of his feelings for Martha. The hot drink and a cigarette weren't going to magically solve those problems; they were just routine intake to keep him rolling forwards until something happened. Then something did happen. A commotion at the front desk brought the clatter of footsteps down the hall. Tiny clicks of heels at speed followed by the clomp of a sergeant's boots in hot pursuit. White caught the girl as she ran around the corner. He steadied his cup of coffee with his free hand and blinked through the smoke of his cigarette at her. She was wide-eyed and looked like she was barely out of High School, but there was something wild about her that caught his detective senses; an aura of crime clinging unmistakably to her desperation.

'Can I help you, Miss?' he asked, his arm a barrier halting her erratic momentum.

'I need to see a detective!' she exclaimed breathlessly.

'Then you found one. Come and sit down in my office, won't you? Tell me all about it.'

No sooner had the girl squeezed into her seat that she blurted out: 'I want to report a murder!'

She was young, pretty, and unmistakably Italian. His instinct told him he'd found the girl.

Chapter Sixteen
The Price of Love

Sometimes these things just fell right into your lap, White thought, but the detective had to be sure. The girl in front of him, despite the panic she exuded, had something else about her. While he wouldn't go as far as to call it wantonness, there was an energy she possessed, a vitality in her way that could only have come from being in love. He and this girl were at opposite ends of the spectrum in that sense, but he recognised the fire in her heart and was more convinced than ever he had found Joseph Walker's girlfriend. If she had information about who might have killed him, that would blow the case wide open. He'd been down this road before though and knew how false a lover's theories could be. So, given that note of caution and the highly-strung state of the girl, he took things one step at a time.

'Okay. As this is a very serious situation, let's start with your name and try to get a clear picture of who did what to who. First, let me get you a coffee to hold onto, you're shaking like crazy.'

She took the drink he made for her and identified herself. 'I'm Isabella Visconti and my brother, Danny Visconti murdered my boyfriend.'

They were sat in his shoe box of an office, and although her Italian name felt like a key piece of the puzzle fitting into place, White kept things methodical and let the girl tell her own story. The hot coffee and the fact a detective was listening to her made Isabella calm down a little and focus on the chain of events that had brought her to the precinct.

'We'd been meeting most nights in Prospect Park. It was a perfect place because it wasn't in Red Hook, my neighbourhood, or in his. We come from different communities, you see? His people and my people, we don't mix.'

A pang of something leapt inside the detective and he asked, 'What neighbourhood does your boyfriend come from?'

'He lives out beyond Lenox Avenue,' she responded, trying to hide the name of the district.

'You mean Harlem,' White confirmed, the connection creating a further buzz in his mind.

'Well, yes,' Isabella admitted.

'Okay, go on,' he quietly prompted, displaying no sign of surprise or prejudice. It threw her a little, but she continued with her tale.

'He never missed a night, not in two and a half months,' Isabella proudly informed the detective. She paused for a moment, the remembrance of her love jarring against the place she was in and her reason for being there. 'The last time I saw him, four nights ago, there was trouble when I got home,' she went on.

'What sort of trouble?'

'My father knew something was up. I'd been telling him I was working late at my restaurant job, but he checked with the owner and found out I'd been lying. They're friends. I guess I should've known it would happen,' she lamented.

'You were in love,' White stated. 'You didn't want to see the danger, even if you knew it was there.'

'Oh, I always felt the danger,' she corrected him. 'Joseph, my boyfriend, is black, but I suppose you'd worked that one out.'

'Well, I am a detective,' White said, flooded with adrenaline at the confirmation the name brought.

'And it doesn't shock you or make you feel disgusted?'

He collected himself and focused on her question. 'Isabella, I've seen some awful things in my time as a cop. Two young people in love was never one of them, regardless of the colour of their skins. Tell me about your father's reaction when you got home that night.'

'He was mad. It started off quietly, but I could tell how angry he was, hurt too. What made it worse was that he didn't even know Joseph was black. I only told him I was seeing a boy.'

'Did he scare you?'

'Yes,' she admitted. 'He's a tough man, lots of pride. Nobody messes with my Papa. He's as strong as a bull from working on the docks for so many years.'

'Your father's a longshoreman,' White considered. 'He must be worried the strike by the Irish might spread to his own crew. I'd bet there was already a lot of tension in your house even before he found out you were lying to him.'

'There's been a dark cloud over our place for weeks, that's why I hated to deceive him, but it was the only way I could get to see Joseph.'

'Were you afraid of him? I mean, physically. Has your father ever been violent towards you?'

'No, but the threat of it was enough. He smashed a bottle of beer and upended his chair. I didn't know what he might do, so I ran and hid in my room, but I wasn't left alone. My brother, Danny, came in almost straight after. We've always been close. He's two years older than me. He's looked out for me ever since I can remember.' She stopped, visibly wounded by something, and White filled in the gaps from what she'd dramatically told him when he'd first got her in his office.

'Danny didn't support you this time though, did he? He was every bit as angry as your father, perhaps even more so.'

'He grabbed my wrist and threatened me,' she said, and White bet he was the first person she'd confessed this to. 'He knew everything apart from Joseph's name and where he lived. He said he was going to tell Papa if I didn't give him the address. I was too frightened not to.'

'So, what did Danny do?'

'He went out straight away and didn't come back for hours. When he did come back, I tried to find out what had happened, but he just got angry again and refused to talk about it. He told me to get out of his room.'

'I want you to think carefully, Isabella,' White said. 'I know you were very upset, but can you remember what time Danny went out?'

'We left the park just on eleven. I hurried home, then there was the showdown with Papa and Danny's outburst. It seemed like it went on forever, but it couldn't have because I remember hearing the clock in the hall chime twelve not too long after Danny had gone out.'

'So, you think Danny went out after half-eleven?' White probed.

'It must have been,' she considered.

'Definitely?' he pushed. 'This is really important, Isabella. How close to when you got back would you say it was?'

'I don't know!' the girl exclaimed. 'It just must have been after half-eleven because it takes me about fifteen minutes to get home, then I was interrogated for a few minutes before things blew up and I ran to my room. Like I said, Danny came in almost immediately. Neither conversation lasted very long, but it had to have been at least a quarter of an hour after I got back. It must've taken that time.'

'You'd be surprised how people can misjudge timings when they're under stress, especially looking back after they think there's been a murder. The mind can play all kinds of tricks on you,' White warned her.

'No,' Isabella said with certainty, 'I'm sure of it. It was after half-eleven and before twelve when Danny went out. I'd swear on my life if I had to.'

White nodded, slowly calculating the timeline as he knew it. The girl said she'd hurried home. He'd need to time the journey from the park to the Visconti house, not that there were any absolutes in this case. He had to factor in one argument with her father that lasted minutes, but how many minutes? Then, an immediate confrontation with her brother before he stormed off to find her forbidden boyfriend. If Isabella could've made it home in fifteen minutes or less, and the sum of the two showdowns was even swifter, it was possible Danny might have left the house as early as eleven twenty-five. That could put him by the docks at about the time of the first police arriving to disrupt the beatings, depending on where in Red Hook the Visconti house was.

There was a lot that needed going over. It was a stretch, but it all felt possible. One teenage boy in a rage, another dawdling the long way back home because he wanted to take in the waterfront in the moonlight on account of him being intoxicated by love. There were so many unanswered questions, and his mind raced with them all. Turning his attention back to Isabella, he asked her, 'What exactly makes you think Danny killed Joseph?'

From her shoulder bag the girl produced a crumpled newspaper. She threw it down upon the desk with agitation. 'There,' she said. 'It's on the front page. I was sick when I saw it this morning, even though I knew something terrible had happened ever since that night. Seeing it in black and white like that...' She broke off, and White was worried she might throw up again, her face had gotten so pale. The headline blared up at them: *Youth Found Murdered in Brooklyn Dockyard!*

'Should I get you a drink of water?' he asked.

She shook her head, staring with haunted eyes at the wrecked newspaper before looking away anywhere but at it. White waited, sensing Isabella had more she wanted to tell him and was composing herself to be able to continue. She looked back at him earnestly.

'By last night I was going crazy not knowing what might've happened to Joe,' she told him. 'My father only lets me out to attend college now, I'm doing a stenography course, but even then, he makes my mother chaperone me there and back, so it's been impossible to make any contact with Joe. So, while my folks were both busy in the kitchen, I climbed out my bedroom window, hung from the sill, and dropped down. Then I ran all the way to Prospect Park. I knew Joe wouldn't be there, but I sat on our bench anyway and just cried my eyes out.'

White listened patiently. None of this was answering his question about Danny, but Isabella was opening up, reliving the hurricane of events that had torn through her life and left it in tatters. The information about her brother would come out soon enough, he felt.

'Did you get back into the house without anyone finding out?'

'I snuck into the yard so I could see Papa in the kitchen. As soon as he got up and there was a light in the bathroom, I let myself in the back door. I made it to my room okay, pretended to be asleep, then waited. I was determined to have it out with Danny.'

'You still hadn't spoken to him since the night he went out in a rage?' White asked with surprise.

'People were always around, and he'd made out he was ill, like he had a fever. He'd done a pretty good job of it too, convincing Mom he had a high temperature so he couldn't go to work. He stuck to his room, and when I wasn't in college, I stayed in mine. When I finally got to see him, it was the middle of the night. This time, he didn't yell at me. It was like he'd been expecting me to come.'

'Like he'd resigned himself to having to talk about it?' White reasoned.

'Yes. He told me he'd gone down to the docks and witnessed a bunch of guys fighting there. He said it unnerved him and he started to think twice about going into Harlem alone at midnight. He still seemed spooked by it when he was talking to me. Maybe he really does have a fever. I don't know.'

'But you think he murdered Joseph. Why?'

'He got mixed up,' she responded. 'He couldn't tell me where he'd been all those hours. He gave me some garbled nonsense about finding himself by the hospital and some black guys picking on him, but it didn't ring true, and all the while I was staring at his hand.'

'His hand?'

'The knuckles were all grazed and swollen. I asked him how they got like that, and he said he didn't know. He told me the fever had made him forget some things about the night, but I didn't believe him. He'd been so angry before, but he was just sitting in his bed, sweating and shivering. It was like some monkey was on his back and he couldn't shake it off. I think what he did out of fury came to terrify him afterwards.'

'Did you confront him?' White pushed. 'Did you ask him if he'd killed Joseph?'

'When I left his room, my head was spinning. I didn't know what to think, but I wanted to believe whatever Danny had gotten up to, it hadn't involved Joe. I couldn't bear to imagine any harm had come to him, and I'd only made it to the park once. I sat up all night trying to convince myself Joe was okay, that he'd realised something was wrong when I didn't turn up to meet him, that he was too scared to try and contact me. All those explanations would seem plausible to anyone else, but I knew deep down something awful had happened to him. This morning, someone at college had the paper. That was when I found out. I ran to the rest room and threw up from the shock of it. Then I grabbed the newspaper and left. I couldn't go home. I couldn't face Danny, but I knew he did it, I just knew.'

White considered the girl in front of him. In all she'd told him, there was no concrete evidence her brother had been the killer. Sure, he'd been down at the dockyard and knew about the attack on the strike-breakers. That at least put him at the scene of the crime. But he'd had to cope with the huge disturbance of finding out about his kid sister, he'd gone off distraught and had second thoughts about being out alone at night. Something he'd seen had scared him, or perhaps he was just in the grip of a genuine fever. Nothing could be taken for granted.

Still, White thought, there was the injury to his hand that remained unexplained, and the rage...an anger Isabella had never seen in him before. It was a disgust and hatred at his sister having a black boyfriend, of the shame it would bring upon the family. In that, there was motive enough. Danny would also have known the docks too, growing up the son of a longshoreman. He may even have had racial prejudice against the blacks for breaking the strike and potentially putting his old man's livelihood at risk. When you put it all together, it turned the boy into a prime suspect. It made White want to interview him and see what kind of boots he wore. He turned to the girl and said, 'I need to write everything down you just told me as a statement. Then, you read it, and if it seems accurate, you sign it.'

'Okay,' she said, still bewildered by all she'd experienced.

White pulled the official form from his drawer and uncapped his fountain pen. 'One more question before we start over,' he said. 'What does Danny do for a job?'

'He's a mechanic,' Isabella replied.

White nodded. A manual trade, he thought, with heavy boots in case a wheel or wrench fell on your foot. Non-slip soles to avoid sliding on spilt oil. Different boots because he didn't work on the docks, but ones that needed a specific tread pattern to be safe. For all her distress, Isabella had given a lucid and detailed account of the events surrounding Joseph's murder. White wrote quickly, recalling and recording everything she'd said. He was burning to get finished so he could get out of the precinct and straight over to the Italian Quarter. In his mind's eye he could picture Danny Visconti stalking Joseph in the hot Brooklyn night, his wrench raised to deliver the furious fatal blow.

When the statement was finished and the girl had put her name to it, White told her to get some air. He'd suggested she sit in the park for a while and then return to college in time for her mother to collect her. Keep out of the way, he'd advised her, so he could have the space to do his job without her having to be there to see it. Isabella had looked crestfallen. While it was one thing to be unburdening herself and seeking justice for Joseph's murder, giving up her own brother to the police carried with it a new kind of torment, the guilt of betraying a sibling she'd known all her life. It was no wonder she left the precinct in a daze. Whatever happened, White lamented, things were only going to get worse for Isabella. She was a kid that had fallen in love, a girl full of dreams who didn't know the destruction it would bring, and he felt sorry for her, but most of all he wanted to find Joseph's killer. The boy and his mother deserved at least that. So, he made his way into the Italian district, but not to the Visconti house. He needed to visit one more place to gather evidence before he started questioning Danny.

Chapter Seventeen
Ragazzo in Fuga

Before he even entered the garage, White was met with a chaotic scene. The proprietor stood outside in the sharp sunshine; his oily hands clamped around a stained ledger while his eyes surveyed three automobiles parked out front of the workshop. Two more vehicles sat inside in varying states of disarray. Several men jostled for the mechanic's attention and the detective presumed these were the owners of the stricken automobiles. The situation was almost comical, played out in a series of exasperated gesticulations, the mechanic shaking his head and pointing between the ledger and the garage. He looked like he'd been born to wear his dark blue overalls, and as White got closer, he could see those hands that held the appointment book were sinewy and capable. The bedlam surrounding him was not this man's fault. This was what happened when your only apprentice called in sick four days running, White concluded.

'I told you already. Tomorrow you can come and collect your car,' the mechanic said forcefully.

'You said it would be ready tomorrow, *yesterday*,' the owner of the vehicle retorted. 'Tomorrow, tomorrow, tomorrow. If I come back tomorrow and you tell me it's gonna be another day…'

'I explained to you, my boy is sick. I'm on my own here. I can't work any faster.'

A third man interjected, 'So, what about me? When do I come back?'

White had heard enough. The vehicles and their owners would have to get in line. Waving his badge at the group, he instructed them. 'Gentlemen, you all need to come back another time. I'm on police business here and it won't wait.'

One of the men opened his mouth to protest, but the detective shot him a look that made him think better of it. The beleaguered garage owner had switched from going on the offensive to wanting to become anonymous, stepping backwards into the security of his premises like a snail retreating into its shell at the first whiff of trouble. White didn't blame him. His day was about to potentially get a lot worse. He was shown past a clutter of tools strewn across the workshop floor, assessing each one as a possible murder weapon as he went, into a partitioned office area where receipts were clipped neatly together into bundles that hung from nails on the plywood wall. The detective took the single chair provided for customers while trying to catch a look at the soles of the boots the mechanic was wearing as he sat across from him.

'How can I help you, detective?' the man asked, still a little wary of the situation.

The boots looked like they could've come from the previous century, White observed. Nothing to be gained from them, he thought. 'I'm here about your employee, Danny Visconti.'

The mechanic gave him a suspicious stare. 'Danny's sick. He's in bed at home with the flu. What's he done wrong?'

'I didn't say he'd done anything wrong,' White countered. 'How long's he been working for you?'

'About a year. He came to me straight from college. He had all these dreams of being a civil engineer, but he's scared of heights. He didn't want to go checking on bridges or skyscrapers, so he came here instead. He's a very good mechanic.'

White was greeted by the imagined image that haunted him from his childhood: his father falling to his death from the skeleton of a tall building while overseeing its construction. The terrible news had devastated him as a young boy, and he was sure it had weakened his mother so much that she succumbed to typhoid just a few years later. He tried to put the horrors of his past to one side and focus on the investigation. 'Has he been off sick before?'

'Never,' the proprietor said. 'He's been totally reliable ever since I took him on. He's a good kid.'

'I'm sure he is,' White replied. 'Does he keep any of his stuff here, overalls, boots, toolkit, those kinds of things?'

The man seemed a little taken aback by the question but answered promptly enough. 'No. There's no room here, and besides, I got broken into a couple of years back. They took everything, so I advised Danny to take his tools home.'

'Have you noticed anything missing from the garage recently, a wrench or a tyre iron, for instance?' White probed. As intended, the dark implication of the question began to make the garage owner more nervous.

'Nothing's missing. I'd know if it was. I've been so busy here I must've used every tool in the workshop these last few days. Say, what is it you're investigating?'

'Routine enquiries,' White said dismissively, getting up in readiness to leave.

'Danny Visconti is a good kid. Whatever you think he's mixed up in, you're wrong,' the owner declared defensively.

White opened the flimsy office door and paused. 'Okay,' he said. 'Then neither of you have anything to be worried about. I'll let you get back to fixing these automobiles.'

On the threshold of the garage entrance, White noted the proprietor's backward glance at the office and added, 'Oh, and I'd appreciate it if you didn't telephone Danny the second I'm gone. That wouldn't help anyone, least of all him.'

The man looked shocked and guilty at having his intentions read so easily, but to White it was nothing, just a cop's reading of human nature. He'd be at the boy's house in a matter of minutes anyway. Danny was unlikely to make a run for it in that time, whether he was sick or not. As he walked the blocks between the garage and the Visconti house, the detective pondered the evidence afresh. Danny was a good kid with a steady job. He was reliable and skilled. None of that meant he wasn't capable of murder in the heat of the moment though. So, the boy had claimed a fever since the night Joseph Walker was battered to death. Killing a person could have that effect on a young man, White thought. Time to see if he was in his bed. Time to take a close look at his boots and tool bag.

White's decision to make the journey on foot had been a deliberate one. He wanted to get a feel for the neighbourhood. His previous trip to Eddie Millarini's general store had shown him the thriving but spiky character of the district's heart, but here, away from the social hubbub, the streets were clean, quiet, and respectable. Although the houses were small and crowded together, each one had been allotted a patch of land at the front and a porch just big enough for two people to sit on. Outside the Visconti house, a woman was tending to a neat flower bed, watering the peonies and begonias that were wilting in the heat, while across the street a boy studied her work as he lazed on his stoop. There was nothing else going on to watch.

Maria Visconti seemed to have a sixth sense about him coming. When he was thirty yards from the house, she straightened up from her gardening and turned slowly in his direction, watching him through the shimmer of heat haze that wobbled up from the road. She knows something, White thought. It might have been a mother's intuition, or else she'd seen something in her son that wasn't right. She could even have read the morning paper and made a connection, but that seemed a stretch to the detective. The garage owner would've had time to telephone a warning, but if that was the case, Maria would have kept checking the street for his presence, and she hadn't done so. No, this suspicion had come from somewhere else, and although it would put the mother on her guard, it would also make her nervous, and that was where something always let slip.

Her expression was easy to read as he reached the house, a thin veil of defiance barely masking the dread that churned beneath. White smiled reassuringly, as if to say: *I know this is hell for you, I understand, but I've done all this before. Trust me, I'll be gentle. I'll not trample the delicate flowers of your dignity.*

'Mrs Visconti? Sergeant Dominic White, Detective Squad. Can you spare a minute?'

A momentary recoil, recovered into more gentle surprise. 'Yes, officer. Nothing's happened to Frank, has it? There hasn't been an accident at the docks?'

'No, nothing like that,' he replied, thinking she'd know they'd send a patrolman for anything of the kind. 'It's about Danny. Can we talk inside?'

She nodded and led the way, White noting that the mention of her son had elicited no reaction of surprise from her. When they were in the house, Maria took him through to the living room where she asked if he would like a coffee. He accepted her hospitality, knowing she was using the delay to adjust to his presence, but also calculating it would allow him time to snoop around a little and get a feel for the house that might be harbouring a murderer. Drifting silently from the room, he noted it was a tidy and cared for place, one step up from Grace Walker's home in Harlem, but still bearing the stamp of poverty in its worn-out furniture and threadbare rug on the floor. There was no sign of any work boots in the hallway, nor did any noise betray another occupant. Hearing the kettle whistle on the stove, White resumed his position and waited for Maria's return.

'There's milk and sugar on the tray,' she stated. 'I didn't know how you took it.'

'Black is just fine,' White replied, the irony of his statement not being lost on him.

'So,' she awkwardly said, gripping the handle of her cup so tightly it made the flesh on her knuckles turn white, 'what is it you want to see Danny for?'

'I called into his work, but they told me he was sick. Is he here?' White asked.

'He's had a fever,' Maria replied. 'He's resting in his room. Can I help you with anything?'

'It's a delicate enquiry. It's best if I talk to Danny alone, if you don't mind.'

'Why, I'm his mother,' Maria bristled. 'Anything he's involved in; I need to know it. It's my house he's living in.'

'Yours and Frank's,' White observed, knowing the mention of her husband's name would temper her resistance. Her eyes went wider, and she pulled up short.

'You don't have to speak to Frank. I mean, he doesn't have to know you've been here, does he?'

'Mrs Visconti, a boy has died. I have information Danny was in the vicinity when it happened. I also know the victim was connected to your daughter, Isabella.' There, let her have it all at once, see what she makes of it being out in the open, White reasoned.

'Isabella? What's she got to do with a murdered boy?'

White took his time. He pulled out his cigarettes and offered one to Maria, even though she didn't look anything like a smoker. She declined, and he lit up, savouring the mistake she'd made.

'The death made the papers today. Maybe you read them,' he offered.

'No, I've not seen any newspapers,' she responded. 'Now, will you please tell me what you think this has to do with my children.'

'Isabella was seeing this boy, romantically, I mean. Danny could've witnessed something bad happening to him...or more.' He let the nuance hang in the air, studying her face for a reaction, but she'd already set herself in the stance of defence. In her muteness, he added, 'Can you show me to Danny's room now, please?'

'What makes you think he had anything to do with the whole terrible business?' she shot back.

'I never revealed it was a *murder*. You knew that all by yourself, and without reading a paper. How so?' White pressed, his firmness putting Maria in a corner she knew she couldn't lie her way out of.

'I knew Isabella was seeing someone,' she finally admitted. 'It's just I didn't know exactly *who* she was seeing.'

'You mean his colour,' White said flatly. 'Danny knew, but he didn't tell you. My guess would be he wanted you to do something as her mother before the situation got too far out of hand, but then it got around the neighbourhood and it was too late.'

Maria was shaking her head now, a tremor coming to her hand. It convinced White she either knew or suspected the worst. Even so, as a mother, she would instinctively defend her son no matter what he had done. 'My Danny is not a killer,' she quietly said.

'I never said he was, but I still need to talk to him,' White steadily asserted, his eyes fixed on Maria's.

She led him to the young man's room and knocked lightly upon the door. When there was no reply, Maria opened it a little way and looked in. 'He's not there!' she said in poorly feigned surprise.

'Maybe he just went to the bathroom,' White suggested, playing along. 'Why don't you go check.'

As she bustled off down the hallway, White slipped into the boy's room. At the foot of the bed were a pair of work boots. Examining the soles, the detective could see the pattern on the treads was very like the imprint made on Joseph's clothing. Before he could look any further, Maria returned.

'He must've gone out,' she declared distractedly. 'Perhaps he was feeling a little better and wanted some air.'

White nodded sagely. Danny's bed had been cold to the touch. He'd not fled upon hearing the detective's arrival. Something or someone had spooked him long before that, and it hadn't been the garage owner. Families, White cursed. They could argue like hell and hate each other's guts, but in the end, it always came down to blood ties. It wasn't Maria that had told her son to flee, but she'd let him go nonetheless, and now, she was trying to cover for him to buy him time. He turned to her; all the pretence gone from his demeanour.

'Maria, I know Isabella called the house. I know you're all trying to protect Danny, but it's too late for that. If he's innocent, the truth will out, he has nothing to fear from me. If not…there isn't any escape. I'll find him eventually.'

Looking suddenly hollow, like all the resolve had been drained out of her, Maria repeated her weak defence. 'My Danny is not a killer.'

'I need to find him. If you know where he's gone, you should tell me. I promise you, it's the best way. Kids can do crazy things when they're on the run. They can cause more harm, get mad ideas into their heads like fixing to die rather than turning themselves in. I don't want any more tragedy.'

The thought of this shook Maria. 'He went about an hour ago,' she relented. 'He wouldn't tell me where he was going so I couldn't rat him out. I gave him twenty dollars. It was all I had saved.'

White believed her. He also knew who'd have the best idea of Danny's whereabouts, and that wasn't his mother. Writing his number down for her, he left Maria, but not before he'd taken the boy's work boots for further examination. Outside on the hot street once again, he ran through what he'd learned. Isabella had blown into the precinct in distress because of the shock caused by a newspaper headline. Whatever she'd been bottling up about what her brother might have done to her boyfriend was let loose in that moment. Then, the reality of making a statement and putting the machine of the law into motion had hit her. She was feeding Danny to the wolves on nothing more than a suspicion, however strong it might have been. So, she'd reflected and given him a chance to run; she'd called the house and warned him. Blood ties, White thought, grimacing as he felt the absence of his own dead parents, and now, his only daughter too.

White felt stupid not to have seen the possibility of Isabella's volte face, but that was done now. The boy would turn up before too long, that was how these things played out. Until then, White had the boots to check and more probing to do about Danny's movements on the night of the murder. He was keeping an open mind. No assumptions could be made from the boy fleeing. The hysteria in the Visconti house, the boy's disturbed mind, and a natural fear of the police might all account for him running. If he was innocent, he'd come back sooner, that much was certain.

Meanwhile, Isabella's revelation created other questions in White's mind. Was Joseph murdered because of the shame an interracial relationship would bring on the Italian family, or could someone else have known and had their own reasons for killing the boy? Grace had been proud of her son's ambitions, but Harold Tubman had recognised he'd gone too far and risked too much in dating Isabella...*you don't brag about being with a white girl when you come from Harlem.* Those were his friend's exact words. You didn't brag because some of your own community saw it as a betrayal of creed, and what trouble might result from that, the detective thought.

He'd need to talk to Isabella again, threaten her with telling Frank Visconti everything, put the pressure on so she'd help him find Danny, but it was best to let her stew for a little while first. He had the boots to analyse back at the precinct and then there was one more avenue to explore further. Grace Walker had wanted to silence Harold, and now White thought he'd worked out why. He needed to visit her apartment in Harlem and tell her what he'd learned about Joseph's relationship with Isabella. What came from that meeting might take him one step closer to the truth.

White and O'Malley were squatting on the roof of the precinct, passing a magnifying glass from one to the other, squinting, cursing, and meticulously trying to examine the boots, the pattern of their soles, and the imprint left on Joseph's jacket. Evidence was everything, they both knew that. White had tried the process in his windowless office, but it had proven impossible. He'd tried the workroom, the canteen, and the vestibule, but always he'd needed more light. The lieutenant had found him on his way up to the roof and they'd figured two pairs of eyes would be better to make the decision that could put Danny Visconti in jail for life. Yet, even in the glorious mid-afternoon sunshine, things weren't made that easy.

'Hmmm,' White groaned, moving between sole and imprint once again.

'Here, give it to me,' O'Malley impatiently commanded, snatching for the lens. 'Fuck. There, maybe. No. I'm too fucking old, my eyes are shot. I can't be sure. You look.'

'I *was* looking. Wait. Hold that jacket tight for me, will ya. These marks aren't so clear.'

'Better?'

'I think so. Hmmm. Fuck.'

'What? You make it?' O'Malley asked hopefully.

'Not for certain,' White replied, taking a break, and lighting a cigarette. Jesus, he thought, why couldn't anything be clear?

'Let me have a go again,' O'Malley said, picking up the magnifying glass afresh.

White let him. The failure to nail down the suspect had sprung his mind back to that even bigger failure of losing Mona and Amy. Out there on the rooftop, he could feel himself beginning to unravel again, a life loosely bandaged by work coming apart at the seams. Still, he hid it from his boss under the disguise of frustration.

'It's no good,' O'Malley declared. 'Even if I say it's a match, you'll argue against it. I just sense it. You've got the girlfriend's accusation, you've got the boy at the scene of the crime, right place and time. Christ, he even ran away! Now, here's these boots and the imprint. A jury could like all this, so why can't you?'

White stared into the unrelenting eye of the sun as if to burn away all the ugly visions he'd seen in the last few days. It was no good. Even if he went blind, he'd always remember Joseph's battered body in the hellish dockyard, Mona and Amy leaving in the Model T Ford. He felt a mess. Throwing his cigarette butt down on the roof, he answered.

'I've heard the girl and I've seen the boots, but there's a gripe in my guts about it all that won't go away. I know it looks like Danny Visconti did it, but I have my doubts. I need to speak to the kid.'

'Of course you do, but just remember the obvious answer is usually the right one,' O'Malley said. 'Police work isn't a conjuring act and criminals don't perform illusions. If it looks like they did it, that's because they did it. Anyways, you lost the boy because you didn't detain the sister while you checked out your leads. Wise up, detective. Find him, bring him in, question him, and stop ignoring the obvious. The kid's guilty.'

White stood his ground. 'Remove everything else and look at the tread pattern and the imprint,' he said. 'Is it enough to present to the suspect? Is it conclusive?'

O'Malley gestured for a cigarette and White obliged, lighting it for him. He smoked while his apprentice waited. 'I trained you too well,' he finally offered. 'No, it's inconclusive. Better go find the boy.'

'After I go see Grace Walker,' White announced.

'The victim's mother?' O'Malley said. 'What more do you think she can tell you?'

'I don't know,' White replied. 'I'm not sure of anything right now, but something's bothering me and I need to check it out. When all else fails, go with your gut, right?

Anyways, about what you said, I don't think you can train anybody too well.'

'It's your case,' O'Malley conceded. 'Even when I tell you what to do, you don't listen.'

'I listen to all the important things, boss,' White reassured him.

'So, go with your gut,' O'Malley reasoned. 'In the end, the gut always knows.'

'Like something you knew all along but just wanted to shut out,' White said, thinking aloud about Mona.

Hearing the melancholy in White's voice, O'Malley toughened again. 'Detective, get the hell off my roof and don't stop moving until you've sorted this case out. Then you might just stand a chance of being okay, whatever it is that's bugging you.'

White nodded and set off to see Grace, then Isabella. As he went, he felt the breath of all his demons on the back of his neck. He didn't want them there. O'Malley was right in that respect. Solving the case would be the first step to making them go away.

Chapter Eighteen
Chasing Down Demons

White drove over to Harlem with invisible doubts and misgivings crowding the inside of the car. The windows were down, and he was glad of a stiff breeze that blew through the cabin, momentarily blocking out the clamour of his demons. Since Mona announced she was leaving it had been hard for him to think straight. Maybe O'Malley was right, the means, motive, and opportunity all sat with Danny Visconti. They'd put in for an arrest warrant, and another one to search the kid's home, but White felt uneasy about it all and he couldn't explain why. He had, of course, already considered just how much his mind was being scrambled by the departure of his wife and daughter. As he dodged around a trolley bus, he almost hit a figure emerging from behind it. He braked, cursed, and reflected that the times of invincibility he'd felt in his young manhood were long gone, and he was only twenty-seven.

He pulled up outside the apartment, scanning the street for the youth who had antagonized him on his first visit, but nothing was occurring other than people going about their business. Even so, today had been full of trouble and things not going to plan, so he'd learned to expect the unexpected. Get to what Grace knows, he told himself, and then use it to help you understand. Still there were too many gaps in his knowledge, too many unanswered questions. Isabella had said Danny knew everything that was going on apart from Joseph's name and address. That meant the couple had not been as discreet as they should've been. They'd put themselves at risk in a white neighbourhood, the most hazardous place for them to be seen together. Harold Tubman had spoken of the danger of such a thing being discovered in his own community, but if it was known in Red Hook, couldn't it just have easily been known here? And, if so, what price the potential reprisals? Grace's reaction would help to answer that.

She seemed surprised to see him. The smell of fresh paint clung to the apartment and the kitchen was still temporarily out of bounds, so he was shown into the living room where he found Du Bois presiding over a sea of paperwork. The activist looked pained by the interruption and his agitation made him start to rise, but White gestured for him to remain seated and directed Grace to the only other chair. 'This won't take long,' he said, standing between the two. 'I found something out today it'd be good to have both your views on.'

'Is it about Joseph's slaughter?' Du Bois asked. Grace remained strikingly silent.

'It is,' White confirmed. 'I have a potential suspect, but it's not one of the Irish dock workers. We're still working on pinning the other night's assaults on them, but nothing points to them having anything to do with Joseph's murder. I aim to take things further today with a search warrant and possibly an arrest.' He turned to Grace and said, 'I really am doing everything I can to apprehend the person who killed your son.'

Grace nodded and quietly said 'I know, detective. I can tell you're a good man who believes in right and doesn't judge the colour of a person's skin.'

Du Bois was a little less charitable. 'What can you tell us about this suspect, detective? Is he white? Is it looking like a racially motivated crime?'

'I'm not entirely certain what the motive was yet, Mr Du Bois,' White replied, processing the way both figures were reacting to him. 'One thing of interest has come to my attention though,' he continued. 'Mrs Walker, did you know Joseph was seeing an Italian girl called Isabella?'

Grace and Du Bois both looked startled, but in the mother's case it was masking something else, and White knew he'd been right to suspect her of steering him away from her family's guilty secret.

'Mrs Walker?' he pressed on.

'I...I'd heard rumours. Tittle-tattle and gossip from no-good people. I dismissed it as jealous slander. Joseph was a bright and ambitious boy who others envied because of his talents.'

'Do you think that was why he was killed?' Du Bois asked. It was a question that could have come from White himself, and the activist was clearly shaken by the revelation. He, for one, had not known the truth, the detective surmised.

'Like I said,' White asserted, 'I can't be entirely certain, but it would help me to know the nature of these rumours, Mrs Walker. Tell me, as precisely as you can, what people were saying about Joseph.'

'They said he thought he was too good for his roots,' she announced with a quiver in her voice. 'They said he dreamed of filling a white man's shoes by being head waiter at the Waldorf, and that black girls weren't good enough for him. He wants to be white, they said, so he chases around white girls. It was all just hate. They couldn't wait to see him fall,' she said bitterly.

'Who said these things? Who couldn't wait?' White pushed.

'Oletta Adams and Constance Gray. They were the main culprits. The others just followed. Their boys never amounted to anything, you see? And their husbands are too drunk or scared to fight in the war, so they make up bad things out of spite to cuss my boy with,' she choked out, tears of hurt filling her eyes.

'How did they know this stuff? Are their sons around Joseph's age? Did their boys tell them?' White continued insistently.

'Detective, Grace is in distress,' Du Bois interrupted. 'Surely, you must have seen enough envy and sourness in your time to recognise the poison it spreads?'

'I have,' said White, noting the activist's use of her first name. He put it down to a good man stung by the suffering of a woman who didn't deserve it. 'I'm sorry to be abrasive, but the fact remains Joseph was seeing a white girl. I'm just trying to figure out if one of the boys from his own community might've known and hated him enough to do something more than spread gossip about him.'

Du Bois clenched his fist and was about to say something fierce in reply. White still surmised this was racial politics, not love. Grace cut him off.

'Detective, we are black. We have nasty things said about us every day an' they don't hold a grain of truth. So, round here, real good folks need proof before we start judging anyone. I wouldn't have had any issues with Joseph seeing a girl who wasn't coloured, and as much as it might have worried me about how some people in Harlem would react to it, I'd be a whole lot more frightened about what white folks might do to him if they knew.'

Du Bois chipped in 'Especially the Italians. They aren't exactly known for their racial tolerance. Is your suspect from the Italian community?'

White held his palms up in procedural defence, not liking the way the pair had shifted the power axis in the room. 'I can't really say any more until I've had the chance to take my investigation further. I hope you both understand,' he added through a head unsettled by how much his wife's departure was affecting his work, his life, his very being. Striving for some kind of foundation, he stated, 'Mrs Walker, I promise to tell you straight away when I have anything more concrete on who killed your Joseph. I'd better get back to work now.'

Grace remained in her seat, too hurt by the conversation to function normally. You and me both, White lamented. Du Bois rose to show him to the door. On the threshold, he touched the detective's arm. It was a move that carried no aggression, but the activist held a different type of power, both morally and politically.

'I hope you won't make this about my people,' he said with a note that carried warning. 'I am a champion of interracial relations, but even in those of colour who are not, their hatred would never drive them to kill one of their own. It's white men who murder blacks for what they see as stepping out of line. There's plenty of evidence to show that in our recent history.'

'In all probability, you're right,' White conceded, 'I just need to explore all the avenues. I'm a detective. It's an integral part of our job. Probability isn't enough. I need proof. So, if you'll excuse me, I'm about to go out and get it if I can.'

'You do understand me?' Du Bois continued, still holding on to White's arm. It was like he'd chosen not to listen to the detective's last words.

'Oh, I do,' White replied, placing his own strong hand on top of Du Bois'. 'I want this killer behind bars more than you could know. What he did to that boy is sickening me. If you don't believe what I'm saying, if you think I'm playing the white man's politics, watch the crowd when your parade takes to the streets of New York. You'll see me there, and not as a cop, but as a supporter.'

With that, he unhanded Du Bois' grip, held onto him to make sure *he* understood, then opened the door and made his way back to the waiting automobile. His demons had slunk away, for now, forced back by the fire he felt inside. He needed to see Isabella. Danny Visconti had to be found.

Early evening and no sign of the boy across the street as White watched the Visconti house through the haze of yet another cigarette. It had been that kind of a day, that kind of a week. It was better not to look further back than that, he surmised, drawing on the reserves of nicotine. Danny's disappearance would have to be explained to Frank at some point, but the detective figured Maria would want to leave that as long as possible. It had been a day of trauma for the family, and Isabella, even if she wasn't in danger from her father, would probably have to vacate the neighbourhood. He prayed they wouldn't try to send her to some backwater town in Italy. It surprised him, he didn't pray for much these days, if ever. He had about as much care for organized religion as a duck.

White figured he should've been angry at Isabella for tipping Danny off and causing more trouble, but she was just a kid caught up in a fairy tale that'd gone very wrong. Now, none of that mattered. He had to speak to her without alerting Frank. Isabella had already escaped her house arrest once. He had to hope she could perform the same trick again.

The window was open in the front upstairs room of the house. White found a small pebble and threw it through the gap. He was gambling this was the girl's room as she'd told him how Frank liked to occupy the kitchen and dropping down to the rear of the building would've been too risky for the kid. The pebble made the gap, but he'd no idea whether it had hit the wall or the floor, or even if Isabella was in her room to hear it. He waited, scanning the ground for another small stone he could use, when his peripheral vision picked up a figure at the window. His luck was in. It was the girl. He beckoned her to come down, and for a moment he worried she might refuse as she stood there in hesitation. Then, she began to climb out the way she'd done before. That was the easy part. The kid was all set for fleeing. Getting her to give up Danny's whereabouts was likely to be much harder.

He took her to Prospect Park, knowing it would make her more vulnerable to his entreaty. She wouldn't go to the bench she'd shared with Joseph, but the place was enough. The sadness of it all weighed heavily upon her young features. Under a broad oak tree, after they'd travelled with a difficult silence hanging between them, White got straight to the point of his visit.

'I don't blame you for calling Danny,' he said under the rustling leaves, 'but it does create a problem. All the time that passes where I can't question him can only make things worse. If he's innocent, it gives the killer time to get away or fake an alibi. It lets a murderer loose on the streets. If Danny is guilty, and I'm not completely convinced he is, he's going to think about what could happen to him, and the fact no one can evade the law forever. You saw how sick he was, that was why you relented. I understand. Whether he did it or not, he'll be worrying himself into a terrible state. He'll be desperate, and who can say what he might do to himself with all those thoughts hammering at his head. I'm with you on this. I don't want the boy to do anything crazy. I don't want Danny to take his own life.'

He paused, watching as she weighed up his words with a terror in her eyes. Sensing he needed to say more, he added, 'You wish you could go back and do things differently, we all do, but you can't. Nobody can. What's left in life is the ruins, but from that destruction, a truth can always be found. You might not want to know it. You might want to flee from it and all the pain it could bring, but without it, you'll never know for sure who killed Joseph, so you'll never be able to rest. That's what I'm here for; to help us both rest. A lifetime is too long to be asking yourself that question. Help me to find Danny, then we can know the truth once and for all.'

A stronger gust hit the leaves of the old oak tree, washing a tidal wave through its branches, and Isabella gnawed at a hangnail in her confusion. 'I know he hurt me,' she said painfully, 'but to kill someone in the way the papers said takes more hatred and brutality than Danny's got in him. My brother didn't kill Joseph, I'm sure of it.'

White was unperturbed by the statement, it was just family, after all. 'So let me question him,' he said neutrally. 'If he can prove where he was then I can eliminate him. The longer he runs, the more guilty he'll look.'

She recoiled. 'I know about the police. You'll get him in a room and scare the life out of him until he confesses.'

'What, and let a murderer go free to do it again? No way. That's not what I joined Detective Squad and risk my life for,' White protested. 'If Danny didn't do it, he has absolutely nothing to fear. I swear to you. I want Joseph's killer. I'm not interested in fitting anyone up.'

Still the girl waivered, so White added 'Joseph's murderer is on the loose. The longer I spend chasing after Danny, the more time someone has to get away, but as your brother's our only lead, thanks to you, we're going to keep looking for him, concentrating all our energies on bringing him in. Is that what you want, for Danny to look all the more guilty while the real killer gets away with his hideous crime?'

White waited as the silence endured. Then, Isabella said quietly, 'We have an auntie over in Jersey. She lives out at Asbury Park. It's a long bus ride away, nearly two hours. That's where Danny will have gone.'

'You're certain?' White asked, fixing on what finding Danny meant to the case.

'Yes,' the distraught girl said, and White was convinced by the strength of her betrayal.

'Okay, you did the right thing, Isabella, you really did.' He handed her his notebook and pencil. 'Write down her name and address for me. I'll head over there by myself and talk to him, there's no need for fuss. Just don't call ahead this time. This thing needs to be over with. We both have to find out the truth.'

Isabella looked at the pad like it might bite her, the pencil like a spear she would strike through Danny's heart, but she took it, and put her brother's fate in White's hands.

'Thank you, Isabella. Shall I walk you back to Red Hook?' he offered.

'No. I'll be okay,' she said. 'Just promise to go easy on Danny. He's my big brother.'

'I'll get you the truth, that much I can assure you of,' White replied.

He watched her go amongst the green leaves, good intentions, and confusing romance the park held for her. Welcome to another twisted version of my life, he thought, and was saddened by it all. She was so young, and had gone through tough trauma with her emotions, from not knowing what had become of Joseph to suspecting her own brother of his murder. She'd betrayed him by going to the police with her suspicions, but to not do so would have stabbed Joseph in his grave, sullying his memory and unquestionable love for her. Now, she didn't want to believe Danny had done it and couldn't stand the thought of him rotting in jail. Even so, she understood the need for the truth to come out, and that she couldn't prevent the police from finding her brother...one way or another. She'd given him up. She just had to hope he didn't do it, White figured.

For his part, the detective hoped Danny was innocent too, because if he was guilty, there could be no mercy and it would do no good, it would just destroy two families and make a New York detective feel nothing positive about the life he was in. It was a shit or bust case, and he knew he was wedded to it, whatever the outcome. Right now, he had nothing else left in his life to fight for. That was his sad conclusion as he headed on back to the car. Asbury Park would at least give him distance and motion from his demons. They could sit in the back seat like the past he wanted to forget. His co-pilot must navigate him on the quest for truth, an imaginary friend, part O'Malley, part Sheriff Masters. He knew he needed someone benign, a guardian angel on his journey through the darkness. Without them, oh, he was gone. He couldn't do it on his own. Not anymore, and not now. Especially not in these most testing of times.

Chapter Nineteen
Light of the Beltane Fire

It was a warm night and White drove with the car roof down, knowing the canvas construction in the Oldsmobile flapped annoyingly when he got any speed up. The seats in the automobile were comfortable, the buttoned leather creaking slightly as he shifted his position, and he could taste the countryside in the air. As he motored on, the detective tried to remember the last time he'd taken a trip outside New York and figured it must've been four years; the period when he was investigating the suspicious death at Columbia Recordings, the case that had led him to joining Detective Squad, and where he'd first met Martha Marsh. He put these things to the back of his mind again, for they only brought him a sense of guilt and the recognition of how sour his life had turned in the present. Count off the miles and pursue your suspect, he told himself, but he knew he couldn't outrun the tragedy of it all.

After being caged so long in the city, the length of the journey struck him, and White thought about that far greater distance Mona and Amy were covering to reach Omaha. It would take days of driving to visit his daughter, back to a state where he had his own mixed memories of growing up in the town he'd left as soon as he'd become a man. The feeling of the orphan train still unsettled him every time he heard a locomotive rattling down the line. He lit a fresh cigarette from the old one he was finishing and blew smoke back across the fields he was leaving behind. The echoes of his past weren't helping him right now. He would have to adapt to the present and grow used to it. Nothing, not even the chasm of miles, was going to stop him seeing his daughter. He resolved that much before returning to ponder all the uncertainties of the case.

Somebody had murdered Joseph Walker with such brutality that the hatred was stamped into his very bones. White's investigation had begun with the dock dispute and the attack on the black strike-breakers which had happened on the same night as the killing. He'd ruled out Pat O'Brien, but had he been too hasty in dismissing all the Irish workers as suspects, he wondered? He was taking O'Brien and the shopkeeper's word that all the boys bought their boots from the same supplier, and Eugene had promised to ask questions on his behalf after White had stopped him taking a bullet back in the Five Points slums, but none of that meant the murderer hadn't been a docker who'd bludgeoned Joseph to death because his skin colour matched those who'd taken Irish jobs. As Du Bois had pointed out, black lives could sometimes be ended for very little by angry white men.

A lack of progress in a case he'd been desperate to solve had been punctuated by Isabella's arrival at the precinct with talk of her brother's fury. So many aspects of Danny's behaviour fitted with the circumstances of the murder, but were Detective Squad jumping to conclusions too keenly? White tossed his latest cigarette out the car and watched in the rear-view mirror as it showered sparks along the road. He thought again. It was a fact that Joseph and Isabella had been seeing each other and that people within both Red Hook and Harlem had been talking about it. If you coupled that to Joseph's ambition and the resentment it had caused some in his community to feel, it meant there was the possibility of other suspects, both black and white, who had means, motive, and opportunity and were nothing to do with the unrest at the docks. *The obvious answer is usually the right one*, O'Malley had said earlier up on the rooftop, but that didn't mean it always was. He'd also told White to trust his gut, but the detective felt all he could do was talk to people, listen, and observe. Everything fitted together somehow, he knew it. He just couldn't see how yet.

Across the plains, a scarecrow caught his eye, a lone figure standing there like some peasant Christ, sagging with the fatigue of protecting the vulnerable, and beyond it a fire carried a column of smoke up into the heavens. White wondered who would go lighting a fire on such a warm night, and it drew his mind back to early childhood where his father told him all about the ancient Gaelic festival of Beltane, where fires were lit that were believed to have special protective powers. It was one of the few concrete memories White had of the man, and the story enchanted him as a young boy. Now, he drove on because a not so different kind of internal fire was urging him to make sense of the case and find Joseph's killer.

The light was already fading in the sky when White arrived in Asbury Park. A dark smudge of imposing night lay above the horizon as he looked out over the vast Atlantic Ocean, and the burnished copper of sunset upon the waves was shifting to be replaced by the silvery play of moonlight. The colours of the promenade shops enticed him, and the smell of cotton candy made White realise he hadn't eaten a thing since breakfast. He parked up, grateful to stretch his legs, and ate a warm roll standing at a stall, letting the juice trickle between his fingers while he chewed on the welcome meat inside. The stallholder gave him directions for the aunt's house and the detective wiped his hands before setting off on Danny's trail once more.

He found the street with ease but cursed the failure of one of the Oldsmobile's headlights because it would slow his journey back to New York. The neighbourhood was quieter than Maria's, a seaside hush settling on it as darkness fell, and the houses were more basic, poor wooden painted constructions that looked like bigger versions of the beach huts littering the shoreline. He knocked, and a stout, middle-aged woman who was an older version of Maria that'd had a harder life opened the door. From her expression, he could tell she'd been expecting him, but not in a good way.

'Maria's boy hasn't turned up,' she said matter-of-factly as she stood in the doorway, 'but I suppose you'll be wanting to come in anyway.'

'Yes. I'd like to hear more about Danny, if you wouldn't mind,' White said, hiding the disappointment his quarry wasn't as close at hand as he'd hoped.

She showed him through to a bare, functional kitchen where she brewed some tea mechanically rather than with any sign of hospitality, making it clear he was an unwanted guest. White didn't mind. He'd already decided Luisa Kilpatrick was the type of person who'd give him the unvarnished truth, and that was what he needed.

The detective sipped the scalding and predictably strong tea, and asked, 'Did you see a lot of Danny when he was growing up?'

'They holidayed here when they could afford to,' she replied, cradling her mug in both hands out of what he presumed was habit because it wasn't a bit cold in the kitchen. 'Maria's always kept in touch and our men get along, despite being cut from different cloth.'

'How so?' White probed, doing anything to keep the woman talking.

'Frank's a worker, whereas my Charlie's a gipsy,' she said without any judgement of either man. 'He'll be better at giving you an opinion on the boy. They spent much more time together when he came down, Isabella too. She's a tomboy, that one, much more of a tearaway than Danny.'

'What do you think of Danny?' he asked, watching the vapour rise from his mug.

'A weaker version of his father. The same tea, but with more milk in the cup, if you see my meaning.'

White nodded, waiting for Luisa to continue, which she duly did after considering things a little further.

'On the surface, Danny's not as tough as Frank,' she went on. 'It's got nothing to do with generations or trades, Frank just has his sensitivities buried deeper, he covers them over with aggression, like he's angry at the world for some reason.'

'And Danny?'

'He doesn't have Frank's discontent, but he's protective in the same way and he keeps everything hidden in here,' she said, tapping a thick finger against the side of her head. 'Yes, the boy's a quiet one, but he knows himself alright.'

'His boss called him steady. I got the impression he was stable beyond his years,' White shared.

'You're either stable or you're not,' Luisa said flatly. 'The boy'll become a good man, someone you can rely on, whatever your lot think he's done. That's what I'd say about him,' she declared.

'Maria didn't tell you why he'd run away?' White asked, although he already knew the answer as he took another sip of the bitter tea. Luisa would've demanded to know what was going on, and she wouldn't have accepted anything less than the truth from her sister.

'She said you think he's involved in a boy's death, someone his own age,' she stated, looking at him steadily.

'But you don't believe Danny could've done such a thing,' White observed.

'No, not deliberately at least,' Luisa replied, adding, 'and I'm saying that based on instinct. I've not had any more detail from Maria, and the boy hasn't shown his face, but sometimes a woman just knows a thing.'

'Where do you think Danny would go if he decided against coming here?'

Luisa shrugged, 'I've no idea. Like I said, Charlie was closer to him. You should go ask him. He's working down at the fair now. You'll find him running the big carousel. There's nothing more I can tell you.'

White left his tea and thanked Luisa for her time despite the bluntness of her way towards him because he figured she was probably like that with everyone, whether they were implicating her nephew in a murder or not. He turned the one-eyed Oldsmobile around and headed back down to the seafront where the lights of the fairground flickered like a larger version of the fire he'd seen out across the plain. Once again, he thought of his dead father and the story of Beltane.

The carousel was the prettiest of all the rides at the fair, bedecked with beautifully carved horses and edged in gilt around its painted decoration. It had an unmistakable air of the gipsy about it, as did the man who was operating it. Charlie Kilpatrick wore fingerless gloves that were at odds with his rolled-up sleeves and open-necked shirt. The skin on his face, forearms and chest was universally brown, the colour of his wife's potent tea, in fact. He was wiry, but strong with it, and there was a twinkle in his eye that turned flinty and suspicious when he saw White approaching. He lent on a lever that slowed the movement of the carousel until it came to a standstill, then he helped one or two small children who were having difficulty dismounting the ride before receiving new customers and pocketing their shiny dimes into an old blue apron tied around his waist. Throwing the lever forward to start the ride again, he turned his attention to the detective.

'The cards told me you'd be coming,' he said.

'I thought Maria had done that over the telephone,' White shot back.

'The Tarot announced it days before,' Charlie grinned, in a way that was more knowing than friendly.

'I see. Did they tell you anything about your nephew being involved in a murder?'

Charlie turned away from him to tend a little iron brazier, poking around inside until the embers burst into flame again. After a pause, he said, 'I wonder if they'll ever teach you cops how to talk to people?' It came out as more of a hopeful question rather than an admonishment.

'Sorry,' White responded. 'I just met Luisa, some of her directness must've rubbed off on me.' He'd judged the use of the remark and its tone correctly. Charlie gave a softer smile.

'So, you do speak my language after all,' he said. Offering him an upturned beer keg to sit on, the weather-beaten gipsy took to his own rickety old stool and asked, 'What would you like to find out about young Danny?'

White was becoming more at ease with Charlie, who danced between combative and cheerful with the beguiling unpredictability of the fire he watched over. The detective was glad of the warmth coming from the brazier too, a cold breeze was coming off the Atlantic now, extinguishing the heat that had accompanied him throughout the long day. A notion entered his head, so he went with it.

'It's funny,' White said, staring into the flames before looking back at Charlie. 'Every time I've seen a fire today, it's made me think of Beltane.'

'The Gaelic festival?' Charlie said, a small note of surprise in his voice. 'All fire is a gift, but there are special fires that when kindled will have the power to protect, heal, and promote growth. The cards suggested you had Irish blood, but they didn't say it was pagan gipsy.'

'My ancestors came from County Clare and my father told me stories that must've been passed down the generations. That's pretty much all I know about being a gipsy,' White conceded.

'No matter. Blood is blood, and there's a restlessness in you that comes from the need to keep moving. You're just a traveller of a different kind. The cards suggested your inner eye sees Danny as innocent. Is that right?'

It was White's turn to be taken aback, but he bided his time before carefully replying. 'I don't know about any *inner eye*, but my cop gut has some reservations. I need to talk to the kid, but your wife tells me he hasn't turned up. What do you make of it all, Charlie?'

The gipsy rolled a cigarette and lit it. He studied White coolly and said, 'Danny has a strong inner fire. He's a young man of integrity. Sure, youth can be a time for great impetuosity, but murder is the devil's work. There were never any demons big enough in my nephew for him to commit such a crime.'

'In the heat of the moment I've known men do things they never thought themselves capable of,' White responded. 'Who's to say there isn't a devil within large enough to turn us all into killers.'

'You believe that?' Charlie said unhappily. 'I know I could no more kill a man than I could mistreat a horse, and horses, in my opinion, are much finer creatures than we are. I'm sorry your work leads you to doubt humanity, but I'm right about Danny. The truth is in the fire.'

'What does that mean?' White asked, becoming frustrated with searching for answers that seemed to want to remain elusive.

'It means that if you look into the fire for long enough and clear your mind of all other thoughts, the truth will come to you,' Charlie explained. 'Not this fire, though,' he added. 'You need to go looking for another one.'

White got up from his keg and offered the gipsy his hand. It was clear Charlie believed in what he was saying, but the detective remained sceptical. 'Do you know where I can find Danny?' he probed.

'Look for the fire, that's all I know. It's all the cards would tell me other than that justice will be done eventually.'

'By me?'

'That, they didn't reveal, but I wish you luck, Mister White, truly, I do. The taking of life is a terrible business and those who do it must be caught,' Charlie declared.

A shiver ran through the detective, and he had the fleeting sensation something terrible had just happened somewhere in connection with the case. He hoped it didn't have anything to do with the missing Danny.

'Are you okay?' Charlie asked. 'You look like someone just walked across your grave.'

'I'm fine,' White responded, trying to shrug it off. He checked his watch. Nine o'clock. It was time to be moving on. 'So long,' he said to Charlie, leaving the warm joy of the carousel behind him.

White left the fairground with the sense something was aligning, but not wanting to be drawn too far into the world of gipsy superstitions, he focused his mind on the boy. If I was a steady, reliable nineteen-year-old that was used to the stability and comfort of family life, and my sister told me to take a bus and seek sanctuary with good old uncle Charlie, but I didn't want to do that because I thought the police might trace me to their house too easily, what would I do? Where would I run to, he asked himself? His thoughts led him down towards the chilly beach, bathed in the blackness of the night and soothed by the hissing of the waves as they spent themselves against the soft sand. There, he carried on walking and thinking.

He thought about Mona, Amy, and Pops Ross. He pondered O'Malley and his links to the cold criminal Eugene. He considered Grace and her terrible loss that had also sent a shock through the Visconti family. He thought of his ancestors, his departed parents, and the fact he was all alone on the desolate beach. Then he remembered Charlie Kilpatrick's words because a few hundred yards away a small fire was glowing in the distance. Somebody had made camp where tufts of scrubland met the sand. Maybe they'd grown too tired to go home, or perhaps they didn't feel the cold air rolling off the Atlantic as they were partially shielded by an outcrop of rock. White walked towards the flickering light, hoping against the odds it might be his Beltane fire.

With the sound of the waves masking his approach and the flames consuming the camper's attention, White was almost upon the figure when he looked up and registered the detective. He studied the man that had emerged from the shadows with caution. White nodded a greeting, lit a cigarette, and tiredly dropped himself down onto the sand next to the fire. He introduced himself and offered his new companion a smoke that the camper accepted. It felt good to not be alone on the beach anymore. After a few moments of the pair gazing into the firelight in silence, White spoke again.

'I'm glad I found you, Danny. It's good to know you're safe.'

The young man shook his head a little in disbelief and the detective noted a half pint bottle sunk in the sand by his side. 'All this way and still you found me,' Danny mused. 'At first, I thought I'd done pretty good, sitting out here and watching the fire as the night came. Then I just figured one way or another I was only waiting for you to turn up. I guess there are some things you can't outrun.'

'Don't worry,' White replied. 'It's fate, and none of us can do anything about that. It's been one hell of a long day, are you going to offer me some of whatever's in that bottle there?'

'It's whiskey,' Danny said, pulling a face. 'I don't care for it all that much. I only bought it to calm my nerves.'

'Did it work? It usually does the trick for me, part ways at least.'

'Nothing's worked,' Danny confided, passing the bottle over once he'd wiped the sand from its base. 'The ocean helped. I sat here listening to its rhythm. I think the fire's the best though.'

'I'd second that,' White said, taking a swig from the bottle and feeling a burn in his mouth he hadn't expected. 'Jesus, Danny. What is this stuff?'

'Some local hooch, I guess. Sorry, I don't know too much about whiskey. I usually just take a beer with my dad.'

'Well, I've had worse, but not much worse,' White considered. 'Hey, did your uncle Charlie ever tell you about the Beltane fires?'

'You met Charlie?' Danny asked.

'I did. He's quite a character. I liked him.'

'I thought cops were meant to be naturally suspicious of everyone?' Danny said.

'I didn't say I wasn't, just that I liked him. The two things aren't mutually exclusive,' White declared.

Danny stared into the flames again, his brow furrowed in thought at their conversation. After a pause, he asked, 'What's a Beltane fire?'

'It's a Gaelic tradition,' White explained. 'They have these festivals to welcome summer and winter. They're good luck offerings to the spirits. The fires are there to protect the community, their crops, and their cattle. They make a big bonfire in the town and then take the embers from it to light a fire in each of the houses. It symbolises hope or something like that. I'm not quite sure. My father used to embellish the story that his father had passed down to him. My family were Irish immigrants originally.'

'It sounds good,' Danny reflected. I don't think we have anything like that in Italy. It's just the Pope, the Pope, the Pope. There's no room for any of that pagan stuff.'

White laughed and the boy scrutinised him. 'You don't act like a cop,' he said.

'What's a cop meant to act like, exactly?' White asked.

'You know, twirling the night stick, slapping on the cuffs, all that type of thing. I guess that's just the patrolmen though.'

'Well, I used to be one of those too, but I only used my cuffs when I knew I had to. I find it better to treat most folks like they're human beings.'

'Even criminals?'

'Even criminals,' White affirmed. 'You want any of this?' he asked, sloshing the lethal mixture round in the bottle. Danny shook his head. 'Wise move,' the detective surmised.

'Maybe my first one in a little while,' Danny replied. He took a long drag on his cigarette, finished it, and threw the butt into the fire. 'So, what happens now?' he asked.

'I take you back to New York and question you formally. We can't do this out here in front of the fire, much as we'd both prefer that. It has to be official and done right.'

'That's a shame,' Danny said. 'Although, I'm real tired and I've drunk some of that hooch so I probably wouldn't tell it straight. I'd mess up, and this is too important to get muddled over. Do you really think I killed Joseph?'

'I can't answer that,' White stated. 'Just tell the truth when the time comes. Before that, we need to get off this beach. I'm not sleeping here.'

'You're not going to put me in a cell, are you?' Danny said stiffly, suddenly frightened again by the whole nightmarish business.

'I got one headlight on my car,' White said, checking his watch, 'and I don't want to head back home like that and have to throw you in the precinct holding pen overnight. How do you think Charlie and Luisa would take to the idea of us staying with them tonight? It'd be like a house arrest or something,' White considered, making it up as he went along.

'Charlie would be okay with that. It's Luisa that'd decide though,' Danny offered.

'One condition. You don't try to run away in the middle of the night, because I'd hear you and catch you. I never sleep well in strange houses,' White said.

'I won't,' Danny replied. 'I'm scared, but I know I've got to face it sooner or later, and you seem okay.'

'I'm not so bad,' White considered, getting up and carefully using the rocks around the fire to extinguish it. He bent down and picked out two pieces of charred driftwood, rolling them in the sand until they became cooler to handle. 'Here, take one,' he said to Danny. 'It's a Beltane offering. It holds the truth and it'll give you hope, come what may.'

Danny took it and put it in his pocket. Then, he hoisted his bag onto his back and cop and suspect trudged their way back along the beach, the moon lighting their way towards the now dark Asbury Park fair.

White lay on the uncomfortable worn-out sofa in the Kilpatrick's living room listening to the rhythmic snoring in the bedroom above him. If he'd had to bet on whether the noise came from Charlie or Luisa, he'd have gone with the former, Charlie had put a few drinks away by the time the detective returned to the house with Danny in tow. The gipsy had made friendly overtures, but it was Luisa who'd made the boy some tea and shown him up to the spare room she'd already prepared for his arrival. She found White a blanket and assured him there'd be no funny business on Danny's part. She'd had words with the boy and told him not to run. White figured it probably didn't matter. Although illegal, he should've got Danny's story while they'd been on the beach by the fire. An interview room at the precinct would see him clam up or dissemble, the detective was almost sure of it. The moment was gone now, however much he might come to rue it.

Shifting on the sofa, White considered how he'd have to tell O'Malley the truth about his trip out to New Jersey. He'd broken with protocol, chasing off on a lead without informing anyone, let alone taking backup. He'd failed to tell the local police he was here, and although he'd not discussed anything to do with the case, he'd spent a lot of time on his own with Danny, something a defence attorney might bring into question if the boy was ever charged and brought before a jury. Even if that didn't happen, O'Malley would point out to his apprentice every single way he'd ignored the rules. White knew he'd already exasperated his mentor, but however much O'Malley was used to him cutting loose and doing his own thing, this was different.

He smoked another cigarette in the darkness of the strange room and considered his position. In less than a week, he'd lost his wife and daughter, been called to a brutal homicide, all but accused his boss of corruption, and been shot at instinctively saving the life of a gangster who didn't deserve it. Now, here he was, sleeping in the same house as the chief suspect in a murder enquiry after he'd shared whiskey with the boy. What would O'Malley make of that?

Fearing his boss would take him off the case, but knowing it was out of his control now, White settled down under the thin blanket on the sofa that was too small for his frame and finally gave in to the tiredness that had been dogging him for days. Before he slept, he touched the piece of charred wood in his pocket and thought of the Beltane fire. 'What will be, will be,' he whispered, drifting on the warm memory of his long-dead father and the stories he'd passed down.

Chapter Twenty
Blood is Blood

'The Blood of Christ,' intoned the priest, as the Catholics at Evening Mass lined up to receive the final part of their Communion. Footsteps echoed in the cool church as the believers moved forwards, sounding to one man's ears like a faulty metronome marking broken time. Johnny Cain wheezed as he approached the priest. He'd not gone to Reconciliation because he had not yet committed the mortal sin that would stain his soul. He wondered if thinking about killing Eugene as he waited in the queue was a sacrilege against the Body and Blood of Christ. He tried to put it out of his mind, but he could not. He took a sip of the thin wine from the chalice and said 'Amen.' There was no time to go to Confession, he would have to rot in Hell, for there was other business to attend to and he felt the fingers of Death reaching out for him. The sands in the hourglass were running out. Eugene must die tonight.

After the difficult journey to and from the slaughterhouse with the searing heat of the sun showing him no mercy and the burning in his lungs starving him of breath, Johnny had not dared to return home. If Patrick had seen him in that state, his little brother would've gone to pieces and that could do neither of them any good. Instead, he'd stopped at a church where he wasn't known, a kneeling wreck beneath the figure of Christ above the altar, the sweat sliding from his face and dripping down onto the tiled floor. His shaking alerted a kindly priest who asked if he needed assistance, to which Johnny simply replied, 'I'm dying, Father. I have consumption, but I'm not afraid. I believe there is more Hell on Earth than there is *down there*, and I will surely face it before I meet my end.'

The priest had looked startled, but regained his composure to say, 'May God Bless You, my son.' He must have sensed Johnny didn't have the time for theological dialogue, must've seen the mark of death already upon his strained features. So, he'd left the dying man there in his guise of praying when all the while Johnny had been using the cool interior of the church for thinking, formulating his plan of murder in the House of God.

He'd crawled from church to church like a wounded animal, the spots in front of his eyes shifting and joining together like spilt blood. He'd swayed, and people had avoided him, believing he was either a drunk or a madman, but he was just sick. Even so, Johnny knew he must stay alive long enough to kill the man who'd betrayed him. It was the only way left to protect Patrick. His plan was startlingly simple, like all the best ones, and there was no need to consider how to escape. Freedom would come in the form of six bullets: five for Eugene, then the last one in the chamber for himself.

On his way out of Evening Mass, leaning on the last row of pews before the doorway, he was caught in a shaft of sunlight shining through the stained-glass window. It cast his shadow across the aisle like a portent of Death himself. You never shook off the spectre once it was there, Johnny thought, but no matter. It would all be over in a few hours' time. He gathered what strength he had left and exited the church. He was on his way over to see Pat O'Brien, the man he'd entrusted his gun to for safe keeping.

By the time he arrived at the bare-knuckle fighter's house, he was sweating heavily again. Pat's snot nosed son let him in, and he dug around in his pockets for a handkerchief to give the boy before realising they were all sullied with his blood from the coughing fits that had plagued him. While he was fumbling, the boy had used his sleeve, and Johnny wondered how a proud man and fine physical specimen like O'Brien could have such a pathetic son, but then he thought of Patrick and came to the conclusion family blood offered no guarantees.

O'Brien was drying his hands on a dishcloth in the living room. There were soap suds clinging to his brawny arms and his hasty attempt to hide the washing he'd been doing had been unsuccessful. Johnny wondered why he'd bothered; everybody knew O'Brien took on his wife's work when she was ill, but no man would ever dare tease him about it, not unless they were wanting a broken nose and jaw. Johnny nodded to his old comrade, ignoring the worried look on O'Brien's face his appearance had caused.

'Jesus, Johnny. You look like death warmed up. Take a seat, will you,' O'Brien said.

'I'm not staying, Pat,' Cain replied darkly. 'I've just come for my gun.'

O'Brien put down the dishcloth and studied his sick friend. 'It's not for you, Johnny, is it? You know that suicide's a mortal sin.'

Cain laughed roughly, bringing on another fit of coughing that did not abate until O'Brien had slapped his back with some force several times, causing him to spit into the empty fireplace. 'Sorry, Pat,' he said. 'As you can see, I'm a little fragile. I just want the gun for protection. I can't defend myself anymore if I get set upon.'

'Sure, but it pains me to see you like this,' O'Brien said. 'You was never the biggest fella, but you've got the heart of a lion, Johnny. You know I'm always there for you. Anything you need, you only have to say the word.'

'You're a good friend, Pat, and I thank you. I'll have that gun now and be on my way.'

Johnny's expression broached no argument, and although O'Brien knew his excuse for wanting the gun was baloney, he went to fetch it anyway, because he'd also seen something in his friend's eyes he didn't want to be around. Sometimes there were storms threatening a man did well to take heed of, the big Irishman reasoned.

Johnny unwrapped the weapon and checked O'Brien hadn't taken the bullets out of it. All the while his friend looked on uneasily. 'Can you put that thing away now?' he asked. 'I don't want the boy seeing it.'

'Look at where you're living, Pat,' Johnny said coldly. 'He'll have seen worse than this before he was smacked off the tit.'

'Now I know you've got dark business at hand,' O'Brien responded. 'You always get like this when there's trouble brewing.'

'Never you mind that. Just remember, trust no one. If anyone asks, I was never here and you haven't seen me for days, got it?'

'Anyone?' O'Brien questioned, 'Even Eugene?'

Johnny gave a sick laugh that unsettled his friend further still. 'Do me a favour, Pat, will you? Roll me a cigarette.

I'm all fingers and thumbs today. Don't worry,' he added, 'I can still shoot straight enough.'

O'Brien took up his tobacco and papers, making a cigarette that looked lost in his huge hands. 'Are you sure you should be smoking, Johnny?' he said with concern.

'I'm fucked already, Pat. One more nail in the coffin won't make any difference now.'

O'Brien handed him the smoke, shook his head in sorrow, then fished in his trouser pocket to produce some pills. 'Take these at least,' he said. 'You need them more than the wife does.'

Johnny stared at the bottle. 'Aspirin,' he read. 'Thanks, Pat. I'll take some now, but you can keep the rest for your missus.'

'A cop gave them to me,' O'Brien confessed, 'when he came to question me about the murder of that black boy. It's been in the papers today.'

Johnny's eyes darkened. 'I heard about that cop. 'He's the same one who stopped Eugene from getting shot.' He put down the unopened bottle. 'Maybe I won't take those pills after all.' He turned to leave, giving his friend a half-wave. 'So long, Pat.'

'So long, Johnny. You're going to be okay, aren't you?'

Johnny hung in the doorway. 'Of course I am. I've got a lot of big Irish bastards to carry my coffin into the church and bury me in the graveyard when my time comes. If there's one thing us Irish boys know how to do, it's digging. Must've been all that potato farming our forefathers did.'

Leaving O'Brien speechless, Johnny tucked the gun into his waistband and left the sorry house.

When he was outside, he surveyed the gutters running with filth and the half-dressed kids covered in grime; a pack of feral scavengers who were beaten before they'd even begun. He knew he'd been right to strive for more, to break the mould of repression. Eugene had done it too. He'd planned to use these people's savage desperation against the Bowery Boys, pitting the most starved dog against one not quite so hungry. Of course, it was the perfect, brutal solution. After all, the gangster had grown up in the Five Points slums. He understood desperation like a scholar did poetry. It was a godless place, that was for sure. Now, the two great men of ambition it had spawned would die in it on the very same day and in the very same room. While Eugene was watching out for the Bowery Boys, keeping his eye on the known enemy, the Pontius Pilot to his Messiah, Johnny would visit him with the kiss of death, his very own Judas ready to spill the Blood of Christ from his deathly lips.

He'd never been one for writing letters, and now, with the urgency of the murder pressing down on his mind, Johnny found this final one to his brother all the more difficult to compose. At first, he thought he would keep it short, a brief explanation of the action he was taking with enough of a coded message for Patrick to comprehend the truth. The bar he was in felt too stuffy and crowded for him to concentrate on the task, so he'd taken his drink into the back yard, spread the paper, pen, and ink the landlord had given him out on an upturned beer crate, and struggled his way through the last words he would ever give to his brother. When it was finished, Johnny read it through carefully.

Dear Patrick,

I'm sorry to have to do things this way, but it can't be helped. The illness I have has hastened the end of my life, and though we both know that, it is not something I want you to have to witness. Forgive me for not saying goodbye in person. You will understand why I was unable to when you know everything that has come to pass. Then, you can put yourself in my shoes and think about the situation I found myself in. At least this way I might spare you some of the pain and sorrow that is an inevitable part of this whole sorry business.

As you read this, know two important things. Firstly, that I am gone from this world. That is my choice, and you must accept it. Second, whatever shock and grief you feel as you read this letter, you must <u>immediately</u> focus on yourself. Pack a bag, Patrick, and leave New York <u>at once</u>. Any delay will probably cost you your <u>life</u>. Get away and take all the money we have hidden in the house — I've no need of it now. You <u>must</u> do as I tell you. Although you are innocent and unknowing of the actions I have taken, the men I strike against will still most likely come for you. That's what these people are like. You know them yourself.

Eugene has planned to frame me for the murder of that young black boy down by the docks. He needed a scapegoat in case the police found out the truth: that his lieutenant, Gerry Flannagan was the killer. Run, Patrick, and keep this letter safe. If the police ever come to question you, it can be used to give them the real facts.

You have been the finest brother a man could ever wish for. Now, <u>get away</u> and keep up the family fight. Promise to enjoy the life I should've had for me. I will be watching over you and my spirit will forever be at your side. Go now, Patrick, and stay safe.

Your loving brother,

Johnny.

He left the bar and found the kid in the park throwing a worn-out football around with a bunch of other boys. 'Tommy,' he called, and the kid left the game to see what Johnny Cain wanted. He was used to running errands for a small reward, fetching beer or tobacco for the men when they had a meeting, carrying messages between them when they were not near a telephone, and he liked Johnny Cain the best because he always paid well and was never grumpy like some of the other fellas. He secretly wanted to be like Johnny, ahead of the pack and with an endless supply of schemes to keep the wolves of poverty from the door. So, when the top man beckoned him over, he went and made sure he listened carefully. He never wanted to let Mister Cain down.

'See this letter?' Johnny said, showing the kid the envelope. Tommy nodded. 'I want you to deliver it to my brother, Patrick at exactly nine o'clock tonight. He'll be at our home address. Go around the back way and climb over the wall into the yard. If you can't see him in the living room, knock on the trap door to the cellar, then call out who you are and why you're there. It's very important you put this letter into his hand. Don't just leave it there. You must do it at exactly nine o'clock too, not before or after, do you understand? Here,' Johnny said, handing the kid three dollar bills, 'this is for your trouble. Make sure you do exactly as I've told you. Now, repeat it to me what you have to do.'

The kid recited every detail of the job perfectly and Johnny nodded in satisfaction. Noticing how he was looking disbelievingly at the dollar bills in his hand, Johnny added, 'This is the most important job I've ever given you. There are grown men I wouldn't trust to do it, but I trust you, Tommy, so I'm paying you a man's wages. Nine o'clock. Don't let me down. Oh, and don't go reading that letter.'

The kid looked shame faced. 'I can't read, Mister Cain,' he admitted.

'You should learn,' Johnny advised him. 'A man who can't read will be taken advantage of and will end up digging or shifting crates all his life. You're too smart for that, Tommy. Have ambition and get yourself out of this sewer. Promise me you'll learn,' he insisted.

'I promise,' Tommy said solemnly. Then, he tipped his cap and ran back to the football game. As he went, Johnny shouted out to him, 'Tommy, how will you know when it's nearly nine?'

'I'll use the church clock,' the kid yelled back. 'Don't worry, Mister Cain. You can rely on me.'

'That I can,' Johnny said quietly, knowing he trusted the kid as far as he could anyone in this town.

Checking his pocket-watch, Johnny saw it was half-past seven. He'd arranged to meet Eugene at eight on the pretext of discussing when and how to resume the attacks upon the black strike-breakers, as well as to get an update on what to tell the men about the N.Y.P.D.'s investigation into the beatings and murder. Of course, none of that mattered now. He would attend the meeting at Frank's chop house with one goal only. It was his very own Last Supper. Both he and Eugene would be dying on a full stomach. Making sure the gun was still housed securely in the waistband of his trousers, Johnny set off for the rendezvous at a leisurely pace. Death would not rush him tonight.

Eugene sat staring blankly at the menu. He always ordered the steak, but he was looking beyond it for an answer. Today had capped off a terrible week, the business of the black boy's death, Zimmerman becoming truculent and disrespectful, Brother Paul's ultimatum and, of course, the hitman from the Bowery Boys who'd tried and failed to kill him. Then there was this latest thing. He took a drink and considered it all. He needed to regain control, and that meant selling out the idiot brother of the very man he was due to meet tonight.

It would've been better if it wasn't Johnny's sibling he was setting up as the sacrificial lamb, he thought, but Patrick Cain had become a liability at a time when it was the last thing Eugene needed. Johnny Cain. Now, there was another problem. Sometimes the balance of things just got tipped over. That was life. As long as he was still in charge of Five Points, Eugene knew he'd always be able to find some solution or other. After all, he'd dodged the blades and the bullets so far.

The bell above the Chop House door tinkled and Johnny walked slowly into the joint. One thing the gangster had always liked about Cain was his punctuality. You could set your watch by the man, Eugene thought, smiling through cold eyes and thin lips at his dinner guest. As they exchanged greetings and Johnny sat down, Eugene was struck by how ill the man looked, but he wasn't here to dispense pity or charity. There was business to be attended to and Cain's presence was necessary. What a day, indeed, the gangster grinned ruefully to himself.

'You seem in a good mood, considering the attempt on your life,' Johnny observed.

'I survived unscathed, didn't I?' Eugene said, putting the menu down and lacing his fingers together.

'Aren't you worried they'll try it again?' Johnny asked, pulling out his chair with an effort.

'They won't do anything for a little while,' Eugene said confidently. 'They'll know I'm on my guard. Don't worry, Johnny,' he added, 'we're not sitting ducks. I've got Flannagan outside in the car keeping watch and he's armed to the teeth. Anyone tries to come in here tonight is going to get pumped so full of lead, it'll take four men to carry the body out.'

The news didn't seem to settle Cain any, and as they ordered and ate in silence, Eugene noted the man was sweating. 'Why don't you take off your jacket if you're hot?' he said.

'I'm fine,' Johnny lied.

'You sure? It's just you don't look too good to me.'

'It's only a fever.'

'In July?'

'I've been working too hard and worrying about Patrick, that's all,' Johnny said dismissively.

'That brother will be the death of you if you don't watch out. What you need is a vacation,' Eugene suggested.

'I'll rest soon enough when our business is sorted,' Johnny replied.

They carried on eating, but Eugene still felt unsettled by Cain's demeanour. Swallowing the last of his excellent steak, he stated, 'You don't like betraying the workers, do you?'

Johnny looked down at his plate where most of the food remained untouched. 'I'm not finding this as easy as I thought I would, no,' he responded. 'But don't worry. I'll make sure I see the thing through to the very end.'

The plates were taken away and dessert was brought over. Cain faired no better with this sickly course than with the previous one, but Eugene's sweet tooth got the better of him and he had an extra helping of the blueberry cheesecake. After the gangster was finished, he lit a cigar and got down to the plans for resuming the assaults on the black workers. Things needed to look authentic. That was imperative if the business was to play out in his favour. So, he gave his commands, complete with dates and times, remaining patient as Cain badgered him over how the police were conducting their investigations. When it was done, Eugene extinguished his cigar. 'So, we're settled then?' he said. 'The cops will step up the arrest rate, the Dock Company will refuse to give in to any form of wage demands, and the boys will get desperate. That's when you'll concede you've lost and point them in my direction as an alternative source of income.'

'We're settled. I could do with a small advance in the meantime,' Johnny said. 'I need to send Patrick out of town for a while.'

Eugene drank a long draught of his beer and got out his wallet. 'Here's a hundred,' he said, counting out the notes. 'That's coming out of your cut, though.'

'Of course,' Johnny agreed, taking the money.

Eugene looked out the window to where Flannagan sat watching the road. Everything on the street seemed quiet enough. In fact, the whole place had fallen into a hush, with only a couple of fellow diners sitting across the way. Things wound down the later it got, the gangster reasoned, and it was nearly nine. He finished his beer and stood up. 'Think I'll go take a leak,' he announced.

'You go ahead,' Johnny said, looking between the clock on the wall and the shady figure outside in the Rolls Royce.

Eugene walked over to the window and tapped on the glass. Flannagan gave him a thumbs-up and the gangster turned away, heading for the john. Out of the corner of his eye, Johnny saw the lieutenant unfold a newspaper, the urgent headline blaring out between his fingers: *Youth Found Murdered in Brooklyn Dockyard!* The coast was clear, and it spurred him on. There could be no other way now. Getting up from the table, Johnny adjusted the weight of the gun before walking towards the rest room door.

His heart hammered in his chest and his lungs burned with a fury. The sweat was running from his brow so much now, he had to stop to wipe his forehead so it didn't get into his eyes. The hand that held the gun inside his jacket had begun to shake as he reached the toilet. Twenty seconds and it would all be over, he told himself. A hail of bullets and then all the pain would be gone, his torture would be ended, and Patrick would be safe. He cocked the revolver and slowly entered the room.

There was no one at the trough and the place was deathly quiet. Johnny swallowed dryly and then noticed one of the stalls had its door closed. He headed towards it, taking care to mask his footsteps on the tiled floor. Still the silence sat in the room. To wait, or to storm the stall, that was the crucial choice, and Johnny knew he had to make it. His finger curled nervously around the trigger, the sweat under his jacket becoming unbearable. An unwanted thought flashed into his head. To die here, among the filth and urine, when he'd dreamed of so much. Was that really how it had to end? The answer came from behind him.

'Jesus, Johnny. What are you doing?' Eugene asked. 'Drop the gun carefully and turn around. I've got my pistol pointed right at you. I saw you heading out the abattoir earlier. I wondered if you'd overheard my conversation. Calling the meeting and the way you looked tonight gave me my answer.'

Though he was sweating and shaking, unseen by Eugene, Johnny broke into a manic grin. What did it matter that Eugene had a gun pointed at him? He was going to die anyway. He just had to make sure he was faster pulling the trigger, for Patrick's sake, not his own. Even if he failed, Pat should have time to get away. So, it had come down to this, dying in a Wild West duel just like he and Eugene had played at as kids. Johnny gripped the trigger and swung round. Shots echoed across the rest room, and Flannagan ran from the Rolls Royce into the restaurant. A few blocks away, Tommy knocked on the trap door and delivered Johnny's letter into Patrick's hand, just like he'd promised. Over at the church, the clock struck nine times and the carnage was complete.

Chapter Twenty-One
Bad Dream Boy

The pain in White's neck that had first occurred when he'd slept on the camp bed in the ante room at the New York Dock Company offices on the night of Joseph Walker's murder returned with a vengeance courtesy of the Kilpatrick's sofa. Lighting his wake-up cigarette, he massaged the area with his free hand and figured he might make it back to the precinct in one piece if he got his passenger to check for oncoming vehicles every time they hit a junction. He walked quietly to the bathroom because it was very early, took in the dishevelled image in the cabinet mirror, and knew once again O'Malley would delight in telling him he looked like shit. That was if his boss wasn't too busy bawling him out over all the procedural irregularities of his one-man mission to apprehend Danny Visconti. *Whatever will be, will be*, the detective thought, echoing last night's recognition there was nothing could be done about it now. He flushed the toilet and headed for the kitchen. It was six-thirty in the morning.

He was surprised to find Luisa and Danny seated there, talking in low voices that ceased upon his arrival. The aunt poured him more industrial-strength tea, *haven't these people ever heard of coffee?* and White winced as the scalding brew burnt his mouth and brought him fully awake. Never one for morning conversation, he sat in the burgeoning silence, hoping the mischievous Charlie might appear and lighten the mood. Nobody, it seemed, had slept particularly well.

'I've no breakfast to give you but some bread and cheese,' Luisa declared, to no one specific and without a hint of apology in her voice. Danny looked like he couldn't eat a thing and White wanted to leave as soon as they could anyway.

'It's fine,' the two guests said simultaneously, White adding, 'We can stop for something on the way back if we get hungry.' He intended to call O'Malley en-route rather than turning up with a suspect and having to explain himself to the lieutenant in person. He wasn't *that* stupid.

The sun made it up properly before they left, warming White's stricken neck, but Charlie hadn't emerged. Luisa put a steadying hand on Danny's shoulder upon parting, her unfussy style of care displaying just the right amount of affection, White thought, to help the boy without over-emphasising the seriousness of his situation. He was a much quieter Danny than the young man who had discussed whiskey and Beltane fires on the beach the previous evening, but that was to be expected and the detective didn't want talk on the trip home that could point to coercing a suspect. An hour into their journey, White stopped at a roadhouse and bought them two bacon rolls. He ate his in a flash and then called O'Malley at the precinct.

'You're where?' his boss said, struggling to process the early morning advances in the case. 'Wadda ya mean you picked up the Visconti kid? How did you know where he was? What're you doing out near Jersey at this time of the morning?'

White had been dreading this response and the tension travelled through his body, setting off the neck pain again. 'It was the sister, Isabella,' he explained, trying to be methodical and stick to the facts. 'I managed to question her again last night. I made her see reason and she gave up her brother's whereabouts.'

'And you went bowling down to Jersey straight away,' O'Malley surmised, knowing his protégé of old. 'So, was it too late to bring him in last night?'

'Yeah,' White replied, trying to sound casual in the affirmative. 'I should be back within the hour,' he added in an attempt to move the subject on.

'I'm surprised the Jersey police didn't leave me a message, check up on your authority to be operating on their turf.'

'That's the one part of my news you're not going to like,' White said, rubbing his ever-tightening neck.

'Hold on,' O'Malley thought aloud. 'There isn't a message and there should be, unless…Jesus Christ, White! Please tell me you didn't detain him unofficially overnight somewhere.'

'He was at his aunt's place. She was there the whole time. See it as a house arrest.'

'You do realise his lawyer could have us on toast for this?' O'Malley hissed down the line. 'What were you thinking? Why didn't you hand him over to the local cops for the night?'

'Because I thought a night in the Jersey cells might've made him clam up and give us nothing. I know it was a dumb move in one sense,' White said apologetically.

'Just bring him in, no detours this time,' O'Malley snapped back. 'Meantime, I'll fetch the search warrant for his place. At least that part of things can be done right and legal.'

Before White could reply, the receiver at the other end had been slammed back into place, cutting the line dead.

With his ears still ringing from his boss' rebuke, the detective slouched back to the roadhouse table where Danny sat forlornly picking at his food. 'Are you gonna eat that?' White asked impatiently. The boy shook his head. 'Give it here, then,' White commanded, and proceeded to cut into the untouched part of the roll, his frustration fuelling his hunger. With his mouth full, White looked across at the boy. 'No appetite and not saying much, you must be worried about your interview. Like I said last night, tell the truth and everything will be okay. You get much sleep?'

'Not really,' Danny replied. 'Every time I close my eyes, I see...I imagine bad things. Then, when I do sleep, I have bad dreams.'

'Want to tell me about them?' White asked, knowing he was possibly veering into dangerous territory, but still addicted to looking for answers. Danny simply looked away, remaining mute on the subject. Maybe that was for the best, White thought. He'd ask again in the interview room. Finishing the second roll, he downed his coffee and, refusing a refill, ushered the boy back out to the automobile. The sooner they were back in New York, he reasoned, the quicker they could make progress with the case.

Another hot day was broiling up from the sidewalks as White headed across town to the precinct. He'd kept the roof up on the Oldsmobile because somehow it didn't seem right to be driving a suspect around in an open top car, and he certainly didn't want to do anything else to upset O'Malley. So, they arrived without fanfare, White bracing himself for a showdown with the boss and Danny looking like he'd just seen a ghost.

As White was booking the boy into custody, O'Malley came down the hall with a piece of paper in his hand that he waved at the detective. 'Step this way, sergeant,' he said. 'They can get on with processing the kid. I've got something else for you to do.'

White wasn't fooled by O'Malley's business-like manner. He could tell his boss was angry as hell but was keeping Detective Squad matters away from outsiders who might gossip. In a quiet corner, he slapped the search warrant into the detective's hand and said, 'I want you to concentrate on turning over the Visconti house. You've been there, you know it. If the boy did it using one of the tools from his kit, he might've hidden it or even tried cleaning it up and putting it back. Either way, we need to find that murder weapon. Take a good team with you, men you can trust. People in that neighbourhood can get a little spiky about police intrusion. I don't want any more trouble.' The blow was then delivered, but not in the way White had been expecting. 'I'll interview the kid while you're gone. Any confession has to be indisputable, and his lawyer won't be able to claim I coerced the boy.'

There it was, no *sorry for taking over your case*, or *that's how it has to be*, but this was O'Malley. He was a blunt instrument, but you always got a second chance to put things right, so rather than moaning or looking crestfallen, White took charge of the warrant and went to see the Duty Inspector about gathering a team of patrolmen to make sure the search was conducted without a hitch.

The sun had become more threatening by the time White and his convoy hit Red Hook. He'd had to wait while a couple of men he knew and trusted from his days as a beat cop finished their patrol, filling in the time by briefing members of the squad on what they should be looking for. He held back the wagon of patrolmen a block away, its occupants complaining the vehicle would turn into a sweat box while they waited for the search to proceed, but White had other worries on his mind.

He was certain Luisa would have called Maria with the news of Danny's arrest and that if she hadn't already told Frank the truth, he would be summoned from work because of the tragic business. As no one from the family had turned up at the precinct, he thought it more than likely the clan were at home arranging a lawyer and getting all the angrier as they waited to strike back in defence of their only son. He was glad of the hand-picked men he had with him, especially the young and fearless junior detective McKlintock who, like himself, would walk through fire to get the job done.

Sure enough, the door was opened by the powerful figure of Frank, who stood firmly planted on thighs the size of a rhinoceros' and crossed forearms as big as two whole hams. The look on his face told White he'd already received the type of news that would both enrage and age a man. White held the warrant aloft and declared his intention to search the premises in as calm a way as he could. Frank responded with a thick finger jabbed towards the detective's chest.

'If you think I'm gonna let you in here when you've got my boy banged up downtown and you haven't even let him phone his folks…' His threat seemed to lose the capacity for words mid-sentence, such was his anger, and noting the clenched fists, White took half a step back.

'Mr Visconti, Danny was allowed one phone call, so I presume he called his brief. As an adult, he doesn't require parental supervision by law, but we've been treating him with respect. His auntie Luisa should've told you that much.'

'Nobody tells me anything in this goddamn house!' Frank spat. 'It's all I could do to get some of the truth out of them before I go down to the cop shop and get my boy back, otherwise I'd have been there already. Release my boy first, then you can come into my house,' he said, fists still clenched.

'It doesn't work like that,' White replied steadily. 'I understand your anger, but let's not go making things worse than they already are,' he reasoned.

'Worse?' Frank retorted loudly. 'You arrest my boy on suspicion of murder and tell me things could be worse? Get the hell offa my front porch and don't come back until you've got my boy with you!'

'Frank!' pleaded a voice from somewhere behind him in the house. 'Let them in. They've got a warrant.'

Maria's attempt at rationality had come too late. Perhaps it had something to do with Frank sensing he wasn't being told everything, or maybe it was just the hatred he felt for the cops who'd taken his son, but something inside of him snapped and the powerful Italian dockworker took a swing at White, whose reflexes from being a boxer in his youth allowed him to dodge the blow by a fraction. It was close enough that he felt the wind from the punch. McKlintock then tried to bowl the off-balance Frank back into his own hallway so he could restrain him, but the junior detective's attempt only resulted in a wrestling match where it was he who was thrown to the floor. White had seen enough. He blew his whistle loudly, knowing the sound of it would carry to the waiting patrolmen a block away. The noise made Frank Visconti pause.

'You can fight six patrolmen from the N.Y.P.D. if you want to, Frank,' White said tersely. 'I'll wait here and search the house after they've arrested you and thrown you in the wagon. It's too hot for this nonsense and I already had a bitch of a week.'

Seven years as police had taught White to be ready for anything, so when, after an initial slump of his shoulders had suggested compliance, Frank charged at the detective, he side-stepped, stuck out a leg, and watched the docker go crashing onto his own porch. The six patrolmen ran up just in time to see White cuffing the prone figure, his arms up behind his back to prevent any more shenanigans. 'I got some heavy cargo for you to transport,' he said to the cops, and then he turned to Maria. 'Sorry you had to see that, ma'am,' he said genuinely. He checked McKlintock was still in one piece and then began the search of the property.

While keeping his focus sharply on the hunt for clues, and more specifically a murder weapon, White couldn't help being affected by the family home he and his team were trampling through. Everything in the house pointed to them being clean and decent people. Barring Frank's edgy temper, everyone else he'd met from the Visconti clan had been respectable and good. They weren't criminals, and as the search lengthened, White had the sense once again they were looking in the wrong place. That was until one of his men unearthed a hastily buried tool bag from the corner of the back garden. One of the pouches was empty, and from the oily imprint left on the fabric, White thought it had once housed a sizeable wrench. It pointed to a murder weapon discarded and a frightened, botched attempt at a cover-up. His heart sank. He was assuming nothing, but he'd have to call O'Malley with the information. Things were beginning to look even more bleak for young Danny.

'...So, tell me, Danny. How do you feel about your little sister going with a black man?' O'Malley blew smoke at the sick-looking boy as they sat in the interview room that smelt of damp even in this, the height of a balmy New York summer. Processed, left to stew for a while in a cell while somebody found him a lawyer, and now sat in the hot seat with a potential murder charge hanging around his neck, the kid was a predictable mess. He was too frightened to show any of the rage he must have felt on the night he clubbed Joseph Walker to death with the weighty wrench, O'Malley reasoned.

'I only went looking for him to warn him off,' the boy said before his brief could advise him on the merits of watching what he told Detective Squad. 'I never found him,' he continued. 'Look, I was angry at the situation and the shame it would bring upon our family, but when I got to Harlem, I began to lose my nerve. It was the early hours of the morning and the only people out on the streets weren't the kind of guy's you'd want to mess with. I got as far as Lenox Avenue and then I realised I was out of my depth, so I turned around and came home. I figured on going back the next day to try and see him, but I woke up with a fever.'

'That's real convenient, kid, but it don't match what we got on you. Your sister came in here screaming that you murdered her boyfriend. She told us all about you threatening her until she gave up his address. Then you set out like your tail was on fire.

'Let's see how you like my other evidence. Next, we got your boots. On Joseph Walker's body there was a shoe print left that matches the sole of your work boots.'

The lawyer protested such a thing could not be submitted as evidence in a court of law and he was outraged by the suggestion a shoe print could be matched. There was no forensic process recognised for such a thing; it was merely a detective's biased opinion.

'Pipe down,' O'Malley told the brief, shooting him a disgusted look. 'I suppose I made the wrench disappear from your tool bag too. You know, the one you buried in your back yard? Now, tell me, why would you want to go and do that?'

Danny's face fell. His lawyer shifted uncomfortably in his seat. He knew there was no hope of requesting a break to discuss this new evidence.

'I don't know. I been sick,' the boy protested weakly.

'Yeah, sick with the guilt of what you did. It's easy to smack a guy over the head with a wrench when he ain't looking at you. It's easy to stamp on him and hit him when you've got a rage on in the heat of the moment. Less easy to live with murder longer term when you see flashbacks of how you caved his head in every time you close your eyes, eh, kid?'

'I didn't do it! I didn't kill anybody!'

'So, why'd you go on the run, then?' O'Malley challenged him. 'Explain that to me.'

The boy looked like he was going to faint. He'd turned even more pale in the harsh light of the interrogation room. His lawyer protested again, this time more strongly. 'Lieutenant, this is harassment. You can see my client is ill. You have a boot print that could belong to a thousand other men, no murder weapon, and no witnesses. The body was found at the docks around a quarter past twelve in the morning. Do you really believe this boy could have left his house, tracked down the victim, murdered him and taken his body to the docks all in less than an hour?'

The man had struck at O'Malley's own momentary doubt as he'd read through White's meticulous case notes prior to the interview. 'He's a mechanic, so he has access to automobiles. It's not a long drive. Joseph would've still been walking fairly close to the neighbourhood after dropping Isabella off near her home. There was time enough for it all to take place. He had the means, motive, and opportunity. What's more, he doesn't have an alibi. Nobody saw him in Harlem.'

The lawyer countered, 'Officer, you know as well as I do the kind of people who are out on the streets in the middle of the night in Harlem are hardly the type of folks to come running to the police in order to provide a white boy with an alibi. You can't prosecute my client on what you've presented so far, it's all supposition.'

Quietly, the broken boy kept up his mantra of saying: 'I didn't do it...Jesus, I didn't do it.'

O'Malley stubbed out his cigarette and looked straight at Danny. 'Your own sister came and told us you did it. Your own sister! I don't believe your story for one second, kid, and neither does she. How do you suppose a jury's going to like it? Now you go back to your cell and take a while to think that one over. I'll come back later and see if you've got anything else you want to tell me...'

The boy was going to cough, O'Malley thought. He couldn't hold out forever. He was a mess. He knew they had the boots, the missing wrench, his flight from the neighbourhood and Isabella's statement about his fierce anger. Add in his lack of an alibi and things weren't looking good for Danny Visconti and he knew it. He was going to have all day in jail to see just how bad they looked.

White stepped out into the street and lit a cigarette. The search was over, and they'd found nothing more. Still, the tool bag was pretty incriminating evidence, if you assumed it was Danny who'd buried it there and not someone else *wanting* it to be found. The detective wasn't sure of anything anymore. The heat threatened by the mid-morning sun had now fully materialised in the early afternoon and squinting his eyes through the haze wobbling the air above the asphalt, he saw two figures had emerged who were sitting on the front porch opposite the Visconti house. One, he recognised as Isabella, the other was a boy around her own age, the one who'd been lazily observing Maria as she gardened on his previous visit. The boy looked relaxed enough, his legs stretched out so his feet were resting on the porch's rail, but unsurprisingly, Isabella seemed more tense. The boy made a move to comfort her, but she edged away. Understandable, thought White, when you'd just lost your boyfriend to a murderer and both your brother and father had been arrested. McKlintock interrupted his moment of musing.

'Sure is hot as hell today. I guess we're all done here, sir,' he said.

White liked both the man's easiness and unfawning respect for his rank. 'We're done. Good work finding that tool bag.'

'I just noticed a patch of earth that looked slightly different. I didn't have to dig too far down to discover why,' the junior detective shrugged. 'My theory is he panicked, hid it in the dark, and didn't realise how shallow the burial was.'

'Maybe,' White said. 'It's a shame we didn't track down the missing wrench, but you can't have everything. How are your ribs?'

'They'll be okay,' McKlintock said, wincing at the reminder of his injury. 'I think that guy was made of iron or something.'

'Thanks for the backup, anyhow,' White replied. 'Let's go. No one ever solved anything standing around on the street,' he said, looking back over at Isabella and the boy, frowning in the light that dazzled his eyes. McKlintock followed in silence.

White climbed the precinct steps slowly. The heat of the day had exhausted him after the sleepless night spent on the Kilpatrick's couch, but he also didn't want to face what O'Malley had drawn out of Danny in his interview. Ever since the callout to the dead body at the docks on the same night Mona had announced she was leaving him; the detective had believed finding Joseph's killer would somehow help him through a difficult time and bring a light into the darkness.

Now, with Danny in the frame for the murder, all it harboured was more sorrow and destruction of family life. One or two things still nagged at his mind, but the weight of evidence was becoming ever heavier. They had everything apart from the weapon and a confession, perhaps only the weapon was missing if O'Malley had already pushed Danny into an admission of guilt. Speak of the devil, White thought, spying his boss at the end of the hall.

'You came up trumps with the search, then. No murder weapon, but that buried tool bag is the next best thing. You shoulda seen the kid's face when I threw that at him,' O'Malley grinned.

'No confession yet?' White asked tentatively.

'He'll cough to it. I'm letting him stew in the cells overnight. It'll give him plenty of time to think about the overwhelming evidence we got against him. Tomorrow morning, he'll talk, and we can inform the victim's family. You did well tracking him down to that aunt in Jersey. It's wrapped things up a lot quicker.'

White stared down at the floor. 'What?' O'Malley demanded. 'Don't tell me you think he might still be innocent. Look at the evidence, for chrissakes!'

'The timeframe for Danny leaving the house, finding Joseph, killing him and hiding his body at the docks is so tight, but it's more than that,' White said awkwardly, knowing he was angering his boss with a line of argument that was on increasingly shaky ground. 'You tend to get a *feel* for killers. There's always something there if you look hard enough that allows you to see how a person could've been capable of murder. I still can't see that in Danny.'

'I've had plenty of murderers who took me by surprise. That little old landlady who poisoned her tenant, not to mention the eminent lawyer who thought he could get away with killing his business partner by setting up a gangster the man had sent down. Remember them?' O'Malley asked. Without waiting for an answer, he continued his lecture. 'Sometimes evil hides itself well, that's why you have to use all your skill and guile as a detective to find the clues and examine the evidence. Also, don't keep referring to suspects by their first name, it makes it harder to turn the screw on them when the time comes, okay?'

Personal trauma, broken sleep, and the relentless heat were all adding to the intensity of the case, so much so

White found he could no longer argue, at least not today. There were too many things going around in his head for him to see clearly and effectively spar with O'Malley. So, he nodded, then took his unshaven and dishevelled self back towards the apartment he didn't want to be in, figuring while a bath wouldn't make things much better, it also couldn't make them any worse. He'd ruled out true rest until the case was over, and even then, he feared his mind would remain troubled. As he made his way down the hall to the exit, White knew something had to give. The pressure was too much for something not to get broken. He just hoped it wouldn't be him.

Chapter Twenty-Two
An Unquiet Mind

Wired on the events of a day where he hadn't stopped moving, White left the precinct and hit the streets, feeling an electricity in the air. The heat of the day was being dispersed by a fanning wind and dark clouds were beginning to mass in the distance. A storm was coming to change the atmosphere, that much was certain. Everything was turning over in his mind. Less than thirty-six hours ago he'd had nothing, then the whirlwind that was Isabella opened the case right up. Had he stood back enough from it, or did he jump straight on the ride because it stopped him thinking about Mona and allowed him to give Grace some hope?

The timings still bothered him. Danny most likely had to get a vehicle, find Joseph, murder him, and dump the body at the docks all in less than forty-five minutes realistically. Also, why choose a dock he didn't know? His father worked out of a different yard and in all the chaos of the killing, wouldn't the murderer want the comfort of somewhere he knew as a child? Could Danny, in all his passion and fury, really be so calculated as to leave the body in a place that would suggest an Irish docker with an industrial grudge as the killer, or was it simply opportunistic? White just didn't know.

The family seemed to be good people, and from the conversation at the beach coupled with what his employer had said, Danny appeared sensible, steady, and mature. He could understand the boy storming off into the night to warn off the lover who'd unwittingly endangered Isabella. Who wouldn't want to protect their little sister in those circumstances? As for Danny's violence towards the sibling he'd never previously laid a finger on, White knew he'd observed no marks of bruising on Isabella's wrists or arms, so Danny definitely hadn't grabbed her that hard. The girl was in shock, that would explain the amplification of her fear.

That he'd headed out to Harlem, was unaccounted for during the hours surrounding the murder, and had run away when faced with arrest did not, in White's mind, mean the boy was automatically guilty. He asked himself, was it his gut, the gipsy Charlie and his tarot cards, or something else that was preventing him from going down the obvious road that Danny was guilty of Joseph's murder, but he had no answer, and the buried tool bag with the missing wrench worried him. That, and the sense Danny had been haunted by something ever since that fateful night. Unless anything else turned up, O'Malley would pursue his confession, and that was where fate seemed to be taking things, but right now, White couldn't think of what he could do to prevent it happening.

The pit of his stomach churned as he reached the apartment and he realised he'd become a man who could no longer face his own home. Feeling disgusting in every sense, he resolved to take the bath he'd promised himself and then change his fusty clothes. The empty space greeted him with a silence that was only punctuated by the ghost of Amy's laughter, so he shut himself in the bathroom and quickly went about the practicalities of getting himself washed. The soak in the tub was functional rather than relaxing, his mind unable to switch off from the demons that continued to torment him. A shave and a fresh set of clothes did nothing to improve his mood. He paced around the space unable to settle for more than a few seconds in any one spot. Noting the Henry Burr record sitting just where he'd left it on the gramophone, he thought about listening to music in an attempt to calm his fraying nerves, but he couldn't find anything that appealed from his limited collection. He gave up, put on his shoes, and headed back out into the night.

The air had become dense, the wind of earlier having dropped to nothing. The sky was pressing down on the city and seemed only to be held at bay by the tops of the new skyscrapers that had sprung up everywhere in the rapid development of recent years. White thought of his father and the fatal fall, and of another dropping body from the Woolworth Building that had begun his detective career and drawn him further away from Mona. Everything was beating against his brain right now. He could find no peace. The world wanted to consume him and suck him into a hellish pit of misery he knew he must fight to stay out of. Still the storm pressed down upon him.

As if to echo his discontent, thunder rumbled overhead. Subconsciously, his feet were taking him towards the home of Martha Marsh. He checked his watch. It was a little late to be calling unannounced, but then that was how they seemed to work and he wanted to see her. Lightning lit up the sky and White took it as some kind of holy reprimand, but given the events of the past few days, he had even less faith than previously, when the job had eroded it through a constant presentation of the dark side of humanity. He continued on his sinful path. The clouds broke and the rain pelted him as a penance. In his shirt sleeves he was defenceless against the onslaught. It felt about par for the course right then.

He arrived at Martha's door pathetically soaked through, his trousers clinging to his legs and his shoes squelching with every step. She eyed him with amusement. 'Come in,' she said. 'You're making a pond on my front step.' Incongruously, the tough detective who'd fought a rabid longshoreman at least fifty pounds his superior earlier that day, now ended up sat in a lady's dressing gown at the complete mercy of his host. His mind was full of scorpions and from out of nowhere, or at least from a place that he'd tried hard to bury, he found himself talking about the different and complicated relationships he'd witnessed over the past few days, spewing forth the torments of the people he'd met since Mona had changed his world.

'To rat on your own brother, when you've been around him and looked up to him for your whole lifetime, because of losing someone who you only met four or five months ago, someone who you knew you could never really be with. It's incredible.'

'That's romantic love for you,' Martha offered.

White sipped his warming whiskey and chuckled because laughter seemed the only way to stay anywhere close to sanity. 'You know Du Bois has a massive soft spot for Grace, but he's an honourable married man so he has to keep it hid. She's got a husband away fighting in the war and a boy lost to a murder. Not the best circumstances for any moral guy to try and make his move in, but with Du Bois I know it's only an unwanted ripple in his emotional lake. I believe he's a good man that's faithful to his wife.'

'I'm glad you see it like that,' Martha said. 'It's good he's helping with her grief out of the kindness of his heart, just like you did for me.'

'Yeah,' he replied, winking, letting loose the devil in him just for a moment. 'It'll all be okay, I guess. Look how we turned out.'

Stung a little by the cheek of his response and how his visits were toying with her heart, Martha countered, 'Hmmm. If you mean that you disappeared for several years back to your wife and only looked me up when she...' Immediately regretting the outburst, she apologised. 'Sorry. I didn't mean to be so cruel.'

'It's okay,' he said, feeling instantly chastened and annoyed with himself. 'Maybe I deserved it. I feel like the king of making stupid decisions at the moment. The other day, right in the middle of my marriage going down the tubes, my big mouth accused O'Malley of corruption. What a smart guy I am.'

Martha shuffled in her seat and eyed him curiously. He was in a strange mood tonight, that was for sure. Playing the subtle detective herself, she gently asked: 'What made your marriage fail?'

White lit a cigarette and exhaled smoke into the room. He looked into her lovely eyes and considered whether he really wanted to be going down this road tonight. Somehow, he felt like opening up. She made him want to tell her everything.

'How far back do you want me to go?' he asked.

'Well, I told you I've been lonely, and I always like to hear you talk, so, why don't you start at the beginning and take me up to the present day. I'm sure you've been through it all in your head a thousand times already, so you'll know it pretty well.'

The permission to air his whole sorry history was somehow all White required to empty the personal contents of his head. He and Martha had shared such intimate secrets before, so any hesitation he had about giving her his life story was overruled by his need to tell it.

'Steady family life went out the window for me at a very early age,' he began. 'I became an orphan when I was just thirteen. My father died in a construction accident shortly after my tenth birthday, and my mother, who was always a delicate soul, succumbed to typhoid three years later. I went off the rails. I was angry at the world and carried a hurt most people could never know, let alone understand. Some of it's still there in me, I guess. I was housed by the nuns for a while. I had an aunt and uncle, but they couldn't deal with me, so the juvenile court put me in the care of the sisters. I tried to be good, but maybe I always knew I wouldn't last there, that I didn't belong in holy houses.'

Martha smiled at the comment despite the sympathy she was feeling for his tale of tragedy.

'Yeah, I don't think I'd have ever made it as a priest,' he humorously reflected. 'They must have reached the same conclusion because they put me on the orphan train heading out to Omaha. I got housed with a husband and wife who couldn't have children of their own. They were good to me. They were never going to take the place of my real parents, but they understood that and showed me a way of life that settled me down for a while. When I got in trouble again, through no fault of my own this time, they took my side. So did the local sheriff, much to my surprise. Up until then I saw the law as something there only to punish me, but big Bill Masters changed all that. He was the reason I decided I wanted to be a cop, that and the growing feeling I wanted to do right by people, to fight the battles that needed to be won for those who couldn't do it for themselves.

'It was a twisted logic, I see that now, but being a cop fits me well. There's something in it I need. As for my relationship with Mona, I just don't know. We drifted apart almost as soon as we were married and having a child didn't help us in the way we thought it might. We never really talked, that was part of the problem. All we seemed to be able to do was argue. I had my job, I liked it, and I felt I was doing important work, filling the gaps in my soul that had needed plugging for a long time. Mona saw it as having a husband who was never really there for her, a man who was married to his career, not his wife. I can't really disagree with that viewpoint. It's ironic, I know, that as a man who wants to right all the wrongs he can, I couldn't prevent the breakup of my own marriage. Now, I've lost my wife and child, my personal life's a mess, and it's all I can do to try and solve the case I'm working on. A kid's about to go down for a murder and I just don't know whether he did it or not. If my head was right, I'd know, I'm sure I would. There's a storm raging inside of me, and it won't let up. It's not giving me the peace to see clearly.'

'My poor little orphan,' Martha remarked tenderly. 'You're a good man. You've got to stop beating yourself up like this.' Her warmth snagged on his tired heart.

'It's funny,' he continued. 'I try to do my best all round and first my marriage and now maybe even my career gets burned to the ground because I work too hard to see the truth. Sorry, I shouldn't be burdening you with these things. It isn't appropriate.'

She smiled and countered, 'No, not appropriate at all. The heroic cop feeling sorry for himself and sat there wearing my old robe.'

He wanted to respond, but the echo of their words distracted him. *Not appropriate*...the phrase triggered something in his mind that had been lost deep in his subconscious. It was an image, a feeling he'd had, but it had been swallowed up in the pandemonium of the day. Martha relaxed a little and rested her feet up on the coffee table. That was it! The boy! The one who had been comforting Isabella on his front porch. There was something inappropriate in the way he was fawning over her in the wake of Joseph's death. Then he'd been almost mocking in his composure as he watched the cops struggling with the heat of the day and the difficulty of the search.

Sitting there with his feet up, for God's sakes; that smug expression on his face. Yet it wasn't his face that White's subconscious had registered in all the mayhem of the scene at the Visconti house. Sitting with his feet up...the soles of his boots displayed to the police. White had been obsessing over patterns for days, but out at Red Hook he'd been distracted. Now, sitting there in Martha's chair, he saw it clearly. The soles of the young man's boots were captured in his mind...and he could swear they matched the imprints he'd found on Joseph Walker's clothes!

Through all his torment, the doubts about the case and the guilt he felt over visiting Martha again, White had found clarity in the eye of the storm. A boy fawning over Isabella; a boy who liked to watch and was observant; a boy whose reactions were inappropriate. A strange and unnerving boy. Sitting in a woman's dressing gown, damp and morally conflicted, White had the damnedest feeling he might've just solved all the things that had been bugging him about the murder. He kissed Martha on the cheek.

'What was that for?' she asked. 'You look like a kid who just found out the circus is coming to town. You really are in an odd mood tonight.'

'It's the case,' he beamed, 'It's you and being able to talk. You've unlocked everything for me. I couldn't see it, but you've opened my eyes. I've just got a lead. It was something you said and did. Look, I won't explain it now because if I'm wrong it'll look foolish. But if I'm right…'

'Then promise you'll tell me,' Martha implored him. She felt happy to have given him some help, even if she didn't understand how. It was good to have the real Dominic back.

'I promise,' he said sincerely.

In the morning, he would go and quiz Isabella about her neighbour, but right now he had a different kind of puzzle to solve. He had no dry clothes to go home in and it was getting very late, but his companion didn't seem to mind. In fact, she seemed to like the situation. He drank a slug of his whiskey. Everything was falling into place, and he was feeling jubilant, but what the hell was he to do about Martha?

He awoke early the next day to find his clothes had dried out enough for him to put them on. The crick in his neck from sleeping on David Young's camp bed a few nights ago, further exacerbated by his spell in the Kilpatrick house, had returned with a vengeance, this time courtesy of Martha's sofa. They had come close, but she was a creature of moral virtue and after the story about his parents and mention of his estranged wife, White was mindful of doing the right thing, regardless of the desire he felt. In the cold light of day, he was glad about his abstinence; it meant he had no trouble facing himself in Martha's bathroom mirror as he straightened his hair and fixed up his tie. Better still, he didn't feel quite so lonely anymore. He had a friend who'd helped him crack the case.

Back in the emptiness of his own apartment, he was relieved there was no time to drink in the ghosts of the place. After a quick breakfast made from whatever he could find in the kitchen, he made his way over to see Isabella. He stopped for a second and thought. Did he really want to be heading for another showdown with Frank Visconti? The longshoreman was sure to have been released by now, White insisting that he and McKlintock didn't want to press any charges. Leafing through his notebook, he found the detail he needed. Isabella was studying to be a stenographer and he'd written down the name of the college she attended. He knew it well because Mona had once studied there too and had pointed it out to him in passing. Mona, White thought, but there was no time for that lament now. He would catch Isabella when she got a break in her class.

It was a bright and humid day, with the sun soaking the moisture of last night's deluge up from the earth to thicken the air. White arrived at the college by mid-morning and fortuitously spotted Isabella sitting alone on the lawn of the campus with a book in her hands, so he wandered over to join her. She looked apprehensive at his presence. 'I had to come and see you,' he explained defensively. 'I don't think your brother killed Joseph.' She looked relieved by this because all along she hadn't wanted it to be true. 'That's not the only reason why I'm here,' he added. 'Tell me about that boy I saw you with yesterday.'

'Benny?' she asked, confused. White waited for her to continue. 'He's just my neighbour. I work nights at his father's restaurant. Sometimes he helps out in the kitchen if we have a lot of bookings. I'm not really sure what else he does. He's a bit of an oddity.'

White considered this information. Non-slip boots for working in a kitchen, he thought. 'Odd in what way?' he questioned.

'We knew him from school, Danny and me. He never really made any friends. He's awkward, you know. He used to talk to himself in the schoolyard. I kinda felt sorry for him. He was bright. He got all top grades, but that just made people dislike him even more. Danny said I shouldn't encourage him. He didn't like me inviting him over to the house, but we work together and he's not too bad when you get to know him a little.'

'He's been over to your house recently?' White probed, an idea beginning to gather momentum in his mind.

'Several times,' she admitted. 'He came over that last night when Joseph and I were out at the park. Danny tolerated him for a while and then sent him on home.'

White hid his growing elation and continued. 'He seemed very interested in you when I saw him on the front porch, if you know what I mean?'

Isabella blushed. 'He's a little too forward sometimes, but he soon behaves himself when I tell him off.'

'Sure he does,' White said quietly, an even greater understanding forming in his head. 'Say, what's the name of that restaurant you work in? I could do with a good Italian meal.'

'Antolini's. It's over on 23rd and 1st. You should have the cannelloni, it's the best thing on the menu. So, will you be releasing Danny today?'

He smiled at her. 'I'm sure we will. Thanks for the tip. I'd better be going now. So long, kid.'

She just didn't see it, White thought as he strode across the campus. She was too innocent to realise the darkness within Benny Antolini. The social outcast was on the outside looking in all his life. What if he'd seen his beloved Isabella being dropped off by Joseph one night? What if he knew she was with her lover when he'd called over on the night of the murder? A well-concealed fury would have begun burning inside of him as he sat in Danny's room knowing he wasn't wanted by either of them. Then a moment's distraction and he snatched the wrench from the tool bag and hid it about his person. He went home and waited, but then he got restless. Prowling the streets, he spotted Isabella saying goodnight to her boyfriend. He hung back in the shadows of the night and then followed the poor unsuspecting Joseph, creeping up behind him on a quiet cut through near the docks...

Back at the precinct, White raced up to O'Malley's office. Bursting through its flimsy door without knocking, the exuberant detective exclaimed, 'I got him, boss! I've worked out who really killed Joseph.'

O'Malley looked tired and frustrated. 'This'd better be good,' he snarled. 'I've been working on that kid all morning and he still won't confess. Okay, start from the beginning and tell me everything.'

His explanation accepted; White made a visit to Danny's cell. The teenager looked dreadful, and the detective bet he hadn't gotten a wink of sleep. Leaning on the doorpost, White studied the kid and then spoke. 'I got just one more question for you, Danny boy. If you answer it really well then you might get out of here in the next few hours. It's real simple but think carefully. I want you to tell me exactly what Benny Antolini was wearing on the night he came over to your house, the night you went out later looking for Joseph Walker.'

The boy's face flooded with a relief he could not hide. 'So, you know the truth,' he said, shaking with the deliverance. 'I don't have to keep it hidden anymore.'

Chapter Twenty-Three
Just Desserts

Patrick Cain didn't flee New York. Time lost all meaning for him as he stood by the cellar trap door with the crumpled letter clutched in his trembling hand. He tried to read it again through a blur of tears, but the writing dissolved, and the dawning of what Johnny had decided upon caused another wave of nausea so he was sick once more in the yard. This second bout of vomiting put something other than the pure shock of the letter into his head, and with a greater clarity, he began to think back over its contents.

Johnny said Eugene was going to frame him for the murder of the black boy down at the docks, but the gangster knew it was he, Patrick who had committed a violent crime and needed his protection. Steadying himself against the wall of the house, he realised Eugene had been set to betray him, and Johnny had somehow found out. That was why he'd gone off to kill the gangster, to stop his brother being thrown to the wolves.

The letter talked of the consumption and of Johnny not wanting a lingering death that would be witnessed by his nearest and dearest. Patrick figured Johnny had decided on it being a suicide mission either because he didn't think he'd make it out alive after killing Eugene, or felt he'd grown too weak to run from Flannagan's inevitable retribution. It didn't necessarily have to be that way though, and Patrick became desperate in his moment of understanding to try and halt the death of his big brother.

Think, Patrick, think! Where would Johnny go to murder Eugene? Not to the abattoir, that would be closed for the night, and if he'd wanted his sibling to run as soon as possible, he'd have gotten the letter delivered earlier. No, the hit had to be tonight, and close to when the kid had brought the instruction for him to leave town immediately, otherwise Johnny would know he'd try and stop him. That meant a rendezvous out of hours. Although it could be anywhere, he felt like Eugene's own home might be his best bet, if he wasn't too late already. It would be somewhere the gangster felt safe, a place where meeting his co-conspirator in the dock strike would see him lower his guard. Johnny was a clever man; he'd have thought all this through. The planning, the layout of the letter to let Patrick off the hook and frame Flannagan instead, every part of the operation had been meticulously arranged. The killing had to be at Eugene's house, he was sure of it now.

Quickly, he went down into the cellar, rummaged in the hiding place for his revolver, and headed out determinedly for the Five Points slum. He had to do everything he could to save Johnny. There would be no more cowering or running. It was time to make a stand.

Eugene sat stunned on the floor of the Chop House rest room. His lieutenant burst through the door, gun in hand, and pulled up short, taking in the bloodshed before his eyes and relieved his boss was still alive. Johnny Cain lay dead in a heap, his revolver resting a yard from his outstretched hand. There was blood coming from his mouth and much more from his chest and stomach where the gangster's bullets had torn through him. Eugene's shirt was also stained, but as he pulled it up to inspect the damage, it became clear the bullet Cain had fired had mercifully barely grazed him.

Immediately, he began to think about the danger of his position in the wake of the event. 'We've got to get that body away from here,' he ordered. 'I'm in no fit state to carry it, and I need you to help me. So, call Nevin and Whelan. Tell them to get here fast with something to conceal a corpse in. They can drive it up to the abattoir and make it so there's no trace of Johnny Cain for anyone to find.' Then, he thought of another potential hazard. 'The restaurant owner! Jesus! Get out there to him now and make sure he isn't calling the cops. If he's not thinking straight, he might've panicked and picked up the phone to the N.Y.P.D. Dammit! There were two other people eating when I came in here. Get out there and see where they've gone. I need this sorting out now! No one must talk. I can't go down for murder.'

Flannagan cleared his head and raced out into the dining area. The two diners had flown, but the owner was standing by the counter, rooted to the spot and terrified about what had just happened in his rest room. 'You didn't call nobody?' Flannagan asked him through hooded eyes. The man shook his head nervously. 'Okay, good,' Flannagan said. 'A guy got shot in there, but I'm gonna call some fellas to handle the situation. What I want you to do is forget anything ever happened in here tonight. My boss never came, you never saw him here. Now, get me some of that cake while I phone the boys, I'm starving.'

Eugene struggled to his feet. The wound wasn't so bad, but he'd need a doctor. There was no way he was going to a hospital, no one must discover he'd been in a shoot-out and killed a man. Flannagan could be relied upon to organize what he'd instructed. He'd get the lieutenant to call the quack and then drive him back home to get the injury seen to. His nerves were beginning to ease, the pain was focusing his mind. Looking down on Cain's prone body as it bled out over the tiled floor, his good fortune dawned on him in the wake of the rapid events that evening. He'd survived another attempt on his life, it could've easily been him lying there dead in a pool of blood. Through the sweat, and smarting from the bullet wound in his side, Eugene managed a sick laugh. Two attempts upon his life and neither had been successful. He felt blessed. Somebody *up there* must like him!

The stately Rolls Royce stood out like an ivory ghost in the quickening dark falling on the Five Points wasteland. It stood incongruous to its poor surroundings amidst the grime and poverty that formed a den of protection around its most famous resident. Out of respect more than fear, none of the feral scavengers in the neighbourhood had ever so much as laid a finger upon the glittering automobile. That recognition of what Eugene stood for, and what he'd done for the local community, meant Patrick couldn't linger for long in the shadows across from his house. Another less ostentatious vehicle sat behind the Rolls, suggesting Eugene had a visitor. Good, thought Patrick. That means he's still alive and occupied. Maybe Johnny was in there too, having to bide his time until the potential witness left. There was no light coming from the front of the property, so Patrick took his loaded gun round the back where a threatening alleyway gave access to the yard.

The houses were identical to his and Johnny's own, so Patrick knew the wooden gate would most likely be bolted against intruders, especially after the recent attempt on Eugene's life. He tried it, but it wouldn't yield, and to break it down would cause far too much noise. He'd have to scale the wall, leaving himself vulnerable to attack as he did so, but there was no other way and if Johnny was inside, he had to save him before it was too late. Scrambling up the wall, he hoisted himself to lay atop of it. There, from his vantage point, he could see Eugene with his back to the window, stripped to the waist with a doctor tending to an injury on his torso. Patrick processed this. There'd been trouble, but it didn't necessarily mean…

As he shifted in discomfort on top of the wall, the gun slipped from his waistband and clattered into the yard below. The noise alerted the men in the room, who looked his way and watched as he dropped down to try and retrieve it. As he reached for the weapon, the back door opened and Flannagan, pointing a pistol at his head, calmly said, 'Reach any further for that gun and you're a dead man. Stand up slowly and come into the house.'

Patrick did as he was bid.

'Thanks, Doc. That'll be everything,' Eugene said pointedly as Patrick was led through the kitchen by the armed Flannagan.

Keen to be out of the house, the physician hastily gathered up his things into his doctor's bag and without looking up said, 'I'll call around in three days to change the dressing and check there's no infection.'

'Better to let me give you a time to come,' Eugene stated. 'The next few days could be busy.'

'As you wish,' the doctor replied. 'I'll see myself out.'

When the front door was closed and the sound of the doctor's car faded away, Flannagan chivvied his prisoner into the room. Eugene had put on a clean shirt and was sitting with a whiskey by his side. The mastiff, Daisy was gently trying to sniff at his covered-up wound. 'Well, if it isn't Cain the Younger. What can I do for you, Patrick?' he asked.

'Where's my brother?'

Eugene gave an elaborate shrug, forgetting how the injury had affected his movement and trying to hide the pain in his side as he did so. 'How should I know? I haven't seen Johnny since a couple of days ago when we had a meeting up at the slaughterhouse. He didn't look well.'

'He told me he was going to see you tonight,' Patrick lied.

'That's news to me,' Eugene coolly replied. Then, changing his tone, 'You're starting to get me worried, Pat. I need Johnny to keep those workers of his in check. They listen to him. I can't afford for him to go missing, not now of all times.' Faking a frown, he added, 'Why were you climbing over my back wall? Couldn't you have used the front door like everyone else?'

'You know what's going on,' Patrick said angrily. 'There was a deal in place to protect me, but Johnny found out you were going to betray us. That's why he was coming to see you.'

Eugene considered this. 'Explain why I'd want to do that when I need your brother's help? This is fantasy, Patrick.'

'He told me you needed a scapegoat for the murder of that boy, the black kid down by the docks. Flannagan did it, but you couldn't afford for him to go down for it.' Patrick knew he was signing his own death warrant, but he was more bothered about getting to the truth of what had happened to his brother. He kept looking at the place on Eugene's body where he'd seen the wound.

Had Johnny caused that, he wondered? Was it part of a fight his brother was too weak to win?

His outburst caused the gangster to change direction. 'Patrick, what're you talking about? You know it was *you* who killed that boy. Johnny told me so himself.'

'No!' Patrick exclaimed. 'It wasn't a boy. I never set eyes on no kid. I told Johnny; it was some old black tramp roaming around near where we'd been fighting the strike-breakers. The police came on the scene before we had any proper chance of retribution. Those bastards had taken our jobs and hadn't been made to pay for it. I was so full of rage I barely knew what I was doing until I saw the old hobo at my feet and felt my boots kicking him in a fury. That's when I came to my senses and stopped. I thought I'd killed him, but I don't even know that for sure. The papers never bother to report dead tramps; nobody cares about them.'

'Well, if that's true, why would you need protecting from anything?' Eugene reasoned, dismissing the story.

'Because I had no alibi!' Patrick shouted. 'I was less than a mile away from where that boy was found. I had grazes on my knuckles and blood on my clothes. I'd been seen beating the strike-breakers too. I've already got a criminal record for assault. The police would've all too happily charged me with murder. That's life in prison for setting on a tramp, so I needed help and Johnny came to you.'

Something shifted in Eugene's mind, and he saw how he'd misunderstood Johnny Cain's plea. With all the other problems in his head, he'd not wanted the details surrounding the frightened request to sort the matter out and had naturally assumed Patrick had murdered the boy. Now, he realised Johnny had come to him with a similar, but unconnected issue. The mix up had been nobody's fault, but it had done untold damage. He hadn't even wanted to help the Cain brothers out, but he'd needed Johnny onside and didn't want to rock the boat at a crucial time. He couldn't help but see the irony of the misunderstanding. Johnny had tried to kill him and ended up dead for nothing. Now, Patrick knew too much, and he would have to be dealt with too.

'Okay,' Eugene said. 'As we're laying our cards on the table, you might as well know what happened tonight. Sit down, Patrick.'

Tentatively, Patrick pulled out a chair and sat. The signal Eugene gave was only a small one, but Flannagan understood and had been expecting it anyway. He stood behind the remaining Cain brother in readiness to perform his task.

'I did, regrettably, get put in a situation where some very difficult people to deal with were demanding your head. I looked out the window just after that meeting had taken place and I saw your brother hobbling away down the lane. It was a hot day, the window in the office had been open, and I worried he might have overheard the conversation. I still hadn't decided what to do about it all when Johnny came to see me at the Chop House. When I went to the rest room, he followed me in with a gun. He made my mind up for me, that's the truth.'

'You killed Johnny?' Patrick said, the words sounding strange as they left his mouth.

'He shot me. You've seen the wound. He was going to finish me off. I had no choice,' Eugene said flatly.

'You killed Johnny,' Patrick repeated quietly, more as a statement of understanding this time.

'Yes,' said Eugene.

Patrick made to get up and lunge across the table at Eugene. He wanted to strangle his brother's murderer. He never made it out of the chair. Flannagan clubbed him on the back of the head with the butt of his pistol and laid him out cold. He was about to finish the job, but Eugene raised a hand.

'Not here,' he commanded. 'I don't want a mess in my house. We'll load him into the boot of the Rolls, take him up to the slaughterhouse, shoot him dead, and the guys can dispose of him the same way they're doing with his brother. That way the Cain brothers can get to be together. I'm sure they'd like that,' he grinned sickly.

They decided to wait a while until it was fully dark outside. Eugene was in no hurry, he wanted to finish his whiskey and if Cain junior woke up, they could always slug him again. He hoped to anesthetize the pain in his side, but as he drank, he became aware of a deeper, sharper complaint in the pit of his stomach. He dismissed it as indigestion. After all, being in a gunfight straight after eating steak and cheesecake was hardly the best way to round off a meal, he thought. What trouble was a bit of bellyache when you'd successfully dodged a bullet, he reasoned.

From the kitchen came the sound of retching. Flannagan had gone to get a drink and could now be heard heaving his guts up at the sink. Eugene got up to see if he was okay and felt a nausea of his own unexpectedly hit him. Putting his hand over his mouth, he too made for the basin, but it was too late, and he threw up violently in the hall. Looking over, he could see a pale faced Flannagan bent double and holding his abdomen. It was then another sharp cramp seized him, and he cried out in agony.

'Jesus, Flannagan! What the hell's the matter with us?' he croaked. 'I think we've been poisoned!'

'But I didn't eat anything you did all day…' the lieutenant reasoned, '…except when I had some of that blueberry cheesecake while I was sorting out the mess at the Chop House. Shit!'

Flannagan felt the stabbing pain again and in a panic, Eugene made for the telephone. He needed someone to take him to hospital, and fast. This pain was…

Patrick Cain awoke with a banging headache and a dog licking at his face. Staring at the table he was resting on; it took him a moment to realise where he was and whose dog it was giving him a wash. A spasm of fear gripped his belly and sweat prickled the back of his neck. Eugene was going to kill him. As the dog desisted and lolloped away, he dared to move his head, slowly raising it so he could look around the room. There was nobody in sight and not a sound disturbed the house.

Sitting up, he rubbed his head where the gun had smacked it. A bump the size of an egg had formed, but he was more worried about losing his life. He began to think quickly. They'd knocked him out when he'd lunged at Eugene. Maybe they'd seen he wasn't about to regain consciousness immediately and had left him to fetch something to wrap his body in after they'd shot him. He had no idea how long he'd been unconscious for, but when they came back, they were going to murder him, that was for sure. Woozily, and with some effort, he got up and began to make his way out of the room. If he wanted to survive, he knew he must escape.

What he saw in the hallway made Patrick stop in his tracks. Lying by the front door, the telephone receiver cradled in his unmoving hand, was Eugene. At his side,

Daisy the mastiff sat looking mournfully at her master. The gangster was dead. Turning away from the awful sight, Patrick saw another body slumped against the kitchen sink. Flannagan was dead too, he surmised. There was no blood and no sign of any gunshot wounds. Whoever or whatever had killed them both he could not fathom. Frightened, he felt for Johnny's letter that was creased up in his pocket. Death was everywhere and he felt it mocking him as he panicked. He took hold of the letter, unfolded it, and read the underlined words that leapt out at him: *get away*. This time, Patrick did as he was told.

Somewhere across town, a chef was receiving an unusually large and handsome tip from the Bowery Boys. 'Good work lacing that cake with arsenic. I guess Eugene got his just desserts,' a shady figure quipped, and a room full of gangsters laughed at the joke.

Chapter Twenty-Four
The Reckoning

Marco Antolini opened the front door to the pair of plainclothes detectives. Through the window, White had watched Benny playing a game of chess against himself. While his colleague acted as sentry, the sergeant took Marco into the kitchen and quietly explained the situation to the man. The father listened, stunned, and then running his hands through his thinning hair, confessed: 'I always dreaded something like this could happen one day. He was never right, never. Sometimes I could reach him, and then I'd think he might turn out okay, but most days...' He made a hopeless gesture with his upturned palms. 'I don't know. So, search his room, do what you have to do, but when you take him in, I want to come with you, because the boy is complex and to him the world is a strange place.' White assured the fraught father he would make sure it was so.

At the kitchen table, Marco explained to Benny what the detectives were there for. A cursory search failed to find the wrench, and the clothes the suspect had been wearing on the night of the murder had mysteriously disappeared. Benny offered no explanation. He rocked gently back and forth on the kitchen chair seeming to lack any emotional reaction to the crimes he was being accused of. When they told him they were taking him to the precinct for further questioning, he simply got up and went along with them in acquiescence. It was as if he was completely detached from the reality of his situation. White had never seen anything quite like it.

In the same damp interview room as O'Malley had grilled Danny in yesterday, the detective had a sense of things coming full circle as he explained about the boot tread pattern. There was no lawyer present, his father explaining Benny felt awkward around strangers, especially when he was in a new or hostile environment. Benny wasn't saying a word. Mr Antolini had offered he couldn't be sure whether the kid was home all night when the attack on Joseph took place, adding that his son often couldn't sleep and had taken to going out at night for a walk to help him rest. Benny sat impassively as this information was passed to the police, even though it removed any kind of alibi he might've used. After presenting the facts, White hit Benny with his theory.

'Isabella tells me you get forward with her sometimes; I saw it happening on your front porch with my own eyes when I came to search the Visconti place yesterday. You like the girl, but she pushes you away. Then, on one of your night-time walks, you see her with another boy. They're holding hands. Now, I don't know him being black made any difference to your jealousy; you just felt hurt and angry. That night, when you went to see Isabella and she wasn't home; you knew who she was with. You got angry again, so you took a big wrench from Danny's tool bag and went out looking for them. Unluckily for Joseph, you found them.'

'You watched him kiss her goodnight and then you tailed him as he headed home. On a quiet street next to the docks, you took your chance. You hit him from behind with the wrench and then you carried on taking your anger out on him until he was dead. That was when the idea of placing him in the dockyard occurred to you. Isabella told me you were a bright boy at school. You'd heard about the industrial dispute, and you saw it as a way to throw the police off the scent. You tossed the wrench into the sea and somehow made it home without anyone seeing you. It was late, after all, and the streets would have been pretty much deserted. Then you hid your bloodstained clothes until you could have a chance to burn them, probably on a night when your father was out at the restaurant and you weren't needed there. Joseph was gone and now you could comfort the grieving Isabella. It had all been working out beautifully until I saw the soles of your boots.'

Benny continued to remain mute, but something had changed in his eyes while White scrutinised the boy's reactions to his story of how the murder went down. They both knew he'd got it right, but without the evidence of those bloodstained clothes or the murder weapon, White would have to rely on getting the killer to confess and Benny wasn't talking. Isabella had spoken of his intelligence. Strange as the kid was, he knew he had the upper hand. Frustrated, the sergeant took a break from the interview and went to get a coffee. In the corridor he came face to face with O'Malley.

'How's the interview going, Dom?' he asked.

White confessed his frustration to his mentor. 'He just won't talk, and by that, I mean he won't say a single word.' Then, because he'd not said it before and felt he should, he added: 'I'm sorry about all the fuck-ups I've made and the headaches I've caused you.'

O'Malley leaned in and lowered his voice so only White could hear: 'I spoke to your wife this morning. She rang here after she couldn't reach you at home for the last two nights. Christ, Dom. Why didn't you tell me about your marriage breaking up? I would have granted you some leave.'

White looked sheepishly at his boss. 'It's not the kind of news I want spreading around this place, and anyway, work is about the only thing stopping me from going insane right now.'

O'Malley nodded. 'By the way, there's a young girl in reception asking for you. It's Danny Visconti's sister. It looks like we're not going to charge him after all thanks to you, so you'll need to release him if you really think he didn't do it. We don't want that girl causing a scene like I heard she did before.'

'She might be here about Benny, my new prime suspect,' White considered aloud.

'Well,' O'Malley considered, 'She's the reason he went after Joseph. From what you've told me, Benny's mad about the girl and must've got in a jealous rage when he found out she had a boyfriend.' Then, having a flash of wily genius, O'Malley smiled deviously. 'So, you should use the girl, then. Give her some time in the interview room with your boy Benny. Get her to say whatever it takes to get him to talk. You know the safest convictions are the ones that have a confession to accompany them. Juries just love confessions, they reassure them. Play this right and you'll make inspector when your board comes up next week.'

'She's an innocent kid,' White admitted, 'but I think she's got enough fire in her over Joseph's murder to have a go at it, especially if it helps with the release of her brother. Thanks, boss.'

'No problem. Now go and get that confession.'

Isabella was waiting anxiously on one of the long benches in the reception area. When she saw White, her first question was about the release of her brother.

Reassuring her, the detective took her down to the custody area after clearing it with the duty sergeant. He entered the boy's cell alone and formally told Danny they would be letting him go shortly, then he explained the situation upstairs with Benny Antolini to the young girl before he let her see her brother. 'Look, you don't have to do this, Isabella, but if you can get Benny to make a confession, it'll speed up Danny's release.' She was just about to ask the detective if he was sure it was Benny who had committed the murder when one of the policemen who had been searching the Antolini property rushed in waving a bag. 'I'm here to claim my whiskey prize, sergeant. I got you one set of bloodstained clothes!'

White left the cop watching over Danny and Isabella while he headed back upstairs. In the interview room, he presented the accused and his father with the new evidence. Mr Antolini grew tearful, but Benny remained unmoved. Leaving the mute teenager with his distraught parent, he exited the room for long enough to smoke a cigarette and let the situation play itself out. Ten minutes later he re-entered with pen and paper. He asked Benny if he was ready to give a formal statement. The murderer shrugged and sat back in his chair, clasping his hands nonchalantly behind his head. 'I did it,' he said. 'I killed that guy. He wasn't any good for Isabella.' The more detailed but emotionlessly frank and spartan confession that followed was delivered in the same bored monotone voice and laid out the basic facts almost exactly as White had deduced them. When it was all written up, the detective got Benny to read it through and sign it. The killer still showed no emotion.

White ran the statement upstairs and then as O'Malley watched on, charged Benny Antolini with the murder of Joseph Walker and had him taken down to the cells.

Five minutes later he released Danny Visconti, much to the delight of both the boy and his sister. O'Malley was all ready to drink a toast to White's latest success, but the detective demurred, quipping: 'I don't want you to accuse me of smelling of booze, sir. Seriously, boss, I promised I would go see Grace Walker as soon as I had any news about Joseph's killer and that's exactly what I'm going to do.'

The lieutenant clapped him on the shoulder in congratulation and then, as he was leaving, called out: 'Don't forget to phone your wife!'

White arrived at Grace's apartment just as another deluge fell from the sky. It reminded him of his soaking the night before when he'd drifted on a disturbed internal compass to the house of Martha Marsh. That had turned out better than okay, he reasoned, so on this bittersweet day where he'd incarcerated an emotionally confused and strange boy, robbing him of the chance of youth because he'd done exactly that to Joseph, White hoped he could at least bring one grieving parent some sense of justice being done. That Danny was in the clear and the Viscontis might be able to count their blessings and be grateful for what they had, a complete family, was the only real satisfaction White could so far gain from it all.

The door was opened by Du Bois, who'd continued to keep Grace's mind occupied by getting her to help with planning for the Silent Parade. Something in the detective's eyes let the activist know he bore important news, and he was ushered into the kitchen where Grace was making tea. She turned, the kettle still steaming in her hand, and stood frozen, examining White's face for the answer she both dreaded and desired. The detective nodded slowly and took the boiling kettle from her shaky grasp, setting it safely on the side.

'We arrested someone for your son's murder today, Grace. A white boy called Benny Antolini. He confessed to killing Joseph out of jealously and we have other hard evidence to support his prosecution. It wasn't a racially motivated crime, which I'm very relieved about. I guess maybe you'll both be a little less hurt too knowing Joseph wasn't murdered because of the colour of his skin. The kid that did it was what some people might term a psychopath. I for one think he's extremely unstable. I'm sure he could have killed again if we hadn't caught him.'

Grace looked confused and fidgeted with her wedding ring. 'Why? Why did he kill my Joseph if it had nothing to do with his being black?'

'Jealousy,' White answered simply. 'The kid wanted Isabella for his girl, but he was too emotionally challenged to go about it the normal way. I guess all his pent-up frustrations came to a head when he saw Isabella with another boy. For the first time it must've dawned on him she wanted someone else, was going to be with someone else, and he couldn't handle that.

'You can't make sense of these things, not fully anyhow. What drives a person to take another human being's life? In all the time I've been a cop, I've never understood it and I don't think I ever will. I'm not sure I want to. I don't know. All I can do is find the murderers and hope a judge stops them from ever doing it again. I doubt that offers you much comfort though.'

'Mister White, you should turn to God as I have. He has given me the strength to carry on and has guided me to come to terms with the bad things that happen in this world. I've had time to think. He has shown me the light of understanding. It is God's will my Joseph has been taken from this life to be with Him. His soul has risen to heaven because the Good Lord wants him there. Ours is not to question the work of God, only to chase out the devil when he appears. You are deeply troubled by your work, that much I can see, but you have taken a dangerous man off the streets and lessened the torment in my heart. You must try to see the good in the world, even if you cannot find comfort in Him. You are a part of the good, at least don't lose sight of that.'

Rendered speechless because of the lump in his throat Grace's powerful words had caused, White was relieved when Du Bois offered his opinion. 'You're both right. It's something Joseph didn't die because of someone's hatred of his colour. You found the killer quickly too, detective. Thank you for releasing Grace from her burden and thank you for keeping your promise and coming over here so swiftly to tell her the news. All along, you've done everything you possibly could. You've cared deeply, showing tenacity and compassion. It's people like you who offer us hope. I take it you'll still be coming to show your support for the Silent Parade next week. You'd be a most welcome guest.'

White shook the activist's hand and replied: 'I most certainly will. I wouldn't want to miss being a part of something like that. In my job I have to take any chance I can to restore my faith in humanity.' Then, addressing Grace: 'I need to tell you one more thing, you've taught me how to cope with loss. I won't explain it any more than that, but there it is. You've made a difference to my life, you've helped me. Thank you.'

'I don't know how,' Grace said, a little surprised, 'But I'm glad I have. Just remember, there may be evil in the world, but there is good also. Find the good people, they will always see you through.'

It was then White thought of Martha and himself. It also let him fully understand the relationship between Grace and Du Bois, and he marvelled at it. These were truly remarkable people and he felt humble in their presence. There was nothing more to be said, so he bade them farewell and made his way back to the car. Just when he was starting to find hope for his and the country's future, the black youth with the old man's face and the scar stood blocking his path. The kid looked edgy, his fist balled in his pocket, possibly holding a blade, or worse.

'I see you ain't got your coloured friends to protect you now, lawman. I told you before, this side of Harlem ain't no place for a white man, even if he does carry a badge.'

White fixed him a knowing look. 'I wonder what Pastor Abrahams down at St. Philip's Church would think of your behaviour, Clarence? Or even your mama, Mrs Parks? I hear she has fierce views when it comes to doing right and wrong in the eyes of the Lord. I know you got that scar falling through your screen door as a child and I know you'd catch hell off of your mama and the pastor if I told them you were threatening a policeman. See, I don't need to use the law on you because I know who owns you, so step aside, kid, and let me be on my way.'

The stunned Clarence stood motionless; his shoulders slumped in defeat as White walked past him to his automobile. He may have failed that evening in the Irish Bar, White thought as he drove away from the troubled district, and he may have made many other mistakes in the course of solving the case, but he was a fast learner and O'Malley, Grace, and Du Bois were the best of tutors.

It was lights out and Benny Antolini sat motionless in his prison cell, eyes wide open to drink in the darkness. People had made mistakes and his dream to be with Isabella had suffered for those errors, but he wasn't giving up. In all her confusion and rush to grow up, the poor girl had fallen for the first boy who'd had the words to talk smoothly to her, failing to recognise the love he felt, and had always felt, right there under her nose. She had tilted their world together off its axis, and in the chaos that followed, he'd made the fatal mistake of not burning his bloodstained clothes. He'd kept them as a trophy after throwing the wrench away, that had been his downfall. Without that crucial evidence, the police would never have forced a confession from him. Now, he'd have plenty of time to lament the single lapse in an otherwise brilliant plan.

He'd stayed silent when they came to arrest him and had still not uttered a word in the interrogation room. He'd bided his time to see what they had on him, but all the while he was recalculating things. This was where he was at, being accused of murdering the boy Isabella thought she loved. To an uneducated outsider, it might have looked like a terrible position to be faced with, but life had taught him how to adapt and conquer whatever circumstances he found himself in. The detective had been clever, guessing almost exactly how the killing had happened, but Benny was already one step ahead when they bought in those clothes that revealed his guilt.

One step ahead because he'd already decided he was going to confess. In an epiphany he'd seen how it was the only way to make Isabella realise he was the right one for her, not that insipid black youth who couldn't even defend himself properly. He'd killed for her, and she hadn't known it, but she would now. The shock might make her detest him at first, think he was an animal, but one day she would see he loved her so much he'd do anything for her. She'd look back and understand the danger that black boy had put her in, how her family would've disowned her for going with someone of a different hue, and how he was weak and selfish in disrupting her life in that way. Then, she'd know that he, Benny Antolini, had acted to save her and no other man would ever make the sacrifices he had for her in his devotion. She'd fall in love with him, and they would finally be together.

Touching the rough wall of his cell, Benny smirked. When the day came Isabella declared her love, jail would not hold him. He'd already begun to make a start on the meticulous plans he'd need to affect his escape. On her word, he'd break free, and they'd run somewhere safe where they'd never be found. Benny knew, drawing the infinite darkness into his rapacious eyes, that it might take years for it to happen, but happen it would. He was sure of it. Isabella and he were meant to be. It would be a marriage to outshine any formal contract or vows made in a church. Doing time was simply marking off the days until that nirvana came about. He would have his love yet. He would have his love.

White sat on the front stoop smoking a cigarette and watching the sun bleed out pink and orange behind the buildings opposite. He'd come a long way in just under a week, finding Joseph's murderer, bringing Grace some closure, and reconnecting with an old friend, but he was still fearful of spending the night alone in his own apartment. It was crazy, he knew, but he couldn't help the way he felt. What he could do to change it though was beyond him. Then, a signal called to him. Just as on the night of Mona's bombshell, he heard the phone ringing upstairs and raced to answer it. This time he knew it wouldn't be work. Breathlessly, he spoke into the receiver.

'Hello?'

'It's me,' she said.

'Mona. It's good to hear from you. How are you both?'

'We're okay. Amy is just beginning to settle, but she's been crabby for the first couple of days. I tried to call you. Where have you been?'

'Working on that murder case; walking the streets; anywhere but here, I guess. I'll have to learn to live in an empty apartment, but I just can't get used to it yet. I miss you both.'

'I miss you too,' she said, 'but it has to be this way. How's the case going?'

'I solved it today.'

'Already? Well, you always were a great detective. Well done. Look, Dom, I know this must be hard on you but it's right for me, and it'll be what's best for Amy. That doesn't mean I don't still care about you, though. You really should come and visit us when you get the time.'

'I will,' he promised, 'I will.'

They said their goodbyes and he replaced the receiver. For all the hurt, the pounding in his head and the pain in his heart, he knew he had to find a way forward. In the daytime he had his job to cling to; it was just getting through the nights. One at a time, he thought. Each one he survived would give him greater hope for making it through the next. After a whiskey and a cigarette, he took to his bed early, Grace Walker's noble words acting as a lullaby to soothe him to sleep.

Chapter Twenty-Five
A Bittersweet Walk into Tomorrow

White awoke the next morning feeling more refreshed than he had done for months. Sleep had given him a better perspective on everything. After too long fighting the sickness in the minds of killers like Benny Antolini and watching it infect his home and destroy his marriage, he was learning to live with the world the way it was. Whether you used God, like Grace Walker, or family as the Visconti brood had done, you found a way of getting through the hard times.

He thought about the phone conversation from the previous night. Mona still cared for him, and Amy would always be his daughter. He knew he'd given too much to the job, but without that, victims like Grace and Martha would never have found out the truth and evil men would've remained at large, more than likely to kill again. He was a lawman and he understood it as his calling. He had been adopted once, by John and Mary Clay, and now he had found a new family in Detective Squad, even if it was the most rowdy, cynical, and dysfunctional clan he'd ever known.

It was supposed to be his day off, but something in his head wouldn't let him rest. In the rush to act upon deduction and evidence, he'd arrested Benny, drawn a confession from him, and visited Grace with the news. He'd also set Danny free to be reunited with his folks, but the fever, flight, and look in the kid's eyes at the beach that night was still troubling White. They left unanswered questions, and the detective had never liked those. He called into the garage first, keen to avoid another potential clash with Frank, hoping against the odds Danny might have returned to work. Most people would've taken a day to regroup and savour their freedom, but White figured on the reliable Danny being better than most people, and as he approached the workshop, he could see he was right.

White watched as the boy leant over the engine bay of a big Buick, fiddling with its insides and focusing intently. He reached for a wrench and the detective was reminded of the fact they'd never tracked down the murder weapon; Benny had simply smiled and remained silent when asked what he'd done with it. A horrible thought occurred to White for the first time. Benny had been over at the Visconti house chatting to Danny on the night of the murder. The two young men had known each other from infancy, and both cared deeply in their own way about Isabella. Danny had it confirmed his sister had been seeing Joseph and had raced out into the night looking to confront him. Mr Antolini said Benny often walked after dark when he couldn't sleep. Danny had protested his innocence over the killing, but what if he'd been Benny's accomplice, the colder boy doing what the kinder one could not? That would certainly account for the sickness and running away, a different form of guilt weighing heavily on the Visconti boy. White desperately hoped he was wrong in his new theory, but he had to know the truth.

'Danny,' he called out upon reaching the entrance. The boy's face dropped and so did the proprietor's, but some things were far more important than fixing automobiles, so the detective pressed on. 'I'd like to speak to you for a minute when you're not too busy.'

The owner stepped protectively over to the boy's side. 'Danny told me what happened,' he said. 'Terrible business. Don't you think he should be given some space now to recover and get on with his life?'

White shot him a penetrating stare. 'I do,' he said, 'but that won't happen 'till there's been one more conversation.'

'Use my office,' the proprietor offered, giving in to the unshakable cop.

'Thanks, but I noticed a small green on my way here. I think we'll head over there.'

Danny's expression was hard to read as they began to walk. He was burdened, certainly, but perhaps not as anxious as White would expect a murderer's sidekick to be. Then again, Benny had shown no emotion at all. Killers came in all shapes and sizes, White reminded himself. One thing bugged him about the validity of his new idea. Benny had taken the blame all by himself. He'd never once hinted at having any help with Joseph's murder. Perhaps he wanted the kudos to be all his own, but in White's experience, once a killer knew he was going to jail, they became all too ready to sell out any partner in crime. He'd just have to see what Danny had to say about it all.

The detective broke the initial silence while they were en-route to the green, asking, 'How're things at home?'

'Difficult,' Danny admitted. 'Dad's still very hurt about Bella bringing shame upon the family, but he's relieved too because I wasn't involved with it.'

They'd reached the green and sat on one of the two benches it offered. The other one was empty. 'The killing, you mean?' White asked.

'Yeah,' Danny responded, glancing away as he did so.

'Something happened that night though, didn't it?' White pushed. 'Something you're carrying around with you. If you don't tell anyone, you'll be bearing the weight of whatever it was a whole lot longer.'

Danny fidgeted in his seat, then out of his pocket produced the small lump of charred wood White had given him from the fire at the beach. He turned it over in his hand, looking at it and considering the detective's words. Finally, he said, 'I guess you're here because you've figured it out. Now, you just want confirmation.'

'That's pretty much it,' White said, playing along, half excited and half dreading what he was about to hear.

'At first, I thought, if you caught him that'd be it. He wouldn't have got away with what he'd done. All that violence, the frenzy…it had to be punished, but I couldn't…' Danny faltered, closing his fist, and feeling the charred wood dig into his palm. 'I was so relieved when I found out you'd arrested him, but it doesn't make everything okay, not in my head it doesn't.'

Two night-time walks, both boys looking for Joseph, hunting him down, but not together, White realised, not as a team. 'You saw him do it,' the detective said slowly. 'Benny was beating Joseph and you came across them.'

Danny gave the slightest nod of acknowledgement. It was out now, and although White wanted to hear more, to know the rest. He waited and let the silence prompt Danny to fill it with his confession. The boy opened his fist and stared at the burnt wood. It took him a while, but finally he gave in.

'I heard it before I saw it,' he admitted, pain etched on his features at the memory. 'It was a quiet night, and apart from my own footsteps, the only sounds were distant shouts and police whistles. It was when I was down by the docks,' he explained, 'after I'd seen the strike-breakers getting attacked by a white mob. Then, I heard this grunting, like an animal only different. I knew it was a man, but the sound, it was so angry, so savage. I turned the corner and there he was, stamping and thrashing down on a body with some tool he held in his hand. I thought it was a hammer at first, but when I got home, I realised exactly what he'd used and felt even sicker then.

'I knew it was Benny. I recognised the jacket he always wore, and his hair, well, you've seen it yourself.' White thought back to the unkempt blonde locks that must've come from Benny's mother's side, and agreed they were distinctive. He gave Danny a look that urged him to go on.

'The body was laying on the sidewalk,' he continued. 'He wasn't moving, only jumping a little from each blow, but even that got less after a while. I just stood there, watching. I couldn't do anything. When he was done, Benny looked around, but he never turned to see me. He noticed a gap in the fence and began dragging the body to it. That was when I ducked back around the corner. I was in shock. I threw up. All I wanted to do was get away.

'I don't know where I went. I must've walked for hours. I was in such a daze, shocked, disgusted, and angry at myself for just watching it happen. I hit out at a wall at one point, that was how I got the grazes on my knuckles, but it didn't make me feel any better. I remember being by the hospital and seeing two beaten and patched-up black men coming out. They recognised me from the assault, knew I'd witnessed it happen. They called out to me. It made me panic, so I ran. I was worried they could link me to being in the area at the time of Joseph's murder. It's wrong, I know, but while I should've been feeling guilty about not going back to see if he was still alive, all I could think about was saving my own skin.

'When I found out my wrench was missing, I got even more frightened. Benny's clever. He took that wrench deliberately when he could've used any number of weapons from his own home, or somewhere else for that matter. I realised he'd done it to set me up. I was scared stiff. Every time I closed my eyes, I could see him killing Joseph, but if I went to the cops when I'd been in the area, my wrench was gone, and it was my sister he'd been seeing, who'd have believed I didn't do it? So, I stayed quiet. Then, when Bella phoned and told me what she'd done, I knew I had to run away.

'When you found me at the beach, I wanted to tell you the truth. You gave me this piece of wood and spoke about Beltane fires, but you can't trust a guy with your life, not when you've only just met him, and not when he's a cop. You caught Benny, he's locked up where he can't hurt anyone else, but I'll always have to live with not knowing whether I could've saved Joseph or not. There, I've said it now, it's all out in the open. Not such a golden boy now, am I?'

White knew there was no saving Danny, but he figured by making the boy give a statement and perhaps even testimony in court, at least he'd be atoning for not attempting to stop Benny or see if Joseph was dead when he was dumped in the desolate dockyard. It was understandable though, what Danny had done. It was all too easy to be outraged and take the moral high ground from a safe distance, but how many people, if faced with the sights and sounds of such brutal slaughter, would've done the right thing? You couldn't know for sure unless you'd been through it, the detective concluded. So, he cut the boy some slack.

'Those injuries,' White said sombrely. 'The only time I saw a body wrecked worse than that, it had dropped out of a skyscraper window. From what you just told me, seeing it so vividly and accurately, I don't think you could've saved him, either at the time or by going back.'

He lit two cigarettes and passed one to the boy. 'Deep down, I always knew you didn't kill him,' White continued, 'but it was obvious something much more than just the fear of being arrested had got you all messed up. Now, I know what that was. You'll need to make a statement. It isn't over for you yet, Danny, but do the right things now and you'll be able to face it better in the future.'

With that, the pair got up from the bench and headed back to the garage. It was better to do it now with the momentum they'd built, so, they gave the proprietor the bad news and moved on towards the precinct. He'd only have wasted his day off anyway, White thought, glad to be back in a familiar groove.

Frank sat at the kitchen table staring down at his large hands. His boss had given him the day off work, the first time he'd not been there to do his shift since he'd started more than twenty years ago. He'd have been a liability at best and a danger at worst if he'd had to deal with hauling crates today. The heavy load on his mind was more than enough to cope with. Angry as he felt at his daughter's disobedience and waywardness, two greater spectres haunted him. Danny had come very close to being jailed for a crime he did not commit. His son's life could've effectively been ended for being in the wrong place at the wrong time. Only some smart detective work and Benny Antolini's confession had averted that disaster. Frank didn't like the cop who'd felled him on his own front porch, but he had to give a grudging respect to the intelligence that had worked out who the real killer was. The cop, Benny, and even Danny's near miss faded into the background when he thought about what might've happened to his precious Isabella, though.

As if summoned by his thoughts of her, Isabella cautiously entered the room. There had been a lot of shouting the previous day and things were still tense as a tightrope in the house, but underneath lay a mixture of sorrow and solace for them all. Danny had not gone to prison, Isabella was not being sent to Italy, and the family would unite against the scandal that surrounded them. Although none of the Visconti family knew quite how they'd make it through the coming days and weeks, they all felt they would stick together and emerge from the nightmare scarred, but somehow stronger for surviving it. Now, as his daughter moved tentatively to get a glass of water, Frank voiced the greatest fear that had been troubling him since the whole truth became known.

'Bella,' he said softly. 'I know I yelled and got angry with you. I'm sorry.'

She stood there in silence, frozen to the spot and needing him to say more. Frank, a man who had always struggled to express his emotions, knew he had to let the frightening thoughts in his head out now, so she would understand and know how much he loved her.

'None of us can change what happened, but something much bigger than pride or reputation coulda been lost: You, Bella. When I think of what that crazy boy did and how he believed you were gonna be together...' Frank clenched his fists and tensed up, but it passed as a shiver of fear through his whole body and Bella was astonished. She'd never seen her father like this.

'He coulda killed you too if you'd rejected him,' Frank finally forced out. 'That maniac, he had no human feeling, only his own interest mattered to him. I coulda lost you, Bella, I coulda lost you and that woulda ended my life too. So, I don't care about anything else. I just thank God you're safe and still here.'

Isabella faced her father, a man with tears running down his cheeks who had never once cried in front of her, and was so overcome she rushed to hug him. They held each other for a long time, silently drinking in the comfort it brought. Then she sat with him at the table, wiping away her own tears of trauma and relief, ready to explain what only the other day she'd never believed he would accept.

'You might think I'm too young to know about love,' she told him, 'but I've felt it. I loved Joseph, will always love him. I've only ever felt that strongly about one other man, and that was you, Dad. I loved Joseph because he was good, kind, and noble. I could never have given my heart to anyone that didn't measure up to you. If he'd have lived,' she continued, a catch in her voice betraying the deep loss she felt inside, 'I know one day you'd have seen what a good man he was and given us your blessing. Even if it took until grandchildren came along, I'm certain you'd have included him in the family because you'd have realised he adored me and lived to make me happy, just like you do.'

Isabella took a long drink of her water, fighting back the grief that filled her heart. 'That's gone now,' she said quietly. 'All I have left is Mom, Danny, and you. I thank the stars I still have that because who else could I turn to?'

Frank reached across the table, placing his big hand, feared and respected by so many in the neighbourhood, over Isabella's. 'You are my *world*,' he said powerfully, 'and as long as I have breath in my body, I'll be there for you. I promise.'

With that, a kind of healing began in the Visconti house.

July 16th. Nancy, France.

My Dearest Grace,

I have bittersweet news to impart. An accident at the barracks has left me incapable of fighting in the war. The stupidity of how it happened is something I will not go into in this letter, other than to say I am ashamed of being the laughingstock of the whole battalion. While I will no longer have the chance to prove myself in battle, contributing to the American values we both hold so dear, there is a silver lining to the cloud of this unfortunate incident as I am being sent home on a medical discharge. This means I will be with you again much sooner than we anticipated, a thought that fills me with joy. Indeed, by the time you have received this letter, I will have been put aboard a medical transportation vessel and be somewhere in the

Atlantic. I cannot wait to be back in New York and see you again.

I love you, my dear wife.

Yours (clumsily),

Charles.

Grace put the letter down on the bureau and stared at it, images flooding her mind of her wounded but merry husband on some military ship in the middle of the ocean, playing cards and swapping stories with other men, who, while they had suffered some misfortune, knew for certain they were going to live and the war would not claim them. The missive had been short, a hastily penned update before they'd moved him off the hospital ward and out of France, she assumed, which was why it carried no mention of Joseph. The happy reunion he was expecting would not be possible, Grace thought. He had escaped the clutches of death, but his son had not.

Grace didn't know when he'd set sail, or even how long the journey took, but she gained some comfort in the knowledge that while Charles' return would see the grief she felt transmitted to him until his very bones ached from it as hers did, they would finally be together in the mourning of their son. Strange as it seemed, she also drew something from the fact he would be able to attend the Silent Parade with her. Somehow it had become an important part of her grieving as well as an essential stand in a country where violence against black people was still all too commonplace. Joseph was gone from this world, but they would march in his memory with the knowledge he would be watching on from somewhere up above.

With the statement written up and signed, White offered Danny a ride back to Red Hook, but the boy declined. He probably wanted to be alone so he could think through how he was going to deliver this latest bombshell to the Visconti family, the detective reasoned. White had told the boy to phrase his statement so that Joseph's body had not been moving when he saw Benny attacking it. He genuinely felt it wouldn't have made any difference to the outcome whatever Danny had done on the night, but if Isabella thought her brother could've saved Joseph and had instead walked away, the detective feared it would create a rift between the siblings that might never heal. Danny had taken his advice. He saw it all plainly enough for what it was now.

White hoped Isabella would be okay, wanting them all to pull through this and move on with life together. Family was so important. It had taken him losing his, *twice*, he realised, to recognise that fact. They had all suffered this past week, Danny's clan and his own, but no one had endured more pain than Grace, facing the death of her only son without her husband present to share the burden. The truth would help the healing, but it didn't undo the wrong. It didn't bring lost ones back.

As he stood there deep in thought, a familiar voice boomed down the corridor. 'So, you couldn't keep away, not even on your day off. Just as well, really. You'd have missed us celebrating the great news,' O'Malley beamed, clearly refreshed by whatever it was that had come to pass.

'Don't tell me, the mayor tripped down the steps at City Hall?' White quipped. 'Anyways, I've got a discovery of my own to fill you in on.'

'Mine first, it's golden,' O'Malley enthused.

'Okay, don't stall anymore, the suspense is killing me.'

'We got an anonymous tip-off this morning, told us we should visit a well-known gangster's place of residence. When we got there, we found Eugene and Flannagan dead. Looks like they'd been there a couple of days too, judging by the state of their bodies. Someone had murdered them both. Two birds with one stone,' O'Malley said delightedly.

'You're kidding,' White responded. 'What was it, a hit by the Bowery Boys? Did they go into the heart of Five Points all guns blazing?'

'Nope. M.E. reckons they were both poisoned, although he can't be sure what with. Not only that, we think whoever did it had the gall to take Eugene's Rolls Royce as well. It was nowhere to be found.'

'Poisoned?' White repeated. 'That's not very gangland. If hoodlums are getting that sneaky, we'd all better watch what we eat and drink.'

'Especially you,' O'Malley put in, 'what with your talent for upsetting people; criminals in particular.'

'I've learned from the best,' White retorted. 'So, they poisoned him and took his Rolls,' he thought aloud. 'Something about this just doesn't add up. I hope today isn't going to be one of those goofy ones where stranger things become the norm.'

O'Malley ignored this concern. 'Suffice to say, the whole of Detective Squad is going out for drinks after work,' he informed White.

'I'm a little surprised you're quite so happy with the situation,' White said cautiously, lighting a cigarette to hide his awkwardness. He knew he shouldn't, but he had to push it. He hated unfinished business and was on a roll after Danny's statement.

'How so?' O'Malley asked, then catching on, 'Oh, you mean the arrangement I had that you looked down your nose at. The one that got you hit in the belly for being so sanctimonious.'

White grimaced through the smoke. 'You might not like it, boss, but I still think I had a point.'

'You're right, I don't like it,' O'Malley declared. 'That being said, I want you to know the reason why I'm happy is that as well as getting two evil sons of bitches off the streets for good, it also gives me the chance of a fresh start. I didn't like myself having to cut deals with Eugene any more than you did. It was an arrangement, it had a purpose, but it always left me feeling like I needed a long bath afterwards to clean off the dirt. Things change, and if you don't keep up with that, you can't police a city. You know what happened to the dinosaurs, right?'

'They became extinct,' White answered, blowing smoke up at the ceiling. 'Okay, boss. I'll say no more about it, and we'll move on.'

'Good,' O'Malley said. 'Now, what was it you wanted to tell me?'

White filled his boss in on what had bugged him after the night at the beach and Benny's admission of guilt, and how he'd gotten to the truth of what Danny had seen. He made a special point of ensuring O'Malley knew he'd brought the boy straight to the precinct and got his statement secured, dotting the 'Is' and crossing the 'Ts' in the process.

'Thank God you're following procedure again,' O'Malley jested. 'Hey, please tell me you phoned your wife.'

White was just about to reply when a flamboyant little man wearing striped trousers, matching waistcoat, and a large silk bowtie that sat like a resting butterfly on his neck, came striding down the hall. On the end of his thin nose, a pair of pince nez were somehow staying in place. He stopped and regarded the two haggard-looking cops. 'Is either one of you Detective White?' he asked anxiously.

'That would be him,' O'Malley gestured.

'My name is Gerwaint Desgranges. I'm in charge of the estate for the very recently deceased Mr O'Grady. He came to see me earlier this week to amend his last will and testament, which was fortuitous given his untimely death. Perhaps he had clairvoyant powers. I understand some of the Irish have gipsy blood in them.'

O'Malley bristled a little, more at the man's way of speaking than the slur on his people, White thought. 'I never heard of a Mister O'Grady,' White responded. 'So, I'm not sure I can be of any assistance to you.'

'Mr O'Grady, well, how can I put this?' the little lawyer hesitated. 'Perhaps it's best to say he was a member of the criminal fraternity who assumed an alias for business reasons.'

'Eugene?' O'Malley guessed, thinking of how White had saved the gangster's life only a few days hence.

'Well, yes,' the lawyer said slyly. 'I'm here because he left you something in his will.'

'Me?' White responded incredulously. 'I only met him twice!'

'That aside, under normal circumstances, much more time would pass before any proceeds from the estate could be divided up among his beneficiaries, but in your case, I'm afraid the matter is quite pressing. Yes,' he said, pushing the pince nez to sit higher up his nose a little, 'Very pressing, in fact.'

'I'm not sure it's right for me to be accepting a gift from the estate of a criminal,' White said cautiously. 'It could be corrupt proceeds or something.'

'I don't believe that could possibly be the case, given the nature of bequeathment in question,' the lawyer reassured him.

'Could you quit talking in riddles and let the guy know what's been left him?' O'Malley barked impatiently.

'It's a bitch,' the lawyer said deadpan.

'What? You mean Eugene offloaded some kinda trouble on me as revenge or he's having a joke at my expense even in death?' White snapped.

'No, you misunderstand me,' the lawyer said with agitation. 'A bitch. A dog. A female mastiff that I'm under strict instruction to pass on to you in the unfortunate event of Mr O'Grady's death. She's in the back of my automobile now, slobbering all over my leather upholstery. There's no one to take care of her and I certainly can't. I'm not an animal type of person.'

O'Malley rolled up with laughter. 'Oh, Eugene! That son of a bitch left you his bitch!'

'I'm glad you find it so funny,' White growled. Then, turning to the insistent lawyer, he said defeatedly, 'You'd better show me my inheritance.'

That evening, after a meal of pork chops shared between them and a beer White kept for himself, man and mastiff took a long walk through the warm streets of New York. The dog seemed happily obedient, and White had to admit he was glad of a little uncomplicated female company, but he'd already made up his mind that with his erratic hours of working, he'd have to let her go. She looked up at him when they stopped at a junction, her big eyes searching his. 'I bet you've seen a thing or two in your time,' White said to her. 'If only you could talk!'

They carried on, White enjoying the rhythm of their companionable steps. It was a shame, he thought, taking a familiar route. He'd already grown quite attached to this sentient, loyal beast, but it was no good, he simply couldn't look after a dog all by himself. Then, realising where he'd subconsciously wandered to, a solution hit him. If it worked out, he'd still get to see his new companion. In fact, he mused as he approached the house, it could turn out famously for everyone concerned.

He knocked on the door and they stood waiting, man and dog on their best behaviour.

She answered looking curiously down at the creature who was doing her upmost to be appealing. 'Dom?' she said questioningly.

White smiled, 'I brought you a present, Martha. Say hello to Daisy.'

Epilogue
The Silent Parade

It is the 28th of July 1917. On Fifth Avenue the heat haze is distorting the sidewalks, bringing out the smells of melting asphalt and sun-kissed skin where thousands of black folks are marching peacefully. Sweat is soaking their Sunday best clothes as they move in a dignified silence, and the sun reflecting off their white attire is making them shine like angels; God's own children are gracing the Earth with a magnificently hushed protest. The power comes from their mute multitudes and the banners they are holding aloft. Slogans such as: 'RACE PREJUDICE IS THE OFFSPRING OF IGNORANCE AND THE MOTHER OF LYNCHING' and: 'YOUR HANDS ARE FULL OF BLOOD' create an almost biblical judgement of racial oppression and brutality that burns into the consciousness of the watching crowd. Those who have seen their brothers sacrificed like lambs are now standing tall like lions. New York has never seen anything quite like it before and may not witness such a moving spectacle again this century.

A parade of children is passing in perfect rows, their young faces solemn and full of concentration. The smallest ones are swaying slightly in the sweltering heat and are being supported by the caring hands holding theirs either side of them. Unity is their strength. The banners they display are less full of violence, but somehow all the more poignant for the simplicity of their messages: 'SUFFER LITTLE CHILDREN AND FORSAKE THEM NOT' is followed by the plea: 'GIVE US A CHANCE TO LIVE.' They render the onlookers speechless. They are the most powerful symbol against racial violence imaginable.

Away from the Parade, one man not in attendance is Brother Paul. The malcontent sits brooding in the basement of a secret location somewhere in the city. New York has not been kind to his plans. His dream of whipping up violence towards the Irish dockers has suffered fatal blows, first through the arrest and charging of a young Italian boy for the murder of Joseph Walker, with the press calling the killing a crime of passion, not racial hatred, then because of a deal struck between Zimmerman and Young allowing a return to work for the striking Irish, and a new expansion project in partnership with a shipbuilding company giving employment to the black strike-breakers too. Fate, it seems, is not on Paul's side.

He knows there is no will for violence in the people of this city, the momentum is all with the peaceful power of the Parade. As anticipation of its unprecedented message spread through Harlem, Paul admitted defeat. He called off the hoodlums ready to travel across America to start another riot. An uprising of the kind seen in Chicago will not happen here, not for now anyway, he concedes. The black citizens of New York have a force that is on a different plane from his own, a shining light rather than a raging fire. There will be blood, and war, and progress, but not in this city, Paul concludes. New York, as always, retains an aura and attitude unlike any other place in America. It is one of hope. It carries a valuing of true liberty and an openness to possibilities that comes from it being the immigrant state, the gateway to America, and the Great Melting Pot. Even he, Brother Paul acknowledges, hasn't the power to corrupt that.

From the proceeds of a swiftly sold Rolls Royce, Patrick Cain is enjoying the high life in a top Boston hotel. He is dining on hors d'oeuvres, smoked salmon canapes swilled down with yet more chilled champagne. Gone are the gutters that ran with filth, the sweat and thankless toil of the dockyards, and the fear of living under Eugene's regime. He knows the windfall will soon run out, but for now it provides him with the means to escape reality, living the life Johnny craved but never managed. He drinks to his brother, but the wounds of Johnny's death still gape in his heart. He is haemorrhaging internally while the bubbles rise in his coupe glass, a man whose outward appearance is one of a carefree playboy, but beneath the thin façade his soul is crumbling. Johnny meant everything to him, and Johnny is gone.

'More champagne!' he cries, and a third bottle is fetched and opened, but Patrick needs air. The heavy velvet drapes press in around him, and the thick plush carpet slows his exit, making him feel like he's sinking into quicksand. Outside, he gasps, hands on knees, and the ghost of the old black tramp he kicked to death materialises without warning before his eyes. Patrick straightens up and flees in fear, dashing headlong across the street. The trolley bus slams on its brakes but cannot stop in time. With a sickening thud, Patrick meets his end under its heavy wheels. Fate is righting wrongs on the day of the Parade.

In the crowd supporting the sea of marchers, Inspector Dominic White is standing overwhelmed by the spectacle. Next to him, Martha Marsh is openly weeping while Daisy the mastiff looks lovingly up at them both. Their chests reverberate to the pounding of the drums as they thunder past. The struggle for equality carries a heady mixture of benevolence and mourning. At that moment, White's eyes catch those of Grace Walker, standing tall alongside her husband Charles as they march past in the throng of protesters. She is displaying a placard that declares: 'THOU SHALT NOT KILL.' It is her own personalized victim statement. She nods in recognition, her gaze, full of warmth and gratitude, directing itself at him before switching back to the sombre expression of suffering appropriate to the parade.

Martha witnesses this and marvels. She touches his arm, although they have resolved to be nothing more than close friends. Finally, White finds a way to release everything he has been holding onto. He cries for it all, right there in the middle of Fifth Avenue, the tears mingling with his sweat in a hot July exorcism. 'GIVE US A CHANCE TO LIVE' is allowing him to begin to make sense of letting Mona and Amy go free from him and all the baggage he brings, but it also affirms his dedication to being the best detective he can be. Today he stands humbled by the Silent Parade, but tomorrow and tomorrow and tomorrow he will fight on against the cruel current of crime, one day, one night, and one step at a time.

Printed in Great Britain
by Amazon